Atomic Cocktail

Atomic Cocktail

Martin Anthony King

To order additional copies of this book, contact:
Xlibris Corporation
1-888-795-4274
www.Xlibris.com
Orders@Xlibris.com
83684

"He then looked at his own soul with a telescope.
What seemed irregular, he saw to be beautiful
constellations, and added to his
consciousness
hidden
worlds
within
worlds
within
worlds
within worlds."

I

"If an atom were enlarged to the size of the Earth, then the distance between the circling electrons and the nucleus would be about the distance between Beijing and Memphis," said Ira.

Goldman closed his eyes and tried to imagine the vast expanse between a panda bear sitting on the Great Wall of China and a cardinal perched on the branch of a maple tree in Memphis. The thousands of miles swept clean the under-constructed psyche of the twelve-year-old, but it was the only way to put it into perspective.

He looked up at his father. "We are nothing more than space."

"We are about as spacious as two-ton boulders and, I am afraid, just as dense," Ira said, laughing.

The laconic pair walked hand-in-hand, their stride in conspicuous contrast to the sub-Saharan rhythm that seemed to pulse under the icy sidewalks. The African beat of American slavery was etched deep into the cracked concrete of Beale Street, trodden and worn by black-stepped souls for over fifty Jim Crow years. It was the only part of town where Ira Goldman could afford housing for his little family with the meager pay he earned as a postal worker.

A small contingent of Ashkenazi Jews had homesteaded the neighborhood, but the Negroes didn't seem to mind; after all, what did the natives know? To them, the Jews were white people who sometimes dressed strangely, and *crackas* was *crackas* and you steered clear of them unless by chance you should become, "one o' dem scrange fruits dat hangs fom souvern treeees." Ira used these morning walks to the bus stop to teach his son the wonders of physics, politics, and philosophy. The boy's appetite for knowledge seemed insatiable and his flair for abstract reflection made his father proud.

"Gimme dem motha-fuckin ci-grits!" Boomed a Negro's voice down the sparsely peopled street. The boy squeezed his father's hand tighter as Ira ushered them right smartly around the curb 'n' gutter bums. There was something about the timbre of a black man's deep-throated anger that could notch the boy's sensitive stock and sand thin his American walnut surface. The sound of heavy fists thumping the melon skull of the Black Jemima seemed interminable. Ira and the boy walked on without once looking back.

"Hobos scare the bejeepers out of me, Pop." The folds of humanity's underbelly always vexed the boy's surcharged sensibilities and only with extreme effort could he disentangle himself from its peevish and melancholy grip. Like his father, he hated when people misbehaved or were impolite, and could not understand the dichotomy of the human condition.

Ira, an unwavering social Darwinist, meticulously cultivated his hard-deterministic garden. Having an overly sensitive nature, he had learned to be cold to the human plight, feeling that the species was like the rest of the animal kingdom: to help the weak, disabled, and aged was utter folly and anyone who adhered to these notions was an irreconcilable fool. But he was intrigued by humanity, or at least by its inscrutable physiology.

Ira often talked about the marvels of the human body; the enormous orchestration of a hundred trillion cells, the mind-warping symphony of the structure of life, billions of brain cells carrying trillions of conversations at the speed of light, but to waste the genius of quantum coherence on witless pitiful souls seemed an utter squandering of natural selection, or so Ira thought.

To Goldman, as the boy liked to be called, street people were the scariest and saddest of the mutant population. No place to live or be loved, dangling by a thread over the abyss of a perilous fate. His acerbic observations were the by-product of a budding acumen that sometimes, like his father's, seemed cold, yet he was moved by the pathetic with the sentiment of a bleeding artiste. Ira was vexed by his boy's susceptibilities, and knew the world was a mean mistress and sensitive souls did not fare well in the face of her bigotry and contempt of new world shakers.

*   *   *

Ira had married Ruth Shultz, who was compulsory Jewish Orthodox, and a certifiable virgin. Not that it mattered to him, but it was nice to know that her body was chaste and unsullied by another man's phallus intrusion.

Ira understood the importance of being a simple husband, but found it complicated to explain to his new wife that she had married no ordinary man. Seriously wounded in the First World War, both of his testicles had been blown off in a mortar accident: a problematic hiccup that was tricky to explain to his young bride who had not the slightest understanding of male plumbing.

With murky minutiae Ira had elucidated that normal erections would be in short supply and producing semen would be categorically impossible, yet Ruth was pregnant within the first month they were married. When David Oliver Goldman was born, Ira was tactically wary, especially as the child did not resemble him in the slightest. He often wondered if his new consort might have gotten entangled in some weird coital misadventure, but her fanatic adherence to her religious credo made that just as unlikely as her getting pregnant by him. Over time, he rested his suspicions and embraced the child that was mysteriously conceived and magically born on May 15, 1920.

From the earliest days Ira knew he had a real humdinger on his hands, a *wild child* that seemed to be a live wire to the universe, and just being around the boy felt like earthen bodies caught in the orbit of a larger mass. Ira would often watch as the babe stared from his crib at the vacant wall, highly entertained as though something was actually occurring. His almond eyes would dart and move one way, then another; sometimes he giggled, while at other times he became startled and cried as if reacting to things that only his young peepers could see.

Ira was fascinated, convinced that the baby was seeing something, but what? And what was his point of reference? The child's neurotransmitters had not been in the world long enough to assemble relative imagery and he was creating a glossary of abstracts that challenged Ira's own acuity. To think and imagine outside the box of solid realism was especially difficult for him. As far back as he could remember his mind had been cast in material monistic concrete. Strong objectivity and causal determinism were the threads that stitched together his wetware quilt, but to watch his boy interact with inexplicable forces, seemingly invisible and unknown, made his toes curl and the hair on his back stand on end.

At the tender age of two, little Goldman heard his mother playing Beethoven's *Moonlight Sonata* on the piano. He wailed so mournfully that Ira feared something was terribly wrong, but he soon realized that it was not a cry of physical pain but something deeply desolate. He had heard babies bawl before, but while most were trying to satiate some selfish need, this weeping was old; a vintage cry squeezed from the grapes of fermented souls, souls who knew they had missed something gigantic in the puny lives they had led and were powerless to do anything about it.

This new addition forced the existential schema of Ira's life, for the first time, into the shadowy realm of intuition. His love for the lad was more than just brain chemistry or epiphenomenon but something authentic that could only be suggested but never grasped.

Trying to understand his boy's abstruseness defied all of Ira's lexicons and often left him piqued and farcically frustrated. It required him to be fluent in irreducible mysteries that seethed in the inner-chambers of his lateral thoughts, and any postulations he had held were ostensibly relegated to the realm of the unknown. But it didn't matter to little Goldman whether his father tried to window-dress the world in Socratic high fashion or Platonic sentiment: just hearing his baritone voice say anything was enough to calm his maverick impulses that kicked the stalls and rammed the walls of his nervous and jumpy imagination.

*   *   *

The two continued down Beale Street until it ended almost at the banks of the black sludge Mississippi River. Ira loved to watch his son walk; his gait proud and sure, his eyes darting from one side of the street to the other, assessing the world as he moved. It was as though he were looking at a piece of his own incarnated self, an eccentric feeling, as if occupying two bodies at once. It was a genuine sentiment that he could neither escape nor try to explain.

His boy could affect him that way and his oblations to him never felt like sacrifice, even when he stressed his son's uncertain forecast. Ira knew what the world could fiendishly spawn and to survive in the first half of the twentieth century required the cunning of a fox. Almost all their conversations were concentric rings around the boy's prospects in the primal struggle of an increasingly hostile world.

They made the bus stop and waited for the 7:45 that was running late. It was peaceful that early in the morning and Ira was fond of eyeing the sparsely peopled streets before the feral world came to life and his trajectory concerns lobbed in. The two sat with a small crowd of black-grape Negroes as the chill of the morning gave way to the warmth of a new-raisin sun. Most mornings, Ira would rattle on about the boy's life and how important it was for him to listen. For Goldman, it was the same phonograph record with a deep gouge that canted and skipped, over and over.

"Son, it's about your future . . . your future. I don't want you to turn out the way I did. You can be anything you want if you just put your mind to it. You understand, don't you? Don't you?"

Goldman's eyes produced a lotus glaze as he stared blankly with savant gapes and nuanced concatenations of oblivion. Ira could only watch as his son seemingly departed to sub-catacomb chambers known only to him. The bus pulled up and the double-glass doors swung open with a mechanical clanging *swish*.

Ira bent over and waved his hand in front of his son's face.

"Goldman?"

II

He stood at the plate, sure that this time he would hit the ball at least the distance of a trickling bunt. On the third strike, Goldman's dream of one day doing the impossible fractured his emaciated confidence and, as usual, he trudged back to the bench deluged with jeers from the opposite team.

"Maybe next time, Jew boy!"

"Did *Jew* really think you could hit the ball?" hollered another.

Goldman sat on the bench, flushed and soggy like a boiled tomato.

I know I could do better, he thought, *if only I didn't have to wear this damned* kippah *and* tallit *sash.* He knew that he could not escape the weighted grip of his all-knowing and ever-seeing mother, the Jewish hammer and anvil of faith, the pile-driving consecrator of his life. She would never allow her baby to step out into a perilous pagan world without the protective vestments of his inherited religion.

"You'll get 'em next time," said the brooding yet gregarious Jonathan Casey, the only Confederate to befriend the little Semite. "Yankees never counted for much down here, let alone a Yankee Jew from New York City," Jonathan would say. But that didn't matter to the young pugilist. The fact that he had chosen Goldman as his little buddy was a dig at the other Baptist offspring, and if they had a problem with the slight Hebrew they would have to go through *him*.

Jonathan was tough, and anything the other boys dished out was nothing compared to the regular pasting meted out by his evangelistic father whose resolutions were to stop construction of the devil's workshop in his boy's rooterish mind. Goldman often noticed the marks of religious insubordination engraved across Jonathan's back. It was God's way or the devil was exorcised at the beating end of a knotted hickory stick. Jonathan wore the scars like proud war wounds, merit badges marking the passage into autonomous manhood.

"I just can't connect," Goldman bemoaned.

Jonathan gave him a crooked grin and stuck his salivated finger into Goldman's ear and then punched his thigh. Wet-willies and charley-horses were one of the prices of a voluntary bodyguard. Goldman glanced at the fireball sun that was threatening to set and jumped to his feet, making a dusty beeline across the diamond as he ran.

"What's the big hurry?" Jonathan yelled.

Goldman snapped his head back. "I'm late for Shabbat!"

*   *   *

Goldman gamboled up the steps of the tenement building and entered the vestibule to be greeted by a wall of warmth and the smell of New York Hebrew comfort food. The aroma wafted through his nostrils and turned the gears of his appetite. "Birdie yum-yum" he muttered under his breath. The blessings of the Shabbat prayer carried down the hall as he crossed the threshold of unit number seven, where his parent's heads were tipped in prayerful deference. As he entered, Ira peeked up and gave his boy a quick wink and a terse smile.

He sat at the table quickly, thinking that if he did it swiftly enough maybe his mother would forget that he was late for the holy Friday meal.

Without skipping a lick, Ruth served up the first course as if her son had been there all along. "Not only are you late, but you sit at a blessed table with the world's filth on your hands."

Goldman glanced at his sullied hands and moved to the kitchen sink. "Baseball," he pushed out of the corner of his mouth.

"So baseball is more important than sharing the Shabbat with your mother and father, the only people who love and care for you?"

He rolled his eyes and sat at the table again and proceeded to dig into the kosher feast. "Jonathan says one day I'll hit that ball clear out of the schoolyard."

"The Shabbat is more important than any ballgame!" said his mother.

Ira looked up from his hot meal and shook his cool head. "Let the boy have fun."

"He doesn't even practice his piano anymore! God gave him a great musical gift and he squanders it on foolishness and even refuses his bar mitzvah."

"He's just a boy. He doesn't care about religious rites," Ira grumbled.

"This is about tradition, and family. Shabbat is what keeps the faithful together. If it wasn't for our reverence to the God of our forefathers then we would be no different than the rest of the godless *goyim*."

"Well, what's wrong with that?" Goldman rhetorically asked.

"We are the chosen. We must remain the salt of the Earth until the Anointed One comes, the Lion of Judah, and delivers into our hands the land of our ancestors," she flustered.

"What land?" Goldman asked.

"Israel and, more importantly, Jerusalem," she said with determined significance.

"Please, the boy doesn't care. Israel is ancient nonsense and there will never be a Jewish nation again."

Ruth stared at her son with unflinching steel-blue eyes and spoke, "'In those days I will carry my people out from the nations and bring them into their own land,' said the Prophet Ezekiel. The Diaspora will end and then *Moshiach* will return."

Goldman jumped to his feet, throwing his *kippah* and *tallit* sash on the floor, and stomped to his bedroom. Ruth started after him, but Ira motioned her back to the table, and then followed the boy.

Goldman sat on his bed with his knees pulled up to his chin, simmering like a stewed matzo ball.

"It's important to your mother, you know. I'm like you, I don't understand what all the fuss is about, but she feels religion keeps the family together and that is very important to her and, for your sake, it's important to me too."

Goldman stared vacantly at the wall and then closed his eyes tight.

"Son, do you understand?"

Like a subterranean mole day-lighting from his manifold interior, he peeped one eye up at his father. "Didn't you say that there is no such thing as God?"

Ira reluctantly nodded.

"Then why do we have to do all these stupid Jewish things? I hate it. We're not like the rest of the people here and I'm tired of being a kike! Yeah, Pop, that's what they call me."

Ira shook his head. "No matter where we go, we will always be Jews, whether we believe or not."

Ira left the room while Goldman lay on his bed with sugar-plum baseballs dancing through his head and lilting dreams of a different life. He picked up one of his books and retreated into worlds far removed from his tiny solar system. Books were his life, pure escapism, pacification for a vivid mind locked within walls of self-imposed confinement. Shakespeare,

Voltaire, Homer, Plank and more seeded the fallow fields of his imagination, but it was a poor substitute for a hormone-bilged pubescent who craved the company of peers and pretty girls.

At school he was alone as well. It wasn't so much that the other kids didn't want him around as it was his own choice. A Hebrew larvae crawling below a sky of buzzing WASPs left him reluctant to let his thin skin get too close to their stingers. Maybe if he didn't have to wear the vestments of his mother's Orthodox creed he wouldn't feel so much a target. That kind of Jewishness might go over in New York, but in the depression-era south it was a mark that said, at the very least, "Put your hillbilly boot up my ass." But that was his fate, a Jewish conscript, drafted into the ranks of an ever-shrinking Gideon army.

*   *   *

The day was biting cold as Goldman and Jonathan walked to school. The first frost of the Tennessee winter loomed in the October air. The leaves were turning day-glow shades of orange, yellow, and brown, and the parts of the sky that were not awash in gray were laid open by broad brushings of piercing cobalt blue. The boys were always talking about growing up, what their dreams were, where they would live and what girl at school they might marry, fulfilling their cartographic destinies. Jonathan would often declare about how he was going to save the world—from what exactly Goldman never knew, but it made him feel heroic and gave expression to his deep emoted secrets.

Jonathan's extroversion was a slim veneer that veiled a brittle young ego and an emerging sense of self, plagued by emotional dwarfism, mainly due to a father who snubbed him like a carrot-top stepchild and all but iced him out of his life. Jonathan envied Goldman, who talked honestly about his own father, a man whom he worshiped even, and the polar opposite of his in every way.

Jonathan's father was an itinerant preacher who traveled with the grand tent revival meetings and healing services common in the South and the Midwest. Jonathan often accompanied him on the soul-saving road, working as an usher, singing in the choir, and even helping to raise the giant tent. Always bright and observant, and over time came to the conclusion that his father didn't really believe what he preached: the love of the Lord, Jesus, salvation, or heaven itself. The hysteria that was the signature of the revival meetings never mixed well with his father's pedantic nature. Even to Jonathan it came across as unseemly, all that broken humanity queuing up for regular whippings from the Bible Belt.

Why would people invite that kind of misery? Jonathan thought. Maybe it was to be pitied by others or perhaps admired for their forbearance.

He sometimes wondered why his father even did it. Maybe because he had put in too many miles over the years, and what was the sense of changing horses in mid-stream? Jonathan, however, still believed, even though he smoked cigarettes, sneaked booze from his father's medicine cabinet, and auto-eroticized to his neighbor's wife's underwear that hung on the clothesline from time to time. He always repented of these evil deeds by his prurient flesh—even the ones that fortuitously blew through his imagination like pulsating balloons in wild pubertal windstorms.

Jonathan mounted Goldman's back and pinned him to the cold sidewalk.

"These are strange days my brother, days when sullen knives are buried breast deep in the ones we love the most."

"And you are a man after Caesar's own heart," Goldman countered.

Jonathan delivered a healthy dose of charley-horses then let him up, limping, and the two continued down the nippy street. Jonathan was rambling on about being crusading knights on God's mission and that the world could only be saved by them when, from across the street, they were eyeballed by a pack of hell-raising boys, those uncircumcised Philistines known as the Caliphs of Baghdad. The gang scurried across the busy street for their routine harassment of anyone who might traverse the straits of their Mecca.

"Just ignore them and keep on walking," Jonathan mumbled.

The Young Turks blocked their path. The biggest boy, Richard Kranium, whose head was clean-shaven and his mushroom-shaped skull could be seen through his thin wool beanie. He grinned to reveal his sparse flaxen teeth, the perfect complement to his overall revolting appearance. He then looked at Goldman with an ear-to-ear, cornrow-gapped smirk and yanked on his *peyos*, the dark tresses of hair that dangled down each side of his Orthodox head.

"Hey, Jew boy, or maybe its Jew girl," he said. The dirty street boys bobbed their spring-loaded noggins and sniggered.

"Leave him alone, dickhead," Jonathan barked.

With a quick roundhouse swing, Richard planted a point-blank cuff to Jonathan's frozen nose with a splat and a wet crunch. Getting punched in the snout is one thing, but on an icy day it's especially agonizing with all that brain voltage arcing through the frontal lobe, eyes flooding, and solid thoughts turning to watery shit. Jonathan dropped to the frosted sidewalk and buried his bloody muzzle in his mitts.

"You stay out of this, you Jew-loving rat bastard, or I swear I'll kick your ass right through your teeth." He then dragged Goldman by his *peyos* while the other boys snatched his *kippah* and threw it back and forth, and ripped the *tallit* sash from his waist. One of the scoundrels pulled Goldman's pants down and used it to floss the split of his violated cheeks. The gang was not satisfied with just miscreant humiliation. They rained down marauding blows, dropping Goldman like a sack of wet wilted potato chips. When it seemed as if the beating would never end, the entire gang was suddenly flattened like bowling pins collapsed in the sweet spot of the rack.

In the spirit of a crusading knight saving his king in battle, Jonathan started pulling infidels off, and they scurried across the street. It was not the first time Goldman had been assaulted and, like always, when he felt his mortal pieces in jeopardy the nearest tree was a good friend. An old soul can always be recognized by how friendly he is to trees and Goldman admired them for their equanimity and willingness to hold their ground. He scuttled up the trunk like an arboreal anthropoid to the uppermost limb, where he held on with the tenacity of a dried leaf in December.

From across the street, the gang pelted Goldman with rocks but soon tired of that, and as quick as the fracas had started, it was over. Jonathan motioned for Goldman to come down but, like any green fruit, it wasn't going to happen until he felt he was good and ripe. For the better part of the morning he remained so still that moss began forming on his north-facing skin. It wasn't until he ate his sack lunch, and the shadows of the day slinked from one side of the street to the other, that he dropped from the safety of his arboreta sanctuary, a ripe coward . . . again.

He hated his attenuated inertia and tried hard to develop an appreciation for the world's wide fairways of aggravation. But when hectoring voices had too much to say he would chide them for accusing him of being a worm who would never be brave about anything. Goldman was cursed with inadequate coping mechanisms, and would administer general anesthetic to an over-taxed nervous system instead of applying first aid to places where it specifically hurt. Like an ostrich with its head buried in sightless sand-traps, he knew that one day he would have to engage the imbroglio of the world's mean game. If he didn't, then it would continue to send pugnacious emissaries as reminders to extricate himself from his chronic rectal-cranial inversion, or it would be left to others to pull his head out of his arse. But for now, that was the only place where it seemed to fit.

Where he really wanted to fit was at school, to find his own nestled spot with the other kids. He just wanted to be like everyone else and take out his garbage like the rest of the white-trash Protestant vanguard; that's where the future was, not antediluvian Yiddish Euro-trash. This was *L'America*, and its fascism was as palpable as Nuremberg torch rallies, idle maybe, but potentially just as dangerous.

*   *   *

Its zero day, Goldman thought. Today he would connect with that leather devil. He swore to himself that if he didn't at least get a base hit he would end it all, though what that meant exactly he wasn't sure. He only knew that he couldn't go on as the Strikeout King.

He was warming up when Jonathan approached him. "Now don't think about the ball or nothing, just feel it. Feel it in the middle of your gut and let it happen."

"Let what happen?" Goldman asked.

Jonathan fabricated a persuasive grin. "The miracle."

Goldman looked at him with a quirk of his eyebrow.

"At my dad's revival meeting a prophet laid his hands on me and said, 'You are a man of miracles and no weapon formed against you will prosper. Whatever you have in mind, go and do it, for the Lord is with you. You are The King . . . the One the world has been waiting for.'"

"What does that have to do with me?"

Jonathan shook his head in exasperation. "Don't you get it? That scripture was from the Prophet Nathan, which he spoke to King David."

"Yeah, so?"

"The prophecy is for you, not me. You are David, David Goldman. I am only Jonathan, Saul's son. Get it?" Jonathan's grin eased into a somber mien.

"Your dad's name is Saul?"

"No, it's Paul, but I think that's close enough." He then produced a baseball with the words *Let the miracle happen*, scrawled on the white leather skin.

"What's this?" Goldman asked.

"You can hit that ball clear out of the schoolyard, if you just believe."
He threw the ball to the pitcher. "Use this!"

The pitcher looked at the ball and guffawed. "Butt monkeys!" He spit
on it and ground in the phlegm, smudging the scribbled prophecy.

Goldman nervously walked to home plate with the conviction of a
hostile witness about to be cross-examined.

"Let the miracle happen!" Jonathan yipped.

Goldman wasn't sure what that meant. He only knew what his father
had taught him: "There are no such monstrosities as miracles." But
something began to stir in his belly, a strange flickering flame that seemed
to get hotter by the second. Oddly, the predictable dread of striking out
lifted and a feeling of rising mystery swept over him and cleared out his
cavorting doubts.

*Today is going to be different. It's the bottom of the ninth, bases are loaded
with two outs and down by three runs . . . a grand slam wins the game.*

The first pitch whipped through his *tallit* sash like a blur and flipped it
over his face. *Strike one*, and then just as quickly, *strike two*. The laughs and
roasting taunts from the other team were ear busting, and Goldman started
to sink under descending negative G's that were pulling him straight to his
molten core. Blood pooled in his extremities and vertigo ruled his wobbly
kippah head. He took a final glance at Jonathan, whose eyes were dilated
and fixed on his every move. He cocked the bat and swung blind at the
next pitch, which fouled.

I connected! I actually connected!

It was a wispy wonder that emboldened him enough to stare down the
pitcher with supreme resolve. His newfound faith shifted from his shaky
head to his steadfast solar plexus, and the possibility of impossibilities
loomed in his beating, bursting heart.

Goldman cocked the bat again. It was then that Jonathan saw something
undeniably weird. From out of nowhere, but straight from somewhere, a
kind of shimmering glitter descended upon Goldman's form. The more
Jonathan tried to comprehend it, the less logical it seemed, yet there it was
in stunning slow motion.

What looked like a tractor beam of white light mist and shimmering
gold leaves seemed to envelop Goldman, like hushed snowflakes silently
settling on a snow blanketed rooftop on a winter's full-moon night.
Jonathan rose to his feet and looked around at the other boys to see if
they too were witnesses to the same spectacle. But, to his bewilderment,

everyone played on as if nothing were out of place. He rubbed his eyes and tried to make sense of the seeming apparition but, before he could shake the vision, his ears were filled with the familiar sound of wood cracking against cork, bound string, and leather.

Goldman smacked the pitch on the Louisville sweet spot. The trajectory was so steep that the other team scanned the marmalade sky for what seemed an eternity, waiting for a ball that refused the natural pull of the Earth. Goldman's teammates screamed for him to round the bases, which he did at a galoot-awkward gambol. To him, rounding the diamond was like taking a run on the moon, slow moving and semi-airborne, as he went where no man had gone before, or at least the likes of him.

He crossed home plate and was greeted by his fellow players with a gush of jubilation, while the other team protested the unfairness of a ball that still would not fall back to Earth. Jonathan stood at a distance, lost in a maze of challenged senses that up until then he had taken for granted. All he knew was that he had hallucinated something über-cosmic or, if the prophecy was true, he had witnessed something soul jarring and holy.

*   *   *

Goldman rushed home, not even sensing his feet touching the ground. He was delirious with dandy joy and couldn't wait to tell his parents the tale of the miraculous. For the first time ever, his fellow teammates treated him like one of them. He knew the only reason he got to play was because of Jonathan, but now he had earned the right to be there. His imagination shook wild, thinking he might have a future as a professional ball player—*Lou Gehrig, Shoeless Joe Jackson, The Babe. Maybe one day playing for the Yankees!*

He approached the stoop of the tenement building and was greeted by a young woman standing next to a uniformed officer. The magic carpet that had whisked him home suddenly sank under the weight of an ominous miasma that loomed in the thickening air.

"Are you David Goldman?" the woman asked. A barely audible chirp of "yes" squeezed from his dry vocal chords.

"My name is Ms. Bowen. I work for Children's Social Services." She then gestured to the officer. "This is Officer Densmore."

The policeman hardly made eye contact. Every time Goldman tried to pull information from his averting eyes he would look away. The officer finally mustered enough courage to cough up what sounded like a cryptic communiqué that no kid except Goldman was capable of decoding. "I'm sorry, son . . . your parents . . ."

In a comet flash he knew his life was patently altered. Goldman dropped like an unsuspecting deer assassinated with a direct blow to his crosshair heart. Open season had been declared and unknown forces seemed determined to stuff and mount his head like that of so many other unsuspecting game, where coterie hunters quip from the cosmic bush, *"Nice shot."*

III

It was one of those icy offices, in one of those public buildings where civil servants carry out their tasks with the inspiration of automatons. The smell of pencils, erasers, freshly inked correspondence, and hanging flatulence wafted in the unventilated air. It left Goldman feeling nauseous, alone and unwanted, like a kid who starts at a new school in the middle of the semester and is received with the enthusiasm of a jaundiced liver. He sat pensively with Jonathan's parents across a large oaken desk from a social worker, with ample doses of buttocks, and breasts so large that they rested on the adoption paperwork. Jonathan's mother held Goldman close with a maternal instinct that comes naturally for some women, even when the kid is not their own.

"It's so sad. His parents were good people and to be killed in that car wreck just doesn't seem fair." She pulled Goldman closer and squeezed him as if she was the only *goy* who could save him now. The ladies talked about how good it would be for the Caseys to adopt the boy, but Jonathan's father was another story. He sat motionless in unspoken disapproval, his beetle eyes darting back and forth from the polished parquet floor to the social worker's gargantuan décolletage.

Amid the loss of his dearly-departed progenitors, Goldman found a shard of levity jutting from his splintered heart. He snickered with a foreign accent and chameleon emotion as he watched Jonathan's father struggle with discretion, and the mushrooming hard-on beneath his trousers that was *growing* uncomfortably noticeable.

"The boy has no relatives that we can send him to, and to just dump him at an orphanage doesn't seem right," Jonathan's mother said.

The Caseys decided that Goldman would be the perfect addition to the family, or at least Mrs. Casey decided. Goldman wasn't so sure, but where else was he to go? He made his concessions with chance and resigned himself to make the best of his new living arrangement, even if it meant feigning gratitude. But he could already feel tremors in his subterranean self, and a fault line that ran just below his crust was starting to show signs of slippage and symptoms of grotesque parody.

*   *   *

Goldman unpacked his scanty belongings as Jonathan went on about how excited he was to have a real brother, but it was all Goldman could do to keep at bay a bout of horror that was molesting his most private parts. The only world he had known had been left for dead and the idea of his parents not being in his life was unthinkable, yet there it was in all its defiant irrationality. All invocations to a higher power were squelched, as if his output signal had exceeded some predetermined level that was not able to give reasonable answers to unreasonable questions of a diminuend fate. The decrees his parents had taught by example now galvanized him to a crucial link, a bloodline he was not fully aware of before. Something more than catastrophic mockery was present and it was hard to enunciate a truth that could not be dislodged from his pinched throat.

His mother, the implacable Zionist, seemed obliging and forbearing to his father's atheism and humanistic obstructionism, as the two hurled together through an eternity of divergence fused in absolution. Their differences now seemed compatible and even understandable. Osmotic forces were seeping through the very pores of Goldman's *raw*hide and new senses he was never aware of before were *listening* to yawning signs and *observing* polysyllabic sounds. He now understood and even embraced his parents' striking contradictions: indifferent cosmic *voltage* versus a divine *Face*. Their disparity felt cold-welded to his hull now, keeling for stability in the nightshift of his drifting young soul.

"Now that we're brothers, are you going to change your name to Casey?" Jonathan asked.

Goldman gave a shrug of the shoulders and put his clothes away as he struggled to keep from descending into a black hole that he could not speak of, but only pass over in muddled silence. He wordlessly swallowed mouthfuls of salted pain and contorted his face until it felt like something reasonable. He reached into his bag and pulled out the token vestments of his Jewish religion, the dreaded *kippah* and *tallit* sash. He remembered how he had railed against having to wear that little costume. At least then he had known that he was loved enough to be fussed over. How gladly he would put them on again, if only his parents would come back.

He kissed the last vestiges of his past, ceremoniously placing them in his new top drawer, when a large hand reached in and snatched out the reminders of his Jewishness. He turned to see Jonathan's father standing over him with an askance smile and a pair of scissors and directly snipped off Goldman's *peyos* curls.

"You know son, you're one of us now, a good Christian."

"I'm Jewish," the boy nervously dissented.

He would not have willingly admitted that to anyone, but now it seemed like it was everything, the final parting gift from his mother, a consolation prize that somehow did console. Jonathan's father never flinched even though the vomitose word *Jewish* resonated deeper than the word *nigger*, both of which he had a special hate for.

"Not in this house," he growled.

"I am a Jew."

Jonathan prickled at an unraveling situation that threatened to get ugly if Goldman did not back down. His father was the house alpha dog and if his new brother didn't roll over and show his underbelly, then a pointed tooth mauling would be imminent.

"God is a Christian and you will learn about the God that your people killed," he said in a monotone murmur.

"How could anyone kill God?" Goldman cheeped.

The question did not garner an answer, and in frustration, Jonathan's father snarled and left the room. It was at that moment that the veiled faces of doom made their presence blindingly clear. A sickening feeling dropped Goldman's stomach, and small electric arcs rippled across his robot-like face. He had hoped that Jonathan's father might be his filial vicar, but the mordant reception by his new step dude dashed any prospects of a potential father figure. In the past, the pea-green boat that kept him afloat through the troubled waters of the world would always wash up on the *land ho* shores of his parents' sanity. But now, his Rubicon journey would require the temerity of his father's resolution and the poise of his mother's firm convictions if he were to navigate the desultory currents of rushing providence. His young life already seemed a perpetual homeostasis of the retrograded and the bleak and at twelve years old, his future . . . a wasteland.

*   *   *

Living with the Caseys meant chores and his duties were the same as his new brother's. That meant helping a tent revival preacher whose livelihood was made on the soul-salvaging road. The boys traveled for the better part of the school break, along a circuitous five-hundred-mile ring around Memphis.

At the first revival meeting, Goldman felt about as comfortable as the muggy evening, a sultry night with humidity as thick as the expectant crowd. Music filled the tent from a gospel group, a kind of blue-grass-meets-the-hillbilly tabernacle choir. The voices rose high into the pergola, lifting the local clod busters like floating dustbowl cherubs. It was Goldman's first foray into a real Southern-fried chicken crusade, and for a Rueben-style New York Jew it was about as comfy as the Spanish Inquisition and maybe just as dangerous if the Southern Templar got wind of a kike in their ranks.

The tent was packed and the congregants settled in and, like a Euripides actor, Jonathan's father entered the footlights, a marquee star making *la Grande entrée*. He wore a blue-sequined jacket off which the stage lights ricocheted like arcing diamonds of dazzling glitter. His hair was freshly inked black crow, his face austere with gestures of heavenly and civic virtue. The bated audience deferentially applauded as he approached the microphone.

Twenty minutes into his hell-fire sermon, he had worked himself into such a sweaty froth that he was soaked to his glistening skin, his face crimson with beads of dyed-black sweat running down his greasy features. Goldman noticed that there was a continual, single globule of sweat dangling from the end of his nose. No matter how hard he jerked his head—which sent sprays of black sweat—there was always that stubborn black bead perched on the end of his beak.

The sermon was potent: God, the devil, heaven, hell, repentance; these were scary issues that ran deep in rural America, yet he had the gifted ability to make it safe for countryside consumption. Too much and the hayseeds would overdose, too little and they might succumb to the virus of indifference.

"Sinners! Sinners, we have all sinned and come short of the glory of God," he belted from the full expanse of his tobacco lined lungs. It was real showmanship injected with a fervent urgency to uproot the seeds of Satan and get a person's life right that had the herd moving through the stockyard of repentance—cattle called, devil-vaccinated, and seared with the white-hot brand of the cross.

Goldman was fascinated by the ability of one man armed with one message who could coax meek individuals from their normal passive selves into blithering, crying dervishes spinning in the aisles and convulsing on the ground. But they seemed happy and only poor folks get happy in church. Although he was moved by the story of the suffering Lamb, it seemed obscurely occult. Still, he held reverence for the ceremony and its persuasive pull made him feel included yet observant and abnormally entertained.

Maybe it was because the revival meeting was such a stretch from his mother's religion, or because the years of his father's indoctrination had indelibly scored deep paths of resistance to things that he considered mythical, but Goldman had a penchant for mystery. Ineffable titillations always left him snake-bit and venomously charmed. It was enthralling to watch someone take sermonic command of so many people—like a cult conductor composing weird movements from some unearthly symphony; obbligato sounds with sway enough to incite peaceful riots. For the first time, Goldman understood the power of doctrinal demagoguery, an alchemic force so strong that it easily guided shoals of humanity to move as one directed body.

After the altar call, the repentant returned to their seats for the healing part of the service. The call went out to the invalid, the crippled, the deaf, and even the blind to come forth. Goldman wondered who would dare to make such a claim as being able to heal these poor incarnated souls. Yet, there they were, in wheelchairs, on crutches, some limping, and Jonathan's father ebulliently waving them to the pulpit.

Jonathan whispered, "When my dad puts his hand on their heads they'll be slain in the Spirit."

Goldman shot him a quizzical look. "What does that mean?"

"They'll be healed and then they will fall. Help me catch them when they do."

The two followed Jonathan's father as he laid his curative palms on the inveterate, and just like Jonathan said, they collapsed into the waiting arms of the boys, who laid them on the dusty sacrosanct ground.

In a short time the area in front of the pulpit was littered with the fallen. Some were in trances, some mumbling to themselves, others praying, while some were crying tears of deliverance. Like a holy bomb, the faithful had been blown to kingdom come. Jonathan's father hovered over the divine carnage, an angel of death, searching for the most critically wounded, laying hands on them again and pummeling their concrete-bunker souls with a language arsenal straight from the Lord's armory.

After a period of hushed weeping and praising one of the faithful stood, a blind man with a white cane hurled it across the tent almost hitting an old woman who had to duck for cover.

"Good Lord Almighty! I can see!"

Another man, who was wheelchair-bound, started jumping and screaming, "I can feel my legs!"

From across the room a deaf woman shouted, "I can hear!"

The hullabaloo was enough to get the crowd revved up again and the band began banging and clanging with true sounds of liberty. One by one, the slain rose to their feet; some danced and cheered, while others still looked about as grim as they had when they first came to the service.

After the revelry, the soaring flight peaked and the descent from the fire-on-high altitude filled the tent with an eerie afterglow that escaped through slashes in the canvas tent. The adjourned then filed out, charged up and revitalized, inoculated with enough of the Spirit to last until the bug of sin mutated into another strain, when they would have to return again for holy booster shots.

While the boys were folding and stacking chairs, Goldman noticed a few stragglers gathered around Jonathan's father. Curiosity moved him to within earshot and he could hear them asking why they had not been healed.

"Sometimes healings don't happen immediately. Sometimes it's God's way of testing your faith. It is not for you to question when and how God heals, but only to believe," Jonathan's father brusquely said.

The unhealed grudgingly fanned out into the bisected world of doubt and faith, where Technicolor hope is reduced to inconsolable gray. Goldman peeped into the back part of the tent, to see Jonathan's father and his assistant, Pastor Jack Butchinski, counting the money from the night's donations. Jonathan's father grabbed a fistful of loot and walked out of the tent. Waiting for him were the first people who had stood up and shouted their healings: the blind man, the man in the wheelchair, and the woman who claimed she was deaf. He paid them in cash; remuneration for a quality performance that is remembered long after the price is forgotten.

It all made sense to Goldman. These people were claque conspirators, plants to incite the doubting heaps into cane-waving blind belief.

Those poor souls who didn't get healed, what do they do now? he wondered.

Jonathan's father headed back to the tent and caught Goldman eyeing him, but continued on as if he didn't exist. Pastor Jack, however, always eyeballed strangers with suspicion, especially prying eyes that might look too deeply into their spurious operation. Jack snagged Goldman's intruding almond eyes and shot him a phosphorous stare that made Goldman's sphincter contract and his sacral spine feel vulnerably exposed. He ran backwards on the balls of his feet, scurrying to hide from the man's seemingly phantasmagoric tow, and nasty things hidden in the devil's bottomless bag of tricks.

IV

The summer moved like the slowly rolling, muddy gray Mississippi, serpentine and thick, and so did the endless schlepping through every Podunk hamlet that catered to the religious addictions of the gloomy, helpless heaps looking for answers to their question-mark lives. Most of the folks that Goldman encountered seemed fairly lucid and of prudent disposition, and it was curious that the tent revival meetings could draw so many reasonable people to such an unreasonable and undignified event.

To him, the services were an exhibition of "primitive culture", as his father would say. Yet somewhere in his own primal cloth he sensed loose threads dangling from the fabric of antecedent gods: Apollo, Hercules, Zeus, the monotheistic gods of Zoroastrianism, Mazdah, and even the singular God of the Jews that his mother so stridently preached. But the melodic delicacy of the suffering Christ struck a tuneful chord somewhere in the requiem of his life and the sad hope of Jesus made such a beautiful dirge. It was hard to shake the melody, and the amorphous song plucked hidden strings from his hollow-body core.

He wanted to fit in, but decided he would not accept the Lord through coercion or some other ecumenical mandate. The more he acquainted himself with its liturgy and notions of benevolent dispensation, the more he felt drawn to the Lamb's saving grace, despite Jonathan's father's brigand example. Jonathan often talked about the world ending and only when the last soul was saved would it end . . . right on time. "All of heaven is waiting for you," he would say, yet Goldman resisted. Even the revolting Pastor Jack, who was at first wary of Goldman, took a shine to him and often talked to him about his aberrant soul that, according to scripture, needed to be salvaged. But Goldman was frustrated with people walking and talking about Jesus. He just wanted to see His *Face*, but that was reserved for dead men.

He wrestled with his indecision. The contradictions of Jonathan's father and other Christian incongruities that were rampant among believers made him even more reticent to accept the parched preachments of pious proprieties. Still, his spiritual scent glands were drawn to the bouquet of the Lamb's rose blood. One evening, he was so emotionally trounced that at the altar call he found himself queued up like the rest of the *Sturm und Drang*. He wasn't sure if he was there because of peer pressure or emotional barometric pressure, but he decided to accept the Christ and to be washed in the water and blood of the tortured Lamb.

*   *   *

Jonathan was happy for his new brother in the Lord, and Goldman was glad to be a believer, but he was still beset with wandering questions that no one seemed able or willing to answer. He longed for a god that possessed a *Face*, not the icy impersonal current of *universal survival voltage* and its cold cousin, *cause and effect*, which his father had advocated. He kept looking for others to provide examples of the personal God, but his ever-inquiring nose smelt something burning in the belief recipes of their *soul kitchens*. Jonathan always talked about the joy of the Lord, putting on his best halo-filled façade, yet Goldman sensed a guarded insincerity that he was never able to bear out. He really wanted, and needed, the love of a god that would call him by name. He needed truth, too, and after the honeymoon of his incubated conversion, trouble was gestating in his born-again belly. Jonathan's father hated the fact that Goldman was now a confessed believer and let it leak that he was of Jewish stock, and soon most people shunned him except for Jonathan and Jack.

As if suffering some Hebrew contagion, he was quarantined from the rest of the faithful. They permitted him to fulfill his Christian duties, but he would never be allowed to sit at their moderate carnal banquets, the blessed *goyim* tables of the New Sabbath Age. The whole thing carried an acrid odor and Goldman's spotless heart was soon showing signs of saturnine poisoning. One of the first symptoms of an apostate is sarcasm, a symptom his father had expressed toward religion. His spirit walk across the irregular topography of his new faith became shaky as his father's *raison d'être* bubbled through the cracks of his new Christian edifice. Goldman hated the feeling of indoctrinated confusion and it bounced off his mental rails like a pointless game of existential snooker. How often he missed his father's tender magic, the sureness of his attenuated spirit, and his ability to quell Goldman's swinging monkey mind that had not yet learned to walk upright.

Ira had been a professor of political science at NYU, an evolutionist who fused an amalgamation of physics, evolutionary biology, and behavioral psychology as a rational counter to the cruel and insane religious and political systems of the world; a vociferous proponent of sociobiology who believed that all life was reducible to selfish gene machines competing with one another for survival. Any pie-in-the-sky prayers, petitions, or belief systems regarding anything other than the terrestrial sureness of man, was archaic daydreaming: "Man was to be his own god if he was to have any say in the formation of his destiny."

He knew that Darwinism and his own solipsist belief was, in a fundamental sense, the antithesis to peace and goodwill, but it was the best he could derive from a world that gave few good answers to the most basic god questions. The dialectic precision of an uncongenial universe stretched and snapped his Orthodox Jewish upbringing, and relegated all religions to antiquated superstitions and potential psychiatric disorders.

Ira had a propensity for spiritual mysteries, but was often frustrated by the vagaries of religious foreplay that were required before any spiritual intercourse. On the most essential level he craved cosmic communion, but the religious institutions that were supposed to point the way left him feeling like a disemboweled ghost, and the place that was to be his sanctuary, in time, felt dubious, aberrant, and altogether suspect. A gamut of blind acceptance was required, but never gave solutions to his open-ended questions. He could see that faith-related standstills came at a heavy price and to continue following generations of divine decrees was ultimately nothing but dutiful claptraps.

What limited tendencies Ira had left in him for anything religious were shattered on the rock of cynicism, leaving him alone to sort through thousands of broken pieces and meticulously reassemble himself into a thinking, reasoning soul survivor.

Goldman, too, would have to test the waters of religious currents that to his father had been psychosomatic tar pits that held many a bone. Even after their death, the tug of his parents' apposing influence was a constant force and, out of duty, Goldman wanted to honor their memory and their beliefs. But he could not serve two masters and he would have to make a choice. He wanted to share his mother's faith, but never saw an advantage in believing in a sky daddy who for some inscrutable reason was imploring his fallen offspring with divine edicts that could not possibly be achieved.

Goldman's ardent blade of logic cut through seeming cosmological tyranny with the scalpel precision of reductionism. He remembered what his father had taught him about hypothetical syllogism: "If God is God then he is not good, and if God is not good then he is not God." This pressed hard against his desire to know the Christ. If He was God, then how could He allow the non-explicating terror of the world to continue? It just didn't wash.

Eventually, he came to the sad realization that this new god was no different than his mother's god. In fact, according to Christians, they were one and the same. For months his mind floundered as he tried to find a reasonable way out of the circular world of saintly semantics. The salt of reason had to prevail if Goldman was to preserve his soul from religion's carrion contamination.

Jonathan's father, in one of his fire-breathing services, groused menacingly that the unsaved would burn for eternity, lapping up the flames in the deepest bowels of *Gehenna*. He made a special assault on the Jews, saying that they were not only "Christ killers" but that they reject the saving grace of Jesus. He went so far as to say that the Antichrist would be a Jew, sired by the devil and a Jewish harlot in a Babylonian brothel, and who was in fact alive somewhere in the world, waiting in the wings of prophetic fulfillment.

Goldman was convinced that the sermon was for him, whose parents died without professing Christ. He was sick of swallowing reproach and nonsense and the sermon was the final thwack that split the spiritual spine of his good book back. After his own unanswered questions as to why a loving god would allow his parents' death, he determined that this was the denouement of his Christian queries, and repudiated his ephemeral faith. He would stick with his father's cobbled reasoning and, whether God was just an old gaffer of *electricity* or the original cosmic painted *Face*, He would have to make Himself known if Goldman was to see the light of a celestial benefactor's truth.

*　　*　　*

The boys were now on different sides of the court, volleying back and forth the deceptive sweetenings of a rarefied existence, and the years of subtle erosion had left Goldman hostile to anything religious. All his natural curiosity and frustrations were buoyed by people who could not, or would not, give reasonable answers to questions about their faith-based twaddle.

Goldman would challenge anyone about religion and loved debating it into the dirt. This pissed off most believers, yet his questions were daring and foolhardy enough to address their own calcified doubts. Goldman was never afraid to question the questioner, butcher the butcher, or bury the undertaker. There was no middle ground for the headstrong spindly teenager and most folks either hated or loved him. But behind closed doors he still found himself wandering down hope-beaten paths of spiritual hypoxia, daydreaming that if there really was a god then maybe one day he would earn enough air miles to see his parents again. False hope can be an anoxic concoction if one drinks too much. He did throw back a shot now and again with an acquired taste for undiluted high-octane doses of the Spirit, but only in secret moderation.

Goldman's essence had vacated his soul asylum, but his young mind was still vulnerable to incurable fantasies and the creative imagination of a schizophrenic that he hoped would somehow vouchsafe his inner-longings. He knew that there was a vast realm of knowledge out there and that you don't know what you don't know. That's what was happening to all those fanatics who came to the tent peepshows, sojourners just wanting a peek at the prime mover, anything to under-gird their insoluble existence.

He had been unaware of the steady drip of time that had eroded the few short years since his parents' death, leaving him on the precipitous slope of sliding nihilism where even the most basic belief systems are battered down. He was wholly convinced that there was no objective reality to which the Bible bore witness, just a consensus reality governed by collective idiocy.

*　　*　　*

Goldman hated working with Pastor Jack, who was an uncouth grizzly of a man with an abundance of bodily noises that percolated from his corpulent torso. There was something beyond his revolting appearance that vexed Goldman. Jack wielded a sickle-eyed look that could cut deep swaths into Goldman's wheaten field and winnow-out his hidden sinful chaff. It was as though every buried secret was exposed to the opaque light of his encroaching gaze: *I saw you torture that frog; You pinched that little baby and made it cry; You stole money from your father's wallet while he slept! You're a real fucker head, and one day I am going to expose you.*

Once, in Nashville, the tent revival meeting had a large take for the evening. Goldman and Jack were counting the donations when gunfire thudded from outside the tent. One of the actors, a black man with gold front teeth, was angry because he thought Jonathan's father had stiffed him on his curative performance. He pulled a revolver and fired several times, barely missing him, then ran into the tent.

"I's a takin' all y'all's motha' fuckin' money!"

He found a burlap bag and demanded that Goldman fill it. As the man was exiting the tent, Jack pulled a .38 and shot him once in the spine, where he folded in half backwards, dead on the spot.

After striking the tent, the body was dumped in a drainage ditch and the show moved on as if nothing had ever happened. A dead Mandingo in 1930's America didn't mean a lot, and no questions were ever asked by the police, locals, church members, or even by Goldman. He had learned that it was just another part of the dirty business of saving souls that taught him to be aware of everything, but affected by nothing and to accept the world's blind spots and its requisite hypocrisy.

Jack's relationship with Goldman over time became almost avuncular, and what at first seemed wholly revolting about the man eventually exposed more complicated aspects to his personality. Jack was not just some Southern-fried hick, but a learned man who held a degree from Ole Miss and enjoyed engaging Goldman's precocious and circumventing wit. Jack always carried a dilapidated Bible by his side and boasted that, "a Bible falling apart belongs to someone who isn't." But Goldman was only too aware of the cracks in Jack's foundation and sensed a malevolent spirit lurking just below his inviolate facade.

His conversations with Jack and Jonathan would go long into the night, duels in abstract disquisitions and discursive philosophy, games of cosmic chicken and quantum dodge-ball—heliocentric rings that orbited around the meaning of the universe's umbilicus. These discussions did not require faith or lack of it, only a sense that there was something bigger hiding behind the everyday grind of mediocrity and life's over-abundant bull-cronky.

For these disputant spars Goldman would gird himself with empirical logic against religious lunges that, in his opinion, manufactured panaceas that still could not cure the world's lead-poisoned ills. Armed with books that taught only cosmic rationale, he antagonistically espoused the view that there was no such thing as the personal God that Jack asserted. There was only an amorphous energy that did not know ones name and was totally indifferent to any religious persuasion. It was heady stuff for a usurping juvenile, whose theoretical reasoning flew over the heads of most adults.

Unlike Jonathan, though, Jack respected Goldman and found their conversations stimulating, but he had learned that if he were to joust with him, he had to be on his game. The pubertal teen had the ability to think quick and talk fast, leaving a person feeling intellectually ham-fisted if they could not parry with logical and satisfactory answers. Eventually, Jack's inability to wrangle with Goldman degenerated into resentment and their once thought-provoking conversations digressed into invective-strewn altercations and mutually-inspired disdain.

Goldman had become an un-credentialed satirist who had learned that life was complicated, cold, and mean, and as he got older the postulations of his father's persuasion cut away any dangling threads about anthropomorphic gods that ruled from the sky. Not only is there no god, but we ourselves are grand mutations, colossal gene machines in a relentless search for more nothingness in a meaningless universe.

V

Regardless of their alloyed dissimilarities, Jonathan was glad to have Goldman as a brother. What he hadn't counted on was that like any brother, there would be rivalries. The boys were in their teens and girls had become a permanent fixation. Things were changing, and waking up with a morning hard-on was something Goldman had to get a handle on. Masturbation had become a compulsion that in one *hand* made him feel like a petulant scrub, but in his other, seemed like a la-di-dah diversion.

Even as a budding atheist, he suffered Bible Belt guilt that came in heavy doses of God condemnation. Not that he thought his flesh fantasies were wicked, but imagining the consequences of someone finding out he engaged in the regular practice made him feel like a morbid deviant. He thought for sure that he was the only one plagued with this gutter behavior, and his single-mindedness to continually indulge in the grimy little act.

Once, after a service, Goldman brought the counted cash to Jonathan's father who was unwinding in his trailer and, walking in unannounced, caught him dressed in women's underwear and high heels, masturbating. Goldman dropped the cash and darted out of the trailer before the scene could emulsify into a fully developed image in the darkroom of his mind. After he caught Jonathan administering corporeal punishment to his own privates, he began to suspect that everyone was preening their genitals.

Hypocrisy would always run deeper than the crime itself, he thought, and the world would always look for ways to pull splinters out of other people's eyes while balanced on their own wooden beams of double standards.

While Jonathan was always forceful and direct with girls, Goldman was timid and prickly, and speaking to them had become a problem. Despite his shyness, the girls loved his striking good looks. His semi-bronzy olive complexion had caused his father to suspect a Sephardic branch in the woodpile, and Ira had prided himself on his own European heritage. Set in the symmetry of Goldman's baby-fat face were deep, dark brown, almond-shaped eyes, a Roman nose, medium lips, and teeth perfectly aligned and white—an anomaly in most Southern smiles. His voice had not yet cracked and there was an effeminate cast to his sugary appearance, which drew the wrath of boys but brought on the girl's giddy affections.

Jonathan was handsome in his own way, being of Black Irish descent, but was cursed with milky white skin that maintained the complexion of a hospital sheet in the winter months and of crisp red bacon in the summer. His somewhat narrow-set, cobalt eyes were the kind of eyes that said, *I don't lie, and if you allow me to peek through your windows I'm liable to see things that aren't covered*. He was a healthy specimen, wide at the shoulders, narrow at the hips, with a strong jaw line that added to the persona that the girls admired and the boys respected, especially those who might have encountered his torrid Celtic temper—a curious lover of his father's God, but often courting the distractions of the devil that twinkled in his Gaelic gaze.

*   *   *

There was a beautiful fawn at school named Rhodesia. She was the new girl and stirred quite the gabber. Nobody knew her ethnicity or where she came from. There were rumors that she was a Gypsy, others said a Cossack from Russia, and still others suspected she was a New Orleans quadroon. She was a rare beauty mark on the world's flawed surface, endowed with a kind of magnetic field that could pull opposite poles into her sphere of influence; an exotic ornament hanging on the tree of life that the *cracka*billies of the Confederacy could not calibrate.

She was festooned with straight raven hair and light-cream coffee skin, bejeweled with jade Siamese eyes that sparkled with flashes of hoary silver. The apples of her face were placed high and complemented her full lips. When she smiled her top and bottom teeth were shallow set, displaying just enough of her pink gum to perfectly cradle her ivories. At fourteen, her body was already flawlessly proportioned and magnificently endowed. At five-foot-five her growing was done, and when she moved her unusual saunter evoked royalty. Grace and style served up naturally for her, yet she acted as if she was not aware of her mythic supremacy. Goldman and Jonathan noticed, and each was determined to win her imperial affection.

When Jonathan spoke to Rhodesia, he had to cover his manic insecurity with clumsy bravado-driven advances. She was polite to him but never interested, though she was interested in his strange looking waif of a brother. Goldman heard rumors of this floating fact, as did his brother and for the first time Jonathan saw Goldman as an impediment, even a threat, to achieving the object of his yearning. He was fiercely competitive but knew he could not compete with his brother's freakish good looks, and this fact burned in his belly like hot irons waiting to be pounded on the anvil of Goldman's head.

One day, Goldman was drinking from the school water fountain when, from the corner of his eye, he spied Rhodesia taking a sip from the other fountain. His head deadened and his faculties flat-lined as he sank into a cupid trance. Could he still breathe? He wasn't sure. The only thing he knew for sure was that he was standing next to the teenage goddess who held the keys to life in her emerald eyes. The two sheltered one another in shifting glances that sifted out the screams and yells of teenage throats bellowing through the school hallway in a hormone-drenched cacophony, but he was sure that he heard her smile.

"You're Jonathan Casey's brother, aren't you?"

Goldman thought for a second and wondered if he could get a word to form in his desiccated maw. He could see Rhodesia's ample mouth move but all her words were garbled and ran together in slow-molasses syllables.

"Y-y-yo you . . . you are, Rhode Island," Goldman blathered.

"What?"

"I mean a road in Asia."

"What?"

He was hurtling to the ground in inglorious flames as he continued to hammer out weird inflections from his thin dry voice, none of which were recognizable as legitimate words.

"My name is Rhodesia." She thrust her silken palm into his sweat-slick mitt and gave him a kiss on his peach-fuzz cheek. He hiccupped and farted at the same time, then made a *deliri et insani* dash out of the school and climbed to the top of the nearest tree.

*   *   *

Goldman had been eyeing an authentic German Iron Cross medal from World War I, which was displayed in the jewelry case in a local pawn shop. He vowed for months that one day it would be his. The day came when he had saved the three dollars it took to free it from the display case and he wore it proudly. To demonstrate his devotion to the princess of his kingdom, he ceremoniously rendered it to Rhodesia as a filigreed token of love and fidelity. From that day on the two could not be separated.

Jonathan was aware of their courtship, and the affection that Rhodesia and Goldman shared hit him raw and filled him with sputum curses. *Why doesn't she want me?* In frustration he chided his brother with psychopathologic jabs, but Goldman's devotion to Rhodesia was immovable and his love unquenchable. The closeness of the boys had eroded with the introduction of the opposite sex and what they had as kids would never be the same. They were older now, and the old familiar world that had been predictable and worn was now being seduced by the delicacies of the new. Boyhood innocence had been traded for something better, at the price of something that was quite possibly worse.

*   *   *

It was late September on an Indian summer evening, a night that would be dunked in the sludge pit of Goldman's psyche for the remainder of his years. It was after a Sunday tent revival meeting and Goldman and Pastor Jack were in a lathered debate about Noah's ark. Goldman was conversant with Christian lore, and argued that it would have been impossible to pair up every living creature on the Earth and pack them into a giant barge. Jack responded that mathematically the numbers crunched, that the ark was three hundred cubits long, fifty cubits wide, and thirty cubits high. That meant it had about one and a half million cubic feet, equivalent to six hundred railroad boxcars. Goldman countered that it would have been impossible to repopulate the world because there were too many oceans separating the landmasses.

"God can do anything," Jack declared.

"So the kangaroo, the koala, and the crocodile hiked down the side of Mount Ararat, then they walked, crawled, and jumped across Asia Minor, through India, Southeast Asia, across the Indian Ocean, and washed up in Australia?" Goldman argued.

Jack enthusiastically nodded.

"And you want me to believe that dinosaurs lived at the same time as man and all the fossilized remains are because of the flood?"

Jack nodded again.

"Then where are the human fossils?" Jack reacted as if he were in full theological arrest and scrambled to pull off a speculative resuscitation.

"And I guess after Adam and Eve were seduced by the talking snake, lions went from eating grass to instantly developing bone-crushing teeth and claws and to hunting other animals?"

"Yes!" Jack shouted.

Goldman threw up his hands and laughed with wild paroxysms. "I can't have anything more to do with your fabled myths or your fabled god, or even *you* for that matter!"

Jack's dry chops stammered nervously about how Goldman was headed straight to hell if he didn't repent for his wretched waywardness and come back to the fold. He knew of his relationship with Rhodesia thanks to the tattletales of Jonathan, who said that the two were regular fornicators. Jack told him that he had taken the liberty to have some of the elders pray for Goldman's salvation and deliverance from his on going carnal know-how and, even worse, for his overconfident, supremely rancorous proclamation to being an atheist.

"It's none of your business what I do, so save your breath and that goes for the rest of your Christian crusaders!"

He had worked himself into such agitation that Jack couldn't get a word in edgewise.

"You're a slave to an ignoramus religious scheme that manipulates ignant asses with the threat of hell. And I'm not having it anymore," Goldman exclaimed.

"The Bible says the wages of sin is death," Jack blurted out.

"And the wages of stupidity is suicide!" Goldman shouted. "The problem with you, Jack, is that you are running from a bad case of doubt. You're a product of self-deception. You create worlds that you want to see instead of worlds as they are."

"You are a child of God, made in His image!" Jack nervously proclaimed.

"I am a child of Darwin, made in *his* image," Goldman confidently exhaling his declaration with secular halitosis.

"Ah, spoken like a true atheist," Jack said with defeated resonance.

"Yes, and thank God for that!" Goldman chimed.

The air quieted as Jack realized that there was no point in arguing with a burgeoning heretic. His pleas left him flushed as puddles filled the pouches of his puffy eyes. He knew he had lost not only a young brother in the Lord but a conjoined friend that he had incarnated as an attachment to his side.

Goldman started to leave but Jack grabbed him by his slender wrist.

"Would you stay and have one more prayer with me?" Jack's grip was like a vice.

Out of pity Goldman shrugged his slight shoulders. Jack pulled him down to his knees and the two knelt in silence. He then rose and looked down at Goldman, who could feel his invasive stare penetrating the soft spot of his fontanel crown. He opened one eye and looked up at Jack, who displayed a barren smile and then began to roll his head like a gimbal-mounted gyroscope.

"I've lost you, I've lost you," he moaned.

The levee gates swung open as he flooded the humid air with a gush of unprocessed emotion. He fell to his knees weeping and put his heavy arms around Goldman. As uncomfortable as it was, he allowed the man to have his moment. Eventually, the hugging and crying became suffocating; he attempted to separate the hulking figure from his willowy frame, but Jack held on even tighter, and like a constricting anaconda, squeezed his coils and was not about to let his quarry draw another breath. The boy's act of consolation had despoiled into a preying upon his kindness and the situation escalated into a bizarre physical struggle.

"*I'm your backdoor man,*" Jack growled.

Goldman was a pathetic match for the oversized brute and the scene had degenerated into the unthinkable. Jack had his pants down to his ankles and his undersized Kielbasa was in Goldman's peach-fuzz face. He fought with what strength his reed body could muster, but he was no match for the likes of a determined sodomite.

The beating and raping was interminable and any fight that had been in Goldman withered after the first penetration. The treachery summoned something inside the teenager that knew no words, only deep guttural growls; a primal man that occupied a remote cave of his psyche, where animals that once lived are evicted by the cunning of a smarter beast. The emerging force did not know subtle notions such as righteous indignation or violations of higher creeds, only primordial survival and a morass of primitive feelings.

The men that Goldman had tried to surrogate into father figures had left him with an ardent sense of betrayal and Freud's parricide fantasy of father-murder seemed potently justified. Even during the invasion of his guano-canal, his mind had been perfectly lucid as a sagacity of moral absolutes devoured him. He didn't believe in ethical imperatives such as right and wrong, only things that made sense or no-sense, and this act of betrayal was utterly senseless. But he could not escape moral outrage and its vile pull that ran him down the mineshaft of an inner-core that he had never known.

As sure as he was that there was nothing for sure, an egregious violation had been perpetrated and unwritten laws that spanned the length of the universe had been breached, semi-incestuous and intimately vicious. He now understood the difference between wickedness and righteousness and men like Jack were the square root of all evil, and Goldman vowed that one day he would make him pay.

Like a freed feral cat, Jack finally let him go. He quivered out of the tent in an altered state that now communicated through the gravity of a new dimension. He felt like the refuse of wine skins and stems after they had been stomped and squeezed and all the juice had been extracted.

As Goldman left the revival tent of holy horrors, Jonathan had to hide from his brother. All through the night he had peeped through a tear in the canvas tent, watching the beating and raping. Jonathan's sufferance for Rhodesia was rat-assed neurotic, and those who got in the way of his obsession—he figured they had it coming.

Goldman walked aimlessly down the dirt farm road, curiously followed by a stray lamb as he disappeared into the pre-dawn darkness. Jonathan watched from a distance, a stone obelisk, ancient, cold and unmoved. Where Goldman was going he didn't know, but he would go it alone, carried by the crucible of a seminal flame that would burn in his belly for the remainder of his rootless nights and for the rest of his wandering days.

VI

The months that followed Goldman's disappearance did not go well for the ministry and the florid magic of the traveling tent revival show had lost its arcane fragrance. Something about Goldman had brought a neo-vitality to the operation that the briny-salt blockheads were not even aware of. He'd been a sharpening stone for those who could not cut theology bait with dull-witted knives and salvation for those who practiced secret secularism in their closets. The newness of his mind was endlessly varied and reconstituted new perspectives on their epoch old religious slants. He had a multitudinous effect on everyone, and they only vaguely understood the hefty footprint his absence left in their mottled mud of mendacity.

He continued to gadabout in and around Memphis. He loved Rhodesia and vowed not to leave without her, but the overriding reason he remained was to exact revenge on Jack. How or what he thought he was going to do would remain unclear until he could devise a reasonable murder plan.

One day, according to legend and lore, Jack was found hanging by the rafters in the main revival tent. His naked cyanotic corpse had been tattooed with rancorous and pornographic graffiti: *Queer, Cocksucker, Fuck me in the ass, Loves sucking dick, I am the devil.* There were gauche illustrations of twilight men and crimes against nature, erect penises strategically placed over his cadaverous skin; inverted crucifixes engulfed in red, orange, and yellow-flames. It was his private inferno, and in that place he had surrendered his Byzantine soul to unclean spirits that he had tried to scour all of his recondite life. The incident was a presage that brought on one calamity after another and the ministry was finally shut down. Jonathan's father was convicted on copious charges of fraud and tax evasion that were remunerated by prison hard labor.

Now that Jack was dead, Goldman had no reason to stay in Memphis except for his devotion to Rhodesia. They were in love, and not just any love, an indivisible love built on the prime number of two. But they had to steal their love away as Rhodesia's parents never approved of him. Her father was Japanese and her mother was half-French mulatto, and Jim Crow laws of miscegenation need not apply. Her parents demanded that she forego giving her heart to the homeless Jew boy, feeling that he was ethnically and socially inferior, which was funny coming from what the rest of white America would have called third world mongrels.

The odds were stacked against the love birds; still they tried to make it fly. Goldman was a peripatetic street varmint who could not rub two wooden buffalo-heads together and when Rhodesia popped up pregnant, the plot thickened. At fifteen, they were thrust into the scary world of onus parenthood and Goldman's prospects never looked so bleak.

Rhodesia's father was rumored to be with the Japanese yakuza and to have whopped-off chrysanthemum craniums in Japan with samurai ardor. After learning that his only daughter was pregnant, he vowed to have Goldman's matzo ball head on a spit. Goldman naturally feared for his young life and there wasn't a tree in Memphis tall enough to climb. With no resources or tribal refuge to fall back on, he figured this was his cue to dislodge from the hodgepodge of Dodge.

He put all his eggs in the basket of California and told Rhodesia that when he got set up he would send for her. She agreed to remain behind and would endure the humiliation of an unwedded pregnancy while he scrounged up a life in Los Angeles. He had heard that he could get work picking fruit in the San Fernando Valley, but even those jobs were hard to come by and every dustbowl hickory-stick had already staked a claim.

Goldman hitched rides with flatland Okies all the way to the Gold Coast, where Route 66 promises of the California dream are rendered verisimilitude and bare. Three dollars a day for ten hours work was just enough to survive on, and survive he did, toiling the picking circuit well. The working conditions were horrendous even for refugee hicks and reminded Goldman of something his father had said: "The laboring class suffers because of its ignorance, and ignorance builds empires and fights wars for the bourgeoisie, who use doctrines of delusion and counterfeit nationalism to herd cattle minds to the slaughterhouse."

Ira had served as an officer in the First World War, the war to end all wars, and was a reluctant witness to the collapse of all reason and the crime of ten million dead. It was during this era that he became a card-carrying member of the American Communist Party, and vowed never again to fight for the cause of imperial kingdoms. Communism became Ira's new religion, but it came at a steep price when he was summarily dismissed from his chair at NYU. A closet anarchist was about as popular as syphilis and potentially just as contagious. A job opened in Memphis where he relegated himself to the lowly status of a postal worker. Government jobs with steady pay were rare during the Great Depression and, with a wife and boy to provide for, he was determined to do anything to keep his little nuclear brood alive, even if it meant serving as a lowly plebian in the dreaded patrician machine.

Goldman felt that the working conditions on the farms could use a Socialist infusion, but he didn't know the first thing about revolution or the emancipation of the proletariat. He was too busy running from the jaws of Malthusian catastrophe to indulge in quixotic geopolitics. He eventually settled in as a regular hand on the only vineyard in the valley, grateful to be a boy doing a man's job. Simpson, the old-timer who owned the farm, eventually made Goldman his foreman. He was given his own bunkhouse and had access to hot and cold running water, which for Depression era America was plush.

He took to rural agriculture and enjoyed the bucolic nature of farm life. After a year he sent for Rhodesia. She had come full term with a baby girl, little Ruthie-Lee, and sent him only one photo. The baby was beautiful like her mother, flawless, except for a small birthmark just below her right ear on the nape of her neck. And not just any random port-wine blemish, but a perfectly-shaped heart about a half-inch across.

Rhodesia said the heart meant she was a God child, that He had put His stamp on her. Goldman pleaded that the two come west, but she said it would be too much for the newborn and that he would have to wait. He begged, but her mind was made up, or maybe it was her father whose mind was made up. After numerous returned letters, Goldman resigned himself to the fact that she was out of his life, and it battered his psyche black and blue, making him ache for months. The maelstrom of his accrued experiences had left him flagellated and raw and for the first time in his vernal life, he had acquired a fondness for the anesthetizing effects of strong drink, and when friendly worlds and lactating loves seemed far away, it became his milk of choice.

In the space of a few deep breaths and many shallow sighs the years stacked up like so many expired Norman Rockwell calendars. By the spring of 1942, Goldman had established himself well at the Simpson vineyard. He even had a return address that had brought him news from a long lost uncle . . . *Sam*. The Japanese had bombed Pearl Harbor and the Marines were looking for a few good men, and maybe they weren't all that picky, even a spindly Jew from the San Fernando Valley would do.

Serving in the military seemed ridiculous to Goldman, even if the country had been attacked. His father's radical beefs with countries that practiced barefaced ascendancy still weighed on his teeming opinions. The thought of throwing himself into harm's way was so disagreeable that he even mulled over skipping the country to dodge the draft. But where would he go? He had become close with old man Simpson, who treated him like a son, which was a genuine departure from his usual reluctance to accept father figures and Goldman regularly confided in him. Simpson was a veteran from the Spanish-American War and had ridden with Teddy Roosevelt's Rough Riders. He didn't want to influence Goldman's decision, but either way he knew he was losing a devoted worker.

After flailing for days in wire-haired, controvert-introvert vacillation, Goldman decided he would appeal his induction as a conscientious objector. It was a long shot, but maybe he could use scraps from his religious past and proclaim that he was an Orthodox Jew and believed in the Ten Commandments, especially, *Thou shalt not kill.* He found a Hollywood costume shop and rented a complete Chassidic black suit and trilby hat. After gluing on a long mystic's beard, he marched into the induction center with terse protestations that digressed into a diatribe of morality, which digressed even more to the evils of war and his religious beliefs that were wholly incompatible with it all. The military shrink listened patiently to his rant, then calmly reached over, yanked the badly disguised whiskers from his face, and stamped his induction papers: APPROVED.

VII

The beginning of the war looked bleak for the Americans with the fall of the Philippines, Borneo, and most of the South Pacific islands right down to the tip of Australia. Wake Island was gut-check time and victory at Midway was crucial, but what the American war machine needed was real estate. Rumors were floated that it would start in the Solomon Islands, an island-hopping land grab designed to push the Japanese all the way back to Okinawa.

The Japanese were building a runway on a parcel of Guadalcanal, and the Americans were determined to drive them off and make the island an unsinkable aircraft carrier. After bitter fighting, the Marines took the airstrip and renamed it Henderson Field. The defeat at Midway had been humiliating for the Japanese and they were determined not to lose another battle, let alone the rest of the Guadalcanal. Some of the fiercest fighting of the war was waged for that muddy, swampy, disease-infested piece of dog-patch, and the myth of the invincible Japanese soldier was sorely tested.

After months of basic and advanced training, Goldman was mentally and physically inculcated to dish it out to the dirty "slant eyes". He had grown a full three inches, gained thirty pounds of muscle, and looked every bit the Anglo gentile that his mother had warned him about—the all-American leatherneck—and a mannish leap from his androgynous Jew-boy years.

The 1st Marine Division was the main landing force on Guadalcanal. Twenty thousand grunts would take the main island, while a smaller detachment invaded an adjoining minor island called Tulagi. A task force of the Imperial Japanese Army defended the little island with a torrid ferocity that the inexperienced marines were unprepared for. There was no time for the young recruits to acclimate to the sweltering climate and the fighting was intense from the moment their boots hit the beach. There had been five hundred Japanese on Tulagi, and in the end, only three who surrendered.

The Japanese capacity for killing astounded the green marines, who could not make sense of the endless banzai attacks, nearly all them at night, directly into heavily fortified positions. Exploding shells, grenades, and machine guns, ultimately hammered out a Yankee victory. The 1st Battalion of the 5th Marines were transported to the main island of Guadalcanal, rested, and re-supplied. Thirteen men from Goldman's company had been killed on Tulagi, and some of them were friends. His requisite courage had been tested, baptized by an ancient primal inferno and he felt grateful not to have incurred any injuries.

*   *   *

Goldman and his squad were airlifted on a DC3 troop carrier. It was his first plane ride and he was utterly enthralled with the experience. From two thousand feet above the Pacific he could see hundreds of tiny green islands peppering the turquoise-blue water. How wonderful and bodhi passive it looked from that altitude. It was remarkable to think that down in that rapturous paradise men were bent on murder with wholesale pomposity.

He and his squad had been attached to a recon unit, assigned the unenviable task as forward observers, and were to be landed behind enemy lines. During the short flight a Japanese Zero caught the transport blind side and pumped a stream of automatic fire that forced the plane to ditch in the Solomon waters. The pilot was killed, along with two men from Goldman's squad. Eleven men drifted in the cobalt ocean for two days before a US Navy interceptor ran across them.

Patrol Torpedo boats monitored the waters as part of an interdiction campaign to keep the Japanese from reinforcing the island. In the middle of the night, as luck would have it, a PT boat almost plowed into the bobbing men. Like waterlogged crustaceans, the eleven were fished from the drink, hallucinating and delirious from saltwater poisoning and shark threats but *shickled titless* to still be alive. They were given Coca-Colas and Spam sandwiches while the PT commander greeted each one personally.

"How's the food men?" he asked.

Goldman smiled and stuck out his hand to shake the hand that had saved him. "Man, are we damned glad to see you, sir."

The handsome lieutenant smiled and ran his fingers through his thick brown hair. "What's your name, son?"

"Corporal Goldman."

"I'm Lieutenant Kennedy, welcome aboard the PT109."

The Commander turned and headed for the helm. The young man's convivial welcome was reassuring and eased the men's water-soaked souls as they fell fast asleep and dreamt of Camelot affairs on the return trip to an island that still refused to die.

* * *

Colonel Kiyoano Ichiki landed on Guadalcanal with the 28th Japanese Infantry and before the day's end had attacked the heavily fortified American positions. A thousand soldiers threw themselves at the marines with traditional banzai night attacks, charging Goldman's company through the Tenaru River lagoon directly into withering gunfire that systematically tore the Japanese lines to ribbons. By morning's light, eight hundred enemy soldiers lay dead.

After the seemingly endless night of grinding carnage, Goldman and the rest of the marines surveyed the battlefield. They were utterly bewildered, not by their victory, but by the doggedness of the Japanese soldier and his willingness to throw soft flesh and porous bone into hot, hardened steel. Goldman thought he could leapfrog two hundred yards from lily-pad body to lily-pad body without ever touching the ground.

Corpses were strewn, twisted, and contorted in every possible position: Arms, legs, heads, and entrails scattered along every bearing. It tested Goldman's senses, and he tried to understand the mentality that would spend life so cheaply. Savages, all of them, but then he remembered the American Civil War, and Gettysburg, the servile obedience of the enlisted men with fifty thousand casualties in that three-day battle alone.

The panoptic sight gave the sentiment of being invisible, and a new mode of obtaining power of mind over existential terror bubbled up in Goldman's core. As morbid as it was, he found himself thinking about the most inane with perfunctory mental mechanics.

When did I brush my teeth last? Is the Government Issue toilet paper single ply or double? I can't remember once ever clipping my toenails as a kid.

He trudged though the reeking massacre like a certified butcher assessing the best cuts, tiptoeing and meandering around the distorted carcasses in a bloodbath ballet. His artistic melancholy was kept at bay with antiseptic analogies—safety mechanisms installed by his father who had always dressed the world for him in conspicuous camouflage.

There was a kind of slipshod aesthetics to the butchery of battle that gave one an abstract appreciation for the art of war. The endless gallons of blood pooling in the glassy blue lagoon was so beautiful to him: torn uniforms, guns, swords, helmets, chunks of red meat, the different colored organs, and the glinting glaze from spattered drying blood in stunning juxtaposition to the tropical sun. It cast an eerie arcane light on the gallery of the dead that was blinding and mesmeric, speaking volumes coded in an exigent language of tribute.

It took six months of gut-grinding battle to shake Guadalcanal clean of the Japanese. American dead were sixteen hundred ground forces and almost five thousand seamen, while the Japanese dead were twenty-five thousand. Both sides lost dozens of warships, several carriers, and hundreds of airplanes.

For the first few months of the fighting, the only thing that kept Goldman's wandering heart grounded was the thought of Rhodesia and little Ruthie-Lee. He hated the idea that she and his baby were not a part of his life. Even after leaving Memphis all those years before, their memory kept him going and brought home the fact that he was defending not just an American empire, but an augury of greater triumph.

The war had taught him about suffering for the sake of something bigger than himself, and fortified his ability to endure almost anything. Mind play of this kind had got him through the worst of the fighting, and like his father before him, he too had become a reluctant witness to the savagery of war and the loss of all reason. Something about living through the honorable terror of combat sifted the sands of his soul and laid in shallow graves any ideas of inauthentic heroism. He had become an efficient killer for the state and found it significant to be a part of these disposable men: guardians of muscle, sinew, and bone, who willingly spend their breath and spill their bowels for tribes they do not know. He returned to California for a well-earned thirty-day leave.

*   *   *

He thought he would be glad to be back in the land of baseball, apple pie, and ten-cent beer. Instead he felt restless and haunted by the phantoms of war, and the peace he so badly needed was hard to pin down. He seized the first train to Memphis and didn't care if Rhodesia's father greeted his head with a samurai blade. If he had to, he would kill him too, like the scores of other Japs he had annihilated on Guadalcanal. He made the two thousand mile journey only to discover that she was nowhere to be found.

There were rumors that her parents had been sent to an internment camp, yet only her father was Japanese, so at least her mother should have been around, but nothing.

Murky, gloomy feelings surfaced and Goldman lamented intensely at the loss. His mind, tumbling in a rolling kaleidoscope, endless geometric patterns of *What?* and *What ifs?* There was an ever-expanding rip in his chest and he hated the feeling of inflamed winds that occasionally blew through that tear, the same tear where he kept his parents' recollection.

To use the rest of his leave in Memphis would be pointless and he left aching with layers of onion tears. He felt that he did not suffer because he failed to fulfill false desires, but suffered because he possessed false desires, and the little family he longed for would be relegated to an extrapolated parable. The idea of visiting the Caseys had crossed his mind, but he hadn't seen any of them since he left all those years ago and the raw recollections of Jack still hung in the balance of his skull. He wondered how Jonathan fared, but it was all pre-his-story now.

He grabbed the first train back to LA and checked into the downtown Morrison Hotel. Loneliness had become his fulltime lover and the two spent their time low-balling their what-cha-ma-fuckers and fondling their erroneous zones. For three weeks he drowned himself in the insulating comfort of alcohol and the sympathetic scaring of whorehouse she-wolves and street screech-owls. It was the only way he could relate to a world where he needed to be fully anesthetized before he could operate in its theatre.

The dogs of isolation hounded his steps with yips of discouragement, and the brothels could only temporarily silence his booby-trapped banshees. He was only aware of the noise as a distraction, sensing that every man who knocked on the door of a whore-hovel was really looking for a God-shaped doghouse to crawl into, and he was no exception.

The war was catching up with him and endless psychogenic seizures strafed his emotional entrenchments. In his alcoholic-induced fog he sensed his very being slipping, a metaphysical *oops*, deporting the man's soul from his body, where eating a pomegranate from the inside out seemed not only reasonable but necessary. Maybe his gestalt ghost was still in the jungles of Guadalcanal? Bilocation; is it possible to be in two places at once? He only knew that he was not fully aware of his immanent now, and just wanted to wake up.

All the self-medicating that was to serve as a general anesthetic could not erase the memory of the war. Even when wide-awake, the unrelenting banzai charges tormented him like a boiling fever that would not break. Sleep was an infrequent extravagance, and when he did get it he was now visited by a recurring nightmare. It was always a little different, but the feeling was the same—unmitigated terror. He would dream that he was sleeping in his bed at the hub of fixed darkness, hearing movement and bestiary breathing in his bookroom mind. An entity of sorts stalked him and would leave him with sensations of utter helplessness. The presence of the thing was palpable and at times he could feel it inches from his face, and if he opened his eyes, he was sure malevolent beings would be unleashed on his molested soul.

At an unconscious level he could not escape fundamental flaws that seemed to underlay his opposing selves. Like looking backwards through a sniper's scope, he tracked his inverted essence with crosshairs of serendipity and malice. There must be something that he was doing, he thought, that brought on the recurring wrath of a universe bent on teasing little cosmic brothers like him. To be a Jansenistic pawn of divine cruelty was wearing him ragged, and he felt there must be a way to impose his will and whittle out some kind of reasonable meaning to his life.

His father had believed in commanding one's own gist, but Goldman lacked the filaments of Ira's hardwiring. If only his pop had lived longer, Goldman might have been better equipped to deal with his infernal continuum of melancholy and its unholy alliance with escalating depression. But he would have to find his own answers, and until then he would endure chaotic nodes that he did not understand. He hated having to clunk along noisily through his banging, clanging world with the feeling that the universe was not even aware of his melodrama or, worse, was conspiring against him.

He was cracking up, and the only thing that kept him from splitting at the seams was the fact that he was going back. Back to the towering jungles, the deadly spiders, snakes, crocodiles, malaria infested swamps, the mud, and the rainforest canopy that could turn day into night and night into eternal darkness. Uncommon valor was a common virtue on those islands, and that's where he would hang his dilapidated hat and make his rotting wet bed.

He had not before been fully aware of the fact that he had survived the torrid equatorial battles virtually unscathed, and the thought of having to fight those "yellow devils" again filled his thorax's cave with parabolic panic and sent him running out of his hotel room in just his underwear. He scrambled up a tree on the corner of Sunset and Echo Park and roosted there for the rest of the night as the traffic along the boulevard moved below him, pitifully unaware of his entropic psychosis and achingly vulnerable new self.

VIII

"Storm'd at with shot and shell; bravely they rode into the jaws of death, into the very mouth of hell."

Eight square miles of volcanic ash, pumice and sand. The reeking of satanic brimstone, pummeled by bombs, bullets, and shellfire, dripping blood from its twenty-six thousand dead; this would be the closest that man would incarnate as the devil, fulfilling vestigial tales of Armageddon in the autumn of 1944.

The Pacific theater was going badly for the Japanese, starting with the fall of Guadalcanal, then the Gilbert Islands, Saipan, the Marianas, and the battle of the Philippine Sea, which all but destroyed Japan's naval and aviation forces. It brought the chronic, rather than acute, reality to the shogun warlords, that any chance of victory was patently untenable.

In his three years as a marine, Goldman had become a marinated and seasoned veteran. Wounded twice, he received a Purple Heart, and the Silver Star. He had been summarily field commissioned as an officer for his natural leadership and his uncanny ability at keeping his comrades alive while still inflicting heavy casualties on a very determined enemy. He had never wanted to be an officer, and could not remember when he had not felt like a frightened turtle. The curse of a coward seemed imbedded in his hide and, even after iridescent acts of courage, he still felt like a forlorn phony, blanketing any recollections of valor. He accepted the commission, halfheartedly but dutiful.

Victories for the Americans had become routine, and as the island rat wars dragged on a sense of cockiness stained the once-pristine marines with hubristic idiosyncrasies. They knew that they were going to beat the "slanty yellows," it was always bloodthirsty pell-mell mania that garnered victories, but suffused with nasty casualties. Goldman liked the *esprit de corps* when the men were humble, when they were not sure if they could beat the ten-foot-tall Japanese soldier.

The marines loved to hate the Nips. They cursed them going into battle and they cursed them coming out; bloody skirmishes often set off madness with sadistic acts of vengeance. The grunts would enter the battle aftermath with spitting, pissing, corpse-defecating desecration, sputum obscenities, shitting from the mouth; it was a rite of passage, savage commensuration for acts of murder perpetrated on their fighting brothers.

The naïve enlisted man, born from the heart of mollified American mores, was baptized by immersion into the Bushido warrior code. The warrior class samurai emphasized self-discipline, courage, and unquestioning loyalty, and defiling the cadaverous shells of their enemy was expected, necessitating the cognitive process of a warrior creed. On every occasion, whether marines were captured or if the dead lay where they fell, the Japanese would dismember the bodies, sometimes while they were still alive. Amputating limbs, gutting and disemboweling, disfiguring faces, stuffing severed penises in trench mouths—bench trademarks that abreacted foreshadows of their own death. This drove the normally rational Americans to mindless barbarism with their own abominable acts of mutilation.

Sometimes the marines experimented with the dead Japanese. They would stand four, five, six corpses in a row to see how deep a fifty caliber shell would penetrate, stuff a grenade in the mouth of a dead Jap and watch it explode, or flame-throw a corpse just to see how long it would cook before it stopped burning. Some of the men decapitated the dead and stewed the heads until the skin and brains boiled out, and then mailed the scoured skulls back to their loved ones. It was a kind of primal trophy, something you put on the family mantel that said, "Don't fuck with us, we've got a killer in our tribe!"

This kind of sadism was understandable and even embraced by the military. It satiated a primeval urge to glorify the cult of war and the rules of some long ago but never forgotten art-of-war protocol that was always just below the surface of an unfamiliar consciousness.

*   *   *

Goldman recalled a particularly brutal engagement where members of a platoon from the 5th Battalion were to relieve a platoon from the 1st Battalion, garrisoned off the Tapotchau heights of Iwo Jima. The platoon had been cut off from the rest of their company, which had pulled back during the night. After the Navajo code talkers lost contact, brass feared that they hadn't survived. When Goldman and his platoon walked into "Hell's Pocket," as the men called it, they were met with the hideous spectacle of forty-two dead marines. They had seen fallen comrades before, but this was different. The bodies were stripped to the ankles and turned on their bellies. Each marine had his ass filleted down to the pelvic bone; the gluteus muscle completely hacked off. The grunts went berserk, crying and aching out loud with clarion shrills and wolf-pack howls, a resonate lexis that only they could understand.

The Japanese were starving and cannibalism was on the menu, with rump roast a delicacy—the most tender and tasty part of the human anatomy. None could sport a rear end like the full-bodied Americans: they had never seen such firm ripe cheeks. For the rest of the day the marines agonized over the far-off smell of open-flamed barbeque of American roasted ass, while the Japs reconstituted and gorged like savannah lions.

The fighting for Iwo Jima was fierce. Every cave, rat hole, trench, and tree had to be sprayed with automatic gunfire, grenade, and flamethrower. Surrender was a Western paradigm that the Japanese could not conceive of. This infuriated the Americans, knowing that they would have to carry the fight to total annihilation, their dirty job made dirtier and more dangerous by the day. It required a coolness under fire if one was to shake off the existential terror of meaningless war, and the marines would forever despise the Japanese for putting them through the bitter and seemingly endless bloodbath of Iwo Jima.

*   *   *

There was a break in the fighting. Goldman's platoon was resting near a sugar mill outside a small village called Higashi. The men were exhausted: cat napping, eating, smoking, and shooting the usual jocular shit—all part of the boredom and panic of war. Goldman had passed out solid. Nothing was to stir him, until he was visited again by the dark dream he had encountered on leave in LA. It was the same creeping, lurking creature that had visited him before. His reaction, paralysis of all muscles and total arrest of his vitals, or so it felt. In the perpetual darkness he could feel the being close to him, and a non-audible shriek percolated from the recesses of his guts until gag reflexes gasped his inanimate form back to the nightmare of war.

It took him a few moments to get his bearings. The platoon looked on but said nothing. Every man had his breaking point, and all knew that those who lived through war were commonly tortured in their sleep. He could still feel traces of the lurid dream slithering through his abdomen, and what had felt like screams were really pathetic moans that required all of his rasping strength to exorcise a cohabitating foul spirit.

A new sound trickled into his head: the collective roar of men laughing, yelling, "oohing," and "ahhing," and he followed his ears to the hubbub. He pushed through a crowd of enlisted men and elbowed his way to the front of the hullabaloo where he was struck by the spectacle of a twenty-foot constrictor, devouring a Japanese prisoner. The jaws of the reptile had the head and shoulders of the scrawny soldier already down its throat, slowly rocking its enormous head back and forth, inching its prey down its pink and crimson gullet.

The marines had caught the snake in the Solomon Islands and it had become the battalion's mascot. Someone got the bright idea of putting it in the prisoners' cage just to see what would happen, and the snake zeroed in on what it felt was reasonable prey. The marines found this rip ass entertaining and would not feed the animal for months so that its appetite would be whetted for more Japanese sushi. After each victorious taking of an island they routinely sacrificed a Japanese prisoner as a propitious sacrifice to the gods of war.

Generally, even a snake of this enormity would find it impossible to get its mouth around the shoulders of a man, even a slender Asian, but the snake had figured out how to eat a man whole. Instead of opening its jaws perpendicular to the shoulders it had learned to open its jaws in parallel, where the body could slip into the reptile's head without any difficulty. The scene was mindlessly repulsing, yet something about the sight fastened Goldman's attention, and he could not look away. Like a good man horrified by the coliseum spectacle of animals eating live human beings, he now found himself a barbaric voyeur and cheered on the snake with Romanesque perversion.

As the constrictor swallowed its way to the midsection of the man, a small black notebook fell out of his trousers' back pocket. The serpent consumed the body down to mid-thigh, and then at mid-calf it stopped and gave what looked like a scaly smile, with the soles of the prisoner's feet jutting out of its mouth. It let out a cold-blooded *hisssss*, then proceeded to work the rest of the feet down its throat until there was only one big toe day-lighting from the reptile's bottomless pit. The toe slipped pass its lipless mouth and the beast robotically realigned its enormous jaw and inched its way to the shade, where the cold-blooded, bloated brute settled in for a two-month-long nap. The marines let out a collective roar and gave the reptile a five-minute standing ovation, shouting, "Author! Author!"

The outline of the Japanese soldier could be seen just below the snake's scaly skin, with his physiognomy features protruding like a nylon stocking mask stretched over a robber's face. The little black notebook that had fallen from the Japanese's pocket caught Goldman's eye and his curiosity. He entered the pen knowing he would be safe, as the monster was as full as it was going to get. The other prisoners trembled at the sight of the American barbarian. He gave the gaunt Japs a surly sneer and headed straight for the notebook. He inquisitively perused its dog-eared leafs, and found it curious that almost all of what was written was in English. He stuffed the notebook in his pocket, gave the prisoners a "sayonara" wave and headed back to his platoon.

He situated himself in his comfort zone again and closed his eyes, but his head was still whirling in the macabre theater of what had just transpired. Unable to sleep, he randomly opened the little notebook and a single line caught his attention, *"What you are looking for is what you are looking with."*

IX

After three weeks of furious fighting and abysmal casualties, Iwo Jima fell. By late March of 1945, US forces were gearing up for the invasion of Okinawa. The 1st Battalion of the 5th Marines would be assigned along with the 10th Army to secure the Ryukyus, a series of small islands near Okinawa. Here, for the first time, the Americans would be invading what the Japanese defenders considered their home soil, and resistance would be mindlessly fanatic. The Marines knew they would suffer heavy casualties, and the Navy, too, would bear catastrophic losses due to Japanese suicide pilots.

Goldman's company was attached to the 6th Marine Division. The military attaché was handing out promotions and medals like beaded necklaces given to women who were willing to flash their tits on a New Orleans Fat Tuesday bender. Men who garnered field promotions and citations for bravery infused morale back home, perpetuating war bonds, which was just as important as winning any blood-soaked battle.

Goldman was promoted to 1st Lieutenant and would be under the command of a man named Henry Courtney Jr., a major and the executive officer of the 2nd Battalion, and no ordinary officer. He led his men in battle by example, and with natural, daring leadership. Under his direct command, Goldman's platoon was ordered to hold a static defense on the slopes of what was called Sugar Loaf Hill. After leading a protracted firefight during the day, Major Courtney weighed the fact that it was getting late, knowing the Japanese preferred to send massive wave attacks under the cover of darkness. Instead of waiting for the inevitable, he resolved to take the fight to the entrenched Japanese positions.

Goldman thought it was insane to expose the men to direct fire from higher ground; it wasn't his place to question an order, but he feared the consequences would be grave and demanded confirmation from the upper brass. The major got permission and the men were ordered up. It was a suicide mission, but the marines were expected to hurl their meat suits into the sausage grinder. Major Courtney yipped encouragement to the young leathernecks, but when the hues 'n' cries of the men were unenthusiastic, he took it upon himself to lead the charge.

He grabbed an M1 carbine, a handful of grenades, and with the heart of a lion stormed the hill, blasting nearby cave positions and neutralizing enemy guns as he went. Inspired by his courage, the men intrepidly followed. Together, the marines braved a terrific concentration of Japanese gunfire to reach the top slope. Temporarily halting, Major Courtney sent guides to the rear to bring forward more men and ammunition. Reinforced by twenty-five more marines, and an LVT loaded with grenades, they attacked the crest of the hill, crushing any planned counterattack before it could gain momentum.

To have an effect on the breakthrough, Major Courtney continued to assault the enemy single-handedly with the ferocity of a man possessed, firing and throwing grenades into cave openings with devastating results. Upon reaching the crest and observing a large number of Japanese forming some one hundred yards away, without hesitation he attacked again, killing scores and forcing others to take cover in the nearby caves. The marines gave chase in an endless blizzard of bullets, grenades, mortar fire, and shrapnel. Determined to hold their new position, Major Courtney ordered the men to dig in. He was a freak of war that remained remarkably cool under fire. He shouted out commands, helped with the wounded and assigned men to different positions, all the while weathering a hornet's nest enemy.

Japanese mortar fire became more intense until one explosion ripped through Major Courtney, nearly tearing him in two, leaving Goldman as the commanding officer. Fearing for the safety of the men against an endless mortar barrage, he retreated with the remaining survivors back down the slope to where they were at least out of range. It was getting dark, and his platoon would have to dig in for the night and wait for the inevitable wave of attacks from a very pissed off contingent of Japanese regulars.

*   *   *

A small gorge ran down the bottom of Sugar Loaf Hill, with a fast-moving creek about sixty feet across separating one side from the other. Goldman figured if he could slow the charge in the rivulet, they might be able to hold their position while *waiting for the sun*. The air was unusually cool for such a sultry island and, for the first time in a long time, Goldman weighed his fragile transience.

How much luck can one man have?

He had been fighting nonstop for almost four years, and the glaring fact that he was not dead yet threatened his hedging bet for survival. He was proud that his natural timidity and cowardly tendencies had not followed him into battle, but he could not take credit for something that he was sure he was not, and that was being brave. He never believed he was courageous or understood why others thought he was, when all he ever wanted to do was preserve his own hide. He had not felt the urge to climb a tree in years, and for that he was grateful. But somewhere along the line he had crossed a fear threshold, and something miniscule, was now emerging from his forgotten shrinking violet nature.

A familiar visitor had been coming around lately, and what was once just an annoying nuisance had become an obnoxious pest. Maybe it was the fact that it was May 15, 1945, and the idea of dying on his birthday wafted through his soul with an unimaginable odor. He felt queasy against the dim vista of eternity that had now become an antecedent bell tolling in his pewter ears.

Is this the last night on Earth for me? What is it going to be like to die, to pass into oblivion? How will I get it? What is waiting for me? God? Judgment? Is He a Face *or only indifferent* electricity?

He had been in many pitched battles before, but this was different, like if he didn't do something to save his own skin then he would never see the morning's light. A reticent but primordial fear of death crept into his fighting creed and hollowed him out like a gutted pink pig; with the apple of his warrior eye stuffed in his mouth, and he dreaded that soon he would be served at the banquet of the condemned. For the rest of the night all he knew was crystal clear blinding terror.

From the first "banzai!" scream, the attacks were relentless. The enemy, exposed by the light of magnesium flares, was obliterated by decimating fire that the marines laid down in a stretched night of endless slaughter. At times he felt the crimson tide would turn and, after seeing stacked cords of Japanese dead, he was sure that they would come to their senses and retreat. They did, but they returned again more fanatic than the previous attack, falling like nodding grain before the bloody sickle. The irksome feeling that they would eventually be overrun was not without merit and the words of Heraclites, "I sought for myself," morphed into buzzwords in Goldman's survival kit.

There seemed to be no end to the waves of screaming, slanted banshees. Goldman knew it was an exercise in nullity before the ammo ran out, and the darkroom where the devil develops his snapshots would be laid before his sinking eyes. The Japanese breached the marines' forward position, and the fighting was hand-to-hand. Goldman spotted a single tree just to the platoon's flank, and before he could talk himself out of it, his neo-simian brain caught up to his body and he had already climbed to the highest saddle branch. He watched blindly as his position was overrun, with every duty-bound marine butchered.

*   *   *

Goldman awoke in a hovering haze of consciousness and the sound of *cooing*. He opened his eyes, which fastened upon a pristine white dove perched on his tree limb, and the sinister pallor of death seemed almost inconsequential in comparison. He couldn't take his eyes off the fowl. It let out another *coo* then flew obliquely away. In the entire island-hopping campaign he had never seen a white dove. The encounter left him with a sense of the ineffable, resonate wordless anomalies that stripped him to his psychic essentials.

He surveyed the battlefield, and the crushing defeat assaulted his sense of moral duty. From his perch he could see that the men of his charge had been decimated, and those that had been wounded the Japanese made surgical work of with their knives and bayonets. The entire night had been laced with screams and howls of the wounded Americans, echoing through the blue-black valley as the men were dismembered one by one, piece by piece, and soul by soul. Goldman had expected to be overcome with a bout of craven diarrhea; guilt and shame should have been the water and feces that passed through him, but he felt nothing, and for that he was grateful.

Scores of Japanese carcasses littered the creek, mixed with the mutilated marines, a ghoulish stew of slow-cooked meat that filled the clammy air with olfactory disgrace. Goldman lowered himself from the tree and planted his boots on the sacrosanct ground, blood-muddy and carpeted by the brave. Almost as far as he could see, corpses were ripening and bloating in the searing tropical sun. The buzzing of insects was accentuated by the sickeningly sweet and sticky smell of burnt, mutilated flesh.

He sat next to his comrades and tried to commiserate with their disemboweled spirits, knowing from this day forward he would bear the shame of a pernicious coward. Any moral high ground he had earned in previous battles would be forever inflamed by the sepsis infection of deceit. No man knows how bad he is until he tries to be good and Goldman knew it would be impossible ever again to occupy the same space with himself. He was a real hookworm, a parasite, and would have to interpolate himself as a spurious host for the remainder of his fraudulent days.

His inconsonant fog was interrupted by distant voices. He feared the Japanese return and readied himself to climb the tree again, but as he listened he made out an American voice. *It must be the reinforcements Major Courtney had called for.*

He was spooked by the prospect of being the only marine alive and unharmed, fearing that his little escapade would be rankly axiomatic, with no way to screed off the obvious. He found the nearest dead Jap and took his rifle, pulled the bayonet off the muzzle and aligned the blade to his right side. If he was to gore himself, he could not hit any vital organs; any infection in the incubator of the tropics would kill him for sure. He strategically placed the bayonet at the oblique muscle, swiftly and painfully pushed backwards and pulled out. He attached the blade to the Japanese's rifle and dragged the body on top of him. His own blood mixed with the enemy's made for a glorious photo-op: The Last Brave Marine Fights to the Gruesome End.

The reinforcements came within sight, calling out to the lost platoon. Goldman groaned and lifted his blood-dripping hand. Marines rushed to his aid and dragged his bloody body out from the heap of twisted dead. A navy corpsman pulled his shirt off and rolled him onto his back.

"So what got you, a bayonet?" Goldman nodded.

Whisky-**T**ango-**F**oxtrot, this was it, the beginning of the never-ending lie. And it wouldn't be just one lie either, because when the lying starts it leads to more lies to support the original lie, and keeping up with all those lies means a never ending mind-sweep of unexploded fabrications. He knew that between death and a court marshal it was the softer option, but the only thing harder was a conscience that refused to give any ground.

The marines fanned out to secure the battlefield and scrounged through the mangled heaps of dead. Goldman hoped that there would be survivors, but dreaded the spotlight as a coward in the face of the enemy. He had heard stories of servicemen who were shot for less. With messy feelings he was relieved when he overheard one of the marines tell an officer that there were no other survivors. He then heard a languid drawl that was recognizable, but distant, and saw the battalion chaplain giving battlefield prayers for the dead.

He looked closer, and then turned to the corpsman, "Who's the chaplain?"

"Why, that's Chaplain Casey."

Goldman's mind buzzed like a beehive of pulsating perplexity and his mouth grimaced with a wary lopsided smile.

"You call yourself a preacher?" he hollered.

Jonathan's ears perked as he turned toward a familiar voice. Seeing Goldman lying on the bloody, muddy ground, he made a sprint to an old friend and brother.

"God Almighty," Jonathan blurted. "How bad is it?" he asked the corpsman.

"Well, Chaplain, looks like the Lord was with this one. That Jap bayonet went clean through without doing too much damage."

Jonathan flagged down two marines who gingerly rolled Goldman onto a stretcher and hoisted his bloody, gauzed body. Jonathan grabbed his brother's hand, and the two traded proverbial vanished stares.

"These are strange days, my brother, days when sullen knives are buried breast deep in the ones we love the most," said Jonathan.

"And you are a man after Caesar's own heart," Goldman witted.

X

For three days Goldman recovered in an olive drab canvas field hospital, and the revenant forms of his dead fellow marines kept an admonitory finger-pointing vigil by his bedside. He tried to ferret out reasons to be alive and contrive rationales to justify his cowardly act. Maybe he had unfinished business in the world? Maybe the wheedled will of providence had coaxed him into saving his own neck for some greater purpose? What good would it have served if he had died? What possible difference would it make if thirty-nine men died, or forty? Crazy questions harassed him with their syncopated rhythms that beat within his inner-chamber and fatigued his tightened jowls.

He had never dealt well with sensory overload or cognitive inflexibilities, and his spineless act of impropriety left his head bustling like a crazy termite mound. Like hives inside of hives he had to put his psychic bugs to rest, or there would no rest for the quick, only for the indebted, dreaded dead. In many a battle he had mindlessly thrown himself into danger's rancorous face and even welcomed the clacking shears of annihilation. At least dying in battle would have had some glory, but the chokehold of fear that had throttled him fore and aft was determined to sink his panicky barge if he didn't do something about it.

Something about Sugar Loaf Hill gnawed at him, like some unsightly spiritual lichen, breaking down the minerals of his very essence, a chemical-induced rat reaction where he could not lay down his life for the munificence of country or his fellow fighting brothers. It occurred to him that maybe there were traces of Christian paranoia about hell stored away in the cabinet of his forgotten files. War was already hell and the idea of being thrown into a worse hell for all of eternity peeved his sense of soul preservation when the door to the other side was as close as the next bullet, bayonet, or bit of shrapnel. The portrait of a God condemned eternity is vivid when framed by the dark corners of death's quadrants, and even resident atheists like Goldman trembled at the prospect of its vituperative grip.

From the corner of his eye's orbit he spied a figure, an imposing outline that he recalled from many years before. He craned his head and the silhouette moved into the revealing light. The two traded scattered smiles as they were lulled by the changed features of what were once boys into seasoned men of war.

Jonathan bellied up to Goldman's cot. "The doctors say you're very fortunate and that you're going to be fine."

"Did anybody else survive?" Goldman asked.

Jonathan shook his head.

Goldman knew there were no survivors, but his forged performance had to look like an original. He had it all planned out, only now he had a glitch in the agenda. Would a long-lost brother be able to see through his wildly-wrinkled tale? He figured the less he said, the less chance he would be spotted as a dog in the manger, tainted by a new breed of flea that now burrowed into his battle-bogus hide.

"I think the last time I saw you was Memphis, 1935 or '36?" Jonathan asked.

Goldman shrugged his shoulders, but he knew exactly to the day how long it had been. The date, the night, the very minute he was raped by Jack had indelibly etched its mark in his dissident compartment, the icy incident frozen and sealed with niggling freshness for the remainder of his refrigerated days. Jonathan knew as well, but he had his own sham to attend to. For years he had felt dipped in the batter of crumbed guilt and deep-fried in self-denunciation, and he was afraid that Goldman would see through his rehearsed subterfuge.

For hours they talked about how their lives had turned out. Jonathan had joined the Navy to contribute his pound of flesh to the war, and to be a chaplain seemed a natural call. He hadn't changed much; he was a grown man but symptoms of his resonate persona remained. He was still a proselytizer, bobbing the dap-bait of eternity on Goldman's surface, hoping he might bite on the line of the Lord. Goldman politely listened to the impassioned pleas of someone he once knew, but was not sure that he wanted to know anymore.

Jonathan wearily rambled on that God had spared Goldman's life for a reason. Goldman knew he had been spared only because *he* had acted, not because some far-off benefactor had pulled cosmic threads to keep him alive. He thought it funny, in a noxious way, that after all the years of watching his father fleece the flock, Jonathan had ever considered going into the same trade. The pittance the evangelist had paid to his only son, and the drunken beatings Jonathan had endured were barefaced reminders of a donkey of a man who always made him feel like an ass. The way he pilfered the fold and his brazen philandering should have marred Jonathan's enthusiasm, instead it seemed to have deepened his convictions.

Now that the looming threat of a firebrand eternity had cooled, Goldman suddenly felt sorry for Jonathan and thought it was sad that people like him needed—even craved—religious concoctions. Even after death's encounter, he had to reiterate to himself that there is no celestial *Face* out there, only us, and ultimately it is up to us if we are to emerge from the cloud of nonsense called god.

Goldman still believed that anyone who took refuge from a meaningless universe into the false embrace of religion suffered from latent psychoses and were pitifully trying to expiate some hidden guilt for just being alive. If his brief experience with Christianity had been a taste of something more, then he was determined never to bite into that crusty bread again. Religion always manifested as self-righteous distortions for people who wanted to feel that they had cornered the market on some great secret. Alert and oriented times zero, most folks lived their lives as castaways, floundering in oceans of uncertainty, waiting to be washed up on any of salvation's distant shores. Truth is more important than facts, yet oddly, Goldman envied Jonathan's faith.

After their long-winded catching up, Jonathan left. Goldman lay back in his bed to rest his weary wagging tongue that cleaved to the roof of his sticky mouth, and clamped his eyes tight. Too much jawboning and too much reminiscing exhaust the soul and disturb memories that should remain tucked away in stroke comas, fast asleep . . . paralyzed. After three days of no sleep he finally passed out, too tired to even recall the jungle battles, and the one part of his mind that knew what was best for him was determined to sleep like a boulder, and dream of nothing.

*   *   *

On a hospital ship destined for the Philippines, Goldman was awakened by the droning voice of a hospital nurse. He then saw a marine colonel with an aide standing by his bed, the wattage of his smile burning his blown pupils. He thrust his hand into Goldman's and shook it with febrile animation.

"Congratufuckinglations. You really had us going."

This is it. They're onto my half-witted farce, he thought.

"I know your type. You don't like taking credit for a job well done," said the colonel.

"What?"

The colonel smiled large. "The fight for Sugar Loaf Hill has given the Marines two more big C's. The decisive battle was determined by the dogged command, leadership, and uncommon valor of you and Major Courtney. The two of you will be receiving the Congressional Medal of Honor. Major Courtney posthumously I'm sad to say."

"There must be a mistake," Goldman dissented.

"No mistake" barked the colonel. The gruff officer pulled out the battle report and read:

"1st Lieutenant David Oliver Goldman, 2nd Battalion, 22nd Marines, 6th Marine Division, in action against enemy Japanese forces on Okinawa Shima in the Ryukyu Islands, 14th and 15th of May 1945. Upon having his meager detachment of marines redeployed along the slope of Sugar Loaf Hill, Lieutenant Goldman and his men made a valiant stand against successive Japanese night attacks. When his platoon was on the verge of being overrun, Lieutenant Goldman commandeered a machine gun from a fellow dead marine and single-handedly beat back wave after wave of fanatic Japanese banzai attacks. Throughout the night he poured relentless automatic fire at pointblank range, while furiously hurling hand grenades into the enemy's ranks. With ammunition running low Lieutenant Goldman engaged the enemy with rifle and bayonet, killing dozens. Although severely wounded, he savagely fought on until the early hours of the following morning. In the local action—against tremendously superior forces heavily armed with rifles, machine guns, mortars, and grenades—Lieutenant Goldman killed at least one hundred of the enemy, but his contribution to the campaign on Okinawa was of a much more far-reaching consequence. Sugar Loaf Hill was the key to the entire defensive line and, due to his utterly fearless and heroic defense, the will of the relentless Japanese eventually crumbled."

While the colonel went on with the chimerical account, Goldman's eyes rack focused on the other wounded in the hospital bay. Men with no limbs, white and red-gauzed mummies, blackened burns, and gangrened features; the true heroes lined up in a pantheon of the brave, and not so much as even a complimentary nod from the colonel. It was nauseating to be the only blight upon the honor hall of the real heroes. Especially when the wounded gave a collective applaud for the merits of Goldman's heroism that the colonel so bellicosely woofed in a litany of the absurd.

"Make any one of these other men a hero, not me." Goldman murmured.

The colonel acted as if he didn't hear. "Heroes that tasted battle are needed back home to sell war bonds."

"I'm no hero," Goldman quietly protested.

"Heroes capture the imagination of the American public," said the colonel.

The accolades were like a rusty trombone blowing through his tinny ears and he could no longer listen to a de-trop melody of the preposterous.

He cut the colonel off with a loud shout that echoed across the hospital bay. "I have no business being in the same room with these men!"

The entire bay condensed into an eerie quiet. The colonel turned to his aide, then to the nurse, as Goldman seethed in a diaphragm-compressed hush.

"I was a coward in the face of the enemy," he plaintively muttered.

The colonel paused then patted him on the back. "Your modesty is eloquent son, but don't feel guilty because you survived. You're going home now. You've earned it."

The colonel left with his aide and the nurse in tow.

Goldman lay back on the hospital bed with his eyes riveted to the ceiling, unable to look at the disfigured and wounded around him, unknown *amis* who shared the same room—and maybe in some way, the same guilt.

XI

After his recovery in the Philippines, Goldman arrived stateside, where he was press-ganged into the ranks of the real war heroes: the flag raisers of Iwo Jima, men from the Normandy landing, and survivors from Pearl Harbor. It was a barnstorming affair with carnival midway panache; patriotic music, hot dogs, beer, and cotton candy for the kids too. The Sunday crowds gathered before the spectacle of war icons; ordinary men who had done extraordinary things in extra-ordinary times. That's what America was selling—a piece of real Minuteman patriotism.

Army Sergeant Sagev, fitted with a hook-claw arm after having it severed just below the elbow by a samurai blade, was the go-to-pro.

The compère introduced him as the first of the heroes. "We have with us today the champion of Guadalcanal, originally from Las Vegas, Nevada, Sergeant Sal Sagev."

The audience bellowed a collective roar as Sergeant Sagev approached the podium with a stage presence that would have made most Broadway actors jealous; a natural orator who could hypnotize snakes with oboe mood control and raised palanquin verse. The blue-collar gentry were smitten by his placid aristocratic voice, and even veterans from the First World War wept by the tablespoons; a preamble politician in all its manufactured glory.

"I want to thank you for turning out today," said the sergeant. "If I can give a limb to the war effort, then I know you can find it in your hearts and wallets to give to this national cause. The future of God, democracy, and the American way depend on you. Buy war bonds!" The crowd exploded with enthusiastic applause and shouts of victory as they raised their fingers with spread-eagle V's to the sky.

The compère spoke solemnly into the microphone again. "Our next speaker is the hero of Sugar Loaf Hill in that terrible battle for Okinawa, one of only a handful of men to have earned the Congressional Medal of Honor. Please put your hands together for 1ˢᵗ Lieutenant David Oliver Goldman."

Sergeant Sagev gave Goldman a pat on the back as encouragement to approach the podium. He reined in his divergent feelings, adjusted the microphone, and looked out onto a sea of candid eyes and sunburned faces. The air, thick with cigarette and cigar smoke, spilt beer, hair spray, and body odor: a floating potpourri of embossed expectation.

He tried to clear his voice, which slightly trembled, the words bumbling over his desiccated tongue. "What is courage? I ask myself that every day. I suppose it is one's ability to rise in the face of fear. People say I am a brave man, but I know I am just an ordinary marine doing his duty, and I am sure that any one of you would have done the same. Your sacrifice is required now, more than ever, for the countless brave men who need your help to whip the Nips. Don't let them down. We're almost there, let's finish the job."

Goldman's staccato delivery did not squelch the crowd's zeal and they let out a collective barmy cheer. He walked back to the honorarium row where the other servicemen were seated and pulled out a piece of paper with words that were similar to what he had just delivered. Looking over the paper he turned to the one-armed sergeant.

"A couple more like this and I think I'll have to go AWOL."

Sergeant Sagev grinned with a *les autres* smirk and again patted him on the back with his hook arm, nicking Goldman's ear, which started to bleed.

"Don't be so hard on your light."

Goldman quirked his eyebrow, "What do you mean?"

"Lightning is faster than sound. That's why some people appear bright until they open their mouths. But you might be an exception." said the Sergeant.

Goldman shook his head and dabbed his oozing ear.

"You're going to fit in just fine."

Goldman pulled out a hankie and pressed it onto his bleeding ear. "Never in a year of Sundays."

*   *   *

Goldman was attached to the Naval Armory in Los Angeles, and would be there until the war machine sent him across the country on the next of numerous bond drives that he furtively dreaded. He felt like an earworm was eating through his brain. Memories from the war could not be scraped from his wallpaper mind, and to pretend that just because he was back in the States meant he was fine was tainted folly. He hoped that in time he might become someone different—a translated man—but in the interim comfort and solace were to be found in long strolls with Johnny Walker or any other blended whiskey that felt as restless as he.

Civilian life was frightening, maybe even more so than the predictable barren stretches of ballooned boredom punctured by short-lived implosions of blinding violence that was the nature of war, and he wished to go back. There was something about fighting for his very survival that seemed to have kept life manageable. Over there, he was a man for all seasons and dialectic truth ruled: black and white, life or death. Here, the gray areas of civilian etiquette were complicated and required diligent self-inquiry, yet his sense and sensibility usually resulted in tactical self-avoidance.

The day-in and day-out tedium of being a hero was brutal; ennui reigned and he needed to keep busy. He was spared the minutiae of degrading details and daily chores that the other enlisted men and officers had to do: policing the armory, KP, and guard duty—these were for unmerited enlistees, not a Congressional Medal of Honor recipient.

Relegated to a sacred cow set out to pasture, he started reading again. He read anything he could get his hands on. He liked comic books: pure escapism, fantasy indulgence, mindless dreaming about living another life. Shakespeare, Voltaire, Sartre, and the three Greeks; philosophy became an obsession and metaphysics a surfeiting preoccupation as he tried to find different ways of looking at a seemingly random and violent universe that hounded existential refugees like himself for answers.

He started reading the little notebook that had belonged to the Japanese prisoner. He read the same line again that was written in English, *"What you are looking for is what you are looking with."*

Why would this man write in English? he thought.

He thumbed through the pages and his eyes fixed on a single line: "Newtonian laws that have stood for three hundred years are obsolete on the subatomic level." The idea intrigued him, as quantum physics had been his father's sideline and one of his own favorite subjects. The autodidact laws of Newton's universe ruled the bedrock of reality, but Goldman's own theoretical slang suspected there was more . . . much more.

A man named Kazuo Kajiki, a physics professor from the University of Tokyo, had penned the notebook. At first glance, the writings seemed symptomatic of someone who suffered from Mystic's Syndrome. Its propositions of consciousness, transcendence, and exegesis unfolding jabbed Goldman's curiosity. He had read a lot about esoteric philosophies, smuggled in from the East, and had some understanding of meditation

from the avatars of India. In the past he had made a few halfhearted forays
into the disciplined art, but without much success. He thought Kazuo's
notes might be an interesting read—anyone who had the guts to look
under the hood of the universe would always bag his attention.

Kazuo had scribbled running commentaries on the works of Planck,
Bohm, Chuang Tzu, Hegel, and Kierkegaard, a kind of Zen meets
inner-expanding space. From just a cursory scan, the writer seemed
bedeviled by attempts to connect seemingly limited degrees of freedom
into a coalesced fundamental template of the universe: the essence of the
building blocks of perception.

The source of all consciousness, Kazuo asserted, was to be found at the
subatomic level and somehow the human brain is the grand receiver and
transmitter of its frequency, the tip of the universe and a portico to a vast
matrix of information, a conflation that tied all things into one. At the
quantum level all could be understood. The micro fathering the macro,
the wellspring that begets the grand rapids of life, the prime creator—the
cosmic delta to an inner world where reality as we know it is deceiving but
appears ordinary to the untrained eye.

Another theme was about karma and cosmic equalization, that all
actions precipitate reaction and bring balance back into a universal harmonic
buzz. In Kazuo's view, the human condition, and its lack of balance, was a
manifested symptom of blocked neurotransmitters that connect the brain's
hemispheres. He theorized that if new synapses could be established, then
the most basic elements of human quality could be restored. Peace, joy, and
happiness, were the natural order of the universe, and the human species,
mysteriously, the linchpin that makes the very cosmos aware of itself.

Kazuo had traveled the world and studied with the great masters of the
Far East, Tibet, China, the Zen Buddhists of Japan, and even the Christian
monks of Europe. The one commonality they shared was chanting or,
more specifically, pitched tones that resonated from collective throats. He
theorized that the notes and the frequencies they generated affected the mind
through the inner ear, drawing the participant into deeper altered states
where penetrating levels of peace and wellbeing thrived. It had nothing to
do with religion or mysticism, but rather a quantifiable phenomenon that
was so compelling that Kazuo had devoted all his energies to find a way to
duplicate it through manipulation of sound.

The Tibetans preferred the monophonic note combination of C, F, A
flat, G flat, and C sharp. The constant hum of these atonal and chromatic
pitches, while in deep meditative states, seemed to have a real effect, not

only on emotional levels, but directly on the brain itself. The Tibetans believed that the brain, at one time, was non-hemispheric and that there was no longitudinal fissure at the corpus callosum, but later had become bipolar, lateralized and almost separate. To them, the bisected brain was really a deformity, a result of aberrant unconsciousness and a chronic sense of separation from the Source, which has hoodwinked the human race in its short history.

According to Kazuo, the original non-hemispheric brain was complete and at one time had total access to the secrets of the universe, the universe being pure mind and the human brain the instrument for its physical reflection. However, it could only be a reflection so long as the surface waters of human consciousness were glass-like and still; energy and matter tangoing for eternity to a cosmic dirge of sound waves, which completed an unbroken circle for eons. Somehow, modern man had broken the biomorphic chain and, ironically, would now have to be the default master-link to its restoration.

He had hypothesized, that initiating a frequency through the five notes to subjects while in deep meditative states might show promise, asserting that the lower the frequency and the higher the amplitude, the more effective the notes. Conscious levels of beta waves could be lowered to alpha waves, which were more focused and relaxed. Still deeper would be theta levels of consciousness such as deep sleep and REM sleep, and deeper still to the delta level where the psycho-spiritual energy of the subconscious ruled the body's motor functions, and even the mysterious gamma level where the infinite recesses of the human psyche leaping between spiritual dimensions could be tapped.

It was at the gamma level that Kazuo believed abstract forms derived from the implicate order where space and time are obsolete, the porthole coupler with the universe that interacted with all creation, a holographic wormhole that made possible instant mental travel and intergalactic communication. If it was achievable then healthy restoration to the human condition could be reestablished, and compendium accounts of the soul's black hole would be washed in brilliance by light spectrums of transcendent consciousness. For Kazuo, everything, including man's sanity, was shaped by compulsory sounds of perfect morphic resonance.

The sequence of notes struck something in Goldman that he had long forgotten. He remembered as a child prodigy playing those very same five notes over and over on the piano, until it drove his mother barmy. For him, it had rendered his puerile angst relaxed and immobile. He was stunned to think that those five notes were significant in Kazuo's meditation techniques. *It sounded fantastic, but what if it were true?*

It was a ponderous cram, but there was something in it that buttered Goldman's metaphysical loaf. The writings fixed his imagination and he decided to read the memoirs from the beginning. In the opening pages Kazuo had written a three-page denunciation of Japan's imperial pursuits. It was a running indictment of not only the Japanese war machine, but a general admonition against any blind aspiration that employed the use of military aggression to achieve some far-flung goal.

Goldman now understood why Kazuo's notes were written in English. It was a treasonous rant, and if his superiors had gotten hold of it, he would have forfeited his illuminated head. Goldman recoiled from this lucidity with unexpected heaviness. He realized that the writer had been a thinking, reasoning human being, a forward-evolved genius even, not some demonized enemy that the military had cold stripped of his humanity. He suddenly felt a mix of queasy culpability stirred with uncharacteristic compassion for someone who had a face and feelings, and had once shared time and space with the rest of the world.

He had to put the notebook down before the charged memory of that day put him in its own snake-like grip. His connection to Kazuo now seemed uncomfortably ensconced in quantum guesswork, yet fixed and precise. The writings were unnerving and exacting in their effect and Goldman needed to return to where vagaries thrived, where his apostrophe self could return borrowed thoughts and mislaid feelings to life's lost and found, where the seer, the seeing, and the seen are one and the same but never owned and never claimed.

XII

The vanguard of the war bond clique had a kinky yen for the watering holes of downtown, and risqué appetites for the local hot tamale female dishes. However, being white servicemen stationed next to some of the Mexican population had its hazards for sot visitors and Anglicized ideas. It hadn't been more than a couple of years since the notorious zoot-suit riots were in full flame.

Drunken military men on their way back to base after a night of drinking were often rolled by Mexican youths who wanted to teach the unruly Anglos some respect. But white America was not about to forgo its presumed prerogatives; first class citizens taking shit from the local "mud people" would not stand, and soon it was an injunction against all people of color. The riots broke out in earnest and servicemen were accompanied by the local white population, a mob of club-toting, knife-wielding Caucasian giants who ruled the land and no one was going to stop them, not even the law.

At first the servicemen were looking for Mexican *pachucos*, young Mexicans who visually defied the norms of unwritten rules that demanded that people of color remain unseen and unheard. The vulgar style of the zoot suit with its broad shoulders, narrow waistline, and ballooned pants instilled a confident, cocky swagger that seemed to emanate from the fashion. The city council adopted a resolution that banned the wearing of zoot suits on LA streets, punishable by a thirty-day jail term. By 1945, tensions were still raw in the city of fallen angels, and every now and again there were border skirmishes, but nothing like the riots of June 1943.

Goldman and Sergeant Sagev were drinking with some of the marines from the bond drive in a rancid little cantina in Boyle Heights. It was a tribal thing, required if you were a full-time functionary of the battle-tested group. Across the bar were three *Morena Floras* squeezed into a red vinyl booth. Goldman had been giving them mooching muchacha sidelong glances all night and thought the prettiest of the three was *breast*iculating to him in buxom code.

His booze gauge was reading full, and he felt he had enough gas to get him across the Strophades bar and approach the fearful Harpies. Like a stroke victim he wobbled to the table as a young zoot suiter delivered him a hefty dose of Latin stink eye and snarled something in Spanish that Goldman did not understand but sounded vulgar enough to be an insult. He ignored the purple-suited punk and kept his focus on the prettiest girl in the booth.

"Ola, my name is Goldman," he garbled.

The Latina shrugged her shoulders, uncurious and unimpressed. He wondered why people like him were instant party killers. Even with a bellyful of beer he could douse the fire of a good time with lockstep efficiency and pathetic squeals of gemmeoutahere! Like a detumescent organ he was about to go soft, but his fellow marines weren't about to let his erected effort go flaccid just yet. They motioned for him to try again. He turned back around, eyes out of focus, jaw out of joint, and attempted to deliver a slurred repartee. Before he could untie the tangled idiom from his tongue, the *konk* of a beer bottle ricocheting off his noggin put him on his back. Hovering over him was the same boonie-rat punk that had been eyeballing him all night. Goldman tried to stand, but another Mexican buckled his beer-filled fulcrum with a kick to the gut and he collapsed.

The cry of "Greasers!" bellowed across the bar, as the marines charged the *pachucos* with thrilled urgency and a lack of unvenial haste. More Mexicans poured in from outdoors, like hot caramel fudge spilling over vanilla ice cream. This was their dirt, their women, their *ciudad*, and they had been planning to jump the Anglos from the minute they entered the beer joint. The other patrons made a donkey-run to the exits as the bar turned into an LA beat down cockfight fiesta.

The pounding, kicking, and flesh smashing whirred in the alcohol air with grunts, smacks, and groans. The fighting was angry and spirited, but good fun for all—provided you were not in the impact zone of a boot or a fist. In the midst of the melée, one of the Mexicans yanked the prosthetic arm off Sergeant Sagev and started swinging it. The sergeant got clubbed by his own arm and almost knocked cold. Goldman came to and started swinging at anything within firing range, so long as it was brown.

Who he really wanted was the little prick who had glass-cocked him with the beer bottle. He worked his way through the skirmish and cornered the punk, who looked to be no more than fifteen or sixteen. He grabbed an empty beer bottle and was about to return the favor, when the teenager pulled a stiletto and started slashing with the vilest of intent. Goldman broke the bottle, and the others stopped the hurly-burly to focus on the broken-bottle knife fight. Like a gladiatorial match they stalked one another in a perilous game of sudden death. For Goldman, it was amusing, which enraged the young *pachuco* even more.

Goldman laughed, bobbing and weaving as the kid swung wildly. In frustration he lunged at Goldman with the knife inches from his eye, and then it wasn't funny anymore. Like the end of a bullwhip, Goldman snapped. In a flickering blur the bar was vacuumed of all sound and movement, as the kid lay on the floor with the knife sticking out of his midsection. A deep-red puddle pooled around his purple suit and, like a motionless chameleon, his mocha skin turned phosphorescent, matching the pale milieu of the cantina.

The frozen quiet was shattered by a commotion of badly broken English: "*Cavrone*, I calling the cops!"

On that cue, everyone vamoosed. The kid was left alone with Goldman, both expanding in dilations of the surreal. The adolescent's eyes, once hot coals blazing with credulous passion, drained into darkened tide pools, round puddles of pollywog mud. The teenager's switch had been turned off, and like a diode indicator, the light was still on but slowly fading to fathomless black.

Goldman was fixed with vapid answers of the weak, and saw nothing but strapping questions staring back. Akin to a bad dream where one walks for miles in his sleep, he wanted to run as far as nowhere would go, but his legs were petrified stumps. Just when he felt his flight instinct pumping juice into his lumbered limbs, *whack!* He dropped to the floor like a sack of beer-soaked sawdust and cracked peanut shells. The bartender, hennaed and hot, paced back and forth above him with a baseball bat, barking out obsolescent insults in locutions of broken anti-Anglo English.

XIII

The static crack of a dispatch radio mingled with the slamming of a concrete-laden steel door jarred Goldman from his stretched stupor of elastic time. He awoke on a glutinous cement floor in the downtown jail, his head and neck pounding with twinges of unwanted memory syndromes. He pulled a blood-blackened, sticky gauze from his head and noticed a flock of wing-clipped jailbirds perched in semicircle around him. He tried to remember how he got there but his mind voided it like an illegal tendered payment, keeping it vaulted where most of his alcoholic blackouts were stored.

Recollections of the night before began to seep into his fermented soaked malaise as he tried to locate the weighing scale of his kaput equilibrium. The words *you killed somebody* tipped his pendulous balance and he suddenly felt wanting. The salted faces from the jail's peanut gallery stared at him like a man on a ledge with *leap mother fucker* eyes and *no one's going to catch you* grins. His skin heated and he stared back long enough and hot enough that one by one the incarcerated melted like weak-flame candles. The sound of a master dungeon key rattled the steel door as a jail guard unlocked it. A plainclothes detective, a military policeman, and a marine officer stood like a three-prong *blivet* in a Gestapo optical illusion, pummeling Goldman's Hebraic varlet face with Teutonic disdain.

"All right soldier, let's go," said the uncombed guard, with a beer gut that hung past his open zipper.

Goldman slowly stood as primal tremors and panic eruptions bubbled through his head, and he almost collapsed under a heavy surge of volcanic vertigo. The men filed into a nearby office where he sat on a chair across the desk from the detective, disconcerted with conjunctions of dreadful import.

"My name is Roberts, homicide. This is Colonel Ortberg from the adjutant general's office. Looks like you got yourself in a real shit-pickle, son." Goldman's jaw locked tighter than a 105 breech block, waiting to fire for effect.

"Miguel Contreras. Does that ring your bell?"

Goldman said nothing.

"Looks like you buried a six inch blade in the liver of that kid. He expired at the scene."

"It was self defense," Goldman shot.

"That might be, but you're going to have to prove that in a court of law. As it stands, you're charged with first-degree murder." Colonel Ortberg's excoriating eyes bored holes so deep through Goldman's mug that the back of his skull burst with blood-stroke apoplexy.

"Military police will take you into custody until the district attorney files charges," said the detective.

The large MP pulled Goldman to his feet, slapped on a pair of wrist irons, and briskly ushered him out of the jail with the cold efficiency of the Waffen-SS.

* * *

He was sequestered in a Quonset hut for the better part of a fortnight. Goldman dreaded the inevitable indictment of a grand jury and the trial that was sure to follow. What he needed was a good lawyer, yet all his requests were suspiciously denied. Objective moral facts require objective moral properties of good and bad, and he couldn't help but feel that this was some kind of skewed karma. It was a strange word for him to use, until he remembered Kazuo's notebook: "Life is a series of checks and balances and there is a cosmic record of people's deeds and a fundamental continuum that form our experiences."

It was payback time, he thought.

Recollections of Sugar Loaf Hill blew through him like skein debris, and memories of his yellow-bellied act left him flayed in red and tangled in blue. He thought it ironic to be court marshaled for defending himself against a knife-wielding greaser, when only weeks earlier they had deemed him a hero for supposedly bayoneting dozens of Japanese.

The clanging of his cell door snapped him out of his censure, his peaking-one-eye blinking through his interlocked fingers.

"Let's go," growled the large marine guard.

Goldman stood and was led out of the cell with only the resignation to his fate as his consular. He was escorted to the adjutant general's office and took a seat. Across from him was the general himself, relaxed and embedded with praetorian weight.

"At the risk of sounding like a quasi-busybody, it looks like I'm going to have to meddle in your affairs," said the general.

"Yes sir," answered Goldman, with a strained voice.

"I once had a midget girlfriend . . . and I was *nuts* over her," the general jibed.

"Is that a joke sir?"

"It's no joke, Lieutenant. The public *is* nuts over you. You're the first American Jew awarded the Congressional Medal of Honor. Hell, you were on the cover of *Life* magazine, and you use it to wipe your ass."

"I'm sorry, sir, I've been under a lot of pressure."

"That's no excuse. I can't accept sloppy thinking. Now, lucky for you, there are enough people in the right places to let your wrongs be buried in a mountain of paperwork, the bottom of which will never see the light of day. Nobody gives a good goddamn about spooks and spics. Now if it had been a white kid, your hard times would come real easy, but we've decided to go light on you. So, do everybody a big favor and levitate your ass outa' here."

"I don't understand sir."

"Go sell war bonds. Dismissed!"

The general waited for a subordinate salute, but Goldman could only stare in disbelief. He gesticulated with an idle military hand maneuver and did a volte-face turn, a reprieved man in a commuted sentence.

*   *   *

The drudgery of the bond drive was taking a dirt-tired toll on Goldman's effete beaten path. He continued to tour the country, but no matter where he went, he was accompanied by a cast of self-indulging pariahs who eat what they crave—guilt and loneliness—eventually strip mining all moral quotients. Whenever he sprayed himself with defoliated feelings, he would run to the bad company of alcohol's rheumy washing of the eye.

The enthusiastic speeches required of him turned into satirical debacles of drunken ribald. Once he was so snockered that he fell into the audience, pulling the podium with him, where it crushed an old lady who had to be hospitalized. Another time, he was shaking hands with the throng when a young mother lifted her baby to be kissed and he regurgitated on the infant like an ovoviviparous human fly. A reporter captured the vomiting incident and the photo was printed in the *LA Times*. He stayed drunk on duty and off duty, it didn't matter. It was all so self-absorbed. Alcohol addiction: chronic repetitious narcissism and Goldman thrived on that kind of self-importance.

To fill his days, he would spend his lotus time lounging at the movie bijous. They were like the books he read, dispersed journeys into extensions yet to be explored; the two-dimensional seduction of the silver screen flung him into vicarious worlds, fantasy kingdoms where he was the hero, the leading man, the savior of all. His imagination thrived in the pictures and he pretended that it was him that the audience loved. The idea of being Clark Gable, Errol Flynn, or Gary Cooper whetted his appetite to be worshiped and adored, stargazed upon by a galaxy of earthbound novas.

One afternoon in Chicago, he settled into a matinée double feature. Between the movies a newsreel from the warfront splashed across the thirty-foot screen. It was raw footage of the American troops liberating the concentration camps of Eastern Europe. "Six million Jews feared dead," belted the fast-talking narrator backed by a ridiculous orchestral score more befitting a bad Broadway musical. Still, the nacreous images of emaciated bodies struck a seminal nerve that resonated down to Goldman's soft cells, which hardened and split in alarmed panic. Acres of fallen brothers and skeleton-like corpses gruesomely bulldozed into mass graves—ghastly images scrawled on his optic nerve, spinning his gyroscopic axis into a torque-induced wobble and his internal security up to DEFCON 4, reverting him to a brain-stemmed creature hurling emoted expletives at the screen.

Not since he was a boy had Goldman thought about being a Jew, but now he felt an ineffable kinship with those desecrated cadavers and was besieged with despotic felony and litigious rage. He stormed out of the theater with the sickening similes still embossed in his mind like stock numbers tattooed on concentration camp forearms. The silver screen made the grisly panorama literally larger than life and gagged him like mutilated morgue meat. For the first time he felt his Jewishness was not just an evanescent dream in some long forgotten life. He realized that he had been functioning in a dream for too long, and to know that one is functioning in a dream is the beginning of an awakening. Goldman kept mumbling to himself, as his mother used to hammer into him: "You're a Jew, you're a Jew."

From that day forward he was determined not to forget his Hebrew pedigree, and if there was anything he could do for his people, he would devote himself to his Davidic branch and its deliquesce cause.

*   *   *

The bond drive was in New York, Goldman liked Manhattan, despite its tendency to make him feel like a diaphanous apparition. In all towns and in all cities, no one knew him from Cane or Abel and he felt that people peered through him like an insubstantial ghost. It's a gloomy feeling when no one knows your name and, as always, substantiation was found in filthy intrigues with maquillage prostitutes. There was a weird comfort in exchanging warm bodily fluids with someone who was a complete cold stranger.

He found it funny that the whores would never let you kiss them, but had no problem sucking your meat puppet, as if your mouth was dirtier. They didn't care who you were, nor did they ask about harrowing childhoods, acts of cowardliness, or miscreant behavior. Just lay the sawbuck on the dresser and say goodbye to your antithetical resolutions. Distractions with alcohol and meat hookers were deleterious spells on an already bewitched self, and he craved a new hex from a superior coven.

He ran into a black pimp outside of Harlem who introduced him to heroin and he never again looked the same at his might-have-beens. Heroin became his new apparatus of encouragement. Never being one who liked needles, it took considerable coaxing before he could perforate his skin with the excitant steel spine, but after his first hit he was a cowboy junkie who rode the *horse* all the way to hell's bell.

There was something about heroin that scratched his scatological itch, and its concentrated affection for his mephitic soul was beyond words. He likened it to a rollercoaster that slowly ratchets up a steep incline, for a moment stalls, and then the bottom drops out to a free-fall opiate-controlled crash. Blood warm leatherette, erotic snarls, testicle tickling, and laughing at your own private joke, caressing, flattening, steam-rolled warmth. Heroin became his *heroine*, and he fell in love after one slurping kiss.

Goldman's penchant for dope was matched only by his ever-running desire to escape the viper of alienation. The trade-off, of course, was that the antidote was worse than the venom. Keeping your heroin addiction a secret was one thing, but trying to get a fix when you're *jakeing* on the road was something else. His symptoms of withdrawal were wound-raw and palpable, and his incessant use left tracks on his forearms that created nasty abscesses that he tried to hide. His veins refused to cooperate any longer, retreating into his muscle to keep from being tapped. Soon he was shooting under his tongue and in between his toes and when he could not find his hot, black-tar ticket out, he would go cold turkey in. It was a wretched experience that required nerves of steel and the rampaging madness of a stampeding elephant. But he did it when he had to.

While touring, Goldman often made punitive expeditions into the netherworld chunks of the cities. He had lived in the roughest black quarter of Memphis and felt a weird kinship with those people, and was even at ease with its vile-hole element. It was in the concrete Congo jungles that he would find his ever-elusive quest for smack easily obtained. Illicit drugs were part of the Negro culture and if you were a white junk-o-holic explorer, that's where you went on safari.

The bond drive moved to Memphis and its psychological imminence felt like infected wounds wrapped in vestures of bad blood. Goldman wandered down Beale Street to the tenement building where he had lived as a boy. He stood on the very steps where he learned of his parents' death, and not since then had he felt his civil liberties so completely violated. Something on the inside cracked, and the watertight compartment that held their memory ruptured. The pressure of being submerged for all those years flooded his being with salted waves of raw emotion that he could not control or understand. He lamented their loss with auditory hallucinations that attached to him like hundreds of leeches sucking his life out, and he needed a fix just to allay the agony of their recall.

A big Black Mariah told him where he could score some high-octane China White. He self-prescribed an anti-bipolar dose for his emotional defection and double-dipped for the occasion. While mainlining in the dealer's drug emporium, a ruckus broke out between a morphine merchant and a disgruntled customer. A Jamaican produced a .38 revolver and two black bucks lay dead, with Goldman out cold between them, a ghastly blood-soaked Oreo cookie. He recovered from the overdose but had no recollection of the double homicide.

When the military got wind of the incident he was thrown in the brig. Brass was only too aware of his incompatibility with the war bond drive, and his failure to adapt to military standards was the final poppy stalk.

They were in a quandary—how do you section eight a war hero? He was a real dandy with no solution, a soiled splotch on the pristine honor of the Corps that felt exceedingly scorned by the mottled character of its bastard offspring stock—Goldman, the world's illegitimate son.

XIV

Being yanked off the bond drive would have been a carbolic burn for most combat veterans, but for Goldman it was a long-sought relief. He could have been demoted and kicked out of the Corps, but the fact that he was somewhat of a celebrity and a notable of the periodicals made the disposal of an undesirable tricky. If the press got wind that a national war hero had gotten caught up in the twilight world of Negroes, narcotics, and murder, there would not be enough damage control in the Marines' spin cycle to save Goldman's incontinent barge, which listed too heavily for the military's dry dock standards. He was a real poltergeist that needed to be extirpated, and brass feared the enlisted ranks were starting to show symptoms of contagion.

He was shipped back to the Naval Armory, and was allowed to keep his grade and privileges, but he was relegated to in-house exile, and a scourge to be shunned by others. He was spared the stockade, but the isolation and tacit orders from his superiors to send him to Coventry wore him threadbare. Every morning he would fall out for formation, hoping for any menial duty to occupy his disproportionate time, but when the others went on to do the day's boring tasks, he was sent back to the barracks to wait for new orders that were always a day away.

*   *   *

In the evenings Goldman found himself a peripatetic leaf blowing through the local saloons and whorehouses, an insolent maniac operating in a void. He was a good-looking man, yet it was seemingly impossible for him to find a woman. He ran into opportunities, but unconscious sickly techniques would scare healthy prospects away. It was always something astoundingly stupid, like trying to put a clever sentence together, that ended up spilling out into a sloppy polysyllabic soup. When speaking to the opposite sex he was so tense that his voice quivered and white foam coalesced in the corners of his rictus mouth. His maladroit mannerisms were so peculiar as to destroy any possibility of social intercourse, let alone sexual intercourse.

There was a woman he had met the first time he came through the armory. She was attractive but not full of herself. Goldman was siesta-ing on the Venice Beach when she inexplicably plopped her plenteous maximus next to him and eyed the *unknown soldier's* Marine tattoo and his rib-bare bayonet wound. She reached over with fingertips of vetted balm and touched his scar. It startled Goldman, who jackknifed up from his somnolent doze.

"Is that from the war?" she languidly asked.

He tried to hide the self-inflicted mark, but she was an intercessor to empathetic scars and with anoxic care calmly pulled his hand away. "I'm a nurse at the veteran's hospital. Was it a bayonet? I've seen a lot of bayonet wounds."

"Something like that," he answered.

Her eyes were gentle and tolerant, and Goldman immediately felt at ease with her. The two talked on the beach for the rest of the day as coronal mass ejections licked their bodies and sun flares squinted their solar eyes, and then sank ninety-three million miles behind the lead-blue LA horizon. They got along well and even went on a couple of dates. At first he didn't realize how lovely she was, the way her full lips pouted, and a smile that exposed immaculately girded teeth, where canines and bicuspids line up tighter than the best military formation.

He was enchanted by her slit eyes, which made him feel occidental and her almost oriental; a delicate nose that rested like czarist nobility on her ceramic face, and the body of a mighty Aphrodite, except larger at the hips and breasts, full of gimlet expressions and thunderings of Zeus. She was a big girl, but the kind of woman that looked right being big. At least she was proportionate, and the fecundity of her fertile basin looked prolific enough to start a small nation. He imagined all sorts of sexual positions with her, but the idea of doing it doggy fanned his lubricious flames. Howls of anticipation rang in his ears as nickelodeon images of bumper-mounting her big caboose shot waves of *sex*pectation through his man-sack. It wasn't until then that he realized he was in a bubble of double trouble.

Goldman's wry sense of humor and self-effacing humility were charming to the woman, but now that he had allowed himself to be dunked in the waters of susceptibility, all those fine qualities vacated with pernicious exigency. He was aware of the subtle deconstruction of their maisonette relation, plagued now with infantilism and a bout of loopy self-consciousness that he was not good enough for her.

One night, the two were in Griffith Park taking in the view of the Hollywood lights. Goldman had been feeling poorly from a severe case of the trots and an unrepentant cold. He had picked up dysentery during the war and never quite licked it, leaving him feeling weird and woozy all night. Often, it would emerge like hot volcanic eruptions, and if he didn't find a toilet quick then he would have to *shizzle* where he could or soil his *pantalones* where he stood. It was one of those dates where nothing was going right. His cold was so harsh that when he coughed his chest percolated with the sound of bubbling fudge and post-mucosa clams that occasionally washed up on his nasal shore.

Because of his pervasive nervousness, he kept saying the wrong things. He knew it was going to be a bad night when he greeted her with, "Hi, how you going." He tried to take the edge off with a few cocktails, but ended up drinking so much that he carried on like an ill-mannered, adolescent jape with garden-variety doses of douche bag. The evening ended with him blowing a snot bubble and soiling his underwear with an *ass*plosion of anal gravy. She never took his calls again.

He went to the veteran's hospital where she worked and tried to curry favor for his venial sin. The plan fell afoul and he made such a rumpus that he was downright threatening. She and the other nurses had to lock themselves in the nurse's lunchroom and call security. Goldman commandeered a hospital gurney and rammed it repeatedly into the door. It didn't matter that there was a patient on the gurney—he was not going to be denied a hearing with her.

The ordeal evacuated all thoughts of love's reinstatement, and he tumbled backwards into the waiting arms of his black dog master. Depression got a hold of calcified stalactites in his subterraneous lobe and sunk its teeth down to the brainstem. He hated these lapses into the realm of insuperable complications and compendiums for reasons not to be loved. To assuage rejections gnaw, the ghost in his machine was evicted and he turned over his carnal mechanisms to derelict alcohol consumption and the improprieties of the local flesh-temples. What he really wanted was the igneous ooze of heroin, his morphine alkaloid lover that never said *No* and never judged. He even dreamed about it, but managed to steer clear of the scintillating syringe and its enchained liberation.

Goldman often requested to be reassigned to the war theater, but the Marines were having none of it. He thought that he might have a shot at redemption if only he was given a second chance. He kept abreast of the war in the Pacific and knew that the combat apparatus was bracing for the eventual invasion of the Japanese mainland. The fighting had been fanatic across the island campaigns, but the invasion of the Japanese homeland would be head-deaden fierce. The military feared at least one million American casualties, and dreaded that total annihilation of every Japanese national would be the only solution. Goldman had hoped to be one of the million casualties—suicide by Jap—thinking his self-immolation would vindicate his uncourageous nature and reintegrate a diapason tone with his sour-chord fraud.

*   *   *

It was another unremarkable day. Goldman was lying on his bunk, killing time that was slowly killing him, when an officer entered the barracks.

"Lieutenant Goldman?"

Goldman halfheartedly responded.

The captain moved briskly to his bunk. "You don't salute a superior officer?"

"I'll salute when I find a superior officer."

The captain grabbed a chair and bellied up to his bunk.

Goldman dragged on a Lucky Strike, and blew a smoke ring that suspended over his head like an ethereal blue halo.

The officer tossed the *Los Angeles Times* on his lap: VJ DAY—JAPS SURRENDER—NEW SUPER BOMB. Goldman took another long drag.

The captain produced a dossier. "I don't get you, Lieutenant. The Corps have been real good to you, and you hock 'em out like a cold loogie."

"The Marines are like a dull knife, just ain't cuttin' it anymore," Goldman insouciantly quipped.

The captain shook his head. "You've been assigned to a battalion in the Bikini Islands."

Goldman picked up the newspaper and read the headlines.

"That's the Marshall Islands. If the war is over, why am I being assigned to an island where the Japs have been run out?"

"You were a real turkey-cock once. Now you're nothing but a chicken-shit. The Corps found a good assignment for you." The captain slapped the orders on Goldman's lap.

"What are the Marines doing in the Bikinis?"

"Read the headlines, Lieutenant," said the captain as he exited the room, patently peeved and temperately ticked.

*　　*　　*

Two days later, Goldman was shipboard bound for a layover in Hawaii. He didn't know it yet, but for the next few months he would call Honolulu home. He came to love Hawaii and made new friends who were surfing enthusiasts, and learned to master twelve-foot redwoods on the Waikiki break and the northern part of Oahu. It was great fun and provided constructive interference where perspired control rode shotgun to a laidback surf attitude, languidly defying all his prefrontal reasoning. *I was drafted for the duration of the war, and if the war is over, why am I not being discharged?* he lamented. His newly acquired surf philosophy boiled down to two choices: "fuck them" or "fuck 'em." One being *aggro*, the other Zen, and now he knew the difference.

Months later, he finally got his shipping orders and left on a fleet transport headed for the Bikini Islands. It was May 15, 1946, his twenty-sixth birthday. He steamed out of Pearl with jostling thoughts that envied the harbor, still laden with the drowned and twisted monuments of December 7, 1941, where the war's memories were submerged for everyone except for him, or so it seemed.

Four days at sea and the *crystal ship* reached the blue sapphire paradise in the Marshall Island neck chain, where the indigenous locals had been stripped of their encrusted jewel lives and evacuated. The Navy had set up a bustling billet on the tiny atoll. Goldman was assigned to a company and soon realized it wasn't just a Marine company but an amalgamation of Army, Navy, Marines and Air Force. The men were all the undesirables from their respective branches, comprising a newly formed penal unit.

The atoll was a hive of activity, an endless parade of naval ships schlepping to and from the islands and the main task fleet. It was a real brainteaser and rumors were adrift that the islands were going to be used for atmospheric atomic testing, but why the men were there was still unknown. Sometimes they murmured among themselves about being "guinea pigged", which created palpable tension that they were reticent to talk about, yet always loomed in the back of regular conversation.

Goldman didn't know much about atomic weaponry, but he did know something about atomic energy. He remembered reading about the giants of physics as a kid. The possibility of creating a bomb from a tiny atom had always been a theory, now it was a tried and proven colossus. He heard that there had been sensitive work carried out in the deserts of New Mexico, where two-billion-dollar *Manhattans* were served up by nuclear barkeeps. Brass never let on about their syllabus intent, but little things gave them away: periodic physicals, psychological examinations, iodine injections.

The military was run by government-inspired dunces, full of woolly talk and moronically disfigured by their insularity, and they were not to be trusted. His own travestied dissent had long ago reached its disagreeable apogee, and left the military untrusting of him. That's why he was there, he figured. The idea crossed his mind that maybe they would all be sacrificed as atomic pawns, and the terror of non-existence suddenly gripped him like a collegiate wrestler. They might be barbecued and the world would never know of their cremated demise. The unrelenting thought plagued him, and after a while he was vexed with bouts of real paranoia.

He was bored and pissed off most of the time, on a chunk of sand thousands of miles from nothing, and he was going nowhere slowly. Panic's single winding column ground-pounded him into the island's white-hot sand, and amid the vast vistas of the sapphire Pacific he felt claustrophobic. Whoever said that living on a tropical island is paradise didn't know what the *fwig* they were talking about. To Goldman it was a wilderness of desolation crawling with rats and poisonous spiders, deadly stonefish, malaria-infested mosquitoes, with temperatures of ninety-nine degrees and ninety-nine percent humidity. He craved arboreal refuge, but the only ones there were coconut trees and their long cylindrical trunks were almost impossible to climb. He essayed a few simian attempts, proved proficient and mastered the ascent. He would roost in the nest of fronds, crack open a coconut, and watch spectacular Pacific sunsets in doggerel verses of a poet in exile: *weathering absurdity*
    in the climate of his
      haiku season.

The palm fronds became his private carrel, and a place to void his clouded mind and eviscerate his jetsam feelings. He would sit for hours in the swaying wind-bent trees, reading about the great thinkers and their radicalized language that cudgeled against the world's collective idiocies and thickheaded postulations. He wanted to understand things, though, not just with processing receptors and clinical reconnoiter, but also with emotional logic that inhabited his excoriated core.

He felt doomed to follow an odd internal rhythm and to a peculiar momentum that emanated from his gene code with a long line of derivative genetic material, grimacing in simpering syncopations. It was an atonal dirge that he reluctantly danced to, a greater rhythm that had hardwired him to a reviled current, cannibalizing his intellect, and often leaving him doddering with symptoms of mental illness.

Whether stranded on an island or wasting away in a dank hotel, wherever he went he carried the same rucksack of metaphysical questions that were hard to grasp in the slippery world of first principles. Goldman could split hard shell notions like cracking sunflower seeds between his teeth, but figured life would keep the meat from him until he had lived long enough to break mysteries that were unwilling to give up without a fight.

His father had been a bottomless thinker, and he had inherited the same affinity. However, he did not inherit his father's constitutional ability to separate feelings from thoughts, facts from emotions, and its inner-discourse that talked in circles of dizzying rhetoric. *I don't know what knowledge I'm missing, but damn, I know I am missing something.* He wished that he could look at life with an objective monocle view, like whenever he found a tree to roost in where he could watch the world go by and not be caught up in its ant-farm entrenchments.

He remembered how his father would take perceived realities and reduce them to biological functions of mind stuff. Ira was a rock-hard Cartesian who believed that the persona and ego were nothing but epiphenomena generated from the wetware of the emotional brain. Raw emotions were the side effect of thought-induced chemical imbalances that had to be tamed with reason, which had its own chemicals that functioned as an antidote and realigned mental equilibrium from foreign tyrannical feelings.

If the mind could not impose its reason, then man was doomed to the inexorable pull of superstition, stupidity, and primitive fears. Ira had believed Nietzsche and his notion of the ideal alter ego, The Overman, embodying the triumph of will to power. Nietzsche had condemned Platonism and Christianity, which long for another world, and deny reality as it is, a never-ending chaos and flux that must be molded in the image of the individual. The only answer was to impose the will and to commandeer aberrant feelings with strategic thought, lancing psychic abscesses, which were the perpetrators of so much mental mischief.

There was order in the universe so long as one was willing to enforce it, but Goldman did not understand cosmic penal codes, celestial laws, and vaguely written rules; they had always left him bewildered, mocked, and bereft of any sure thing. He felt demoralized and powerless in the face of his emotional hurricanes that randomly appeared, never knowing what damage they would do before they ran their course. That's where he and his father diverged.

Nothing meant anything to Goldman if he didn't feel it, and the uninspired pursuit of knowledge was somehow diluted if the experience did not include the joy of exploration. Jung had said, "Knowledge did not enlighten, it only stripped us of our birthright to the mythic world where man was once at home and every new declaration was followed with a dance by the tribal fire."

For Goldman, it would take emotion to counter emotion. Not that it was brain chemical warfare, but warfare of consciousness. The secondary consciousness, and its sense of separation, could only be countered with primary consciousness if implacable notions were to shift and if he was to tailor fit his own existence.

For now, he resigned himself to his open-ended misfortunes, suspecting that it had something to do with nature's ways of chemicalization. "All dead wood from the past must be cleared before new consciousness can come forth." So wrote Kazuo. What that consciousness was, and how it was to be found, Goldman did not know, but he did know it would require a lot of scratching if he was to dig its seeds from caliches theories. He had become a wandering pilgrim, beseeching a universe that seemed only to whisper, *that's for me to know and for you to find out*, and yet coaxed him down dim-lit gangways where primordial acquaintances lured him into unmapped labyrinths and aging mental viruses; a delicate high wire act between sepia dreaming and lucid waking.

*   *   *

Goldman and the others were called out for formation and told to get ready to ship out. Where they were going, no one knew. Goldman didn't care. He just wanted off that damn island where he felt like a dried turd in a sandy cat box. To him, the atoll had shrunk to a fraction of its size, and the beautiful turquoise water had become a treeless wilderness. The men were ferried back to the main fleet and boarded onto the USS *McKinley*, moored about ten miles from the atoll.

XV

The Navy announced that all personnel were to witness two atmospheric nuclear weapons tests, which sent everyone's sundering instincts into compressed peals of nervous laughter. The first explosion: code-named ABLE, the second, BAKER. Vice Admiral William Blandy boldly proclaimed: "How fortunate for these men to witness this great destructive force that will do something good for mankind." The military wanted to study the effects of a nuclear blast on ships, equipment, and live animals. Covertly though, they wanted to study the effects of radioactive fallout on their uninformed witnesses.

It was July 1, 1946 when the mulling multitude was ushered deckside. The men were issued special sunglasses and ordered to look due west into the prosaic air that was odorless, colorless, and noiseless except for the far-off lamenting of a B-29. Instantly, the night's India-ink sky exploded into brilliant white. Even with special sunglasses, the men had to shield their fried-egg eyes. The blast was followed by an enormous thud that ruptured the humid air, and spewed forth concussions splitting the auditory meatus' of ten thousand sets of ears.

The thermal flash lit up the ships with its iconic mushroom illumine as the men's irradiated skin-cells sizzled and their broiled retinas faltered in optic recoil. Goldman was curious, and his shipmates' reaction to the blast was almost as intriguing as the detonation itself. His senses fell inchoate at the spectacle of hundreds of skeletons radiating through soft tissue temples like translucent Vishnu gargoyles. As if from a giant X-ray machine, anyone whose skin was exposed looked like intergalactic chaos, molecular solar systems observable with the naked eye. Goldman pulled the sunglasses from his glowing head and could see every man's face, luminescent green and transparent to the bone. A phantasmagoric scene; legions of shimmering skulls sporting black Ray Bans, all staring blindly like stone obelisks frozen in a nuclear moment that would haunt them with the atomic bug for the rest of their short lives.

As the blast subsided, the concussion laid into the observing ships. The fleet was rocked with fifteen-foot swells that sent the men reeling. Five test ships were sunk. The next day, Goldman's company was ferried out to the test site to make onboard inspections. The massive vessels were burnt and twisted like tenebrous iron leviathans. The tethered animals were blistered and scorched and millions of blue pellets blanketed the ship decks. At five thousand degrees the sand from the islands had melted and crystallized into turquoise ingots, raining over the entire armada.

After inspecting the ships, the men were ferried back to the flotilla to witness the next explosion. In operation BAKER the weapon was suspended beneath a dirigible auxiliary craft. The blast sank eight ships and did more damage than ABLE. According to the experts, the area would be too contaminated for several weeks, before anything more than brief onboard sorties could be conducted. Goldman and a handful of men were ordered onto the radioactive ships for more damage inspection. The destruction astounded them, and not just the vessels, but the obliteration of the once-beautiful waters of the atoll, which were reduced to an enormous brown underwater crater.

The sight of one hundred and fifty thousand-ton ships twisted like giant iron toys battered the senses. The fact that there was a Prometheus power at mortal man's disposal that could deliver that kind of ruin seemed otherworldly and unholy. Goldman remembered the Vishnu poem: "I have become death, the destroyer of worlds." The myth of atomic energy with its potential for total annihilation was a hardened fact, chiseled from the rock of *Manhattan* and now more than just a *project*. The unleashed fury from something as basic as the building block of matter, which was now the destroyer of all matter, seemed indecently ridiculous and fraught with fiendish irony; like quantum potential that pulled on ourselves long before we arrived in the physical form, the ever fluxing of chaos and order, where we are both spectators and actors of the same averse opus.

As the men approached the scorched flotilla, they were sickened by the sight of burnt and scalded goats, sheep, pigs, and dogs. Most of their hides had been vaporized, parts of the flesh had peeled away exposing bones and their swollen tongues flopped from their mouths. Even worse, some were still alive. Goldman could not get his mind off the pitiable livestock and felt something had to be done. He noticed one of the military escorts carrying a carbine and figured it was for putting the animals out of their squealing misery. The men had been on the ship for more than an hour and the pathetic wails from the critters were a barbaric shrill to any moral ear. When he could take no more, he approached the task officer.

"When are you going to put the animals down?"

"They stay the way we found them," he barked.

"Then what's the gun for?"

The officer pointed it at Goldman and moved crabwise away.

These men don't answer to anyone; the lords of the new Earth, and now they stride the world's neighborhoods with a big nuclear stick, and are not about to walk softly, he thought.

It was official: the atomic countdown to a black velour midnight had started with Zulu time charging hard on twelve. The men were ferried back to the task fleet, showered and checked for levels of exposure. It was no surprise that they were shrouded in radioactive decay and as hot as nuclear frying skillets. Like the angel of death the Geiger arrow thrashed with degraded zeal as it passed over the men, but Goldman's shell hardly registered a tick.

He was taken and isolated. The military needed to know why his phosphate casing seemingly remained non-radioactive. For days they poked and prodded his fleshy sheath, but in the end were left as clueless as when they had started. They argued that there had to be a consistent radioactive law, yet Goldman was proving to be a progenitor of a bizarre frame-shift mutation, leaving the military stupefied yet giddy with super-anomaly conjectures.

The Navy concluded that for the next few weeks the ships would remain too radio-hot and there would be no more forays onboard. The men didn't know it, but the levels of contamination would prove deadly, and in short course they would become symptomatic of a surreptitious neutrino virus, but they were shipped back to Hawaii and discharged before the ill effects were borne out. Goldman, however, was proving to be a nucleotide glitch, and the military wanted to crack the mystery armor that seemed to protect him. If there was something in his biology that could be decoded and replicated, then there might be a eugenic defense to the ravages of electron decay. For a week, the endless tableau testing went on; a relentless collage of dissection and loathing for Goldman.

The military then got the nasty idea that he and a handful of other men would be isolated on one of the target ships. Brass wanted to know how long the men, and Goldman in particular, could survive before crumbling under sustained radioactive contamination. The men were issued emission tags, and ordered onboard one of the cruisers.

The first order of business was to throw the rotting test animals overboard, where a pack of atomic-laden sharks devoured the mutilated carcasses with agitated zeal. The men settled into a stay of inactive drudgery and weren't expected to do much more than kill time, that in the end . . . would kill them.

Goldman tried to delude himself with default mechanisms, but he knew the assignment was a veritable death sentence. There were days when he wanted to throw himself overboard like a worn-out ionized rag, while on other days his survival pendulum would do anything to stay alive.

Being on the death ship snapped something between his ears, and he realized that for too long he had been unaware that he was unable to live within the boundaries of his own space. Living as a victim has its perks but he had reached a point where being a victim wasn't worth the fight anymore, and his last days on the atomic fleet seemed a reasonable alternative to living in a universe where billions of other possibilities to his life would not be optioned.

Goldman spent most of his time topside, where he could be closer to the sky's sidereal clock. He would eat his canned food, drink a military requisitioned beer, and take in the view of the sun as it sank over the horizon, the same beautiful horizon that he remembered from the perch of the coconut tree that had now vaporized into trillions of dissenting electrons. The gray, burnt-orange sunset would showcase its atomic colors for the next century, a pathetic imitation of the original. The sight left him oddly sympathetic toward the other men, but he didn't want to get close. They all knew that it was a *ship o' fools*, and whether it was symptoms of death ray emissions or symptoms of dread, they were reduced to genetic revenant arks, like the ghost ship that would eventually take them down with it into an ocean of atomic rot.

*   *   *

The days turned into a week, and the men were fittingly symptomatic of uranium embalming that was corroding their endocrine systems and gutting their sallow souls: loss of appetite, chronic fatigue, and swelling of the joints. Their hair started to fall out, and after a week most of the men were putrefied walking colostomies of gross physical trauma. Goldman became the onboard custodian of the dying, and if help didn't arrive soon he feared he would be the lone survivor.

The men's decant isolation poured out contagions of madness. One of the men jumped ship and tried to swim back to the fleet. He didn't get more than a hundred feet before the sharks zeroed in on him. The curdling screams of a soul being devoured alive were unimaginable. In the glacial graveyard of radioactive ships, the wails were patently surreal as they caromed off the iron walls of the giant vessels, echoing terror in the contaminated torpid air.

The fact that the fleet did not respond to their daily radio pleas was too much, and Goldman simply turned off his hope valve that was already reduced to a psychotropic drip. He figured the military was going to wait until they were all good and baked before they took them out of the microwave, steamed and served like so many multi-eyed potatoes.

The men's radioactive tags reached capacity and they started to drop from the nuclear branch like radium-rotted fruit. It was then that it really hit Goldman that he was not succumbing, and his immunity was inscrutable. By the end of the second week, four men out of the ten were dead. Goldman thought it disgraceful to watch them expire and felt that they deserved some dignity, even in this cadaver-inspired place. He found a sickbay gurney and laid each body on it with a small American flag draped over the dead men's faces, ceremoniously sliding them overboard with a nauseating splashing *kerthump,* where the patrolling sharks made quick work of the remains.

It was only a matter of time before he would be alone, and the idea of being stranded on the giant deserted ship taunted him with lurid fear, and he worked harder to save the others and forestall the inevitable. If he were somehow immune to these levels of radiation, how long would it be before he would succumb to starvation, thirst, or just madness?

For Goldman, implacable rage was a perfectly normal reaction, but who was to pay, and where was revenge to be sought? The system was a colossus that had no head or tail; like a giant recluse worm, even if cut in half it would only continue to grow. The ubiquitous power of upper echelon imbeciles who seemed to be everywhere and nowhere, and easily moved expendable pawns in their strategy to control the board, whispered a shade louder in codes of diabolic government conspiracy.

By the end of the second week every man, like his emission tag, had expired and Goldman was now alone. His macabre days became a game of hide 'n' seek with his igneous particles and terror-thriving molecules.

His hyper-imagination was running at full tilt and if he didn't get it under control he would be the final fatality, even if it were by throwing himself to the fatted sharks.

Having to live on the twisted hulk of floating steel bent his senses and left him with austere feelings that the ship's glory days were relegated to fate's contortions. It had probably served well during the war, though, like him, was now reduced to disposable refuse. All along the oceanic horizon the vast graveyard was a premonitory vision, where enormous ships that were tossed about like playthings from an atomic tantrum were a new testament to an insuperable apocalyptic countdown; a living treatise of the end times.

Being on the cruiser drove the stake deeper into the farce of Goldman's life, and the more time that passed the more tangled the years had become. If he were to sidestep his ever-accumulating chaotic nodes, then he would have to do like his father said: "Impose your will and the circumstances that are seemingly intent on inflicting harm on you will eventually have to give." He had waded in up to his waist, and now he would have to submerge himself into a muscular river that pulled at him with currents of unequaled satire. He didn't care anymore, and resigned his fate to destiny's oblique view and the universe's obscene entelechy force.

XVI

To keep his unraveling head wired tight, Goldman's castaway days and monomaniac nights were spent with his revolving collection of books and a singular obsession of darting meaning's bull's-eye. What really fixed his attention was Kazuo's little notebook. It was a devouring cram, of which the more he read, the more he flexed his metaphysical muscles, and he admired the wispy Jap's ability to dead-lift abstract weight by the ton.

Kazuo had been raised by his grandmother after his parents died of mercury poisoning from a copper mine that contaminated the village's water supply, and almost extinguished the boy's own flimsy vermillion flame. His grandmother was deferentially pious and practiced a cross of Shinto and Buddhism. It was her creed, and she was determined that little Kazuo would do in kind. But when the gears of his inductive machinery inevitably turned, he could not calibrate his beliefs to his grandmother's hybridized religious torpor.

By the time Kazuo had reached his teens, he had developed an abacus-fast mind that was skeptical of any religion. As a budding scientist growing up in the first half of the twentieth century, he found it to be archaic fever-dream nonsense: the idea that the Japanese were direct descendants of the sun goddess, or Shinto with its nationalistic reverence for traditions, ancestor worship, and military chivalry that required all Japanese to be ritually purified under its tenets, and to serve only the Emperor as god. Most Japanese fused this belief with Buddhism and its never-ending quest to reach nirvana, and if you didn't get it right in this life then you could re-enter as a *peace frog*, or a dirt rat, and start all over.

Darwin had proposed that all life forms were nothing more than actualized protoplasm, as there was not a scintilla of evidence that those who did not reach enlightenment came back as frogs or vermin. Science had dispelled these myths with imperturbable facts, and Kazuo's perfected art of dissimulation broke his grandmother's hot sake heart.

Kazuo had thrown in his lot with science; however he did not like the idea that science had appointed itself the new high priest of absolutism. With its almost fanatical disregard to the subjective experience that religion facilitated, it entirely eliminated the God quotient, and reduced the human experience to merely better living though chemistry, and the universe, a cauldron of isolation and cosmic indifference, which offered no meaning, no context in which to take comfort.

Still, for Kazuo, any spiritual tendencies toward religion, including religions of the West, were reduced to whether he was an atheist or agnostic. But as much as he tried to neuter theocratic notions, he still had an affinity with theosophical ideas and a penchant for blending science and government with faith; a credentialed contrarian who secretly trained in Tibeto-Burman rights.

The Tibetan offshoot that used chanting in the five sequenced notes of C, F, A flat, G flat, and C sharp, were combined with a peculiar pentagram configuration that Kazuo had borrowed from a Hungarian sect of cloistered monks. They would sing Gregorian hymns for hours with their arms stretched out from their sides and legs spread wide like Leonardo da Vinci's Vitruvian Man. With eyes shut and one palm turned up and the other turned down, forces were supposedly pilfered from the heavens and grounded to the Earth through the claymation of man.

For the monks, the practice was more than just a mystical rite. It was neuro-scientific and quantifiable. The appendage pentagram, representing the five elements of the Earth, created a kind of living human conductor, a transmitter of sorts, where all vibratory light recycled in particles of vivid consciousness, crystallizing into the spectacle of one; a kundalini coil that concentrated corporeal energy through the golden ratio. For them, physical bodies were nothing more than low-voltage capacitors and the Vitruvian pentagram functioned as a stepped-down power transformer, otherwise the human psyche would roast on the brainstem stick. With the hybridized five-tone Tibetan chant and the thermal-chemical coupling of the Vitruvian pentagram, Kazuo had satiated himself with his pseudoscience, but believed the effects were real and measurable.

Kazuo was not just a shade tree quantum mechanic but an epistemological engineer that had recalibrated Goldman's timing-chain beliefs. Knowledge is just a rumor until it lives in your muscle and Kazuo's theorem penetrated Goldman's contractile tissue and even his bones. He thought how odd it was that a few years earlier they were probably trying to kill each other. Now he felt Kazuo a friend and was saddened and ashamed about his unseemly demise. Goldman sensed a requisite obligation to steward Kazuo's writings, and that they were supposed to be in his hands. Maybe it was up to him to matriculate the metaphysician's work, to apprenticeship himself to the writings. Maybe this was why he had survived the war.

Goldman then remembered the coincidence of him playing the same five notes on the piano as a kid, which were so hypnotic and calming, and now he was reading how Kazuo had employed the same notes for transcendence. In fact, according to Kazuo, the five notes were part of a sound therapy that went back twenty-five hundred years to Pythagoras and his mathematical musical certainties and their auditory medicinal application. It was all too fantastic to be just coincidence, and for a moment, he felt it to be by divine edict. Could Kazuo be right? Could the practice actually connect the finitude of man and the immeasurable universe into a choral morphic buzz that could tumble down walls of ontological separation?

Out of curiosity, Goldman configured his body into the standing pentagram. He raised his arms out to the side, spread his legs, turned one palm up and the other palm down, closed his eyes, and proceeded to hum the five tones. After repeatedly *oooohhhmmming,* he tired and lowered his arms. He checked his watch to discover that three minutes had passed, yet to him, it had felt like . . . four. He felt restless again and started wandering the ship. He still couldn't get over the damage that was done to the vessel. Fourteen-inch guns bent like giant reeds in the wind, with wax warped one-inch iron bulkheads, like something out of a science fiction tale.

The ship seemed to have its own personality, and specter voices echoed through its heavily riveted walls with primeval plangent groans: "At one time I was big, brave, and beautiful, and all who boarded me felt my weight through their sea legs. Now I am marooned in the fathomless abyss, abandoned, and remembered no more." Walking on the wreckage was like walking on an exhumed voluminous iron corpse in need of a decent Viking-fire burial, but the only proper death was to die in battle. He sighed as if he and the great ship had something in common, an opened atomic brew that had sucked down the suds of their collective fates, belching pneumatic exorcisms, slandered gases, and vain premonitions, devil sounds never heard before, a progenitor of something original but worn like sniffed wind forever lost in the wrong.

One night on the cruiser was particularly bad. Goldman found himself spasmodically yipping out loud and tearing at the thin air, certain that there was something alive on the ship. He heard tapping noises, subterraneous creaks, and slamming bulkhead doors. At times, from deep in the vessel's belly, he thought he heard tenebrous voices of men talking, a corruptive collective laughter that maneuvered and echoed through the hull's inner-quadrangles. He was too alone, and it was hard for him to separate gasping injustice from his encroaching dementia. Nerves of steel cable were required to be on that ship, and he struggled to keep his taut wires from snapping.

* * *

It was a full-moon's sea. The ocean's surface was glass and the water's language had never been more unvoiced. He couldn't sleep in the lower decks another night. They were stygian black and it felt like malevolent beings could thrive inches from your face without your knowing. He decided to retrieve his things and start bivouacking topside. It was still light enough to venture into the chilling entrails of the ship and as he moved he felt as if eyes mimicked his actions, the kind of peepers that cut through his dense matter like infrared lasers where photon emissions and radio waves expose his deepest, sweetest vulnerabilities. Yes, most assuredly, he was being watched.

He crept into the lower berth where he had watched the men succumb to the advances of their virulent radioactive pathology. He then sensed someone or something standing close to him, and he froze like a marble headstone. He heard a breathing *wheeze* and jumped back, only to tumble over something . . . alive. He reached out to break his fall and his hand landed in a tepid goulash membrane. The sound of a flimsy guttural moan punched his panic button and catapulted him deckside, seemingly without touching a single stair step. He then looked at his hand that was covered in gooey coagulant blood, and was knocked sideways with witted hysteria.

* * *

He tried to sleep on the upper deck, but got only brief catnaps. The chilling encounter had left him lost in a bestiary of satanic creatures and gargoyle glyphs were carved in his excitant imagination. It wasn't until he saw the light of day that he finally passed out. His limbic system was once again invaded by the sorcery of his recurring dream; like the thing in the belly of the ship, there was something lurking in the backwaters of his psyche, a haunter who moved close to him but said nothing. What was in the dream that made the marrow of his bones liquefy and his skin move like an adder's belly? It hovered close and as always, he couldn't find the strength to return to the land of the awakened. But with blind rhino will he bolted upright and alert. Peering down was a monstrosity like nothing he had ever seen. Like a blood-soaked tattered rag, a rawboned creature scarcely balanced on four legs postured before him. Goldman dashed for the starboard side of the cruiser. Behind him he heard the same pathetic groan that he had heard in the ship's bowels and realized that it was not a groan, but a feeble *bleat*.

XVII

His short-term memory had forgotten about the livestock that had been tied onboard. All the other animals had perished, yet this little lamb had somehow freed itself from the upper deck and survived the thermal blast from inside the belly of the ship. The creature was a calamitous sight. Much of the mouton flesh had flayed from its boney frame and its tongue was so swollen that it panted hard with fragile grunts just to get air. Goldman tried to hydrate the barely living thing with a can of beer, but it foamed up and sputtered out of its mouth like an empty keg on its last frothy pump. He then grabbed it by the neck, tipped its head back, and poured the beer down its inflamed gullet.

The animal swallowed just enough to momentarily revive itself. After a while it was able to drink not just one beer, but two, and then collapsed. Goldman clambered down to the infirmary and found some towels. He wrapped the bloody cashmere in white terrycloth and laid the lamb in the shade of the ship's conning tower. He retrieved some water that he had collected from a recent rain and soaked the towels, and then wrapped them around the animal's weeping wounds.

It was a fulltime job just keeping flies off the lamb and changing sticky blood-blackened towels. The hide was still intact in places, but for the most part was little more than raw meat. Flies had laid eggs in the gaping lesions, and in the following days maggots festered like tiny white zombies feeding on the exhumed. At first Goldman tried to pull the wriggly live rice out of the pus-infested meat. Then he remembered that maggots feed only on dead and infected flesh and that during the war field surgeons had allowed them to do the dirty work of consuming putrefied tissue in soldier's wounds.

The two creatures were in it together: side by side, stride for stride, and deep to deep in un-communicated appreciation of their collective fate. It was cathartic to minister to the little mutton and it kept Goldman's mind off his own congested inertia. The lamb cried throughout the despairing day and well into the vaporous night and, like a butcher shop that was closing a little more each day, Goldman knew the lamb chop's number was up.

*   *   *

The moon waned in seeming collusion with the ebbing of the lamb's life, and under a Pleiades blue-white sky Goldman lay stripped, feeble, and powerless to help. In a few short days he had become so attached to the little varmint that he gapingly grieved with bottomless flummery words, obsequious hymns, and aping groans, beseeching any force in the cosmic backwaters that might hear his entreaties. They were wild pickax prayers that swung at anything that moved in the Pantheon of Greek galleries and zodiac carousels. The cosmos' pitiless indifference exhausted his pleas, which eventually collapsed into petitions of a morpheme feather, and with a lulled sigh of resignation he surrendered the stricken animal to the unknown custodian of life's forgotten creatures.

He dandled the animal, then closed his eyes and seemingly transformed his inner-profile into an algebraic Gautama-Sanskrit shape. It was a dreamy conflation where his body conduit sensed his volume but without the mass. Finite steles and vascular chords streamed Kazuo's five notes through his carbon nitrogen core. How long he had been doing it, he couldn't say, but something discharged from within like tantric lightning, and his jangled interior instantly became unclouded and centered. The lamb hushed and sifted through his arms like refined white flour and the two drifted into common azure sleep.

Come sunup, he was awakened by the sensation of something soft and wet against his burnt Roman nose. He pried his eyes open and saw the lamb standing over him like repudiated sin, gaily licking his face. Its fat blistered tongue had shrunk enough to retract back into its quieted muzzle. He gave the animal a cursory inspection and noticed that some of the wounds looked as if they were scabbing over.

He fetched some water, which the lamb drank, yet it still cried for something more. Goldman opened K-rations that held any kind of vegetable or fruit, and the lamb devoured the distilled goods with gibber and gestation. Altered mutton vowels mixed with carrots, peas, and peaches—a mishmash of sorely needed nutrition whisked with melancholy bleats about its predicament. The lamb then lay on the dry-blood towels and resumed its convalescence. Goldman could not give satisfactory answers for the animal's dramatic improvement, but he was glad to have the company—even if for just one more day.

*   *   *

Goldman started his days by scanning of the indigo ocean with government-issued telescopic eyes. The task fleet was still on the horizon, but no shuttlecrafts: situation—normal—all fucked up. The sutured hope that soon he would be rescued tore a little more each day and shook his wits unaccountable. His vitiated time had been filled with disseminating blame and clout tedium, but looking after the little lamb seemed to lessen the crime. The sight of something friendly and alive, sharing his quandary was a consoling freest that expended something in him generously.

After two days, the lamb's wounds had completely scabbed-over, thick black protective scabs like earthenware clay packs that sealed in therapeutic moisture from the baking Bikini sun. On the fifth day, the chunky blood crusts started to crack and fall off. Underneath, new flesh had formed and even small seedlings of white wool rooted like tiny cotton samplings. By the end of the week there was not one visible sore, only patches of healthy pink skin. Except for a few places along the lamb's back where wool had not returned, the animal seemed the picture of health, and abnormally normal.

How could something so grave make such a turnaround? he thought.

Soon the entire fleece had turned to snow, and everywhere Goldman went that lamb was sure to go. It was his constant companion, always astride his flank, a white shadow communicating with silent epigrams of devotion, permeating Goldman's secreted defenses where he was alert, ascetic, and receptive.

A sense of impending dissolution shifted, as his own molted layers seem to shed before the animals' magnanimous gaze. He pitied and venerated the lamb with collective penitent confessions, and divulging of the world's unsolved crimes. It was wrong for the lamb to be there, and the treachery of it having been sequestered on that insolvent barge left Goldman importuning bronze gods standing in the niche of inconstancy. Abandoned questions piqued his dolorous Greek tale, as he watched his own saga as seen through a lamb's eye, speaking un-perfumed truths of *why?* But he was running as short on answers as he was running on supplies and, after taking inventory, he figured he and his new wooly friend had maybe another week. They might not die of radiation poison, but they would die nevertheless, the last casualties of a new forgotten war.

* * *

It was late afternoon on a Sunday when, from a distance, Goldman heard the far-off droning of an inboard diesel engine, and he scrambled for the binoculars. A small ferrying craft was moving their way and he could hardly believe the amphibious apparition. It pulled next to the cruiser and a detachment of men boarded, dressed in radioactive protective suits, and armed with contraptions and arrogant devices not seen before. One of the men approached Goldman.

"Where are the rest of the men?"

"Dead," he answered pointblank.

"All of them?"

Goldman nodded then started swinging like a crazed belligerent. He punched the guy in the protective suit, and then punched another until he was wrestled to the rusty deck. He was lunatic livid and enraged with crimes of felony for leaving them all to die. The man in the suit ignored his rants and fixed his attention on the lamb. He made passes with another arrogant device, but the gadget would not register.

"Where did you find this animal?"

Still discolored, it took Goldman a while to answer. "Down below."

"Like this?"

Goldman explained how he found the lamb in its butcher-shop shape, and its miraculous recovery. The man in the suit shook his head with incredulity.

"Impossible," he said. He figured Goldman had gone stark raving glitter, but the fact remained that the lamb was unscathed and, in fact, looked about as vigorous as Goldman. He ordered Goldman to get his things; they were leaving. The doltish galoot grabbed the lamb and dragged it across the deck. Goldman slammed the suited goon against the ship's rail, gently hoisted his little friend over his shoulders and kept the space-suited lout at a wing's length with a middle finger's *bird*. He disembarked the ship, like passing under a Roman triumphal arch, with no glory or tribute, hardly believing that hell's summer camp was over.

* * *

After returning to the task fleet, Goldman was whisked to a decontamination room. He was scrubbed with a solvent that was supposed to wash away any residual infectivity, but only stripped him of his basic dignity. No levels of electron mischief were detected. They gave him a change of clothes and a quarantine room, where he was treated like a prisoner of an undeclared war. Eight hundred men on the ship, and he was more alone now than ever. He missed the little lamb that had attached itself to his atria pump like a quadruple bypass stitched to an aging swollen heart, its goodness still streaming through his veins.

Early the next morning, he was roused from his bunk and escorted to a medical examination room, where two doctors waited and a couple of salt and pepper suited men armed with paltry documents and military arrogations.

"Strip," one of them commanded.

"I ain't stripping for no one! I want to see the adjutant general."

One of the salt and peppers produced a villainous smile. "You will, son. As a matter of fact, you'll be heading home soon."

"Home?"

"That's right, Lieutenant, you should be proud of the work that you've done for your country."

Goldman wanted to lash out at anything that moved, but after his ordeal and all that orotund talk about being ready to die was just so much puffed-up peacock shit, and he was glad to be alive and squawking.

"I want to go home, now!" he shouted with run amok resolve.

"And you will. We just need to conduct a few more tests."

"Enough!" he roared.

"Just a general physical and some blood samples and your obligation to God and country will be fulfilled, an honorable discharge with hazardous duty back-pay too."

As pissed off as Goldman was, he was relieved to know that he would finally be released from the obsolete slang of his military service. Not that he had any place to go, but he wanted to be done with the government and its shadowy imps that operated with blanket impunity and acted as if its military surplus store population was devoid of any inventoried rights.

*　　*　　*

Goldman was shipped back to Hawaii, where it took a few days for him to be processed out of the Marines. He was questioned by different people, mostly civilian cadres under the secret employ of the military. He was taken to expensive lunches and dinners, shown the town, and was even given a fine-looking Hawaiian prostitute whom he mounted with as much hostile regularity as he surfed Oahu's waters with placid frequency.

These secretive people were highly intrigued by the specimen now known as Anomaly #66-6. The fact that he had been exposed to lethal amounts of gamma radiation and was seemingly unaffected pricked their curiosity and filled their repository with possibilities yet to be explored. They were starting to accept the fact that he was a supreme oddity but the question still remained, what about the lamb? How did the animal recover so magnificently? Goldman's semi-concise yarn was irresolutely doubtful, but what else were they to think?

Unexplained phenomena always made the military uncomfortable. If something could not be explained then it would have to be relegated to a threat. With the war over, and the Soviets and their satellites rising from the ashes of Europe, American intelligence knew that, in time, the Communists would possess the bomb, too. If there was something inert in Goldman's fabled flesh that could help Uncle Sam beat a new enemy, then they were going to have it.

Goldman received his discharge papers and returned to the States an unsung hero. He didn't care. All he wanted was a long vacation from military machinations and heavy doses of government-inspired malfeasance. The world's nuclear clock was ticking, and in a tacit way he knew he was part of its crucified countdown.

Resistance is hell, he thought and pretended that St. John's Revelation was just vestigial tales of delusion, but from his spinal cord reasoning his ears rang like a five-alarm fire and it scared him spit-less.

XVIII

Goldman returned stateside with an honorable discharge in one hand and a small stipend in the other. LA had always been an enchantress for him, a foregone lover of untried things, and he decided it would be as good a place as any to set up shop. There were plenty of jobs, but a yearning to return to an agrarian existence clung to him like pieces of an arcane dream. After spending almost five years yoked to *bollock* circumstances, he needed time to reassess his life, his purpose, and why he was even here—the world, that is. He had stayed clean, no hard drink, only a beer now and again, and all but forgot his fentanyl penchants for heroin.

It was back to the familiar furrows of loneliness though, where the commandeering of will was required to plow through the night shift of the soul. Being alone again made him feel invisible, like an apparition in a vacant house—but if no one is there to haunt, then what's the point.

By late 1946, LA was changing; the days of the constabulary command of the Anglos were now being threatened by people of color. Freeways were built, and the charm of a two-hundred-year-old cottage metropolis was expanding into an industrialized megalopolis, where future phantoms taunted its elongated heritage with the mechanized hum of mindless driving progress.

When Goldman could not stand his isolation, he found himself nagged by whorehouse compulsions and ritual acts of pagan harlotry. Not so much that he was horny, he just liked being around bankrupt sluts who weren't uptight about being naked and could freely chat about their *cock*pits, arses, and wambamboozles; the cavalier way they would break down methods for giving head or clinical techniques for taking it in the blowhole. He was most comfortable with *breast*osterone gorgon-like felines who salivated like Greek dogs.

The grind of abeyance was a relief, initially, but became tedious. He still had a bit of money and didn't have to work, however he needed to feel useful. He decided he would go back to work for old man Simpson, if he was still around, and re-stake his claim in the San Fernando Valley.

Goldman found contentment a trite concoction, but when he was working on the farm it permeated all of his prevaricated parts that quibbled about what he really needed. He remembered the succulent grapevines and how they would go fallow in the winter. It was so bedeviling; their twisted knobby branches looking as dead as petrified snakes, yet returning again to the land of the living when spring had sprung. With deep-green leaves the twisted serpentine vines would race down the strung-up baling wire, connecting tentacle networks, weaving between constructive interference and syntonic connections to a promised solstice.

Examining nature had the ability to settle Goldman's impetuosity and schismatic factions. He loved continuity and the predictable cycles of planting and harvesting; the way the vines responded to water and sun, the smell of rancid manure mixed with cloddy dirt. It made him feel as if something was in control, something you could depend on. Like fifth-dimensional clockwork unconnected to man's time; nature responding to the call of hope that maybe this year will be better than the last. His recollections were alive again with the saffron scent of ripening grapes, its sweet pungency wafting through the warm air, the sound of June bugs buzzing well into the night; drinking a beer and watching the sun set over an endless sea of berries, making the sudsy lager taste that much sweeter when mixed with salty sweat and resplendent body ache.

Being close to the soil made the very matrix of his anatomy buzz; to actually walk, work, and live close to the dirt was electric for him. Goldman was fascinated with magnetic fields, and the Earth was full of them and he loved the symbiotic connection when fertile loam squished between his toes and grounded his renegade dearth. Most people strutted through their lives self-wired for low-voltage animation, and Goldman believed that if people could not actually plant their feet on the ground, then their natural charge would run out leaving them to operate on dry-cell involuntary drudgery. Like pregnant women who find solace in mineral rich soil, Goldman craved farm dirt that kept something alive and growing in him.

He was welcomed back to the vineyard as a conquering Roman god. Simpson had read about him in the periodicals, and was privileged to have a Congressional Medal of Honor recipient in his employ. The last few years, things had not been going well for the old man. The vines were yielding less, and in fact whole sections of acreage were producing nothing. Simpson was hardly making enough to cover working expenses.

The valley itself was changing, too. Where once there had been endless trees and lush farmland, there was now low cost GI tract housing systematically pushing out the farmers. Simpson was being pressured to sell his two hundred acres, but he was a farmer at heart and to sell the land would strip him of his meaning. With Goldman back onboard, the old man was going to give it one more season, one more shot, armed with the magic he hoped the returning hero still possessed.

Goldman recommenced with the running of the farm as though he had never left. His first order of business was to walk every acre and bless the soil with his fecundating benediction. It was an absurd twist that after five years of world war and some seventy million dead, everything on the farm remained virtually unchanged. He remembered having buried one of Simpson's favorite dogs and strolled by the barn where he had interned the animal years before. The shovel he used to bury the mutt was still leaning in the exact spot he had left it in 1942; a bereft snapshot of a day that still refused to die.

Getting his old digs back and combing through his belongings felt like a homecoming. He grabbed a book and dusted it off: Jung's, *The Archetypes of the Collective Unconscious*. He remembered those insomniac nights, wrestling with his trenchant insights, perilous adventures that cut deep swaths through the center of his own unconscious core.

He picked up *Plato's Republic* and recalled the story of the cave: humanity facing the interior wall, back-lit by a fire, while the universe puts on a dazzling shadow show. We are only shadow watchers that mistake the ethereal for the real, while truth is always behind us but we are too frightened to look. The only real truth is light but we are seduced by imagination and immanent manifestations of archetypal realities that keep the true transcendent world at a distance. It was significant to Goldman that in all religions was the common thread of partition, with truth on one side and humanity on the other. It was an irreducible mystery to him.

Thorny thinking always pricked him off. He remembered how determined he had been to penetrate the canard shell that blocked the road in the hero's journey, fantasies of cutting its Gordian knot in one bold stroke to reveal the Great Within. It was there that his predatory imps were summoned; his darkling-darlings that barred the light, casting long shadows on his wall, silhouettes of meaningless human existence.

He wanted to find his constellation, his own brilliant stars framed by the vastness of the eternals. He barely understood anything, but he knew enough to know that it had to do with transcendence and, according to Kazuo, he could not embody a new form until he jettisoned the old. If he wanted meaning badly enough, he would have to arise and hunt down game he had never seen before and lay claim to its shadowy cave, where psychic dispositions form the basis of human emergence.

He rummaged through more books: Shakespeare, *The Collections of Dostoyevsky*, *The Oracles of Nostradamus*, and more—books that made him feel mystical yet pretentious. He had always wrestled with the supernatural and, like his father, tried to reduce it with empirical deduction. It was his father's wiring that had helped him navigate the treacherous waters of no hope, but it had never been enough. He could not dismiss inclinations to believe in something more than libidinal materialism. Those myths and mysteries appealed to his secret sense of wonder, and the possibility of meeting Ali Baba and rubbing magic lamps was his *bon vivant* to the inscrutable joy of tasteful exploration.

While thumbing through Nostradamus, he recalled how he had fantasized what it would be like to be a self-styled seer. *What could you do with such a talent?* He imagined being famous, people clamoring for his every word, loving and fearing him. Women would fall to their knees in his presence—a compound supernatural force to be reckoned with. Endowed with such a gift he would acquire all the wealth in the world; an earthbound god commissioned straight from Orion's constellation. He shook his head with embarrassment, recalling such stupid fantasies from his earlier years—years before the war rattled his proclivities for unbridled imagination and youthful sentiment.

He then picked up a book his father had given him, *The Communist Manifesto*. To his father, Karl Marx was the world's messiah, a messenger not from God but from man. He remembered how Ira postulated the virtues of Communism, about equality for the masses and liberty for the proletariat dregs, and how the world that he reviled could only be changed by revolution. Yet he would say, "Real revolution is a steep slope that has the potential to turn into a runaway train. True revolution has to be done with exacting measures if there is to be a real utopian society. Speed would be its demise, and like any train that cannot slow down at a sharp turn, its own momentum would end up a pile of philosophical wreckage, if not engineered with temperance."

Goldman never entirely understood the philosophy of the Manifesto, but years later he gained an understanding of the benefits of doing away with the insane, irrational, and inhumane systems of ravenous Capitalism. He believed Marx's assertions, but his key argument that the economic situation of the laboring classes would deteriorate as Capitalism progressed proved his ignorance. America showed that Capitalism was thriving and the working class was healthy, while the middle class shored up the difference between the oppressed and the oppressors. Nevertheless, it was a good idea, he just never liked the idea of the few holding power. The muscle of Socialism was still based on money, and all struggles are about money, but the people with money never do the heavy lifting of waging revolution.

Reminiscing about his past made him think of his parents, and his memory of them was as vivid as ever. It made him wonder if there was life after death and where they might be now, Heaven? Hell? Were they burning for eternity, as Jonathan's father said, just because they were Jews? Or is it all recycled compost? Once the spiral staircase is broken, oblivion, not a trace of existence to be found upstairs or down? *Weird scenes from a gold-mind* flooded his mind. All those men on both sides of the war silenced forever. *Where are they now, paradise or eternal torment? Where is Jonathan?* he thought.

He shook his head, baffled that of all the places in the world and all the islands in the Pacific, he had been on Okinawa. And not just on the same island, but the same battlefield, the only battlefield where Goldman had proved a coward. What were the odds of Jonathan walking into his charade? Had he survived the war? Tragedy or statistic, he wasn't sure he even wanted to know.

Time, the great assassin dovetailed into the memory of Rhodesia and baby Ruth; they, too, would remain a mystery. *Hell, Ruthie Lee would be ten years old.* He often daydreamed about his daughter. What she looked like? What she thought like? What she felt like? He remembered the little port wine birthmark in the shape of a perfect heart, just below her right ear, God's lovechild branded with His mark. He wished that he could have come home to a family, something bigger than himself that would flood his *mind*-shaft with streams of liquid light and wash away the pejorative nature of his meaninglessness.

Goldman thought about Miguel Contreras too, the kid that he knifed years ago. Did he wreck someone else's life by killing him? From the corner of his conflagrated thoughts a herd of existential quantifiers trampled his begrudging daydream garden: *Elephas maximus,* stampeding reminders into his plot that he didn't deserve a healthy life. He put down the books like he had put down himself, breaking from null-zone reminders of his *runnin' blue* past and old realities that no longer mattered.

*   *   *

After a few days on the farm he settled into the rural routine. He liked the discipline of waking up early and getting the wetbacks ready for the day's work. There was something inexpressibly satisfying about running around the farm, towing flatbeds of grapes, and the persistent aroma of ripening fruit mixed with the smell of the Mexican laborers that almost defied description. It was a cross between laundry detergent and shitty baby diapers that, when mixed with the morning dew, smelt right in a weird way. The peculiar potpourri settled his wispy senses, and for an ephemeral while all would be well.

XIX

It was one of those velvety days when the Santa Ana winds blew insistently and hot. The inaugural tent revival meeting was that evening and daylight was running short. Every time they hoisted the main tent the quarrelsome and devil dusted gusts would blow it over again. When the pergola was finally erected, the church workers prepared for a night of a thousand stars. Since the war, something had driven Jonathan to pick up where his father's venal nature had failed, and he obsessed with breaking its imperious spell. He may not have inherited the old man's gene for showmanship, but what he lacked in charisma he was determined to make up for with ideological sincerity.

He worked hard to be transparent—transparency to God—where the full working power of the Spirit would do anything he asked, even miracles, if only he could really believe. His father's contumacy to faith had left its welts over Jonathan's once-pristine spirit that needed to believe that everything was a miracle or nothing was.

He deemed that his father had once possessed an iridescent conviction in the good news of the glistening gospel, its angelic crystal-ball powers of prophecy and even to heal all in need. He remembered times when his dad laid hands on the invalid who did indeed recover. Not all the time, but sometimes they really did. Those were the memories that he wanted to recall, not those terrible days when healings were staged gags by flop-sweat actors performing for the beguiled and gullible pre-millennial fanatics.

The Great Depression made men do desperate things, even men of God, and when the crowds of the faithful thinned out so did the offerings. Jonathan remembered times when his father languished in financial despair, which furtively angered him as he believed he was doing the Lord's work but felt shortchanged in an LLC partnership that dumped all the liability on him. It seemed to have been the catalyst that turned Jonathan's father from the straight and narrow, and ditched his faith into the drainage strait of perdition. His convictions, in a penumbra, had teetered for years, and the Great Depression hastened the tipping.

To keep the money flowing, Jonathan's father felt he had to stretch the truth for the sake of the corralled fold. It was all justified in his corkscrew mind and what at first were only mild white lies soon turned into all-out deception. In the end, the only thing he could see was the money and the survival of his indulgences, and what was once a triage unit for bleeding souls had become a hambone performance for profit, and Jonathan vowed that one day *he* would be the real deal.

To him, the proactive rhetoric of Revelation had to be preached to a dying and decaying world, and Jonathan took it upon himself to single-handedly strike the law of entropy from Satan's books. He was a stalwart soldier for the cause, an obdurate reed in a world of hurricane opposition. He had bleak days of doubt, though, with suboptimal symptoms as common stalking shadows. There were a thousand and one God questions that failed to be addressed, and he wrestled with philosophical entanglements that were subtly eroding the murky underworld of his faith with dissenting fatigue.

He secretly feared that there was no objective reality to which the Bible bore witness, and Goldman's discriminating arguments from years before still plagued him with bouts of epistemic vexation. Jonathan had brought many of Goldman's questions before his father, which only perturbed the man, whose ill temperament was never equipped to counter scathing theological inquiries. He remembered how he would throw up his hands, yelling, "The Bible says not to lean on your own understanding," or, "To open up your mind is to open up to the devil!" Jonathan was smart enough to know that these were poorly patted answers for an anecdotal defense whose only authority was the Bible itself. "Why?" was the harbinger that Jonathan's father hated, for he too asked the same questions, and over the years the unanswered "why?" would become the reason for his recidivism, amoral behavior, and spiritual melancholy.

Reckoning such as that would never fit in the breadbox of Jonathan's beliefs, but it was the only bread the church was serving: a steady diet of working out your salvation while dodging flames that licked through theological gaps in faith-filled fireproof floors. Jonathan worked hard to love God, even when it seemed that He didn't answer his prayers or honored His word. To be embraced by a cosmic father who responded to *humus-sapien* prayer vouchers that one day might be redeemed was fine for spiritual neophytes, but he needed more than just chestnut platitudes.

God's hand still hung heavy despite Christianity's theological potholes and frat-funk-flaws, but to Jonathan, it was still the only game in town. The years resigned him to the fact that many things could not be explained, and to continually dig for magic worms would be an exercise in morbid ad infinitum and the fatal extraction of objectivity. Blind faith was required, yet it languished under a tide of shunted skepticism that Goldman had planted in his plot long ago.

*   *   *

The upcoming meeting was his maiden voyage on the ship of salvation in the artesian waters of California, and Jonathan wanted it to be special. As he was preparing for the service, he dug through his traveling trunks that held some of his personal effects. A box fell out, dumping a handful of photos onto the ground. He collected them up and saw a photo of him and his parents, both dead now, and for a moment the slight prick of a concealed needle perforated his heart. He still loved them both and on occasion, they were missed with a toad in his stomach, a frog in his throat, and lily-pad puddles in his eyes.

As he put the last of the photos back in the box, another one fell to the ground. It was a picture of him and Goldman as boys. He picked up the photo and remembered the baseball game where during which Goldman had hit the ball that rocketed into the sky, never to return. *Impossible*, he thought. Only at that moment did he wonder for the first time where his adopted sibling was and if he had survived the war.

Something caught his eye in the black and white photo. There was what looked like tiny gold specks in the general area of Goldman's image. He rubbed the slick Kodak surface, but it was part of the original snapshot. *How did a black and white photo show the color of gold?* Jonathan then recalled the gold leaf incident before Goldman hit the homerun, and the words of the prophet still thumped in his cochlea shell, *"You are a man of miracles and no weapon formed against you will prosper. Whatever you have in mind, go and do it, for the Lord is with you. You are The King . . . the One the world has been waiting for."*

After the prophecy had been declared in front of the entire congregation, he remembered his father pulling him aside and whispering in his ear,

"That prophecy ain't for you, kid. You best give it to someone else." He wanted that divination bad, but his father's tongue seemingly had the power to put the kibosh on God's ballot. Jonathan hated how the old man had the repressive ability to make him feel paltry, insignificant and utterly inconsequential.

The years had hollowed out his father like a rotted log, where the meanest creatures in the wilderness would burrow for long stays. Regular beatings were common, and Jonathan's ability to cope was shored up by an ever-expanding imagination that pretended to suffer for the sake of the gospel. Often he feigned deserved punishment, and in a bizarre way even looked forward to it; for him it was a *rite d' entrée*, where saints are mauled in the spectacle of the coliseum and bleed in tortured bliss. After all those years, Jonathan's umbrage to the glut of one man's cruelty—a father who resented a son that he perceived as a better man—trampled his sentiments with foisting blame, and still pissed him off something bitter.

Yet he felt furtively guilty about his dad's faith-filled farce. It was sad to think that somewhere on the highway to heaven his father had become lost on the back road of perdition, and a ministry that had at one time felt like a divine calling had turned into an offensive command.

XX

1946 passed with the ease and the breeze of a warm summer sneeze. It was the first year of peace for America and brought the country out of its *cordon sanitaire* and started to assert its confidence at home and abroad. Goldman held his own without falling into alcohol, heroin, or slag temptations for brazenfaced cocottes. For now, his addiction was the farm, but he knew it was only a holding pattern until he decided who or what he wanted to be when he finally grew up.

The only thing he did know was the rhymed malice of the lonely and that he couldn't get a date if his life depended on it. Something about him scared normal, reasonable women away. This fact was corrosive to his self-esteem and caveats of abnormal admonitions made him feel borderline queer. *To be rejected from time to time is one thing, but every time?* It just didn't make sense. Whenever opportunities presented themselves they'd backfire, like Wilhelm glycerin.

A young woman worked at the local grocery store. On their first encounter, Goldman hadn't really noticed her. It wasn't until he sniffed the wind of her saffron scent and fixed his carnivorous gaze on her rolling figure—that made her feel sullied and him a satyr—that he realized he was even attracted to her: the natural undulations of her smooth body and delicate swiveling head, the way her hands femininely moved when she counted change back to her customers, the way her proportions rested on her silken frame, her effervescent smile, and the diamond sparkles that flashed from her eyes when she laughed. And not just any laugh, but a deep soulful chortle that harbored no deceit. She was a real testicle tingler, that girl, and she left him filled with annotations of concupiscence.

After bestowing diadem tribute, the secret ceremonial touching of his sword to her oblique shoulders was complete and she was crowned by his abdication as a man. She didn't know it, but he had armed her with a premeditated force that could lop his corona with a single glance, and what was once a passing fad had become this year's furrowed fashion, a transfiguration that dropped him to all fours.

It was uncanny how his perspective had changed. Before, they had made small talk and had chitchatted about things that didn't add up to Jack squat. He was comfortable with her, and inanely nonchalant, making her laugh with the most idiotic humor. But time spent sequestered can make any prospect seem unattainable. Maybe it was because he had not been laid since before he could remember and the prospects of phallus resurrections were rolling his heart of stone, and she didn't even know it.

Little by belittled, the insipid effects of his floating anxiety wrinkled his dissolute self. Each time he queued up to her register the magic and spontaneity faded more with every vitiated visit. He made feeble attempts at restoring pheromone links, but the more he tried, the more bizarre the interaction and what were once lighthearted and pleasurable encounters had become nervous and clumsy spectacles that left him a stammering simpleton and the register girl perplexed.

He avoided her for weeks then finally worked up his twitchy guts to pay for his foodstuffs at her register again. He made sure not to buy awkward things like toilet paper. He didn't want her to think that he actually pinched mud sharks and wiped his sludge hole. Or things like antacids for his nervous stomach or hemorrhoid medicines for those bleeding barnacles that breeched the sanctum of his rectum from time to time—typical items he would purchase when she wasn't working.

On this occasion he bought inconspicuous things: a bottle of wine, spaghetti, lettuce and tomatoes, cereal and milk. Things that looked inoffensive and she would unconsciously ring up without affording them a single thought. As the register line shrank so did his stunted sense of self. The cool, at-ease air that had temporally inflated his thin membrane nature started to escape like a pin-holed balloon and a barely perceptible seepage had expanded into a hemorrhaging gush.

After the previous bizarre encounters, she wasn't sure if she should acknowledge him or just ignore the "spaz" and try to get him in and out as painlessly as possible. By the time he reached her, his inflatable self had flattened, and instead of a puffed-up peacock, he had deflated to a squawking chicken, boil-dipped and feather-plucked.

She said hello, and he let out a freakish Tourette sound, a cross between an insect buzz and the screech of a chimpanzee. She didn't acknowledge the mangled verbiage, but continued robotically with her job. When it came time to pay, he reached into his pocket and pulled out money that exploded onto the floor. After gathering the change and bills, he handed her a ten spot with a quivering perspired palm. She told him that he was ten cents short. He reached back into his pocket, trying not to dump his money again, and pulled out a pocketful of change which, for no apparent reason, had a big black pubic hair in its midst. As he fished around for the dime, the pubic hair that had so mortified him, and her, was now pinched between his thumb and forefinger. And for reasons that will be warehoused in mysteries never to be solved, he handed it to her. Horrified, she abandoned the register, goaded and anvil weighted with the affront. Goldman left the dime and the pubic hair on the counter and grabbed his groceries, never to return.

*　　*　　*

It was harvest time and, with Goldman back, old man Simpson had experienced a glorious season. The grapes were bigger and more succulent than ever and twice the yield of any of his best seasons. Despite Goldman's soul desolations, he possessed a bountiful affinity with flora and fauna. The crop was so plenteous that extra Mexican laborers were bussed in to fill the demand.

Goldman was making the rounds, towing flatbeds of grapes, while Simpson rode shotgun. He never had a son, and took to Goldman as a quasi-progeny and a potential contributor to his limited gene pool. He had four daughters who were all grown and still unmarried. He tried to get Goldman to date one of the fillies but he thought them rough on the eyes, vinegar to the lips, and sourpuss to the penis. The old man had hoped that he might marry one of his offensive offspring, which would have made seamless the transition of keeping the farm in the family, but for Goldman, he would remain a gelding in their company.

With a full load o' grapes, there was no reason to take the farm road with its bumpy, dusty hedgerows, so Goldman peeled onto the sparsely trafficked highway. While driving he noticed a flatbed truck with a red banner strung across the length of the bed: WORKERS UNITE. Standing in front of the truck was an eye-popping *contesa* with a bullhorn blurting out provocative castigations in Spanish. The Mexican workers craned their spellbound heads and, like Goldman, were beaten stupid by her exquisite bludgeoning.

"What's that all about?" he asked Simpson.

"Commie bitch troublemaker. Been tryin' to get the wetbacks to unionize. I've been running her and her pinko friends off, but she got a court injunction and can spout her filthy propaganda so long as she keeps a hundred yards from the property."

For the first time, Goldman saw a real Communist. She was an exotic beauty, a mix of makeshift pageantry and seditious party line cant. He had heard about these people and remembered how fondly his father had talked about them, and to see a provocateur of her urbane caliber was exhilarating.

"She's beautiful," Goldman spluttered.

"Yeah, she's one hot tamale, but don't let that fool you. She's all business and downright mean. Mina . . . *Mina* than a motherfucker!"

The tractor lurched past the truck, and she turned the bullhorn directly on the grape train and blasted a broadside volley of inflammatory Red rhetoric. Goldman's almond eyes tangoed with hers, and he thought she returned a libidinous glance.

*   *   *

The harvest moon was rising just as the sun eased onto the amber horizon. Goldman unloaded the grapes and turned the tractor back onto the highway. He hoped that the Commie femme fatale would still be there. At the very least, he needed one more peek. As he came within eyeshot he was relieved to see the flatbed truck with the red banner. It had a flat tire, and the only people there were Mina and another Latina, or at least he thought it was a woman. No, it was a lesbian, he could tell by the tattoos on her thick biceps and the way a cigarette dangled from her taut lips.

He tentatively edged up to the truck. "You got a problem there?"

The butch scowled, "No, *maricón*, we don't have a problem! You got a problem?"

"I don't have a problem," he said politely, "I just thought you might need some help."

The women eyeballed him with feelings of rising Anglophobia as he pulled the tractor over. He walked up hot, flushed, and hesitant, seeing their shaded silhouettes more clearly against the twilight lumen. The lesbian was clinching a star wrench in her chubby fists and, even with brute torque strength, could not bust the rusty lugs from the corroded tire rim. Goldman figured she was trying to impress the Latina goddess with feats of physical strength and aping male know-how. When he got within firing range she hocked a glob of phlegm and saliva, missing him by inches.

Seeing Mina up close and uptight, he was besotted by the sexed apparition. He could hardly keep his eyes off her, yet could only hold eye contact for the briefest of moments. White-hot, blue flames leaped through his sunburst body, dangerously close to subterraneous combustion as his heart minced blood clots, palpitating clangors in uproarious thumps. His hands went limp and perspired like damp rags, but he was relieved to see his usual female-fawned comportment vacated and, for the moment, he felt confident, assertive, and boyishly appealing.

"Let me give you a hand with that." He reached down to grab the wrench, but the butch resisted.

"I can do it, so why don't you run along back to your slave master."

With a playful simper he threw up his hands. "I was just trying to help." He looked at Mina and shrugged his shoulders and headed for the tractor.

"Hey, don't run off so quick. She's been cranking on this thing for an hour."

"I can change it if you like," he said as if honor bound.

"I like." Mina said.

Goldman busted loose the rusty lugs, pulled off the tire, and replaced it with another. He tried to make small talk, but the two were as responsive as sphinxes. Two millennia of Egyptian sandstorms could not erode that kind of limestone.

"Are you Communists?"

"No, we're a traveling circus looking for freaks to put in our sideshow. Do you want to join?" the butch sarcastically asked. Goldman chortled with delight.

"Who says we're Communists?" the beautiful Mina temperately asked.

"Old man Simpson says you're trying to get the workers to revolt."

She nodded her head, at a loss. "Simpson, the great exploiter of the peasants." Goldman smiled and handed the star wrench back to the bull dyke. "So, you are Communists."

Mina smiled back. "You catch on real quick."

"Do you work for the Russians?" he naively asked.

"We work for the oppressed few who have their dignity stripped by the gringo money shakers."

"Sounds like you really enjoy your work," he quipped.

"And you are a comedian?"

He chuckled. "Only when my life seems like a joke."

Like an arachnid corsage, a black widow had crawled up Goldman's shirt. He wasn't aware of it. Mina watched until it was almost to his neck. She moved close to him and dragged her red Commie nails across his perspiring chest. He froze in simmering silence as her fingers crept close to his neck, and then flicked the spider off.

"Work for the vulture Capitalist and you will be a joke, work for the American Communist Party and your life won't seem so tragically funny." She pulled out a business card, scrawled something on it, and handed it to him. He shook her hand and their pressed palms made his stomach salsa and his testes churn in factorial whole numbers.

"My name is Goldnads, I mean Coldman . . . Goldman. Nice to meet you."

The women entered the truck, the lesbian rolled her eyes and turned the engine over. It belched a loud V8 rumble as she double-clutched and pulled up the incline of the shoulder, crunching gravel beneath the tires with a popping sound. Mina stuck her head out the passenger window.

"We meet this Thursday at the address on the card. Come by, you might learn something."

The flat bed rolled down the rural tarmac, grinding every gear, until it was a single dot on a vanishing pinpoint. He stood alone on the blue highway and squinted at the card: Mina Contreras, District Representative, American Communist Party.

XXI

For three days Goldman could not shake the scouring impression of the regal revolutionary. His hollow realm and idle interior felt stonewashed in a vicissitude of the unexpected and new life pumped into his sterile basket of eggs. Mina possessed a quality that could eviscerate something that Goldman needed to shed, or maybe it was something she could add. In just one encounter she had rearranged him from a coma-stroke chrysalis into something new. He would become what she had become to him in a super-symmetry, where what we awaken in ourselves stirs a similar awakening in others.

Mina's image moved with kinetic friction through the quarries of his mind, stretching sublingual muscles into lisping tongues of adoration. Her long, jet-black, draping hair with short-cut bangs that rested on her high brow; her full red lips and straight white teeth: her slightly protruding black doe eyes cradled in heavy lidded orbits, perfectly balanced in her visage; her lean body and muscular limbs. Everything about her played on Goldman's keen sense of aesthetics. He remembered that she had worn sandals, and how the symmetry of her toes complemented her high athletic arch.

He thought she might be South American. Her Spanish was etched with titled prose and she lacked typical russet skin. Like something out of a Hollywood movie: Rita Hayworth meets the Jaguar Mayan Queen, only dissident, mythopoeic, a living revolutionary propaganda poster: Zapata and his fearless female companion, her cleavage exposed down to the nipples of her conical breasts, heading the charge with a rifle in one hand and the Mexican flag in the other—*La raza, y el reconquista de los Anglos del Norte!*

Why someone so beautiful would throw that away to be a commissar in the Communist movement not only intrigued him, but her cause suddenly felt dangerously persuasive. With the heat between the United States and the Soviet Union boiling at 212 degrees, her activities put her in a class of her own. Sedition was some high stakes poker and, in the country's current political climate, she was playing with a short stack.

*   *   *

It was Thursday, the first Thursday since his Communist enculturation, and fragmented pieces of her countenance still rampaged through his brain. He wanted to go to the rally, but doing so would put him in a pinching vice. If old man Simpson or any of the locals got wind that he was attending, he would be squeezed right out of a job. They were opposite palpitating poles, but her opposing current was inescapable to him. He thought that if he could slip in unnoticed he might be able to make some time with her, and then who knows? He fantasized about licking those toes and feet-fucking her before bedding her down. A thousand and one kama sutras to explore, fueled by the wild lunacy of love; a sizzling fantasy, which left him flushing hot like a semiconductor sub-straight plugged directly into her three-phase current.

He got to the building where the meeting was being held, an abandoned fruit packinghouse that had been used to bottle moonshine during the Prohibition years. Entering, he was instantly assailed by a menagerie of the Red Nation. Those that gathered included the upper crust of the Communist elite, liberal lefties, failed artists, free zone thinkers, mamy jammers, *vag*etarians, bone smugglers and a garden mélange of anarchists. A speaker was bellowing a flame-throwing diatribe on the evils of Capitalism, which riled and reddened the ruddy dissenters even more. Behind the podium Goldman could see the beautiful Marxist queen placed on an iconostasis alter where the other unorthodox Communists promptly sank out of sight. She looked like a primrose growing in the middle of a shit patch, the belle of the Bolshevik ball, and her halation illuminated the lesser Commie candles that surrounded her.

Goldman stood in the back of the crowd as the amplified rant rang through his head like a bad case of tinnitus. She looked like a displaced princess in her green fatigues and black beret. Around her arm was fashioned a red band, emblazoned with a yellow hammer and sickle. She approached the podium with an air of *radieuse royale*, and the packinghouse crowd stilled like ascetic loyal subjects.

Her physical presence was alluring, while her oratory skill surpassed that of the most seasoned speakers; eccentric doggerel canto, like a page scripted from *Evita*, where imperial torment leaks between the texts. She looked out of place. Maybe it was her striking beauty that was so incongruous with the oddballs, loony tunes, and misfits. Like the Statue of Liberty towering over the decaying boroughs of New York City, she embodied freedom and, to Goldman, was the only legitimate landmark.

Her affricate ability to hold a crowd with limpid prose was one thing, but her real talent was the silence between the words—pregnant pauses mused with accented syllables and hard guttural consonants growled out like so many fevered Nuremberg speeches. The cult of personality has its place in the chronicles of anarchy, and her image alone could ignite a fireball of holy panic.

God, she's sexy, he thought. *With that kind of persuasion, she could start her own religion.*

She was an astute propagandist and gave rousing supplications for the cause of the working class, mainly the Mexican migrant workers, and educated the audience with a short course in the philosophy of Communism. She tangoed with Engels and Marx, a dance with the bourgeoisie elite in two-four-time that was driving the proletariat to the ballroom doors. Goldman was hopelessly lured by her amalgam eloquence as she hammered on about inequalities and implementation of equal liability with ethno-lingua rhetoric and luscious sibilant sensuality.

She asserted that suppression of private property was needed and, as a transitory measure, advocated compulsory labor for the idle, the rich, the bourgeoisie, and the non-proletarian class. She argued that state Socialism must inevitably become the master of each man. It sounded like confiscation of individual liberty, yet hearing it from her sounded perversely persuasive, even to the mercantile privileged. Her words, spinning like silkworm sonnets, a masterwork of Machiavellian madness and, to Goldman, it was a pedagogue aphrodisiac like nothing else.

After the meeting, the crowd spilled out of the hall. Goldman scuttled crabwise between the packing crates like a slinking *lizard king* hoping for her heat-sensed glimpse. When she was almost within eyeshot he raised his hand, but her head turned as she exited the packinghouse like a fandango celebrity. A train of lackeys followed her across the street to a coffee shop. He figured that if he were to manufacture an opportunity to talk to her, then he would have to take the poet's path and do something wily. Who knew when their happy trails would cross again.

He entered the establishment, scanning the peoplescape for the unsolved mystery of his morning star, and saw her sitting in a booth with her Communist consortium. He sat at the counter and ordered a cup of Columbian. Without seeming awkward, he eyed her, trying to play it off as if he didn't know she was there. They exchanged sheltered glances and he hoped that she still remembered him, but she gave no sign, only the indistinct flaunting of deadly elegance. Maybe she was trying to ignore him. After all, she was beautiful and dangerous, and he, a floppy wet blanket. What expectorated line could he cough up that some other miasmic vapor-filled gasbag hadn't used before?

Now that he had turned the flame up on the performance pressure cooker, he fretted about finding a reasonable strategy. How could he approach her under the guise of being interested in the cause without coming across as a gristle-lobed bonehead? The table looked like it was filled with left-winged intellectuals that could outsmart him with a single slice of semantics. He had read the *Communist Manifesto* and now tried to remember some salient points that might make him sound complicated with a splash of regale. He bravely prepared himself and, like the marine that he was, adjusted his gentleman's equipment, and walked into the gnashing jaws of his psychotic imagination for a surreal woman that he was now sure he loved.

The group was caught up with boisterous interposes, verbal barbs that would not fit with any other topic, but the only topic for Goldman, was Mina. He cleared the nervous phlegm from his arid throat and the table turned toward the interruption, including Mina who detachedly watched his peril as if seen through the untamed eyes of a Bengal tiger.

"I'm not interrupting anything, am I?"

Mina gave a half-derisive glance, and he suddenly felt like someone who throws rocks at the fat side of the moon.

"We were just talking about working stiffs who gun down aristocrats," she said.

Goldman cleared his throat again. "I have a working stiff that would like to gun you down, I mean . . . I'm a working stiff that is tired of being gunned down by the . . . you know . . . Capitalist pigs?" The silence of the table erupted with undisguised hilarity. "I mean, I am just a working stiff and I'm enthusiastic about you, I mean your cause," he babbled.

Mina smiled cruelly with mundane expressions of decadent power. "No, I like what you said the first time, that your *stiff* is working and that you would like to *gun* me down."

Goldman's face blushed and his guts went watery.

"If you're interested in my cause, don't bring your pistol half-*cocked*," she tersely teased.

He felt as if anal-beads had been pulled from his mouth as the table burst into affable confusion. "I believe in the new social order," he said in a hissy fit.

"Marx is the messiah," said one of the Reds. The table roared with domineering jollity.

"Do you believe that?" asked another Commie.

"Well, if Marx is the messiah, then Engels is God," Goldman responded.

They all laughed harder, except Mina who seemed determined to maintain an arrogant propriety and a stunted sense of humor.

"Very good answer, my friend," shouted one of the Communists. "Sit down and let us conspire together." Goldman squeezed into the red vinyl booth. "So what brings you to this table of rabble rousers perched on the lunatic fringe?" asked a boozing revolutionary.

"Just another dissident son looking for the right cause," he answered.

For the next hour he endured the ritual hazing of a potential recruit, putting down shots of vodka with the Red Guard. Two other Communist separated him from Mina and a third was putting stumble fuck moves on her. She was polite, but Goldman could tell she wanted nothing to do with the Bolshevik ape. Now and then she would look at him with transient curiosity but tactical avoidance. Maybe the drinks were getting the best of her estimation and he was starting to look better as the night wore out, or maybe he looked good compared to the mountain gorilla that was mauling her. Goldman figured if he kept up the pretense as a possible enlistee, maybe she would eventually take a shine to him.

The large simian left to use the monkey crapper. Mina seemed uncomfortable sitting with Goldman, and any conversation was better than suffocating silence.

"You must have thought about what I said?"

"In regards to what?" he asked.

"A new life with the Party . . . Comrade."

"Well, if you're the life of the Party then maybe I'll join."

"I think your employment on the Simpson farm might be a conflict of interest."

The front doors of the coffee shop blasted open, and there entered a boisterous group of sulfurous men, mostly local farmer rednecks, along with old man Simpson. They'd been plunging hard into clear jars of John Barleycorn and knew that the troublemaking Communists were having a rally in town. They had come to let the subversives know that this was an all-American community with strong xenophobic backbone, determined not to be intimidated by the pink provocateurs. The men bellied up to the bar and Simpson immediately spotted Goldman, who tried to slouch into the booth, casually lifting his hand to cover his face, but he knew he was already boiling in Dutch fudge.

The rednecks were spouting off about how the next Communist they saw they were going to beat some Red ass. The big Commie ape returned from the toilet, heard the threats from the rowdy clan, and sounded off with a loud Stolichnaya-inspired challenge.

"Fuck all you hickory sticks!"

It was an open invitation to move the pack of star spangled Americans to the table of hammer and sickle-celled Reds, as the posturing went from malice aforethought to a harum-scarum blood opening.

"What the fuck are you doing sitting with these Stalin scum?" asked one of the farmers. Goldman stammered something unintelligible. "What was that?"

Simpson penetrated his good friend with filmy downcast eyes. "Yeah, what was that?"

"I was just having a drink," Goldman murmured.

Simpson looked at Mina then back to Goldman. "You mean you're having a drink with that Commie bitch that's been shittin' in my yard?"

Before he could answer the big ape butted in, "Hey, buddy, watch the language. Don't be calling that *bitch* a Commie."

Simpson ignored the big Red primate and kept churning Goldman like buttermilk soured in the belly of betrayal.

"I'm going to tell you something son. Why don't you leave the table and we'll handle these ringworms, eh, boyo?"

"He wants to stay," Mina snarled.

"Why don't you let him make up his own mind," Simpson growled. He looked at Goldman again. "If you're smart, you'll get up and leave while you still have a job and a future."

"He doesn't need your fucking job!" Mina shouted.

Like a drunken prank she threw her vodka glass and it exploded on Simpson's forehead. The table emptied and the two sides erupted into a full scale bar war. Goldman caught a wild punch on the chops and dropped to the sticky linoleum floor. The beating, stomping, and kicking went on until the defenders of the American way had bloodied the Reds with a complete shellacking. Goldman came to and could see Simpson wiping blood from his wrinkled brow. The old man then pointed his admonishing finger at him with ruminations of a lost son and a firebrand new name.

"Judas!"

XXII

A month had passed since Goldman's dishonorable exodus from the Simpson farm and his deference for the man was missed as much as the grapes. He missed the routine of working the vineyard and his Hippocratic fidelity to the soil. He missed the smell of diesel fuel from the tractors, cloyed with heavy doses of sweet 'n' sour manure. He missed the peppery cayenne relationship with the vines, and even the wetbacks with their bad bitter body odor. He missed the hum of mechanized energy that was part of the routine of tending a farm, like bees around a frenetic hive where every drone carries out their chemical orders in bustling buzzing bliss. He missed the fact that the whole was bigger than the sum of its parts. And most of all, he missed being a part of so much unfinished business.

He may not have known his purpose in the world, but on the farm he didn't have to—the pastoral existence it offered was not ridiculous but was the priest-craft of something sublime. He was saddened by the loss and felt forked tongued and blameworthy for letting the old man down. Simpson had been better to him than any other; he had treated him kindly and brought him into the fold as a real confrere. For once, since the death of his father, he had been able to speak with another man in the tongue of equanimity, but it had ended in a colloquial exercise that left him feeling like an elliptic guest in a ciphered language.

If only Simpson could understand Mina's edge—a cutlass spell that had sliced through Goldman's protective hive, where sweetened honey flows from his hexagonal years and scarified wounds are laid bare by her reluctant smile and waxing balm lips. Simpson was stubborn, though, and would never compromise with Goldman's point of desire, but he missed him, too, and like a leaky sieve, only when he was fully parched would he value the loss.

The LA chapter of the Communist Party had set up shop downtown, and was printing a Socialist rag called *The Daily Worker*. It was an internal combustion engine of politics and propaganda that disseminated cant, organized demonstrations, and rallied local workers to demand better working conditions and pay. How they bankrolled their operation no one knew, but people were on payroll and the lights were always on.

Goldman threw all prudence to the gusts of fortune and donated his grab bag of surfeit talent to the call of Communism—or at least that was the stratagem. His real agenda was the improbable barbaric sacking of Mina's *labia majora* treasure. He wasn't sure he believed in the movement, but he was sure of the saccharine venom that pumped through his veins; her fangs went deep and her bane had the ability to arrest common sense and fill men with hyperboles of greater callings, and for Goldman, it was love at first bite.

*   *   *

It was an unseasonably and unreasonably warm day. The Party had organized a march that would commandeer the downtown streets and end with a rally at MacArthur Park. The demonstrators were armed with protest signs deriding the evils of Capitalism and Mina was to lead the protest. Goldman figured that if he could slink his way to the front of the throng and sidle up to the Marxist dealer, maybe he could win chips for the revolution game and cash them in later for her affection. She had hardly spoken a handful of words to him since he had joined the Party, and giving attention to a new pledge was the least of her priorities. He knew he had to earn her interest and muster street-cred as a jackbooted revolutionary or he would disappear into the ranks of the undistinguished.

One of the demonstrators handed him a protest sign that read: VETERANS OF THE WAR UNITED AGAINST AMERICAN CAPITALIST PIGS. His insect tendencies were provisionally down for the cause, but this was tantamount to treason.

"No one else has a sign like this," he objected.

"You're the only veteran in the march. Anyone who served in the war adds special significance. Besides, Mina made this sign especially for you," said the volunteer.

This put a new spin on his halfhearted pall. If Mina did this: how could he ignore such an obvious sexual gesture? Although he was only trying to impress her, he still needed to plow though his maundering disinclinations and drum up some genuine revo-social-enthusiasm.

The protest moved through the streets with furrowed brow earnestness. The onlookers were mostly reporters, police, and counter protestors who didn't appreciate the dirty Red devils making such ado in the free enterprising City of Angels. The demonstrators had marched no more than a mile when the milieu turned murky and mulish. While the leaders were loud and boisterous, most of the rank and file was timid and inconspicuous, marginalized laborers who turned their cause over to the radicals, who in turn pulled on their reluctant snouts like a ring in a sheep's nose. Some of the volunteers, however, were a different story, wannabe brats with rich parents who relentlessly pressured them to achieve, and this was their way of rebelling with imprecations of blasphemy. Others were *no*cialists and epileptic anarchists who thrived on convulsed confrontation just for shits 'n' giggles.

Deluged with catcalls and expectorated threats, Goldman carried his sign with circumspect conviction. Had he joined the Party because of his father's sagacity it might have made sense, but there was nothing selfless about his ri*cock*ulous farce. Like the sirens from *The Odyssey*, Mina's tune twined around his head and rattled like loose pagan coinage, and he would follow like a dumbstruck sheep to a close-to-the-skin shearing. He elbowed his way near to the front of the marching fracas where the heads of the Party were prominently displayed. Mina glanced at him with a quizzical expression, which to Goldman, looked like a backhanded proposal to win her over if he showed enough inclination.

Other war veterans did not appreciate his protest sign and vocally attacked him as he marched. One marine in full dress blues plowed his way through the crowd and tried to pull down Goldman's sign. The scuffle caught Mina's attention. The marine delivered a roundhouse but Goldman ducked and countered him hard on the chin, knocking him rapt silly and upside down. Mina reacted with undisguised astonishment, and he now felt qualified to move to the front of the demonstration.

Something about mob mentality always brings things to the surface that are normally buried. Counterintuitive assumptions that are passed off as decent moral behavior are really imposters hiding in the collective herd. Mob anonymity: the great tempter of the intra-species, mauling mayhem, and sport-spilled blood—entreaties to a collective sense of tasteful violence.

The rally got to within sight of MacArthur Park and the police were waiting, flanked by just about every right-wing, all-American Joe Blow that could tote a stick, bat, or beer bottle. Goldman moved close to Mina and she finally acknowledged him with a questing face, conferring a serious love-of-risk smile that was patently persuasive to his veiled neo-con nature, daring his shade to find her light.

"You okay?" she asked.

He smiled back with a dislocating effect. "Like tap dancing on land mines."

While marching with new flagrant defiance, he caught a glimpse of a face in the crowd. The face caught a piece of Goldman, too, and for a teetering moment they looked at one another with evocative sliding stares, but he kept moving. Goldman couldn't place the mug, but his muscle memory flexed, thumbing through the Rolodex of his past.

Lawless excess was at a frenzied pitch. Glass bottles, stones, and anything that wasn't nailed down were hurled at the demonstrators. Goldman saw someone throw a rock directly at him. He ducked, but it knocked Mina cuckoo and she swooned and collapsed to the asphalt. He hastily picked her up and handed her off to one of the Reds, then proceeded to beat the stone thrower in retribution. He had been in fights before, and had even killed, but the thrashing he was meting out was filled with torque-rage, rigor, and reason.

Mina came to and turned to one of the Bolsheviks, "Where's Goldman?"

"He's beating seven shades of shit out of the crowd!"

She ordered the rearguard in after him and the opposing sides degraded into an inrush street riot. The police detonated tear-gas canisters followed by nightsticks a-swingin'. Goldman was at the bottom of the conflagration with a pile of skirling humanity pounding and kicking his turncoat hide with red, white and blue welts and fifty swirling stars around his head. By the time the Reds pulled them off, the police were already there, and as one gave Goldman a civic crack across his melon, he simultaneously recollected the face in the crowd . . . *Jonathan.*

Traversing the celestial equator that bisected his head, Goldman reentered the world of the cognizant with an atmospheric flameout and a loud *bang* from the police paddy-wagon doors. Blood leached down his bespattered features as Mina pressed a bloody bandana to his lamenting crown. All the beatings in the world were worth this one moment. In fact, he could not imagine a more befitting end to his fantasy: broken, bleeding, and bruised, held in the arms of a dream woman tending her suckling with the affection of a sex-sated nurse.

*　　*　　*

The Communists were indexed, booked, and flopped into holding tanks like radulae creatures to lick their innumerable wounds and set their idle bones. Four hours later someone posted bail and they were back on the street. Goldman caught up to Mina, who was giving hand signals in weird geometric angles and wrenching out orders to her underlings with the authority of a trade unionist.

"How's your head doing?" Goldman asked.

"I should be asking you," she said, as she hand gestured her last command to a subordinate. He pointed to the bloody bandana that was wrapped around his oozing brow like laurels of victory.

"This is a trophy."

"I think you need stitches."

"I'll be fine."

She reached over and delicately pulled the bandana off to take a closer look at the purple-mounded gash.

"Let me clean it so it won't get infected."

Before he could feign a coy rejoinder, she grabbed his hand and led him to her car. A short distance later, they pulled in front of an aging downtown building.

"I have some disinfectant."

She led him upstairs and opened the door to her somniferous den, which felt narcotic and instantly made Goldman's eyelids heavy and relaxed and his dick aroused and leather hard. The building's phlegmatic exterior was in striking contrast to the sanguine interior. For someone who touted the virtues of Spartan living—forgoing bourgeoisie opulence—she had every creature comfort that Capitalist dollars could procure. Like a labyrinthine bazaar, there were hand-carved baroque furniture, antiques, marble statuettes, jade electric cigarette lighters, fine paintings, and other lavish collectibles that were tastefully arranged and elegantly displayed. The environ seemed charged with obsequious infelicities, sybaritic indulgences, and concubine sex, leaving a bittersweet tang on Goldman's tongue and reticent sounds of past orgasms dripping from the Venetian plastered walls. In these surroundings she looked like what she was, voluptuary . . . regal.

She went to the bathroom and returned with a bottle of antiseptic and a wad of white mesh gauze. She proceeded to clean Goldman's wound with appropriate care and indulgent looks while wrapping his wobbly head, which occasionally tipped as if he might slip into a doze. An abnormal libidinal energy followed Mina. She was a labiate flower, seducing insects into her majora folds where bugs like Goldman manifold into altered states of super-consciousness and the personification of lofty ideals are wondrously attained. She was a true archetype, a kenotic being that moved in counter-transience and could equipoise his instability with a scanty hundred and ten pounds of Argentine clay.

His head gash dripped onto his sweated shirt. Mina leaned over and slowly unbuttoned it. *I am actually being seduced by this woman? Will wonders ever cease?* The idea so completely washed over him that he blushed like a prepubescent as both of his *heads* levitated in her command, and he was afraid that he might pass out before she could spread her flying-buttress invitation. She brandished a steel-plated smirk.

"Don't get excited, Comrade. I just want to wash the blood from your shirt."

She dissected situations with perennial strategies and Machiavellian intelligence whenever sizing up a potential threat or a seasonal lover.

"Darwinian law is my article of faith. To weed out the feeble and malformed who by natural selection would be unfit for mating rites has preeminent precedence. I hope you don't take it personally," she said with shrewd detachment.

Goldman reacted with the incisive query of a Neanderthal. "Huh?"

With prescient interest she noticed the scar that marked his right side. She was fascinated with physical wounds. There was always an inescapable story behind everyone's injuries, and a scar is a tattooed reminder of an event that never lets one forget.

"How'd you get that beauty?" she asked.

"That was from the war."

She then lashed him with conjoined eyes of sympathy. "You don't have to say anything. Most men from the war don't want to talk about it."

She had an auspicious appreciation for those who braved wounds, inside and out, and was moved by his modesty, a quality she found both attractive and admirable. Not admirable enough though to breach the strict criteria for selective intercourse and cultivated gene swapping. She then noticed the marine insignia, skin labeled to his shoulder like an epaulette stamp.

"And you were a leatherneck?" Goldman nodded. "I never cared much for men in uniform, especially marines, but you might be the exception."

He boiled in the poach that his wound was a fetid fraud, but the sympathy ingredient was part of the recipe—if it could get his dick wet then what would be the point of killing the moment with wordless exclamations of truth. The fact that he had joined the Party with tactical motives was a fraud in a litany of frauds, and he would use every scheme, scam, and con to keep her looking his way.

"My brother was killed by a marine. It's true, right here in LA."

"I'm sorry," Goldman said with feigned anguish.

His memories collided in retrograded irony as he looked in the split rearview mirror of his past. His pretend grief promptly turned genuine, and then promptly turned alarming.

"What was his name?" he asked with mounting unease.

"Miguel. We were very close."

The name slapped his ears and left his cartilage-flap quivering and his stirrup-bones a-swinging. Electric head photos flickered into the unfolding revelation, and the very woman who could change his life was the very woman whose life he had changed with the killing of her brother.

Why did it seem that spongy circumstances could effortlessly absorb him, and collective impossibilities manifested with osmotic ease? It seemed to be one of nature's fetishes to ensnare his life with its tentacles, too unbelievable even for the wildest fiction.

He was crestfallen and languished in shreds of imponderables, but he didn't have time to process the unquantifiable quirk as she now drew close to him. She was in control, and wanted to see if he could converse in subtle sexual communiqués. He had not been with a woman intimately since his teenage days with Rhodesia, he had shagged many a hag, and pig-piled many a sow, but ladies of negotiable affections don't count. Prostitutes never kiss, and that simple pleasure had eluded him all of his adult years. Often he thought how nice it would be to just kiss a woman and forgo the sex. It seemed vastly more intimate. A kiss is just a kiss, but for Goldman, a kiss was a demagnetizer and a restorer of his elusive cognitive parts.

He knew he was close, but Mina's tactics were complex. She could be with any man she desired, and the fact that she might be desirous of the very man who had knifed her brother, winded him with fiendish irony and a nasty bout of reflexive dissonance.

There was a primordial hierarchy working in unspoken social Darwinian code, where aggression and libido rites are established even in familial killings. His heart eclipsed the impossibility of verbal tales and would only have a non-fictional chance so long as he responded to the way she wanted to be read. The idea of her rejecting him snagged his pride and made him shudder in his psychosexual skin, but blood continued to rush to the aid of his *upright organ* that he still hoped she might play. She moved close to his lips with her open flower mouth, but didn't touch. She traversed to the nape of his neck with a *whirr* percolating from her choral cords.

"I would just as soon shoot a marine as kiss one."

"You wouldn't shoot me."

"I'd shoot you in two secs, no question."

She negotiated his body like a heat-drawn viper which sent his semen-producing testicles into overdrive, and he was now sporting a hard-on the size of a blue-ribbon cucumber. She pulled away from his ear and cracked the windows of his soul with her lazy eyes of liquid black, the same liquid black he had seen in her brother's eyes before he expired on the cantina's sawdust floor. Goldman's mouth had dried to cardboard and, like the back end of a sonic boom, his hearing flattened with a low-level ring.

His body leaned dangerously into her. "I'm devoted to your cause."

He thought those were the finest words he could assemble; words that might open the gates to her garden, where labium two-lip petals spread and invite insects like him for fertilizing deeds and cross-pollination rites. She seemed unaffected and continued to stare dryly into his simian eyes with the aridity of a desert mirage.

"Somehow I doubt that. I think you are a swordsman and that is your devoted cause."

Goldman rolled his head in a wanton circular motion.

"Don't be shy Marine. I know that if I unsheathe that rapier that you have so conspicuously tucked away, that you would run me clean through."

Her cryptogram was succulent, but still at a distance. The sounds of Goldman's inner-workings were potent and he was ready to pounce like a fork-tailed fiend.

She moved to his crotch and ever so slightly touched the outside of his zipper, diddling just enough that he feared he might ejaculate—and he did, voluminously. His pants sour-soiled and the musty scent of esperma filled the room with a twinge of ammonia. This delighted Mina, and it satisfied her to see that she could brandish sexual proficiency without having to engage in the dirty business of lovemaking. She got up as if nothing had happened. Goldman sat on the edge of her couch with his sodden pants and bloodied head, soaked in humiliation. She returned from the kitchen with a hand towel and tossed it to him.

"I'll see you in the morning. We've got a lot of work to do tomorrow."

"You want me to leave?" he asked, mystified.

"I need to bathe and get some rest, and so do you." She walked to the bathroom and started to fill the tub.

Grudgingly, headed for the door, Goldman turned and watched her strip down to her tawny skin. He didn't know if he should look away or if it was just another level in her ongoing game.

Her image was ethereal and meta-sexual, jiggy with gothic poise—how perfect those dimensions, how firm her breasts, and how tight her arse: the shape and proportion of her hips, long legs that supported her chiseled torso, her beautiful feet and ankles, those arms, muscular and tight, the curvature of her neck and shoulders that faded into raven silk hair, framed around a face that could launch a thousand and one boners. As he was drawn toward the bathroom like a rodent to a piper-rat drowning, Mina turned, brandishing a Colt .45 and pointed it directly at him. Her threatening face locked onto him with surly intolerance slowly easing into a capering grin and she shooed him away.

"I'll see you in the morning. Please lock the door on your way out." She lowered the gun and leisurely closed the bathroom door.

He was left standing alone, his dismal manhood as flaccid as his ego. He exited her apartment with his usual existential scheme, booby-trapped by someone who had just played his diminishing scale . . . in the wrong key, but somehow for Goldman, all the right notes.

XXIII

Jonathan tramped the main highways and the back low ways, crisscrossing the Golden State in the putative business of harvesting *fruits* and *nuts* and any other bad seed that needed to be supplanted from the world. Unlike his father, he had not made a name for himself as a star on the soul-saving circuit. He had a modest following though, and the congregants were easily rapt by his exegete studies, folk eschatology, and the Americanization of the Apocalypse; augmentations of Protestant virtue and caveats of sin, judgment, and the secret sect of damnation.

His sermons were gripping enough to lead the wayward and even the ambivalent to repentance, but he often wondered if their lives had been demonstrably changed. Did drunks really stop drinking? Did fornicators stop fucking? Did homosexuals stop gobbling cock? Did thieves stop stealing and get real jobs? Often Jonathan fell into moribund lows where his religious plotline seemed antiquated, dank and boggy, with runaway feelings that the Kingdom of God was always coming but never arriving. His perennial anxiety would often leave him fugue-funked, where the best he could do was feed his sheeple with breadstick promises of some faraway hope and pray it would be enough to satisfy their ascetic tastes, and his.

Maybe they were all caught up in the same claptrap game: the game of being on fire for something that they didn't really believe, but to believe in nothing would be far worse. That would mean having to "stand erect and alone with nothing and no one to lean on," as Goldman used to argue. Most people can't do that. The idea that there is no hand in the sky waiting to take hold of yours is devastating, and only the most fortified souls can bring that truth to bear.

Could it be that religion was the intoxicating agent of erstwhile lots, the same craving for meaning where inherited corkscrews in the heart of generations futilely tug on a vintage cork that never was? The idea of bottling God is too tempting for just one fermented sip, and the illusion that one is drinking from the bottle will, in time, conceal the fact that the bottle is drinking from you. Jonathan sensed this and sorely craved any divine arbiter to right anathemas of theodicy, and to come clean of its former haunts.

What was really needed was power—real power—the kind of power that Jonathan read about in the New Testament. A walking Jesus, with His roaming disciples, healing all that He touched, casting out entrenched demons, feeding the thousands with a handful of peat-bog fish and morally inflated bread. Jesus said "Why do you marvel at such things, I tell you, you will do even greater things." But Jonathan was not to be conned. He knew of no man who had attained such feats, and furtively pitied those that would throw themselves on the altar of cosmic indifference to be forgiven, healed, and changed—lives utterly starved without a shred of proof of the *Face* of grace or a drop of extraterrestrial blood.

Even the dullest of wits knew that this plane of pointless endurance was meaningless, and that without at least the mirage of a better life over the horizon, existence would be insufferable. A child is born into the world with a wet slap and one day that child exits the world with a formaldehyde slap—the final humiliation, the indignity of death—and buried in a Britannica box of the world's unanswered questions, when all the sojourners wanted was a real and sober experience with the supernatural, to be tuned to a sound that they had yet to experience, but had waited a lifetime to hear.

Jonathan was obsessed with rectifying the scourge that had tainted the name of the Caseys. His father's notoriety went further than just the tent revival meetings. He also hosted a radio program: "The Paul Casey Gospel Hour". Jonathan remembered how he used to sit by the radio and listen to his father's voice boom through the speakers of tens of thousands, possibly millions, of radios across the Bible Belt. It made him proud that his dad had accomplished so much for the Lord. But the excitement and mystery of a celebrity father was eclipsed by his father's fickle, feeble flesh—a far cry from an unshakeable piece of consecrated granite, the noble and fearsome warrior of God who did not know the meaning of moral infidelity or temptations of Hellenism. He was ashamed by his dad's profane, selfish descent into ethical decay, which turned the Lord's address into a holy house of horrors.

His father had bought airtime on the *Texas Radio* and the *Big Beat* and sold prayer cloths cut from hotel towels; holy water pulled from public toilets, and anointed oil from the deep fryers at the greasy spoons where they ate. How cash contributions were skimmed and put away for safekeeping in his hole-y pockets. How the healing services had degraded into sleight of hand magic shows, where deception was a prized skill. He hated the old man's lurid taste for the melodramatic, sot heathenism, satyric tales of unholy sex and the reckless spawning of bastard offspring.

He remembered once, seeing his father indulging in full-fornicated knowledge with one of the newly converted. She was a beautiful woman, profoundly touched by one of his snake-persuasive sermons, and one of many who gave her bleeding heart to Jesus that night. His father was so smitten by her Grecian profile that he had her come to his private room, for special *preying*. A couple of hours later, Jonathan went looking for him to turn in the night's offerings. Usually, after the sermons, he could be found in his trailer sour mash stricken; the spirit of Jack Daniels diluting the streams of his pious confluences, rock-hard consonants and desiccant vowels slurring in alien tongue well into the wee hours, but not this night.

Jonathan was checking the parked cars when he heard the rhythmic squeaking of a chassis' leaf springs. He approached the sound and was assailed by grunts and moans of sloshing copulation. His father had the woman pinned in the jumper seat of a 1928 tin Ford. Her head banged and his full moon-ass glowed phosphorescent white, plowing fallow ground that had not been seeded in years. It was episodes like these that challenged Jonathan's own imbroglio and manacles of hypocrisy. As revolting as it was, it was *he* who secretly wished he was nailing all the unsuspecting fair maidens that his father coroneted into the Kingdom.

There were endless questions about a father hell bent for leather, where moral ascetics erode into alcoholism, masochism, and spiritual autism. His mood swings were like those of an unbridled ass that requires a master skilled with a whip. Jonathan suspected that he had inherited the same symptoms, and often flagellated himself with straps of pagan distaste in the hope that it would be enough to satiate his God—who was suspiciously becoming more symptomatic of a capricious potentate. All the same, he knew that there was still something real to it. At times he would be so filled with the Spirit that the very marrow of his bones testified to the Nicene Creed. Other times he was bedeviled with demons of ambivalence and would skirl for days until the spell of apostasy had been broken. He remembered the long talks he used to have with Goldman, the budding atheist arguing about how preposterous and unbelievable Christianity was, and how—over and over again—science had shut down the myths of that or any other religion.

For Goldman, the Christian story was like a person who knew from hearsay that dodo birds existed but had never actually seen one, and was trying to prove they existed purely by argument alone. Like a cosmic joke, it frustrated Jonathan with irrational larks. In the end it was about faith, and did he have enough to get him through his assumptions without any validity or proof. More often than he dared to admit, he felt fragmented with splintered doubts, where he doubted even his doubts.

Goldman had been persuasive enough to lead him down the slippery roads of religious dissenters and into potential ministrations of mendacity. What if all of this was nothing more than a tormented world's way of coping with its own imminent finality?

The specter of termination and annihilated consciousness left a rift through the middle of Jonathan's compressed guts and rattled his bare bones that would one day be the only testament that he ever existed. The fear of non-being could reduce the most reasonable mind to stark terror, and he was no exception. *Are we really just electrical wetware that ends when the bio-clock hits midnight, pumpkins and mice and all that's not nice? And what will it be like to be dead?* Goldman used to laugh at the notion, saying, "You will be just like you were in 1905, ashes to ashes, never were, never was. Nonexistent, da dit, da dit, dat's all, folks."

There had to be a way of mopping up the prospect of a chaotic and meaningless soup, and the seemingly impersonal purpose of cosmic mechanical mirth and its ever-elusive punch line. Faith could not just be an arbitrary invention made to weave meaning from life's frayed threads. A god that did not know your name could not be tolerated. To even entertain such a notion would send Jonathan spinning like a dog chasing the tail of flea-bitten imponderables. Goldman had said, "The inability to accept a meaningless universe is the fundamental flaw that underlies human history, and the indifferent cruelty that nature embraces makes the quandary of meaning all that more illicit. To expect something more is ambition that exceeds even the talent of God." But for Jonathan, that's where man had to pick up the slack.

Goldman had taught him how to question and how to reason, "Reason is what dignifies our humanity. To settle for anything less would be violence against the intellect and a senseless assault on the heart." To set religious belief against rationale was to challenge human decorum and, in a sense, to set man against God, which always pinned Jonathan between the brick of logic and a *heart* place. Sometimes he wished he could just flush the entire leaf-mold muck and sluice his mitts in ablution. He knew he didn't have enough faith to be an atheist, but he had just enough of the world's dirt under his nails to be symptomatic of an unwashed agnostic.

No matter how serpentine his fanged queries or his unanswered slinking questions, eventually his circuitous trail would wander back to fundamental bulwarks that could not be breached. From there he would wait out his attenuating suspicions and emerge to rebuild his faith-eroded ramparts. His questions were like asymmetric ellipses where oblique planes could never intersect at the base of quantifiable truth, but he was relentlessly determined to plow through his stampeding uncertainties and thrash his father out of him. If he was going to preach the message, he would do it without holy smoke, and mirrors, even if that meant presenting it with all its warts, shit, and blubber, as well as his own enumerated doubts.

There was something grand about his commitment, where his Custer heart would make its Little Big Horn stand and balance on the borderlands of the great unknown. How then would he measure his faith? He would measure it before an ever-declining laity that would appreciate the oratory skills he mimicked from his father's scarlet miter, but laced with the originality of an essential heart.

He finally understood why his father could never quit. It was the thrill of holding an audience in his hands and manipulating them into any emotional shape—like earthenware clay thrown on spinning machinations, hand-pressed vessels to pour himself into—and that thrill ran through Jonathan's veins, too; to fight even for a losing cause, infused his anemic self with white cells of meaning, resistant enzymes to spiritual amylase.

The knack of a tent revivalist was a vanishing art, but Jonathan was still convinced that this was his highest call—God's call—and would be the trade he would ply for the rest of his dragging locust days. Even if he never healed one human being, even if he never brought one soul to the saving grace of Jesus, even if in the stellar scheme of things he amounted to nothing but a pile of cosmic shit dust or a carbon-mulch sandwich, at least he would scrap for something, and go down to the cold, cold ground, swinging.

XXIV

Goldman was a dependable hand at *The Daily Worker*, however he had not seen a paycheck in months. It was hard work running a Socialist rag and even harder to find subscribers sufficiently peeved to want to read it. By 1947, there were just too many contented brigands and privateers to fan the flames of collectivist anarchy. The only interested were the expropriated and warbled farragoes. It was the cream of the slop and Goldman had stepped right up to the bottom.

With the Communist scare and rumors that the Soviet Union was close to detonating its first atomic bomb, the gematria code of the world lay suspended. The seconds swept and the minutes jerked as theological calculus closed in with the precision of a nuclear clock, *novissimis diebus,* and the apocalyptic new age. Bona fide paranoia shook the globe as the tectonic plates of the US and the USSR were colliding with geopolitical convection.

The realpolitik of the Cold War had every good American looking for Reds under their beds, Commies in their coffee, and building bunkers in their basements, where the grapes o' wrath would soon be stored. The threat was real enough that Congress had enacted The Subversive Activities Control Act, which demanded that Communists, and members of Communist front organizations, register as agents of foreign governments. This put *The Daily Worker* in the white-hot spotlight, and everyone associated with it, including a very reluctant Goldman.

There was nothing subtle about the FBI's constant surveillance. They would stakeout for hours across from the nerve center, intolerably obvious. Maybe that was the point, to warn any malcontent who might want to challenge the American vision that the dream police were watching. Since his experience with the indelicacies of the military, Goldman had developed a real paranoia about the government. He knew he would draw exacting flak from the FBI, the Justice Department, and even the military junta, but Mina beat a heavy drum in the rhythm section of Socialism. Her syncopated fandango was so good that even club-footed dancers like Goldman could be turned into sure-footed pinko flamencos.

His job as a press operator was tedious and left him feeling like a muted yak *Ptui!* He hated it and didn't like taking orders either. Mina believed, though, that was where he could do the most good. For now, he would settle for just the privilege of laboring under the same roof with her. His Mina-monomania was alarming, even for his shibboleth standards. He was addicted to even the most fleeting glances of her, and it was a dreary day when she was not around.

Demonstrations had become too dicey and Goldman missed the opportunity to march. It was in moments of potential danger that he shined and she seemed to pay attention to him, unlike the invisible press machinist he had become. He hated feeling mothballed and craved a way to bleed off his aggressive inaction. He prized the whiff of street battles and their mawkish taste—that's what made his grenadier soul go off. He loved it when he could impress Mina with acts of puerile bravery, and the thrill of being labeled a subversive gave him a sense of schoolyard magnanimity. The demonstrations were unpredictable and nerve racking, but invigorating as hell and it was the only time he felt imperious. It was like the days with his fellow marines, fighting in the South Pacific jungles. With the eccentricity of death all around, he never felt more normal.

New federal laws were putting the squeeze on fraternal Socialist orders, and anything else that might be considered un-American. If the Feds wanted to interdict, they could charge any Communist branch with conspiracy and start making arrests, and Mina's organization was too anemic to fight that kind of infection. Goldman wondered if circumstances really got thorny, would he be able to hang in there? The whole thing was so ludicrous. He didn't believe in their cause or anyone's cause, just his cause. Yet it felt good to be a part of something that was bigger than him.

Maybe the years of his father expounding the virtues of Socialism had laced his blood, or maybe it was just polyps of conscience. Ultimately, someone had to be the grand conductor, even in Socialism, and he had learned not to give the devil his due or anyone else in positions of authority.

His excursion into the Communist movement was creating considerable discomfort in his wallet, and if he wasn't compensated for his proffered toil he might soon have to temporarily switch sides just to mitigate his penurious condition. *How are these people supposed to take over the world if they don't pay their workers? If this is how Communism works, then no wonder it's a struggle. No one can afford it.* Revolution is healthy and everyone needs a little anarchy, but eventually reality gnaws through any lofty goals, and bills are still waiting for you at the end of a hard day of revolting. It felt tainted with sarcastic insolence, and anyone who thought that entrenched world systems could be changed ultimately suffered from naiveté and bouts of chronic gullibility.

The hours at the press nagged Goldman with shuck 'n' jive dodging calls to a real purpose, but he was scared to dream big. Tall aspirations are potential high falls from unfulfilled desires, which gore the heart and vitiate the soul. Finding refuge in never-ending fantasies of some greater calling was safe. In that castle in the sand, Mina loved him and was devoted to whatever steamy dream he enlisted her in. The truth was that the embers of resentment smoldered more than the fanned coals of her succubus seduction.

Ever since the day she had diddled his dipstick and pulled a gun on him, Goldman felt snubbed nosed. He remembered her implied insult that he was genetically unqualified to breed with her. According to her, natural selection did not favor his genetic material. The shoe was on the other foot, and he was suddenly aware of the muckety muck that he had dragged old man Simpson through by rejecting his ugly daughters. They, too, were unfit for natural selection, and he was not about to forgo his reticence to three-meter dives into shallow gene pools.

No doubt, every swinging Red dick wanted to plow Mina's lush acreage. Maybe that was her luxuriantly tame *modus operandi* for sucking in new recruits. All those penis-wagging slags hoping that, one day, she would approach them with desirous eyes and American cream dreams of entwined eugenics.

Why was she doing all this? he thought. *Does she really think she can change the world? And how the hell does she afford a new car and that nice apartment with all those fancy things?*

According to rumor, she was an heiress to an Argentine oil tycoon who made his fortune as a wildcatter in the Mexican oil rush of the 1920's and through corrupt government land grabs from the Indian farmers of Guadalajara. She was said to be a trust-fund brat who had issues with a potently rich daddy, and revolution was her way of lashing out.

It's so typical. Those who look like they have the most to lose, really don't. It's all Gucci baby—her beauty and charisma are backed by status and birthright power, and if all goes wrong she can fall back into the open arms of a silk-padded sanctuary and rest up for her next crazy obsession.

*   *   *

Goldman put the last touches on this month's run of *The Daily Worker* and was getting ready to lock up when another worker on his way out said that he believed Mina was still in the back office. Goldman hadn't been aware that she was even there and it startled him to think that the two of them would be in the building . . . alone. Chaos and tentacles of desire intertwined like strands in a cyclone. Was it possible that he might perform an overture for her?

If so, he would have to play it cool and easy. It would be a delicate situation that would prove disastrous if not handled properly. He started to pace back and forth with lockstep summations and disputations of a lame game plan. His internal-combustion dialogue was dogging his elusive lighthearted nature, again, and women, especially beautiful women, always made him feel queasy, moody and morbidly solemn. Why couldn't he just act normal? Why did he have to always be so dad-gum nervous and self-conscious? He was tired of being a busy body in his own life, trying to understand contortions that passed themselves off as him. He knew he was good looking, attractive even, yet he feared that permanent scarring from female rejection would eventually turn him into a porn-core misogynist, resigned to a shameful life of infantilism or homosexuality.

Why couldn't he get out of his own way and just let it happen? Life is a natural—just let it stream where it naturally flows. But it had always been that way for him. At the most critical moment, when a beautiful thing lined up, he would find a way to derail a train that was right on schedule. He didn't even have to try, his inured wiring was so solid-state that it spoke its own language, a demotic script he had yet to decipher, but the programming was always the same: disaster!

He couldn't work up the courage to walk over to her office and say one word. He knew that once his mouth opened, his vocal chords would constrict and the tightness of his stomach and his pounding heart would conspire in pinching his voice an octave higher. His mouth would become cotton dry, and bazooka-like clatter would spittle forth without a single word resembling modern English.

"Futhermucker!" he mumbled to himself.

His nerves were jangling and, to help take the edge off, he quietly started jumping up and down like a capering gnome, contorting his face in various obscene gestures. He was sure that even his penis was ducking and taking cover, so he dropped his drawers and tried to revive Mr. Winky that was DOA. He pulled on the elastic scrotum, stretched his penis out as far as it could, then let it snap back. He shook his pud so hard that he hit his testicles on the edge of a table and let out a baffled *yelp*, but was still not enough to revive it. He tried one last time, with a tug and a pull, a twist and a shake, but nothing was to charm the one-eyed snake.

He pulled his pants up and sat with his pounding head cradled in his shuddering hands. For some time he didn't move, until he noticed that he was humming an odd tune that seemed to reconstitute aberrant particles whizzing through his inner stellar system. Kazuo's five notes played in his amphitheater skull like an arcane string quartet and, in a short time, the psychic gale he had fallen into seemed to release him. For a moment, he stood in the "I" of his cyclone self, and with a dose of requisite valor, walked directly to her office.

The desk light was still on and her paperwork looked abandoned. *She must have already left.* He threw up his hands in resignation and proceeded to the front door, fully relieved that she was not there. He thought he heard a voice. He stopped and looked over the vacant building, blanketed in black. He turned to leave and then heard the voice again. He turned back around and was startled to see Mina approaching from the vestibule of the dark. She stopped, illumined by a single pool of light, completely naked.

"I've been watching you. You put on quite a show Marine."

"I was just . . . you know . . . ah . . . talking . . . to myself."

She looked directly into the beam that spilled on her like a stage spotlight waiting for a soliloquy to be delivered.

"Some of my most inspiring conversations are with myself," she said with smoky resonation.

"Do you always go traipsing around naked, eavesdropping on people?"

She smiled oddly. "Sometimes."

"You're not going to pull a gun on me again, are you?" Goldman asked.

"No . . . but I like what you said before, that your *stiff* is working and that you would like to *gun* me down. But after watching you, I'm not so sure. If you're interested in my cause, don't bring your pistol half-*cocked*."

He was leveled with her apparition. Like a mosquito hawk drawn to an incandescent bulb, he walked into her light. He stood face-to-face with blood-squeezing capillary attraction, but remained calm. The only thing

that could sink him was the illumination that flooded from her visage. It
filled his dinghy with rapture, a *rider on the storm*. She slowly raised her
arms and wrapped them around the thumping carotids of his neck.

"I want you to talk to me, but don't say a word."

It was an eccentric tongue he knew he could not speak, but an idiom
he now understood. Alone in that empty warehouse, they spoke in elated
code, like sounds that foreshadow a coming event: a portentous moment
that bore the full weight of her mass . . . straight from a boy's dream.

Their diaphragms fused hot and glowed fanciful in the dark, two
sojourners swimming in an ocean of beatific bliss where parallel universes
are separated by the thickness of their stardust skin. In a kinesthetic flash
they touched in incandescent wonder, and their mirror neurons brought
order into an incongruous world where spirit and nature collide, smashing
atoms . . . lunaception—larks' tongues flickering in fellatio-fused aspects,
intercoursing something new from the ad infinitum of something old,
where the skin-starved devour in gustatory haste, and aristocrats are finally
gunned down.

XXV

Goldman awoke from a dragging doze. Morning beams shot across the press machinery casting slanted geometric shadows against the cinder-block wall and, like an unsubstantiated rumor, Mina could not be confirmed. The whiff of lilac and spent orgasms still hung in the exhausted air, and her simulacrum aesthetics were still heavily present. His back was stiff and he wondered how he had been able to sleep so soundly on the concrete floor. Like Adam awakening from a god-induced nap, he gazed at his oblique muscle, the bayonet scar suffused in a shaft of sunlight. The wound from the separated *womb*man was still fresh, but where was Eve? She was a curious bird that always flew the nest at a wing's flittering inclination. Maybe it was just a dream. Had his dislocated mind manufactured the entire event? He felt cold in the empty warehouse and longed to thaw in her clinch again.

He rustled up his clothes, locked the doors of the building, and proceeded to walk the long way home. He was sure that the encounter had happened; it was just too tactile, too splendidly vivid. It was no wet dream; he had actually accomplished the impossible dream, and made love to the woman of his dreams. He leapt with toothsome delight, but just as quickly sank under the tasteless feeling that she had been unwilling to bring in the new day with him. Had she been so disappointed that she cast an enchanted spell of sleep so that she could slip away? She had pulled the coyote, and he unexpectedly laughed with a heaving surge. Then, just as unexpectedly, bawled himself out for wallowing in saccharine feelings like a syrupy sap.

The streets were deserted as the sun softened the early morning's bite. He slinked down the vacant avenue like a cat that had just eaten the house bird, when a car's engine started and accelerated. He heard the thump of concrete, rubber, and steel meeting at high velocity. The sedan bounced over the curb like a two-ton torpedo, pointed directly at him. He darted across the street only to see another car moving toward him at a colliding speed. He dashed back to the other side again, but the first car had him cornered. Men in black suits exited the cars with ID badges and cobalt plated revolvers. They flung him in one of the sedans, stuffed his head in a black bag, and drove to a building not far from where he had been shanghaied. He was locked in an icy room that felt like a colloquium sarcophagus, where recollections of government threats sundered his chicken heart and he wondered what was on tap. A short time later the door opened and a man wearing a suit entered, accompanied by another man in a military uniform.

"Good morning, Mr. Goldman," said the man in the suit fitted with an acrimonious smile.

The officer handed him a cup of coffee and offered him a cigarette.

"My name is Special Agent Muller, assigned to the Foreign Subversives Detachment of the FBI, and this is Colonel Ortberg, you might remember him."

Muller carried an old copy of the *Los Angeles Times* and tossed it on Goldman's lap: REDS TAKE TO STREET AND INCITE RIOT. The cover displayed a photo of Goldman marching side by side with Mina. Muller grabbed another paper, *The Daily Worker*, and threw that on his lap as well.

"You believe that propaganda?"

"I believe in the First Amendment," Goldman stoically answered.

"Well, I believe you are part of a Communist conspiracy, which means you have no First Amendment," Muller sneered with blind authority.

"I'm a citizen of the United States and I have every right to exercise my freedom, and that includes what kind of society and government I want."

"You're an agent and a fulltime functionary of the Soviet Union, someone who advocates the overthrow of the United States," Muller said, as if it was a matter of fact.

Goldman tensely laughed as he swigged the coffee and dragged on the Lucky Strike.

Muller bent down and faced him with curls of rapt expression.

"You ever heard of Jewish Bolshevism? You're the first Jew awarded the Congressional Medal of Honor, who chimp-fucked his service record by becoming a little Red monkey in Mina Contreras' Communist zoo."

After a few gulps of the black Joe, Goldman's eyes abruptly hung, heavy lidded and lazy, his tongue thickened and felt unruly.

Colonel Ortberg chimed in, "The Red threat is real enough and the last thing we need is a turncoat like you going public. It makes the American way look bad."

"It's not a crime to try to create an egalitarian society," Goldman slurred.

"You're a real dippity-doo shitwad and *The Daily Worker* is about to be smashed into itty-bitty Bolshevik pieces. Knowing who you are, we've given the professional courtesy of extending a fair warning. If your life means anything to you, you'll say goodbye to your little escapade in the Socialist movement and get on as a productive American," said Muller.

"I am a productive American."

Muller leaned into his echoing ear. "If we see you with that little Red bitch or any of her operatives again, I'll turn your little Communist dream into a drop-kicked nightmare, and that ain't no *bull*-shevik. This is a preview of things to come."

The two men left the room.

Goldman picked up the *LA Times* and stared at the photo of Mina and him, embossed on the front page. *God, we're a good-looking couple*, he thought. His eyes then moved down the page to a smaller headline: JEWS FIGHT FOR THEIR OWN NATION. It read: "Returning Jews from around the world are fighting for their very existence in the land of Palestine." The article touched something genuine in him, and his closeted Hebrew pride brimmed with selfless pseudonyms and rhetorical questions of no doubt.

The idea of fighting alongside his associate brothers felt like a homecoming and eclipsed any desultory inclinations he may have had for the Communist movement. This was something that was real, a real struggle, a real revolution, and a chance to participate in a thing that had every right to be. He remembered what his mother had said: "When Israel is a nation again, the Anointed One will come." He suddenly swelled with a dose of revenant pride, like a poltergeist that has finally found a numinous house to inhabit. The prospect of his people fighting for a homeland infused him with brazen obligations to abandoned tribes that stood insanely alone. He was so excited that he jumped to his feet, but fell over with his head hammering and whirling, and it scared him noisy. He tried to stand again, but there was the same swooning sensation, and then a quick sinking, out of sight, out of mind.

*   *   *

Goldman came to, with no idea how much time the clock had eaten, lying face up on a hospital gurney. His head was still spinning, he tried to sit up, but found he was strapped down tight, big-papoose style. The quiet of the room was interrupted by his dysphonic objections as gossamer images hovered around him like arch diabolical specters. He saw a man in a white gabardine coat, and Muller, and Colonel Ortberg standing near. He closed his eyes again and felt a sharp pricking pain on the tender side of his forearm. A hypodermic needle exuded hot gamma juice into his vein like liquid gall, and he drifted back into idiot's paradise.

* * *

He awoke in a room that he had never seen before, beneath a brocade coverlet in a brass bed with squeaking springs. It was a chicly appointed space, accented with the smells of lilac and hot broth, and sexual subterranean feelings filled its vacancy. His head still hurt, but not as bad as before, and his arm was slightly numb. He gathered enough strength to sit up and tried to step out of bed, but collapsed to all fours atop an eighteenth-century Persian rug.

"No you don't."

He turned and staggered at the prospect of Mina. She put him back in her brocade-covered brass bed with the squeaking springs.

"We found you unconscious and naked in front of the doors at *The Daily Worker*. You were covered head-to-toe in red paint. There was a sign hanging around your neck."

She picked up the dilapidated cardboard with the words: BETTER TO BE DEAD THAN RED, scrawled across it.

"You were off your rails, talking crazy. You've been out of it for two days."

She went to the kitchen and returned with a sterling silver tray, upon which was a seventeenth-century china bowl filled with bouillabaisse, and set it on his lap. She slid silver spoonfuls of broth down his craw, treating him with uncharacteristic care. They didn't say a word, and their muted faces remained veiled, communicating nothing of discernable significance. Their relinquishing of words conjured up libidinous recollections of the warehouse episode and pseudo-sexual reservations. She then stood, like a beautiful effigy stuffed with indifference and flimsy gestures of scarecrow ennui, and left the room.

Goldman heard the stifled closing of the front door as he lay back in her squeaky brass bed. The room, darkened by window shades and extinguished lights, blended with the cloying smells of a far-flung lover who was gone . . . again. He teetered on feigning gratitude, but he really was glad to be there, even if she was not. Delicious apparitions and cream-like events ran down his gut while uncorroborated sweets and iridescent feelings bounced in his head as he tried to separate fixed truths from opaque phantoms—and root out the red paint still embedded in his fingernails.

XXVI

There was a helium rumor floating around in Jonathan's head that one day he was going to come to life, but for now he would wait in insipid benefice tenure. The tent revival meetings were a rolling live-wire act, but being on the road left him feeling anything but alive. It was hard work trawling for followers and benefactors, converting feral goats into domesticated sheep. After a while that's what it felt like, a bad job notice, not a good God calling. He so wanted God's christening, to feel piously raised yet equally keeled, to know that he was the divine instrument of substantial matters. He was chary, though, when other people purported to hear the God voice and considered them sanatorium prospects, excessive and delusional.

There were exceptions for intermediaries between divinity and mortal dust and he liked to think that he was one of the elect. That was his hope. Hope—God's static potential waiting to happen. Maybe that wasn't even God, but sublingual laws that responded to prolonged static friction: prayer? Nevertheless, Jonathan didn't like to leave crucial circumstances to caprice and serendipity. Coincidental quirks always left a quavering taste on his limerick tongue, a ticklish waft in his Constantine nose, and a sour squirt in his Celtic eyes.

He had transfused the blood of the Lord into a *B-positive* attitude for most of his *A-negative* life, but he just couldn't get the blood components to gel. Still, no matter how anemic his cause, he had determined to spread the good news of the blood-soaked gospel for as far and as long as God would tolerate it, and if the Almighty was on his side, then no man could get in the way of his magisterial authority. But the bills did, and the overhead of running a tent revival was leaving the operation in the red. His Technicolor dream of a magnanimous calling was starting to cave, and he struggled just to keep it from collapsing. For too long he had languished as an insipid yawn, and was furtively tired of orbiting the biggest Boss in the universe as an inconsequential satellite.

He didn't like stodgy realities that were tough to chew, let alone gestate, and their ecclesiastical tutelage seemed bent on teaching him lessons deficient of any spiritual nutrients. Why would God not throw an extra bone his way, and why did the business of doing the Lord's work seem vouchsafed, yet exasperating and vacant? A divine calling that is worthy of the dignity of human persons, and yet is seemingly thwarted, leads to sub-standard beliefs, cold stripped of anything real. Faith, without the conscious filling of the presence of God, is not faith but freeze-dried *thug*ology that requires immense human effort and flesh-hammer devotion.

Jonathan questioned the motives behind his compulsion to pick up where his father had fallen. Maybe it was to right the old man's house of perversion. He knew why his father had failed—because *he* had failed, not God—but how he had gone from a son of God to a son of a bitch he would never know. It angered Jonathan to think that the Lord did not honor *his* attempts when he had proven himself a crusader who suffered and plodded on in futile ignominy. God always seemed to have protected and even blessed his father. So what is it in those people that morph decent prerogatives into cupidity but still come out on top?

He swore he was going to be different and sever generational ties with moral rectitude. He was the *primus inter pares*, sanctified and maintained a model of sightless faith that had few equals; a consecrated man who, unlike his teenage years, never touched alcohol or tobacco. He was faithful to his new wife and never cast a roving eye on another woman; a fabulist practiced in liturgical bread and fermented wine rites, an impregnable bulwark against the seductions of Baal, proficient in the art of self-mortification, a hanging celestial light in the chandelier of God's ceiling. He did everything right by the big black book, so why was his call not sanctioned but afflicted? Why did the people come to the tent revivals in ever-shrinking numbers? He knew his message was good and the doctrine sound, so maybe it was the messenger? Or maybe because the horrors of the war were over, the economy was strong and everyone had composite roofs over their heads, a Dodge in the garage, and a chicken in the pot, so who needed God?

The pressures of keeping his *Spanish caravan* alive, and the endless days schlepping on *purgatorio* highways, relegated him to a role in an importuning allegory. The fruit he carried would always be unfinished business and he knew he was souring on the limb. He had a devoted wife, but she wanted to settle down and start a family, which of course would be incompatible with the divine diktat of a soul-saving troubadour. His nightmare of being a failure leaked into his calling, and he could hardly look his own life in the eye. Maybe it was the healing services that were so frustrating? He was sure in his artesian well that God wanted, and even commanded, him to lay hands and heal the fold, but the crowds always left the services as physically broke as their wallets.

He could recall only a handful of times when people seemed to recover from some minor ailment that probably would have gotten better in the natural course of events. He feared the word had gotten out that he was a schlockmeister and a tin-pan prophet. But in the center of his artichoke heart he was absolutely convinced that God had given him the gift of prophecy and healing, so why did it not come to pass? These issues were neither benevolent nor maligned, but arid facts and fine-line schisms that did not take sides. But the matter grated relentlessly against the grain of his milled paradigms and teetered on the suspicion that faith was a vestigial word almost irrelevant to his experience. His convictions had degraded to rooted dualism and discursive twaddle, a wandering relig-holic in a waterless search to quench the parched expanses of his epistemic uncertainty.

*   *   *

Jonathan's tent revival was in Pomona California. A grief-stricken mother had brought her beautiful blond daughter whose femur bone had snapped from the ravages of a cancerous tumor. The doctors said there was no way to salvage the leg, and that by the end of the week they were going to amputate. With clarion wails the mother begged Jonathan to get God on the line. He was lachrymosely moved by her pleas and asked her to give him time to pray. In front of the entire congregation he dropped to his knees with invocatory petitions for God's wisdom in the matter. He soon felt in rapport with divine flow and redoubled the intensity of his prayer just to make sure. With liquid fire eyes, he arose with his arms outstretched and *Rex Judaeorum* beams of assurance radiating from any crucified doubts.

"It is not God's will for this girl to lose her leg," he confidently proclaimed.

He asked the entire congregation to direct their hands toward her and declare the healing, and on that cue the worshippers exploded with peals of heavenly thunder. The giant tent expanded and contracted with bellowed hot flames, heated tongues, positive confessions, binding the devil, and direct verbal attacks on the cancer itself. When the service was over, everyone, including the little girl, was filled with radical confidence that she was cured. Jonathan's conviction was real enough that he challenged the mother to have X-rays done and, with a God wink, assured her that there would be no trace of the cancer; in fact, the bone itself would be mended.

*   *   *

Three months later the tent revival was again in Pomona. In the middle of Jonathan's service, a sound like an air-raid siren slowly turning, peaked with an earsplitting skirl. From the back of the tent came the woman who had brought the little girl for healing, pushing a wheelchair to the front of the congregation. The girl's right leg had been amputated mid-thigh and the stump—not acclimated to the phantom pains of a lost appendage—was sticking straight up. The doctors had done the test but sadly, nothing had changed.

The child's mother wept with lamenting yowls, pointing her reproving finger with accusations of fraud and deceit. Jonathan was stunned, bewildered and flattened like road kill. In the marrow of his bones he was sure that the little girl had been healed, but the cruel fact was self-evident. The hub of his soul gushed black crude of the deepest, sweetest corruption that he was a hoax or, even more unimaginable, that his God was.

It wouldn't be the first time he got excited about something holy only to have it be another mirage, but this was especially vulgar, and once again, God was a no-show. It shook his faith so completely that he scrambled to find some egregious sin in his own life that could account for such a calamity. The occasion was one of many wrecking balls that threatened to dismantle his tumbledown shack of faith, and one of many penumbras that circumscribed his ever-shrinking beliefs into epileptic fits of diminution, grand mal seizures in a pig's eye, where spirits of trichinosis search for wandering swine like him to inhabit. The word got out that he was a flim-flam man and the crowds thinned to a trickle, as did his spirit.

He had to get over his malaise and man up to the fact that life was deadening, and maybe it's the nature of evil to keep split-hoofed men close to the ground, but if this was God's modality then he could not serve such an impetuous idol. It left him feeling grotesque and deserted with the horrible sentiment that there was no objective reality, and his subjective self was nothing but debagged nonsense—a growing crisis of the ages. His beloved tent revival ministry was abandoned. He was low on money and moved into a small apartment just outside of Hollywood. A fellow pastor told him about the downtown mission that was in desperate need of a fulltime minister and kept bugging Jonathan to take the job, but he was despairingly reluctant.

The milieu of skidrow would be apocalyptic. He had never been cut off from the obscenity of the human train wreck, but this was mortal carnage: alcoholics, dope fiends, street whores, homeless malignant walking corpses, and the insane; a constant cycle of broken humanity revolving through the mission's turnstile. The logistics of caring for the destitute would be of biblical proportions, and it would require a Moses-like fiber to lead these people. The sullied business of warehousing street souls ridiculed his dreams of holy higher callings, but he grudgingly took the position.

*   *   *

It was something Jonathan feared and everything he loathed. Sometimes he returned home staggered by the sickening condition of those people. They were the ugliest of the ugly, and it would always be that way. The equivocated sermons he had to give rang hollow to the street refugees who were required to sit through an earful of religious rhetoric before they could eat. His curdled faith blighted the significance his convictions once held and his acerbic contempt for the homeless filled him with rancor for anything humane. He felt betrayed by life, and the hard sternum that once buoyed a soft heart had inverted and his elastic old self was showing new signs of decrepitude, where wrinkled convictions and timeline creases are in need of a serious *faith* lift.

XXVII

Mina presided over Goldman's revival with ministrations of a sycophantic nurse, although her bedside manners were to resurrect *him,* not his phallic inclinations. His penchant for seconds on the warehouse sex buffet was not to be. He fiddled with cross-connecting thoughts and the features of a simulacrum sex matron who looked the same, but acted patently different. He assumed the days spent in her squeaking brass bed would be raw-dog healing time. It was clear though, that her pejorative fire-hydrant valve was private property—not to be opened again.

She was a mercurial specimen that stayed in fighting shape with conjectural gymnastics that made his eyes cross just to watch. He tried to reacquaint himself with her sexual Sanskrit text but, to her, he had become the bogeyman, and she shot him down faster than a well-oiled Norman Rockwell virgin. He didn't understand her schizophrenic behavior and thought the natural declivity down the slippery slope of intercourse would be the normal run but, for her, his post-sex protocol need not apply.

They slept in the same bed, but they might as well have been on opposite coasts separated by four time zones and a continental divide. Maybe his breath stank? Maybe he was a *bitte le petite?* Then why was he there? She could have dumped him at any hospital, or his own place for that matter. She acted like a sexual litigator playing the back nine, and he, an asexual spore, and the thought of not being on par with her game left him feeling like a slub-fuck handicapper. To walk blind and backwards through her sand-trap course, and having to caddy her gnomic irons, was like trying to drive icy metaphors into hole-in-one shots. He was a diddler-on-the-roof, and her unreserved rejection dunked him in a vat of self-conscious ooze. To occupy the same space with her relegated him to a lark scolded for his dimwittedness by an ass and he would not whinny in her bed with a half-mast of wood and a matching set of blue donkey balls.

The arm that had been injected was still swollen and tender, even to the slightest touch, and he felt persistent flu-like symptoms and whirling nausea. He stumbled into the front room like someone tripped by a *gaucho bola*. The first thing that caught his pink eye was a Steinway baby grand, and he moved to the piano with practiced thoughts of a forgotten prodigy. He remembered how his mother had drilled his refined motor movements until his hands had a mind of their own, tickling the 88's as if they didn't even belong to him. She was a natural and so was he, a genius even. He loved music but hated the discipline required to truly master the instrument, "His natural talent makes him lazy and deprives him of potential excellence," his mother would carol.

He went into Beethoven's *Moonlight Sonata*. It was so beautiful that he forgot about the gnawing pain in his arm, and was relieved to know that his hands still maintained muscle memory. His rational process seemed particle and his intuitive process, a wave, as he deftly deferred to German melancholy, and with legato ease finished the first movement. For no perceptible reason he started playing Kazuo's five notes. Over and over again, it was the same C, F, A flat, G flat, and C sharp. The notes were ruefully hypnotic and his body seemed to resonate into one monophonic hum.

In his cortex theater mind, scant imagery flashed across his movie screen like auteur phantasmal wisps. He saw beautiful fiberglass cars coming off the GM assembly line: futuristic automobiles with three hundred horsepower engines. There was a magical land with delirious rides: children and cartoon animals, castles and monorails, where a giant mouse ruled from atop a mountain of cash and grown men slavishly obeyed his every command. He saw a handsome raven-haired hillbilly dancing on stage with mechanical carnivorous sounds of a rolling locomotive, *sixteen coaches long*, before a crowd of teenage girls screaming something about his pelvis. General Eisenhower was sitting in the White House smoking Camels and drinking Grand Marnier. Then there was the old city of Jerusalem, drenched in gunfire, smoke, and blood . . .

He mentally reentered Mina's apartment with his muscle of love beating in his left hand and the five notes pounding in his right as if they were mutually exclusive, automatic . . . anticlimactic. He took a shower, called a taxi, and was driven home with only a bathroom towel wrapped around his waist.

For days he did nothing but sit like a slack-jawed hillbilly eating paint chips. He wanted to be grateful for something, anything, to put his outré life in perspective. He wanted to be thankful to feel nothing, but for now heaps of hurt was the only thing that made him feel alive, baleful pain that pierced the seven veils of the alleged persona. He hated how people could brandish saber tongues, cutting through the tender parts of the heart—and Mina possessed a vicious mouthpiece that could vivisect four-chambered ventricle emotions while the patient was still alive.

The fact that she made little of their union irritated Goldman to all fuckery, and cavorting with animus agitation; to him, the two were now one in body and force. Maybe it was over-censorious, but her haughty disinterest left him feeling duped, and gripped him with a drooling-drone dismissal spell. He thought that if it were the other way around he would probably feel the same. He longed to own the power of *No* that she so blatantly brandished, but the word only has power if you really mean it and, to him, she really meant it.

It was all his doing. He knew he had stepped into a cage with an intra-ovulating beast, a devoted Darwinian survivalist of solipsist absolutes. Self-seeking gene machines like her rightly demand what they qualify for, and canine-mating rites would always be alpha-dogged and deferred. If Goldman couldn't hack the pack, then that would be one more deficient gene link isolated and one less revolutionary who was not down for her cause.

Her natural selection sacking made him feel like a hopeless waste of protoplasm, and his lack of adaptive evolution filled his hominid nostrils with the smell of a wet dog. The more he drank, the more he thought, and the more he thought, the more he sobered to the fact that his half ass endorsement of the Communist Party had been for a succubus woman that would never be his. She was living proof of the fallacy of the consequent: one is treated superior because one is superior, and to him, she really was.

His room had become a torture chamber of torque tedium and he could hardly disconnect his arse from the couch, moving only to take shots of Tequila and to drain his blowfish. She had hoodwinked him hard with a bout of down-right, down-left, downhearted furrows that wrinkled his emotional lobe and siphoned off synaptic pathways of wholeness. His conditioned mind had scattered and left him with only emotional compressions of the gut, and he knew he would have to reassemble his concatenated parts, like some laboratory monster, just to get his brain back.

It wasn't just Mina who dragged him into darker waters, but the shadowy figures of the government that he towed in train. He started to fear for his life with agitating wings of terror, just wanting to fly away.

Maybe if Mina had showed more interest in him it might have been enough to plow through any perceived threats. He may have even been willing to go down for the Communist cause with the right woman, but her ambivalence was not enough for him to become indictment fodder. If the one skin encounter they had was nothing more than a *porneusal* bone session, then he was determined that his oblations to her would cease.

His mind raced back to the abduction. He remembered being stripped and strapped to a hospital gurney, a doctor reading his chart and injecting him with a cocktail of plutonium and uranium, *"Ten times the amount that anyone would receive in ten lifetimes."* He recalled how voices in the room mumbled and chuckled with low-pitched, petulant laughs as the hot radioactive liquid coursed through his arm. He was a fertilized nuclear zygote and his cells were dividing with atomic shock—an isotope seed, and he feared that one day it would show its fruit. He hadn't been this spooked since the night on Sugar Loaf Hill.

He marveled at how his system could tolerate heavy metal, mortal doses. The government wondered too, and if there was something in his bioplasm that could mutate its way around radioactive decay, then they were determined to develop it as a potential antidote in the nuclear showdown that was heating up in the new Cold War. He needed to think clear, and free himself from his tied-to-the-mast situation, and if he didn't get out of town soon, he was sure that government socialites would be throwing more Atomic Cocktail parties for him.

Recently, he had sensed something changing in his constitution, as if the chemistry of his inner-workings were turning like a nuclear centrifuge. Or maybe it was just his imagination: flights of sparkle fuck, trying to find something unique in his chicken-hearted banalities and symptoms of wanting to be someone more than he really was—anything to impress Mina. He was out of his gourd with clacking love for the proto-feminist, except that now the call of his catacomb logic shouted louder than his entombed sentiments. He wanted to leave the Party, but feared that he would go straight to nowhere. Employment at *The Daily Worker* was the only life he had known for the better part of a year, and to vacate suddenly made him feel misplaced.

*   *   *

The days ticked by like the metronome of a grandfather clock, and his cuckoo-bird brain mocked his companionless hours with primeval chirps and *Homo solitarius* angst. The times when he did leave his place he was sure he was being followed. His paranoia became so chronic that he believed even little old ladies were secret operatives for the FBI. One crone happened to ask him to help put her groceries in her car, but he suspected she was a disguised agent and when the old woman reached into her purse to give him a tip, he thought she was going for a gun and he proceeded to rain down blows that tweaked her blue wig and sent her dentures flying. Bystanders came to her aid and tried to make a citizen's arrest, but Goldman had a twinge of suspicion that they too, were working for the FBI, and bolted. The vigilantes chased him down Sunset Boulevard until he scaled a thirty-foot palm where he nested in its fronds and steles, howling like a lotus position blow-monkey. The fire department brought out a hook 'n' ladder unit to get the coco-nut case down. The event created a rouse that the papers and television ballyhooed as: THE PALM TREE SCALING, OLD LADY THUMPING MANIAC. He was in the limelight again, and that was the last place he wanted to be. After posting bail he knew what he had to do.

*   *   *

He put his meager possessions in his '41 Chevy and took one final gaze at the little Hansel and Gretel hovel he had called home. Standing there, he was seized by the aroma of lilac. He turned, and was struck by the enameled shine of Mina's pearly ivories.

"Hello, Marine."

He hastily put together a disguise of nonchalance, but her female knowing bored holes through his flimsy masquerade. He stood on the other side of the car as light reflected his image in the retinas of her heavy black doe eyes and she fixed onto his form with fiat command.

"We have an edition of *The Daily Worker*, and you're the cover story. I've written an in-depth article about your valiant struggle with the government."

"Well, I don't want to sound like an unsubstantiated scoop, but I'm done," he said. Mina gave her head a curious tilt, stiffened by the gout proclamation.

"You're leaving?"

"That's right."

He threw the last of his possessions in the car and moved his self-conscious body around to the driver's door where she was barring the way. He felt clumsy and nervous as he tried to negotiate around her inviting curves. She looked him in the face with vesper bell notions.

"Don't let the Man scare you. Every cause has its martyrs."

He nervously laughed. "I ain't nobody's martyr."

"You think you're the first mark in a government conspiracy?"

She was a funny one, this girl, a vampire without a shadow and a mind like a steel-trap spider door, a numinous creature who knew how to pick her moments. Even her colloquial jargon had dramatic flair, and she fired for more effect.

"This is part of the struggle. If the cause is going to stand, then now's the time to close ranks. Oh, my naive Marine, divide and conquer is so obvious."

She continued to petition her case, and for a while it almost sounded like she was copping a plea. He felt flattered, if only it was about him and not about the Party, he could nearly make the case that he would be missed. Her consternated pleading almost jumbled his neatly made-up mind. All he wanted to hear was, "I just want *you* to stay," but she was too slippery, and her alimentary concerns were always about nourishing her cause and nothing more.

"What do you care?" Goldman said.

"I care about justice." Mina affirmed.

"I care about . . . just *us*." Goldman stoically countered.

She scrambled to deflect. Her mouth opened but all words were seized. The only resonance that emitted was a peculiar silence and an inscrutable veneration for the man. She would never let on, but she admired men of humble strength layered in chthonic mythical stratums, and it was clear to her that Goldman was a man of obscured quality. She knew he grappled with inner-demoniacs, and that he was self-conscious and a left-footed stumblebum around her, yet there was an attractiveness in his buffoonery. She sensed something that not even he was aware of: an eminence, pregnant with potential. But her own bolshie pride would only allow her to feel with distant fingertip clarity.

If he was looking for her to throw herself under the tires, it wasn't going to happen, and if she thought he was going to give one of those *Casablanca* goodbyes, that wasn't going to happen either.

She noticed on the car seat his passport and a newspaper article with the headlines: JEWS FIGHT FOR INDEPENDENCE.

"What are your plans?" she asked.

Goldman shrugged his shoulders. "I found an operatic opportunity for flamboyance."

"Whippity-do! The Palestine Jews!" she drolly remarked. He nodded with an embarrassed flush. "What about our cause, the cause of the people?"

"These are my people, and this is my cause."

She stared long with vacant lights, and then dredged up a low-voltage smile, reached into her purse, and pulled out a manila envelope.

"This is all the back pay I've . . . we've owed you . . . in cash. I thought about using it to coax you back, but it looks like your mind's made up."

He tossed the manila envelope onto the seat and smiled wistfully, then politely nudged her out of the way and got in the car. For a split-end moment she looked dainty—breakable—and for an even thinner split, they ceased maneuvering and traded crystal-cave stares. For one more fleeting split, he was filled with the magnanimous power of *No*, and she broke with spellbinding sagacity, that the sagacity of her spell had been broken.

She then produced an official Communist Party pendant, engraved with Lenin's bust and the hammer and sickle red flag. They both forced smiles with miles of preface regret as she pinned the pendant to his lapel like a sacred scarab brooch, and volleyed with a valedictory fist and an ode to sonnets yet to be spoken.

He clunked the Chevy into gear. The car jerked backwards and almost ran over her foot—squashing any hopes of an urbane and memorable exit. He put the car in drive and she curiously faded in Goldman's blind spot as he made a hasty departure into the void of Pollyannaish sizzles and blue vaulted sky callings.

Mina stood motionless, dumb as an idol, watching the span of their separation grow until he disappeared between the lines of a wispy rhyme in a soliloquist's fading tale.

XXVIII

After selling his car and with his back pay from *The Daily Worker*, Goldman bought a plane ticket and caught a TWA Constellation, flying coast-to-coast in about eight hours—which was an astounding feat. It carried fifty people in its aluminum belly and could outrace and outdistance any other prop planes. He had flown a couple of times in troop transports, but had been in the air for only brief jaunts and never higher than twenty-five hundred feet. The Constellations, in contrast, were pressurized flying tubes that took away the sensation of being airborne, even at the unheard of altitude of twenty thousand feet. It left him feeling hypoxic, and simultaneously unbounded and claustrophobic, as he wrestled with sedentary feelings at three hundred miles per hour.

He flew transatlantic from New York to London, then to Beirut via Paris. He was in Lebanon for three days before he realized that he was not in Palestine. Goldman didn't have a clue about how to plug into the Palestinian milieu, so he bent any foreign ear that would listen. He found some locals and proudly proclaimed, "I am a Jew looking for the fighting brothers for the independence of Palestine." An Arab who understood English produced a scimitar and chased him half a mile, slashing wildly and blaring, *"Allah Akbar! Allah Akbar!"*

Eventually he crossed into the land of his forefathers, Palestine—Israel, as the Jews were calling it—and got as far as the coastal town of Haifa, a beautiful port city that juxtaposed Roman ruins, mud brick structures, baroque buildings and the sapphire Mediterranean that lapped its white-hot sands with unwarranted inflections of tranquility. It was a frenetic little haven, awash in capering opportunists and enterprising street vendors who were selling everything from fish and American cigarettes to guns and contraband, and every kiosk seemed to be having a clearance sale.

The city was a whirling cauldron of Jewish Zealots, Muslim Holy Warriors, Christian Crusaders, and the garrisoned British that tried to function as a bushing between the impinging and discordant parts. It seemed every anti-quest fanatic was perpetually preparing for some holy day or holy event, where wars and rumors of wars seep through cryptic prophecies readying for bloodshed that no one wanted to admit was coming.

The British tried to impose *Her Majesty's Royal Order,* but were relegated to the role of an aging junkyard dog with worn-to-the-root incisors. The flood of post-WWII Jews betaking themselves en masse to the holy land overwhelmed the British, and now the Arabs as well. Skirmishes were common, and by March, 1947, there had been some one thousand killed. Palestine would remain de facto until new borders were drawn.

Goldman arrived in early December—about the same time the United Nations approved a plan to resolve the Arab-Jewish conflict by partitioning Palestine into two parts. Like Solomon who was willing to cut the contested babe in half, only the Arab mothers protested, arguing that the partition was unfair to the population balance, and rejected the UN authority like cud-chewing ruminants forced to eat spoiled meat. Although some Jews criticized the plan, the resolution was welcomed.

The Arabs saw the intrusion of the Jews as another humiliating vestige of European colonialism, where the Arab population had always been seen but never noticed. Goldman could not have timed it better or worse. He had only been in the ancient land a week since the imposed partition when bloody violence broke out in earnest. Murders, reprisals, and counter-reprisals: hundreds were killed on each side with preambles to greater slaughter, and ancient lines were being drawn . . . again.

From 1947 to 1948, the fighting escalated and more Jews streamed into the land, pestilent clouds of Euro-locusts and, for the Arabs, one of seven plagues yet to come. The British had made feeble attempts at stemming the Jewish influx but were unable to run screen against the tsunami tide of lost tribes and holy land divested prophets. Rusting, soggy ships with cadaver-like Ashkenazi ghouls were being turned away like uninvited guests not on the party list. Jews who tried to cross illegally into Palestine were arrested, and some were even shot as they made paint chipped metal-antelope dashes through the British arcade lines. Goldman entered the country disguised as a Bedouin sheep herder, riding in the back of an Arab bus that shuttled Mohammed-commissioned pilgrims to their third holiest shrine: Jerusalem.

His semi-Sephardic complexion had bronzed in the Middle Eastern sun and his beard had grown almost full. When British checkpoints inspected the bus they never once questioned him. Like a loyal British subject, Goldman would greet them with a tip of his *keffiyeh*, and in a badly mimicked Middle Eastern LA-Memphis-brogue exclaim, "*Allah Akbar! Allah Akbar!* And so is mother England!"

Traveling through the holy land was like riding econo-class along the rich toll roads of simultaneous time. All those ambitions, glories, and passion pursuits, interred in the shifting dunes of perpetuity: skeletal ruins and chaparral peaks, where splendid armies and bejeweled-encrusted kings reincarnate as rocks, lizards, and thorny thickets . . . But Jerusalem was the objective. He didn't know why, but the city seemed to tug at his navel-pierced soul with a primordial draw and confounded notions of higher holy callings.

There were two other Jews on the bus, a man and woman, who like him were trying to make Jerusalem. When they could not produce the right papers they were escorted off the bus by two armed guards at a remote British checkpoint. The soldiers were questioning them when the couple suddenly darted off into the desolated expanse. One of the soldiers began firing.

Goldman watched from the bus as the other soldier drew his pistol, pointed downrange, then placed the gun to the temple of the other soldier and blew his crown off. He collapsed into a contortion that made his lifeless body look agonizingly uncomfortable.

The soldier entered the bus and began shouting with an upper class British accent, "Are there any other Jews on the bus?"

The Arabs shouted in parroted unison, "*Allah Akbar! Allah Akbar!* And so is mother England!"

"Fuck mother England!" shouted the burley Popeye-forearmed soldier. "I'll say it again, are there any Jews on the bus?"

Goldman found his tremulous hand levitating from under the Bedouin sheets.

"I am a Jew."

The soldier approached him with pistol-pointed precision. Goldman tried to deflect the nine-millimeter, but the soldier pulled back, and then handed it to him butt first.

"You're going to need this."

Goldman sat cobble-stoned, trying to assemble rational pieces that didn't fit a concocted puzzle. The soldier stood by the driver and motioned to Goldman.

"Follow me if you want to live."

He grabbed his bag and exited the bus like a confused chameleon trying to adapt to his changed environment, and his listing doubts all but gave his lizardarian appearance away. The soldier yelled in Arabic at the driver to leave. The man obliged post haste as the other Arabs stuck their *keffiyeh* covered heads out the windows of the silt-blanketed bus, shouting, *"Allah Akbar! Allah Akbar!* And fuck mother England!"

The soldier turned to Goldman and extended a meaty hand. "Ronan Goetz."

Goldman presented his reluctant mitt and they pressed their dusty palms. In a gratifying way they each felt satisfied with the other's portrait presence.

"I don't understand what's going on?"

Ronan moved to the body of the pretzel-twisted soldier and stripped it of weapons and other valuables.

"We're at war, or haven't you heard?"

"The British?"

Ronan slung the rifle over his shoulder and put the sidearm in his holster.

"The Jews and the Arabs," he blurted out.

"You're a British soldier, I don't get it."

"I'm a British officer in her Majesty's Royal Guard, and a decorated hero from the European theatre."

"Why do you gun down fellow Brits?"

"I'm an Israeli patriot. That's my allegiance."

"You're a Jew?"

Ronan produced a terse smile. "And a rabbi working for the *Haganah* underground."

The two walked to a jeep that was loaded with a cache of small arms and hopped in.

"And you? Are you here to midwife the state of Israel? Because she's starting to crown. And take those sheets off. It's bad enough I'm a two-headed coin, I don't want anyone to think I'm courting the bloody Arabs too."

Goldman began whipping off the *thawb* sheets, letting them fly into the desert as Ronan drove at an impendent speed toward the man and woman who were still running, and almost plowed them flat. They begged in broken Pole-English. "No shoot, no shoot!"

"I am a freedom fighter for the Jewish resistance. Get in."

They hesitated, then jumped into the jeep with pallid faces and desiccated bodies, but soaked in sweat beads of relief. Ronan double-clutched and fanned the desert with baked flying sand.

It occurred to Goldman that the muscle of Heraclitus was fluxing something new. British steel that once routed whole continents was now enervated and anemic. Right before the world's eyes the mighty little-island empire was smelting like molten ore into another chapter of fallen kingdoms, where hundreds of years of moral impurities form slag for extraction. The European war had been a bankrupting bombshell and had done more damage than the *Luftwaffe* or *Wehrmacht* ever could. It had stripped England of her grandiloquent title as *Civics Brtitannicus Sum* and a world-class power. Even the Jews that were initially a mere scarecrow threat were overwhelming the fighting Tommy's fighting spirit, like Russian assassins, dropping British soldiers with *Vasily Zaytsev* proficiency.

Goldman didn't know, nor did he care to know, about political modalities, but he knew enough about military realities to understand that the Jewish birds that were flying in were nothing more than a cluster-flock of budgerigars who didn't even speak a common language. Leadership was lacking and anyone who had mastered at least minimal gross-motor movements was promoted to pack leader: patrolling marked territories, unseen boundaries, and cordillera vantage points that churned any perceived enemy into wine and meat sauce. There was a converging sense of urgency that justified bloody retribution, and the Jews felt that without their own state, self-preservation would always be at the hands of outside forces. For once, the Jew wanted to be the master of his own destiny, in his own land, with his own parlance to God.

The jeep raced down a dusty bumpy trail at breakneck velocity. Goldman felt oddly at ease with the strange man who seemingly lacked any trace of conscience for unscrewing the cranial lid of a fellow *pommey*.

Ronan was a peculiar specimen. Like Goldman, he had fought in the Second World War, and was now stationed in Palestine to police the breakaway British territory. He had been born and raised on a kibbutz near the shores of Galilee, and when the war broke out in Europe, David Ben-Gurion had ordered the Palestine Jews to fight anti-Semitic fascism, wherever and by whatever means.

When Ronan helped to liberate the concentration camps of Eastern Europe, something gouged the deep hallows of his dry-rot Hebrew apostasy, and he understood something that could not be known by walking around it, only through it. The camps were the devil's workshop, where his handcrafted voluble obscenities snickered and whispered scorn into Ronan's Leviticus ears: infanticide, pogroms, Zyklon B, the sanctioned annihilation of his very brood; German mythical séances that drum up ghosts of unfinished business and carry out Jewish exterminations with jackbooted, Aryan efficiency. Ronan was only nominally associated with his religion, but the phantasmal experience of the death camps dazed him into a dry-cry wail of an apostate, where his very nature seemed to have betrayed him.

From that day on he was wholly devoted to the cause of building a Jewish state, and never again would he allow henchmen of anti-Semitic despots to fasten slave collars on his Zionist *Hebros*. After the war, he secretly defected from Her Majesty's Service and joined the outlawed Jewish Haganah organization to work as a covert agent in clandestine operations against Britain and her Arab allies. As a British intelligence officer he was privy to highly sensitive information that was critical to the Jewish Intel underground.

The heads of the convergence, including Ben-Gurion, Golda Meir, and Shimon Peres, depended heavily on Ronan's information; he was their go-to *mensch*, indispensable to their secret operations. He later created a hit squad at the behest of Meir; machinated like-minded Jews that assassinated key figures in the British and Arab field chain of command. Ronan was a dependable killer and an expert assassin who could drop a target at a thousand yards or gut a man with a dinner fork.

After a forty-minute wild ride through the narrow and rutted back roads of Galilee, Ronan pulled into the Jordan Valley, where the shores of Galilee shimmered histrionically, beckoning the weary and heavily-laden to surrender to the delirium of the senses: the view, the sapphire clarity of the water. Ronan crash-landed in the camp with a blizzard of sand and a dust devil that had followed the jeep for the last mile. The occupants exited, digging out the sand that caked in the corners of their eyes and gritted between their popping teeth. They seemed gratefully lost as their acclimating wits sucked in the kibbutz with a dry air hiccough.

What had been a social experiment in communal living now served as a makeshift waystation for those who would be hastily trained for the ordure of war. Some people look good in the rough with no need to knock off the edges; Ronan was a barrel-chested warrior who gave the impression that he might have been a bear in another life, with thick butcher's fingers, webbed wrinkles around his narrow eyes, and deep-throated growls. He corralled the three newcomers in a hefty grizzly hug.

"Welcome to our little kibbutz by the sea, where all Jews are free, so long as they are willing to fight!" He patted them on the back and pointed to the mess tent. "Get yourself some food and I'll show you where to bunk."

After scarfing down a sparse meal of cheese sandwiches and sweet tea, Goldman was directed to a man who fitted him with khaki shorts, a shirt, and a vintage WWI helmet. He was given a bedroll and sent to a scorpion and tick-infested tent. He had no sooner entered when Ronan followed with a rifle and a side arm, which he tossed to him with a cross-purpose grin. Goldman let go of his new baggy khakis that were so loose they dropped to the ground, and caught the weapons midair.

"If you can prove to me that you know how to shoot 'em, you can keep 'em. If not, I'll give 'em to someone who can."

Ronan led him out to a marksman's range with multiple targets. Goldman examined the old rifle while trying to hold up his loose khakis.

"WWI, bolt-action, Italian 6.5 mm Manlicher-Carcano," Ronan authoritatively said. He grabbed the rifle, aimed downrange, dropped a target at one hundred yards, and handed it back to Goldman.

"If you can hit another target at the same distance the rifle is yours."

Goldman chambered a round, let his khakis fall again, steadied, and fired, dropping a target at two hundred yards.

Ronan slowly turned to him. "Hell of a shot." He seized the rifle, fired, hit a target at three hundred yards, and handed it back.

Without bothering to pull his khakis up, Goldman chambered a round and fell a target at four hundred yards.

Ronan smiled. "You've had some experience with firearms, no?"

Goldman nodded.

Ronan then grabbed the sniper rifle and aimed at a seagull circling overhead. He tracked the bird through a gale of Kentucky-windage, and fired. A plume of feathers exploded in the far-flung blue canopy, and it plummeted five hundred feet to the ground. Never had Goldman seen such devilish marksmanship.

Ronan nonchalantly spit. "So where did you learn to shoot?"

"I fought in the Pacific campaigns with the US Marines." Goldman pulled up his baggy khakis as Ronan's face lit up like an overcharged tungsten lamp. He approached Goldman gripped with compressions of respect that melted his sense of being mutually exclusive.

"I never did get your name."

Goldman continued to examine the old rifle while still holding his slack khakis. "1st Lieutenant David Oliver Goldman, 22nd Marines, 6th Division."

Ronan tilted his head slightly and tried to peer through Goldman's growing beard.

"I know you. I mean, I don't know you, but I've read about you and seen your photo in *Life* magazine, the first hymie awarded the Congressional Medal of Honor." He vigorously shook Goldman's hand as if he were a dignitary due all pomp and protocol as torrents of good fortune whirled through his head like a spinning top. He grabbed Goldman by the arm and marched him to a nearby tent where a thin, distinguished-looking man with a black patch over his left eye was going over terrain maps.

"Moshe, you must meet this man."

With his one good eye he made a cursory inspection of Goldman.

"And who might you be?"

Goldman tipped his head in obeisance, looking past his sandy eyebrows. "I'm Goldman, and I am here to fight for the Independence of Israel."

Ronan blurted with ebullient joy, "This man was in the US Marines, a Congressional Medal of Honor hero, too."

The man with the eye patch gazed at him as if he was suddenly worth spending his one good eye on, and jutted out his hand. "Moshe Dayan, Field Commander of all Jewish forces in the Jordan Valley."

*   *   *

Goldman's clout as an American war hero and committed Zionist made him an intricate part of the military kibbutz, and Ronan made sure that his prized recruit would be plugged in as deep as his political extension cord could go. In a short time, it was apparent to Ronan that Goldman had natural ability to lead and an intelligence that tempered a ferocity he sensed was just below the American's skin. He was soon familiar with all the main players: David, Golda—Goldie as she was known to those close to her—Moshe and Shimon, the authors and forefathers of a birthing nation whose water was about to break.

Goldman attended high-level meetings and was confided in by the Jewish leadership with persistent regularity. He became a permanent fixture at top echelon powwows, and was often asked for advice on tactical strategies. Goldman loved working for Ronan's intelligence apparatus, and felt appreciated like never before. He liked living on the kibbutz too, which he tacitly endorsed as Communism at its best, which added significance to the cause and weight to his steps.

For the first time since he could remember, his life seemed in sync, and inaudible ascension filled his ears with sounds of opportunity, with chance coming in numerous disguises. He had read many a story where circumstances and dealings were designed to bring certain men into uncertain times, and it seemed that providence had put him in the passenger seat of a bourgeoning country's affairs and soon might be ready to give him the wheel to a greater destination.

XXIX

Goldman's soon won confidence of the Israeli high command, garnered him a commission with the Haganah Corps. Unlike his field commission with the marines, he felt that this would not be an impediment to his elemental nature but a way to express some secret self that was to be found only in war's ascension. He was assigned the task of training the Ashkenazi recruits. It was tough going, with little cohesion in the ranks, and most of the immigrant Jews spoke dialects of Judezmo, Yiddish, Judeo-Arabic, and other languages from the Diaspora. A common lingo was needed to winnow out alien consonants, obtrusive foreign vowels, and hieratic scriveners in the national tongue. Out of the forgotten blue he felt his mother's belly-cord presence, and recollections of his past converged on scripture that her secret dream might at last be born: *In the last days they will speak their ancient language again when the son's of Jacob return to the land of their fathers.*

The idea of having the immigrant recruits learn Hebrew excited Goldman, and buzzing thoughts swarmed in his head with the ridiculousness of it being unimaginably real. He found an English teacher, and was thrilled by the fact that she could speak and write Ben-Yehuda Hebrew. Jews born in Palestine learned the new form of Hebrew from the turn-of-the-century Zionist Eliezer Ben-Yehuda. He taught a lexical modernization of Hebrew that slowly spread, but now was needed if the country was to coalesce as more than just a cozy metaphor. Goldman grasped the Ben-Yehuda Hebrew with uncanny command, and soon spoke the language with such eerie fluency that even his variant dreams and caroming thoughts were immersed in the resurrected idiom.

Classes in Hebrew, military training, Jewish religion, and customs were a fermented blend of sour mash and ancient spirits waiting to be uncorked. Goldman, of course, could care less about pious incantations and religious rites, but it helped with the morale of the troops and would come in handy should a Judeo born again find himself in a foxhole with a firebrand atheist. Goldman had been in many a battle without calling on a god and this war would be no different, even in the most heavily mined god-trap in the world. Yet there was something authentic about being in the ancient land that lent itself to ancestor worship and religious liturgy. The idea of embracing his mother's God almost seemed befitting of the primordial terrain, where the very rocks were like funerary sarcophaguses encasing the spirits of a million lost prophets.

Goldman's Goats, as they were known—partly because wherever they went feral goats and sheep would follow—waged a tumultuous Zionist assault against an anti-Semitic menace not seen since the days of Nazi-chic sadism. At first the ill-prepared fighting Jews were a bungling dervish act, but they shortly turned their comedy of errors into a genre of holy terrors that the local Arab militias were incapable of withstanding.

Ronan was proud of his imperialist Yankee prodigy. A find like Goldman was a lottery ticket leveraged with dizzying odds and a winning pennant in the winds of future glories, but he felt a foot shorter and a diluted imitator when succussed in Goldman's company. Ronan's counsel to the high command was now deferred to Goldman, who didn't know anything about the terrain, yet he had a supernatural sense of its topography mysteriously wired in his head, and an electromagnetic military bearing that was proving critical to every battle.

At numerous junctures, Ronan's mulish tactical insistence had proved disastrous, with much loss of life and critical setbacks. Now, when Ronan presented a military prospectus, Goldman often objected with thickening insistence, and their differences soon bordered between acrimonious lip-flapping and jaw-breaking fisticuffs. When Ronan's tactical deck dealt one too many losses, the upper brass stuck to Goldman's game, which proved in practice—running straights and suited flushes. Goldman shot up the ranks in the secretive inner-circles like a prized pledge in some long-forgotten monastic order. He had proven to be an indispensable asset, and after Moshe Dayan was put in charge of the disintegrating forces in and around Tel Aviv, Goldman was subsequently commissioned field commander of the Jordan Valley Forces.

Ronan had wanted that position badly and Dayan had promised it to him. That was, of course, before the extruded tendrils of Goldman's commonsensical wizardry pushed out Ronan's petulant lack of judgment. Goldman was worth his weight in enemy dead and favorites had to be played, even if it mocked the afflicted. "Ronan has killed his dozens but Goldman has killed his hundreds," was the new battle cry. Goldman's swift assent descended Ronan into full-throated enmity, and with boa-eyes, he would never look the same at his newfound prodigy.

Goldman commandeered so many martial victories that a number of Arab Liberation regiments conducted interventions into Palestine. These were considered Muslims of the new holy war, who put a *fêted-fatwa* on his head and vowed to drive the Hebrew pestilence into the sea. It was a survival instinct broil just to secure a toehold in Palestine, but under every Israeli *kippah* head was Jerusalem; the house of matins and evensong, where Jerusalem vespers call in the wee hours to God's chosen. The order was given and all military efforts were to forge ahead to the holy city, to make Jerusalem the capital, and bring the rest of Palestine into submission under the umbrella of a new Jewish state.

It was early 1948, and the *Yishuv* powers sensed in their hallow wells that this would be the year that the state of Israel would be poured out. To wait on the good graces of the impotent United Nations would be folly; there were just too many Jews swelling within a borderless de facto state that lacked a national identity or central command. Key cities and a contiguous landmass would be critical if the complex task of statehood was to be realized. Haifa, Tel Aviv, and most importantly Jerusalem would need to be under Jewish control.

The Arab army of Abd al Qadir al-Husayni, the charismatic leader from Egypt, along with several hundred Arabs of the Army of Holy War under the command of a young officer named Anwar Sadat, organized a blockade to kill or starve the one hundred thousand Jewish inhabitants of Jerusalem. Ben-Gurion personally ordered Goldman's Goats and the Haganah Brigade the enviable task of taking the city.

Goldman took the initiative. He ordered the splitting of his force, with him leading the Goats and Ronan leading another, but Ronan resented the dawdling order and felt it dangerous to weaken the fighting force. Goldman's strategy was to be fast and nimble and hit the enemy on multiple flanks, as opposed to Ronan's narrow-scopic dirt-pack-scrum in the face of overwhelming numbers.

Ronan acquiesced with the ordure of a bastard son and, between the two, the mission proved a stunning success and filled the unsuspecting Ishmaelites with excrement fear. Nevertheless, the city was still starving. Ronan petitioned the high command to allow him to supply the inhabitants, despite Goldman's protests that it was too risky, and after unremitting wheedling they gave in. Under Ronan's leadership the Yishuv Brigade attempted to supply the Jewish population with convoys of armored vehicles, but the operation degraded into a debacle with scores of Jewish volunteers killed and almost all the armored vehicles destroyed. This was yet another blight on Ronan's competence. Even with the help of Goldman's Goats, it was the first time the Yishuv organization had been stopped by the Egyptian Husayni volunteers, and Jerusalem remained un-liberated.

Failure to unshackle the city was another chapter in the endless rotation of would-be liberators that continued with unremitting vigilance in an overextended dream. For Ronan, Jerusalem had to be in the hands of the Jew and, according to scripture, the proto-messianic republic could not be established until it was. He did not believe in polysemantic interpretations or compromise to ciphers and coded prophecies of the Torah: It was Jerusalem, or nothing.

Goldman also sensed an explicated convergence in his quad-chambered heart, like the four quadrants of Jerusalem: the beating mandala of man's very existence was somehow to be found in that sinkhole city. Something inconceivable needed to pass through a porthole in him, and it was seemingly only to be found within those forbidden walls.

He tried to correlate his emotional orientation to the fluttering aches and taciturn wails of his fellow Jews when all the fighting and bloodletting failed to breach the city's parapet. Jerusalem: the city of constant spinning chaos in a universe that favors order; a polynomial vortex where disorientation reigns and a single substrate underlies her axis, where electron clouds of eleven dimensions converge in concentric patterns—wheels within wheels circling its wailing walls.

Jerusalem was abandoned and Goldman's force—still gutted from their failure—was needed to save Jewish settlements in the highly isolated Negev and Northern Galilee regions, which were hanging by an arachnid thread under the webbed assault of reconstituted Arab attacks. Goldman's men attacked the small villages in and around Galilee with the ferocity of depredating maniacs, and the local Arab population was soon overwhelmed.

This was typical of the Zionist campaign: like the Germans of WWII, overwhelm one's opponent with swift blitzkrieg efficiency and rout the enemy into stampeding panic. Goldman's Goats mastered the technique and soon the Arab population left to seek refuge abroad. With a series of Jewish victories, the British felt a shift in the political climate and in early 1948 decided to support the Jews and the annexation of the Arab part of Palestine.

It looked like the momentum had swung, but the neighboring Arab states soon rearmed, determined to put the pointed-tail Jews back on their cloven-hoof heels. Like a case of national eczema, the seesaw skirmishes began to overwhelm the Jews with scaly, crusty anxiety and a nasty itch that failed to be scratched. The fledgling country was growing tired of clawing for the same piece of dog-patch, and the Yishuv defenses were soon corroded by doubt that there could be any lasting victories. Goldman argued with Ben-Gurion and Meir that an all-out assault on Jerusalem was the only way to rally the demoralized ranks.

*　　*　　*

With funds procured by Golda Meir from sympathizers in the US, there was now enough money to stem the tide of well-supplied and trained Arab states that had broken every ceasefire and were able to draw Ashkenazi blood like an annihilating angel. The ineptitude of the United Nations and its inability to enforce ceasefires pushed the conflict into the second stage of the war, and Israel had to go on a relentless offensive if she were to survive. After incessant cajoling by Goldman and Ronan, the high command resumed its strategy to stop the blockade of Jerusalem.

Ben-Gurion ordered Goldman and fifteen-hundred men from the newly created Haganah's Givati Brigade to free the in-route to the city. At last, Goldman felt destiny yanking his chain and pulling him through fate's foyer. It was as if he had been born to do this one thing, the ablution of his people from infidels that had contaminated the holy city for too long. It seemed sycophantic, yet his connection to steles he had never been aware of was now feeding the undergrowth of an ostensible Davidic line that was mysteriously branching through his generational ringed core.

Goldman led by example, and was on the front line of every pitched battle, but slithering fear still slinked down his spine with reticulated shame. He hated the feeling and all requisites to self-preservation wanted him to weigh his possible misadventure. But a peculiar thought buzzed in his head: *I am immortal so long as I am alive.* Even the sight of all the mutilated and charred corpses that littered the battlefields didn't mirror him as mockingly as the Japanese war had, and chimerical glories were to be found in the shattering violence with closeted adulations and dispositions of compliant masculinity.

Goldman's Goats were relentless in trying to crack the city, but Arab resistance was dogged. It seemed the only part of the city that was out of mortar and gunfire range was the East Gate, which had been sealed off by the Ottoman Turks some four hundred years earlier to thwart the prophecy that the Jewish Messiah would cross its threshold. As a further deterrence, a Muslim graveyard had been planted at the entry, as no Jewish holy man would walk through a burial ground. Goldman determined to use an artillery piece to blow open the East Gate, but Ben-Gurion ordered him to stand down, "The gate is holy and to molest it would do more harm than good." Goldman could not understand the touchiness associated with that crazy city. It seemed every rock, tree, and wall was sacred, and to not recognize the East Gate as a consecrated doorstep was tantamount to desecration. He thought it was ridiculous, but acquiesced with secular frustration mixed with a proprietary sense of seneschal stewardship over the landmark and its promulgated piece of prophecy.

Goldman's forces continued their strategy of bleeding attrition. The Arab forces outside the city were finally broken, but at a heavy cost to the Haganah's Givati Brigade, which put Goldman in a disagreeable mood for the remainder of the battle. In their possession they had some Arab prisoners, and one bargained that if Goldman would let him go, he would tell him where the ever-elusive Egyptian leader Hussayni was. The man was freed and Goldman took it upon himself to personally take out Hussayni. For two days and nights he crawled on his belly through dense scrub and sand like a camouflaged desert serpent. He made his way to Hussayni's field headquarters and, when he was sure he had spotted his mark, leveled the Manlicher-Carcano and put one round through Hussayni's forehead. Hussayni's death was so demoralizing to his forces that Anwar Sadat and the Egyptian Arabs abandoned Jerusalem.

Ronan was reluctantly impressed by Goldman's successful mission, and even donned the full regalia of his religious vestments, ceremoniously giving a rabbinic blessing over Goldman and the Malicher-Carcano with Torah-inspired proclamations.

"With this weapon the enemies of God are overcome and whoever uses it will slay the adversary of His Kingdom."

Goldman took the blessing to heart and never entered a battle without the Italian sniper rifle by his side. By the end of April 1948, Jerusalem's enroots were finally cleared and the last pockets of resistance collapsed. In the battle, Goldman caught a piece of shrapnel for his troubles, and was unable to walk under his own power. Someone found a donkey and propped him on it, and he entered the city a conquering hero with palm fronds and blankets laid out on the cobbled streets, followed by dozens of goats and sheep.

A moment of intersecting serendipity bespoke a weird transference as a flock of white doves fittingly flew overhead, beautiful like a white curlicue staircase to heaven . . . and strafed him in bird shit. It spooked the donkey, which kicked and reared and crashed headlong into a Turkish coffee stand. But it was not to curb the crowd's enthusiasm, which cried out in jaunty mime, "Blessed is Goldman who comes in the name of the Lord." With a sullen pallor, Ronan stood on the glory sidelines, beating his chest and clawing his tonsured scalp as the failed high priest liberator, while Goldman entered Jerusalem in transcendent triumph. The entire city suspended as the Jewish inhabitants surged around him like a rogue wave of tear-watered humanity.

There was something about passing through the holy walls that heightened the senses, many millennia of unexcavated ghosts percolated from its crusty formations and ancient worn dirt. It was oppressive and exhilarating at the same time, a spiritual jamboree covalently bonding and unbearably painful, stretching the cage of Goldman's thorax, winded by millions of bygone sighs. It was as if kinetic forces had removed all moral instincts and justified sacrificial slaughter that was required before holy shrines could be sanctified, where endless bloodletting was necessary, and even seemed reasonable.

The capture of Jerusalem pushed the leaders of the neighboring Arab states to turn their sharpened teeth against their ancient enemy again, but they needed a new battle cry. Suddenly, Palestine, a piece of forgotten third world dirt that never had statehood nor was ever consequential to the Arab psyche, was now the new Islamic holy land, and Muslim screams for jihad were bull-horned from every minaret.

*   *   *

Anno Domini, May 15, 1948, arrived without fanfare. It wasn't until Goldman had finished his breakfast of figs and unleavened bread that the news had spread: Ben-Gurion had declared the Independent State of Israel. *In all the chaos, how could something like this happen so quickly? How is a nation birthed in a single day?* It all started to make sense. For days, British columns had headed out to bordering areas, and on this day the last of the

British had left and it was official: Israel was on her own with gnashing hostile nations on every one of the newly-defined borders. Snap raids into foreign possibilities suddenly animated Goldman, but the emotion soon turned to terror as he realized that he and every Jew in the land could very well be exterminated.

In a panic, he ran through the Old City and straight up the Mount of Olives. He reached the summit and clambered up the tallest olive tree. He spent the next hours in bipolar swings of concave depression and convex exaltation, cacklings of a killer and cries of a lover swinging from every emotional extreme limb. Eating olives like a dumbstruck chameleon, and changing emotions to suit the environment as chaste tears and virgin olive oil ran down his manic face in a dripping love potion, soaking his khaki shirt to his spellbound skin. From the tree's perch he could see the entire city, and for the first time in all its panoramic ferocity, a didactic sweet sadness whispered lessons in his ear that a fabled city had yet to learn. The sun beat on the Golden Dome of the Rock and the light glanced from its sphere, enveloping Goldman like foreign entities exchanging electro-transmissions, the two fusing almost into one.

Serial recollections of the Apocalypse raced through his mind: *Was this the beginning of the end, or the end of the beginning, or the beginning of the end of the beginning?* Was this the countdown to Armageddon, a preamble to epochs yet to be declared? It was his twenty-eighth birthday, and the gossamer of his mother's ghost drifted through his memory and filled him with gauzy declarations of prophetic fulfillment. But she would only experience the revelation through the descended line of a son who did not yet understand its passages of greater complexities or the significance of its episteme consequence.

XXX

There would be no maternity leave for the newly birthed country. Following Israel's declaration of independence, the war entered its second round with wind-milling psychotic fists from the Arab states, twisting and squirming with a hatred that had been part of an ongoing feud between a clan of peoples as far back as the "playing favorite" days of Abraham. Utter annihilation was the Arab cry, and all the newborn could do was try to survive a full-throttled Muslim attack. Israel's supreme fear was of another Holocaust—the Shoah was still fresh in the emaciated psyche of the Jew.

The final battle to determine if Israel would remain a state would be decided by the two formulating sides. The Arabs committed twenty-three thousand well-trained and well-armed troops to fight Israel's sparsely supplied and under-trained Yishuv recruits, who sometimes had to share weapons and even food rations. The only comfort the Israeli army had was its core paramilitary Haganah fighters, an elite unit of two thousand maniacs that had been garrisoned in Israel for years. The unit had been headed by Ronan's reckless modus but now was replaced by Goldman's sure-handed invulnerability and his rubicund charm to speak battles into rosy victories against crushing odds.

An amalgamation of Iraqi, Syrian, Jordanian, Egyptian, and Lebanese forces hurled themselves into the Israeli lines the day after the new state was declared. Like North African arthropods whirling around infernal regions of hell, fire, and damnation, the Arabs were relentless. They overran the Jewish defenses but soon retreated after suffering huge losses to Goldman's Goats, who systematically sniffed out weaknesses in the enemy's lines and exploited them with devastating effect. Over the next few months, as both sides increased their manpower, Israel's advantage grew steadily as a direct result of a nationwide mobilization and the massive influx of thousands of new Jewish immigrants.

To achieve parity, the Israeli Defense Forces were officially established and all Jewish battalions were integrated into one army. By the fall of 1948, Israel had achieved air superiority—ironically with refurbished WWII German Messerschmitts. Arab ground forces were under constant bombardment, which stopped them from destroying any major Jewish settlements.

Jerusalem was still the trophy and that's where the most belligerent fighting occurred. Goldman's Goats were attached to the newly formed Sixteenth Jerusalem Brigade and they fought for the holy city like wild men possessed with morbid grace. But with no reinforcements and supplies running low, they were forced to abandon the sacrosanct boroughs, and on May 17, the Trans-Jordan Arab Legion entered Jerusalem. It was maddening to lose the prize, and the broken dream of Jerusalem becoming the new state's capital was an instantiated reminder of Israel's frustrations.

Goldman felt a musty kinship for that dusty ancient town and altarpieces to him seemed to raise everywhere, tacitly endorsing him as a secular god. There was something about its nocebo effect that permeated his resistant pores—which did not allow anything religious to penetrate—but his immune system was left defenseless against pious osmosis. It was the City of David in all its horror and glory, and most of it was seen through the scope of Goldman's Manlicher-Carcano. He wanted to walk the Old City with the ambulated elegance of an expunged reprobate without the threat of sudden death and the possible shit-canning of his soul.

In the close street fighting, he saw the Via Delarosa, the East Gate, and the West Wall, where he dodged snipers; the Garden of Gethsemane and the Mount of Olives, where he watched mortars explode, splitting the sky like blossoming transience. It was hard to declare, but despite the war he felt Jerusalem a largesse homecoming, yet the gift was dashed by fate's vicissitudes. There just wasn't enough manpower or weapons or providence to keep the vision alive, and vision without resources is delusion.

The IDF was ordered to vacate, but Goldman was given a final mission, a conceding parting shot for the road. He was ordered to take out Jerusalem's Grand Mufti, the religious leader that had created so much mischief for the IDF. He was holed up in the Al-Aqsa Mosque, surrounded by a retinue of fanatic martyr-aspirant Muslims. The only way to grant him a *shahid* witness would be with a 6.5 mm aerogramme, straight to Allah The Merciful. Ronan was the superior shot and the mission should have gone to him, but it went to Goldman, and again, his lustrous boots treaded on Ronan's ever-deserting glories and he fumed with roasting umbrage.

He reluctantly dispensed rabbinic blessings on Goldman's mission and the partisan hunt was on.

The Grand Mufti was going about the city surrounded by orotund tales of an Arab-liberating savior and was heralded by the local population as the deliverer of Jerusalem. For days, Goldman mixed with the city's populace disguised as a Turkish rug merchant. He rolled the Manlicher-Carcano in a kilim and patrolled the rooftops like Aladdin, waiting for the right moment to unroll it. At two hundred yards he cracked the quiet of the city with a perfectly placed shot and the Grand Mufti was not so grand anymore. The assassination was the beginning of endless reprisals and revenge killings that would dog Israel for the rest of her days.

Goldman still could not get Jerusalem out of his mind. For him, the city could only be understood in big anthology chunks—volumes of history to be sorted, indexed, and measured by epochs, armies, and competing gods. The loss of the city hit him like a living, breathing stone, massively still—inert yet moving at the speed of a protean prophecy. *What kind of city goes through gods like that?* He strolled idly out of its gates, leaving its Arab inhabitants wallowing in crumples and whines, anathematized wails against the Jew. Like King Saul in his final battle, Goldman wanted to fall on his honorable face or sword, but he had neither.

*   *   *

Operation DANI commenced in the middle of the country, while operation DEKEL was carried out in the north. Nazareth was the new objective of the IDF, along with all of Galilee. Goldman's Goats reinforced positions in Tel Aviv and then were reassigned to the Golani Brigade and ordered to take Megiddo and Lejjun in the Jezreel Valley. The battle raged until early June when Iraqi and Syrian forces were finally expelled. Goldman gave Ronan command of his own company and with his two hundred men he fought valiantly, almost single-handedly ousting the Syrian forces. Goldman was impressed and could see why the Jewish leadership was so rapt by Ronan's fighting ability—when he got it right. He was a dependable warrior but was bespoken with the *Lymantria* loyalty of a gypsy moth—unpredictable and always looking for his glory bulb. After the long-fought battle, he and Ronan walked the heights of Jezreel and surveyed the endless Valley of Megiddo, or as others had called it, Armageddon.

Goldman looked up at the steep incline and took in the eerie image of a single lamb at the summit, beckoning with haunting bleats to scale the sheer grade. Brilliant white, with a fire-eyed glint, the lamb pulled at Goldman's reluctance. He shinnied the almost perpendicular grade but just before reaching the top, a whirlwind of sand blasted him in a pulverizing tempest. When he could see again, the lamb was gone. He stood on the summit and turned toward the panoptic view, and from the vantage of Mount Taber was awestruck by the vastness of the valley.

He was then overcome by a sensation of disembodiment and bedeviled by a spiraling phantasmagoric vision: tens of millions of men in a vast conflagration of fire and smoke; raging sulfurous torrents of smoldering blood coursing through the valley like a roaring plasma river. He tried to shake the seeming hallucination but could not disentangle himself from the apocalyptic movie and its corpulent plot. It was a maddening mix of wee-hour morbidity and night sagas of unimaginable terror, but he remained obstinately sane even when he went briefly out of his mind.

Ronan saw Goldman caught in the trance-like current and tried to throw him a reality line, but he did not respond as he stood stone-like, a neoclassical pediment gabling in revelatory slopes not fit for mortal eyes. Ronan looked out onto the valley, and then turned back to see Goldman standing next to two Israeli soldiers who had not been there a moment before.

Something stirred in Ronan and, like a cosmic sentry in a belvedere tower, he suddenly saw Goldman as more than just a ponderously gifted man, but a rhapsodic icon, a kind of multi-dimensional Rosetta Stone decoding hieratic revelation, both carnally and spiritually, with curses of flesh and graces of blood that tabernacle as one. A scintillating pool of energy encompassed Goldman, and seeing him standing with the other soldiers spoke to Ronan in Coptic tongues of grand elucidation. The experience left him with visceral jealousies, and he wanted to appoint himself Goldman's official assassin, yet he knew there was something extraordinary about the man that he could not put his trigger finger on. Goldman resurfaced from the diaphanous daze, the coherence of the soldiers talking him back to reality.

"Who are you?" Goldman asked.

One smiled with raised splendor. "My name is Elijah Dori."

The other soldier looked at him with a lotus-beam grin that made Goldman feel drowsy and comforted at the same time. "My name is Moses Shemen."

Goldman, still stuffed from biblical portions, could not disentangle himself from the premonitory apparition and its ensuing afterglow. He stared down at the immense valley and then turned to the soldiers.

"The hour is coming and it will be a time of great affliction," he said in a weird vulgate translation.

The soldiers acknowledged with grave nods. They put their arms around Goldman's shoulders to escort him down the hill, but he collapsed, unconscious, and they had to carry him like a limp rolled carpet. Ronan looked on as Goldman was placed in an armored carrier, and the two soldiers were inexplicably never seen again.

*   *   *

The following day the Israeli forces consolidated and prepared to take Nazareth. The fighting was intense, but on July 16, Nazareth fell. It was a gloomy affair with Arab refugees huddled en masse—beaten, thirsty, and starved. The IDF soon had them fed and watered, and like livestock they were loaded onto trucks and were relocated. The Jews returned to Nazareth and Goldman's brigade was assigned to their new objective, the maintaining and governing of a new nation. The Israeli forces had lost the Jerusalem crown, but they had managed to not only maintain control of all Jewish-held territories but expanded their holdings by fifty percent.

By July 1949, Israel had signed an armistice with Syria. The Israelites had staved off their enemies despite overwhelming odds, and an ancient people that had been dispersed along the world's frontiers had managed to keep their sense of national identity. Two thousand years adrift and now they were a living, breathing organism again, and Goldman felt this would be his old home for the rest of his newly-forming days.

XXXI

With the cessation of hostilities Goldman was put on active reserve and Israel was thrown into a flurry of in-house construction. The building of the new state would require the expertise of social architects with fanatical foresight if it was to evacuate the indistinctness of national visions and its spellbinding doubts. The task of assembling the country's aircraft while in flight was daunting, but soon the forces of denouement released their hold and the internal workings of a totter fledgling were turning as smooth as a rickety gearbox. The wheels were revolving but grinding and would require oiling by foreign money if it were to keep from seizing. With the dawning chill of the Cold War, the Americans and the Soviets were jockeying for geopolitical pose in the international starting blocks with the anticipation of a hundred-yard dash starting gun. What kind of government would Israel be: a free Capitalist machine, a Socialist dream, or a Communist scheme? Who knew what was birthing, but superpower money poured in as fast as their dilated ideologies.

With the armistice Goldman was elevated to a full-bird colonel in the IDF reserve with fishing rights to the inner-power pond where the biggest kosher cod swam. He loved the idea of a budding nation bulging with new possibilities. He couldn't help but think that he was a real patriot for a new egalitarian society and he vigorously voiced his opinion about the type of government Israel should be. He saw himself like the granddads of the United States, a nation father armed with neoclassical notions and middle management control. He was walking in high cotton and filled with flights of imagination where his name would be stitched like hook 'n' needle point in the hearts and minds of quilted generations yet to come. Elevated with penchants of stateliness, Goldman believed that this was his purpose in the world, to forge a new country, with his name anvil-stamped on its shiny hub.

The prime minister position naturally went to David Ben Gurion. Goldman, too, wanted to hold a skyscraping roost. He sensed something changing though, and the derogate cabinet that at one time was so considerate of him, was now standoffish and embraced his contributions with unspoken disapproval. He had become a coriander leftover from the war and his loyal following demanded that the government share the mixing bowl in the country's new recipe, but Goldman was not even allowed in the kitchen. They understood his gonzo zeal for a country to function like a state-run kibbutz, but to initiate it on a national scale would ruffle too many feathers—namely the feathers of the American eagle, which Israel was determined to nest with.

Leadership had been within earshot of rumors and had heard the Communistic proclivities spouted by their prized champion. They ordered Ronan to dig up turds from Goldman's litter-box past. He produced a dossier from the US State Department that all but labeled him a Communist agent, and Ronan subsequently clued-in the FBI that their man was in Israel. Against Goldman's single-mindedness, Israel had determined to embrace the West, which included its unashamed anti-Communist loathing that doglegged between the whiff of free enterprise philosophy and revulsion of odious Socialist schemes.

Goldman believed Communism was the only reasonable future for the new country. The experience of living on a kibbutz, with its communal sharing and equal distribution of work, had appealed to his collectivist tendencies. But he suspected that somewhere in his sexual nuclei that it had been a flaccid way of demonstrating to Mina that he was a legitimate erection in the international Socialist boudoir, and hoped the news of his firebrand politico foreplay would arouse her.

Goldman had harvested a huge political following that threatened to burst the grain silos of farm league politicians. He had a strapping effect on his people, and not just the Jewish population; the local Arab inhabitants took a shine to him as well. He buffeted the Israeli government by befriending, despite formerly being acrid enemies, an Arab representative of the newly-formed Palestinian National Authority and his ever-present sidekick, a young Egyptian named Yasser Arafat. With Goldman's help he lobbied for Palestinian rights, which were overwhelmed by the new government's decision to expand Jewish settlements and to clandestinely continue waging war against the Arab population. Because of Goldman's association with what the government considered "seditious elements", he was banned from running for any central office or from having any association with government officials. It finally hit hard that un-repudiated bigotry was the function of all power.

He so wanted to be a rosy-glow thespian in the footlights of Israel's history, but the FBI and forces cloaked in black were systematically splicing out Goldman's fanfare and any trace that he had ever been onstage with Israel's fight for independence. His battle deeds were attributed to fictitious characters, bad stand-ins meant to blot out any evidence of his contributions to the play. Even his beloved Goats were edited from the script as if they had never been, thanks to the FBI, who sent Special Agent Muller to pressure Israel to deny Goldman any participation in their government. The Knesset obliged its new master and politely asked Goldman to leave Tel Aviv and Israel proper.

*   *   *

Goldman moved back to the little kibbutz by the sea, which had been transformed from a military training base to a social epicenter for his new Communist utopia. His knack for green-thumbing the desert revivified the land into a vast oasis of corn, wheat, and beans. He even planted orchards that in record time produced oranges the size of softballs and grapefruit the size of bowling balls, but the bumper crop that made the kibbutz a household name was the vineyard. Acres of succulent running vines produced a flash-pasteurized sweet concord, the likes of which the Mediterranean growers could not compete with. Something about his "golden touch" as the locals would say, pumped magic into the dead soil that even produced two harvests in a single year. A sanctuary of life sprang from desolate ground and verdant greenbelts thrived in a land that had always eluded the Bedouin clans.

The living legend of Goldman caught the attention of an androcentric clique that lived in caves close to the Jordan River, the Magi Essenes, ascetic separatists who devoted themselves to social division, and the study of fire retardant scripture and its combustible prophecies. Israel was now a nation and, according to their interpretation of the ancient text, the Chosen One would have to return. An ardent eye had been kept on Goldman from not only the Israeli government, but also the Essenes who suspected that he might be the One. After all, he was a national war hero, liberator, and leader, and as prophecy had declared, "The One whom the very leadership of Israel would reject, but the One whom the government of the world would rest upon."

Goldman had a routine of bathing every morning in the Sea of Galilee; for him, symptoms of hidden defilements and unclean spirits were purged by the ritual washing in its waters, and countermanded his ever-skulking feeling of shoddy legitimacy. One day as he stood on the sandy shore, drying off in the musty hot air, triple silhouettes of depth and delicacy approached him, clad in camel-pube tunics, with frowsy long hair and cult-of-the-dead streaked beards.

"Who are you and where do you come from?" one asked with a prying trim.

"And who might you be?" Goldman probed.

"We are the Magi Essenes, and we believe you might be the One that we have been waiting for."

"I doubt that, I know none of you."

"Yes, but the stars know of you."

Goldman gave the three heat-image phantoms an askance smile and started to dress himself. One of the Essenes moved in close and made a cursory inspection, then nodded to his obscured associates. The oldest one walked up and did a fine-line examination and then raised his hands like pinnate fans shading Goldman's face.

"Greatness has come among us."

Goldman dressed in a silent bustle and was about to leave, yet found that he couldn't slip the grasp of the proclamation.

"Greatness?"

The white-maned one smiled with heavy doses of completion.

"Your star testifies on your behalf. You have come a long way to birth our country and now you are here. We have been waiting for you to fulfill scripture."

"Scripture?" Goldman queried.

"The redeemer shall come in the clouds from the land of the setting sun. You have done this?"

Goldman shrugged. "Well, I caught a plane from California."

"It is your turn to save the world," the old one poignantly declared.

Goldman tried to dismiss the bombshell declaration as a fizzled dud, but there was something about its explosive potential that appealed to grander glories and *What ifs?* He gave the three the once over, the twice over, and on the thrice, smiled.

"Do you like wine?"

*　*　*

The three fell into exhaled perorations of gold, frankincense and myrrh, and discursive twaddle that left Goldman's ears ringing and their yap muscles aching with cramping delight. The Magi Essenes were an obscure Zoroastrian sect and the keepers of a hidden knowledge of the Talmud known as the *Kaddish*, which was based on the ancient Aramaic language with its loaded divine levels in Kabbalist coded translations. For them, the very Aramaic prayers themselves had deeper meanings. Each combination of words was impregnated with the potential to invoke universal powers and supernatural beings in a never-ending rotation of infinite possibilities—even the individual words went far beyond the text, and were often magic in and of themselves.

For once, religion made sense to Goldman, or at least the Magi Essenes religion. They taught that the interpretation of scripture as it is known was incorrect. There was no sky god in some far-off place, or punishment down below, where we walk on the roof of hell while taking in the view of heaven. There was only amorphous abstract energy, an infinite encompassing matrix that included all things, an ocean of God filled with billions of human holograms where even a single drop of humanity is loaded with the business end of its creator. The problem was that the true God had been buried under countless generations of mortality, and the purity of the sacred text had been adulterated by religious systems practiced in the slave trade of souls.

The Magi Essenes arcane proposition seemed to be uncannily similar to the teachings of Kazuo. The fused paradigms from the Kabala, the Talmud, and the writings of Kazuo coalesced into a simpatico cauldron of vulcanized illumination, where the very profundity of man could potentially be freed from the beguiling serpent of space and its reticulating cold-blooded time. Every few thousand years or so, a divine incarnate would arise in the world as the point guard ball handler of the universe and the illuminator of all humanity, a single terrestrial touchstone linking the abstract to the tangible, the integral coefficient and king of all quantum potential.

After days of elucidation, the Essenes had no doubt that Goldman was everything they had suspected. The sweetened writings of the Magi mixed with the salted text of Kazuo's theories were a potent conjugated compound, and another confirmation to God's elect, that had to be proclaimed from the world's rooftops. The awakening truth was not only for the Jew but for the whole world, which had been sleepwalking in the compulsions of the artificial self for too long.

"Only if we dare the darkness can we find the light in our psychic slumber and, if we can awake, we will find stirrings of happiness and the mark of cosmic sense," the Essenes said.

Goldman had always assumed that he was spiritually asleep. All of his life seemed like unconscious robotics and gross-motor movements of the soul, but the time spent with the Magi Essenes had made small but definite explorations into his Einstein awakening, "Life is an illusion, albeit a persistent one," and, at least for the three sojourners, Goldman had come into the world to conquer the illusion.

The liberation of Israel was just the beginning. Soon the whole planet would need to be liberated from spiritual domination and exploitation. To the Essenes, the kingdom of heaven was truly within, and for eons most people had searched for something that had been under their turned up schnoz's all along: humanity, forever swimming in a sea of God and not even knowing that they were wet. The Magi Essenes were convinced that Goldman was indeed the One they had waited a lifetime for, the *homo luminous maximus*, the savior of the world. Even Goldman wanted to believe, if only he could dodge his soul desolations and unlearn everything the world had taught him.

The three desert wanderers had completed their mission and now they could sleep in the bosom of their forefathers, knowing that God had moved into the neighborhood.

"We thank thee, oh Lord, for revealing The King, the liberator of mankind. He will go forth and bring truth to the people. All knowledge and power will be revealed to him and 'He will destroy with the brightness of his coming'. The blind will see, the deaf will hear, and the lame will walk. The dawning of a new world order will come forth from his scepter. 'May all kings fall before him,'" the oldest Essene prophesied.

The odd triplets turned east and walked back into the mirage of the thin air desert. Goldman watched until they disappeared behind a headland on the vanishing horizon and through diaphragm gates of delirious apparitions—they were gone. There was a technical mental glitch in Goldman that wanted to abrogate the three, but to lampoon them as religious loons might forfeit his deeper inclinations to transcend his ego's overarching ambition for success and his yearning for magic lamps that never get rubbed.

Could it be that he was the Chosen One? Was it possible that he was here to save the world, and if so, from what? Their sins? Their belief systems? Their gods? It was all too fantastic. For days it left him with a holy inebriated hangover that throbbed between his ears with pile-driving bouts of pious vertigo. Eventually, he blew off the matter as revenant desert delusions, but his eagerness to believe indicated a keen insight into his present helplessness, for to see what is false is also to see what is real. But the real world was closing in again and, as always, he would have to fight a rearguard action against his unexamined assumptions.

*   *   *

Goldman's kibbutz was thriving and expanding with juggernaut notions of manifest destiny. He owned large chunks of land in the Jordan Valley and built a corporate-like operation that fed an ever-growing kibbutz that employed and housed more than two thousand inhabitants. Hefty sums of money were being made, but every cent went back into the operation. Goldman's personal net worth never increased, and he tried to pretend he didn't care. True Communism was the antipode to profit, but the amount of money that was coming in was tantalizing and snaking thoughts of cooking the books tempted him with the swallowing of his own tail.

He thought that if he were to run his organization like a real business, *hell, I'd be rich*. The lure was great, yet he stayed disciplined and made sure that all monies and shared assets were distributed equally to one and all. He secretly resented it though. After all, it was his vision, his energy, and his drive that made it succeed, so why not the lion's kill? His firsthand exposure to free enterprise made perfect sense and, for the moment, his own argument was persuasive enough to convert him into a Capitalist of the nouveau riche.

With enough money and influence he personally championed new Socialist causes and lobbied the Knesset for the rights of the shrinking Arab population, who now loved and supported him like their Lawrence of Arabia. Goldman had become such a menace that the Israeli government threatened to have him deported, or worse. When his hyacinth flowered followers got wind of the threat they determined to forgo their collective social meekness for violent resistance and national revolution. Both Jew and Arab shouldered up and swore they would fight his deportation to the death, if need be.

By 1950, Goldman was the dark horse who was now leading the pack closer to a finish line that kept changing as frequently as its riders. There was the Likud Party, the Mafdal, and the National Unity Party, and Goldman wanted to create the Goat Party, which to the government was a euphemistic tag for Jewish Bolshevism. He had become such a force that the powers that be were willing to make small concessions, if only to keep the peace. But the more the administration faltered, the more public opinion leaned toward the underdog Goats. The Israeli government was continually prodded by the mordant stick of the FBI to do something about the Communist provocateur, and to do it PDQ.

*   *   *

Goldman had returned to the kibbutz after a full day of sweet concord harvesting when he was visited by an old friend, yet an alien to his essence. Goldman had not seen Ronan since the war.

"You have done well for yourself Kemo Sabe," Ronan dully commented.

Goldman reacted with cartoonish excitement. "This is just the beginning. The whole country can be like this if only the government would open their eyes. Why can't they see it?"

Ronan shrugged his shoulders with a stoic weight that symbolized his assent.

"I suppose the word Communism scares them more than the fact that you seem to know how to make it work."

"I don't get it?"

"Politics, my friend. This may be a new country, but I am afraid it is business as usual."

"Then what did we fight for?"

"I think you're getting patriotism mixed up with other 'isms.' The only 'ism' that matters is Judaism. That's what the country is about and that 'ism' has chosen Capitalism my friend. Don't let it dilute your soul."

"If only they would give it a chance, I could change the world."

Ronan smiled with a sad sigh and pitied the seeming effects of a disordered mind. He looked into Goldman's face with augur premonitions and suddenly felt his own internal disfigurements somehow exposed just by being in the same room with a man that he suspected might be more—much more. Ronan smiled again, this time with a glint in his Hebraic eye.

"Altruism, now that's an 'ism' I support."

The two walked to Goldman's office where there were scores of photos and other war memorabilia hanging on an honor wall. There were guns of all types, helmets, uniforms, and even the shrapnel pulled from Goldman's leg in the battle for Jerusalem, framed in glass. The Manlicher-Carcano riveted Ronan's attention.

"May I?" he asked, as if beholden to it.

Goldman pulled the sniper rifle down from the wall and handed it to him with a befittingly formal display.

"I remember how you put your blessing on this weapon, and said that it would always find its mark. I never once missed my mark," Goldman proudly said.

Ronan went over the rifle with a rapt expression. "I always loved this weapon, but you brought something to it that it never had before . . . destiny." He attempted to hand it back.

"Keep it. It belongs to you. You never know when you may need the guarantee of a blessed target." Ronan smiled and slung the rifle over his shoulder and rested his weighty forearm on Goldman's collarbone. He pulled him close and whispered into his bulls-eye ear. "There are forces at work that want to make sure your legacy is cut off. You have served the house of David well and many generations will thank you. I'll personally see to that. But your services are no longer required. Be a good American, and quit while you're still behind. It's time to go home, Yankee."

Ronan walked out with his trailing doubts in tow, leaving Goldman with a purgative dose of fear that regurgitated in his belly like gastronomic cud and reduced him to navel gazing for hours. He knew he was a marked no-good-nik and his far-flung ideas were murder to the state. Ronan had been appointed the head of the newly-formed Mossad, and when the head of Mossad asks you to leave the country . . . you leave.

*   *   *

There was a Communist Party rally in Haifa, attended by some of the world's most influential Socialists, and the heavy hitters demanded Goldman's attendance. He was resolute in being there, even if it rattled his symphonic interior and blew his stoic exterior with operatic terror. Oddly, he didn't want to be there any more than he thought that he wanted to be a Communist, but he was going to do it for one reason . . . Mina. He pinned the official Communist Party pendant that she had given him to his lapel and, despite his familiar stress response, determined he would attend.

The rally would make international headlines, and she would read about him and finally have to surrender her heart to a real revolutionary. *What a glib monkey*, he thought. Did he get so caught up in his flytrap realities that nothing in his life was authentic anymore? He had only thought about her a million times since first setting foot in the holy land.

If only she could see me now.

He was once again a war hero, only this time he thought he really deserved the triumph, but his participation in the birthing of a nation left him feeling like a *caesarean section,* a suburb of Rome.

Goldman was the key speaker. After red banner waving and vitriolic podium squawking, it was his turn. It reminded him of his days on the war bond drive, how panicky he felt to be in front of so many people, and he was even more nervous knowing that he had become a surreptitious target. He gave what at first was a timid sanding of the Knesset, which then ramped up into blistering accusations that the Israeli government was really xenophobic neo-fascists that wanted to exterminate all Arabs. He threw everything at them from the devil's house, including hell's kitchen sink.

He had worked the crowd into a lathered gush, when a single gunshot echoed from one of the adjoining buildings that looked down onto the plaza. *Splat!* A red mist peppered the podium. Before Goldman could capsize the event he was on his back with his security piled on high. The stage was bedlam as the roaring crowd pointed to an open sixth-floor window. Goldman was quickly ushered off the stage under a thickening pall as the crazed mob hunted in vain for a phantom gunman that was not to found.

He lay on a gurney in the hospital emergency room as the doctors bandaged a perfect 6.5 mm hole, which had precisely pierced the fleshy lap of his ear.

"Lucky for you your shooter was a bad shot," said the doctor.

Goldman gasped. "He was a brilliant shot." *No one could have made that bulls-eye but Ronan.*

He knew it was a warning, a gesture of professional courtesy, and feared the next one would be through his almond eye. He had come halfway around the world to fight for a cause that in the end was almost death by misadventure. In another universe there were billions of possibilities to other options in his life, but this was the one that the scudding winds of caprice had him play, and who else could play Goldman better than himself? He left Israel with holes in his pockets, a quarter inch hole in his ear, a one-way ticket to the America he had forgotten, and to a future burned almost beyond recognition.

XXXII

Exigent times were whetting the appetite for aggressive Socialism and the Soviet Union was flexing its cephalopod muscle across the postwar globe. Its tentacles reached well beyond the newly-acquired land grabs in Eastern Europe and slinked into third world countries where mud people empires, neck-corseted to European masters, snapped like jungle-rot leather. The Soviets had high aspirations for world domination, but it was a hard sell to the free-enterprising West. Every revolution that was ever seeded grew from the dirt up, just as every perennial carrot pulled from the West was stunted and small. There would be no healthy prospects while the crops of Capitalism bulged from profit silos.

Mina Contreras was a case study. Born into a flush mainline family and one of two children ushered into the world by a wealthy oil and land magnate who owned or controlled large parcels of land in Mexico, Panama, and Argentina. She was naturally endowed with a keen intellect and educated in private schools around the world, but she wouldn't have to work a day of her privileged life.

She was a trust-fund toddler, fed with a silver ladle that would take her from the valet's cradle to the chiffon grave, and bequeathed with enough disposable cash to ascend the ivory spiral staircase to heaven, but that was the problem. Her curse was the dispensation of leisure, and the luxury of struggle would always exceed her meager means.

Nature designs some folks with heavier fiber than others, and Mina was triple woven hemp. To be content is to twiddle a life of laziness and mediocrity, an apple-stuffed pig without questions, devoured by middling indulgence. She could not be the best of the worst or the worst of the best, average meant death. She was destined to never feel more alive than when she was involved in a cause that exceeded her grasp, or in a struggle that was bigger than the paradox of her inherited lies.

Her early years were spent on expendable fun and wallowing bliss. Sugar and spice and everything her father's millions could slice. However, she suffered emotional beatings from the abrogated blows of rejection. Her father, Ricardo, was never comfortable with affection, particularly towards his offspring and his aloofness weighed heavy on the brood, especially Mina. She was willful with an introspected cosseted interior, but veneered with thick crocodile skin—psycho-genetics inherited from her father's epidermal aspects. To be picked up and coddled, or even to be placed on his lap was rare, and to be kissed was rarer still. Her soft eggshell mind could not understand why the only man that meant anything to her was so artic blue and icy distant. She gathered a million reasons in her over-developed noodle as to why her father was so adverse to any type of affection towards her. Maybe her precocious alacrity made him feel ill at ease and elliptical around her oblong wobbly nature—or maybe it was just the simple fact that he didn't love her.

From her initial years, little Mina sensed that he knew that she could see through his bridled veneer. There was no hiding his thinly veiled avarice from the X-ray vision of her immaculate eye. The prospect of being a healthy, happy, well-adjusted child was unhinged by an absentee paternal transient, that remained a gift showering shadow in the backlit annals of her unhappy little girl days.

Her earliest recollections were of living on plantations in the tropics of Mexico, with bananas, rice, and sugarcane as far as the naked eye could see. To maintain these great expanses of produce required an army of workers, but the laboring class was treated like ants, and her father, the great formicate wrangler, ruled the workers with the iron fist of a salivating sadist. He was never the one to swing a club or crack a bullwhip, but he made sure that his minions did. These were mercenaries by every definition, paid cadres that were given carnal *carte blanche* to enforce his will at the end of a beating stick. Like the military, it was a chain of command, and like the military, if the rank and file did not toe the line, then corporal discipline was executed right down to the child laborers.

Mina was insulated from this dreary reality when she was sent off to private schools in Argentina. The summer months, though, were spent on the sweltering plantations, where she began to understand its deplorable realities after she befriended a peasant girl who worked her father's fields. She was one of seven children who lived in the communal barracks. Her parents and siblings slavishly worked the fields six days a week and Mina discovered that it was under the most dreadful conditions.

Mina's parents insisted that she not befriend the little Indian, but she liked her company so much that she would often sneak away to help her cut sugarcane and plant beans. Sometimes she even brought her back to the mansion, where the two would talk and play well into the sultry Oaxaca evenings.

Even as a kid, Mina's moral night vision could cut through stygian oppression. It was clear to her that the peasants were not beasts of burden, laden with the weight of the rich, but sentient beings held under the waters of submission for entire generations. When she reached her teens, her empathetic distress for the workers became so fervent that she had determined to do something about it. She persisted in improving the working conditions and better food and water. Their only source of water was from the local streams and ponds and many had become sick with typhoid and cholera.

Her father reluctantly acquiesced to some of her demands, but it was only because her mother insisted. These luxuries that her father had grudgingly agreed to began to take a toll on the plantation's bottom line. The healthy profit margin from turning sow's ears into silk purses was now being cut into by the cost of maintaining improved living and working conditions, medical care, and periodic pay increases. The peasants loved Mina for it. Many of the devout sainted her *La Madonna del Trabajo*. She was so revered that one of the workers gave her a hand-carved figurine of her graven image, along with Marx's *Communist Manifesto*.

She had read the book years earlier, when it had been given to her by a classmate, Ernesto Guevara, or "Che", as he was later canonized, the future Communist demigod of Castro's Cuban revolution. She had read the *Manifesto* only because she had fallen giddy for Che's dashing good looks and ardent intellect. She just wanted to share something special with a boy that seemed to be impervious to her freakish beauty. Even at sixteen, Che commanded a flamboyance that inspired nicknames like *furibundo*—furious one. He was enormously popular with the boys as well as with the girls, unusually bold and dripped with handcrafted confidence.

Mina tried to corral his jingoistic nature with expensive gifts, but he rejected her procured overtures and, once again, she found material offerings a shallow substitute for the sanctum of love. It wasn't that he didn't appreciate the gesture, but he was from a working class family and had a deep appreciation for Socialist causes and an abiding hatred for religion and the bourgeoisie. Secretly, he adored Mina, but before they could be one, she would have to renounce her advantaged position and become a soldier for world revolution. When she finally said yes, the two became undividable, like subcontinents separated only by the thinnest isthmus. She lost her virginity to him and was subsequently pregnant. When her father found out, he went *chango*-shit *loco*. Ricardo had close ties with the Argentine military junta, and at his behest Che was beaten to within an inch of his young life. He forbade Mina from ever seeing the Communist lecher again, forced her to have an abortion, and shipped her off to Spain. Mina never looked at her father the same, and no longer did she care to gain his admiration or affection. Whatever link she might have had to him was killed with the death of her unborn baby.

Years later, she had almost forgotten the meaning of Socialism, but after reading the *Manifesto* again, she was determined to implement its tenets. The plantation laborers were not just the working proletariat, but Indian slaves of a European feudal master. In her own way, she had created a microcosm of a Communist society that actually worked; the peasant class functioning with the aristocracy—although it wasn't exactly what Marx had advocated.

To Mina, the systematic duress imposed on the plantation workers, was nothing less than poaching protected game. It roused something sleeping in her, an un-manifested syndrome played off for years as artificial duty. The issue was not about class distinctions or the improvement of one class over another. It was about the whole history of man since the dissolution of tribal societies that held land in common ownership. Since then, it had been a narration of class struggle, the exploiters and the exploited. The stage was set, not only on her father's farm, but the entire human race. To her avant-garde susceptibilities, the world was reaching a tipping point where the exploited and oppressed could not be emancipated from the ruling class without emancipating whole societies and the world at large.

Only radical revolution could bring real change, she believed, and the idea of drastic transformation mixed with fiery passion coursed through the chambers of her firebrand heart. She would be waging war on her father, but for her it was a righteous betrayal; still she wasn't naïve enough to think that a hidden schema didn't exist.

She loved Che and her heart was still badly mangled. Maybe this was just another way to prove her allegiance to him and to get even with a father that had so brutally dismembered the two. Still, she wanted to do it for the right reasons, and after self-barbed examination, she felt her motives were genuine. It was not about revenge or teenage angst over a disembodied father, it was about emancipation from a recalcitrant landlord.

Years later she learned the truth about her father. He was not a self-made man who had built an empire with his wit and cunning. Rather, her mother had inherited the fortune from her own father who had used *his* wit and cunning to build an empire.

Ricardo had been a playboy all of his adult years and a caddish philanderer of the worst breed. It wasn't until he met Mina's mother that he surrendered his crown as a skirt-chasing monarch to become her queen, never the king, Mina's grandfather made sure of that. The fortunate marriage would cement the deal and Ricardo would be entitled to all rights and privileges as her husband. Coming, going, and spending as he pleased, however, would be out of the question. Mina's grandfather never trusted him.

Ricardo was a jet-setting international matador who made a living at the expense of tortured bulls. He dazzled women with his death-defying dance in sand-bowl arenas and spread his libertine seed from Madrid to Mazatlan. Mina's mother, Juanita, fell hard for him. She was semi-good looking and by Ricardo's standards, would be nothing more than a consolation prize for one night of routine debauchery. But when he found out that she was the heiress to a dazzling fortune, she went from plain Juanita to *La bonita amor.* The marriage was consummated and Mina and Miguel were relegated to byproducts of nuptial convenience. Ricardo never wanted a family. But to an aging matador who had not one *peso* to show for the years of his profession, Juanita was the golden parachute that would bring him safely back to Earth.

Ricardo was allowed to work the plantations and the oil fields and whatever money he gleaned he was allowed to keep. The once-dashing, free spirit of a chronic womanizer was relegated to running farms and monitoring balance sheets. It was humiliating, but he was determined to turn his degradation into self-copulating profit. Money was the only thing that mattered to him and he would crush anyone who got in the way of his insatiable bottom line.

By the time Mina was of age she had gained complete control of the labor force, thanks to her grandfather. She understood that for people to live and eat that they would have to make their efforts pay, but to expose them to inhumane treatment was where she slashed and burned a line in the jungle. She moved out of her parents' mansion, built a shotgun shack close to the workers' quarters, and like a Roman tribune held court and enforced her *de jure authorité*

Ricardo implored his father-in-law to do something, but in his eyes, his granddaughter could do no wrong. He was a diehard Capitalist, but in old age it didn't seem nearly as important as in his younger years. He had a heart for the disenfranchised, even when it thinned his wallet, and it was clear that his granddaughter was special; a burgeoning ideologue and the coals of passion burned white-hot in her revolutionary bosom, and he was not about to quench it.

*   *   *

The plantations had not fared well, making just enough to be solvent, and for Mina that was a profit. Ricardo wanted to make money, and lots of it, as he had all the years before she interfered. To him, it was more than money. It was about pride, deep-seated Latin male pride, and a woman stepping on the neck of machismo dominance was enough to justify honor killings, even if it was his own daughter.

Mina had warned him about the excessive working hours and continual harassment of the workers by his goons and that if it didn't stop she would lead the people to defend themselves. When the harassment continued, she organized a general strike. It put the hurt on, as there was only a small window of time to harvest the vast acres of bananas. If they weren't picked soon they would turn into millions of rotting pods. The strike was so effective that her father was forced into a position either of capitulating or commencing with the vile routine of seal-pup clubbing, and his matador pride would never agree to the former.

One night he bussed in a band of thugs from Chihuahua. They stormed the workers barracks with clubs and axe handles, but Mina had known they were coming. They entered the barracks and were greeted with empty bunks, when from out of the jungle the workers charged, armed with sticks, clubs, and machetes. With Mina leading the way, they fought with the ferocity of a people possessed. Ricardo watched from a distance as the rogue intimidators he had sent retreated like squealing pigs, beaten and bloodied. With his personal guards he charged the workers, ranting with apoplectic fury, clubbing and shooting anything that moved.

Six lay dead and fourteen wounded. Among the dead was Mina's childhood companion. Among the wounded was Mina herself, who caught a round that tore through her inner thigh. She was bedridden for weeks with a nasty case of jungle wound-rot and the doctors were afraid they might have to amputate her leg.

No charges were ever leveled against Ricardo, but Mina would never forgive him. After she recovered, she and her younger brother Miguel moved to LA. She never returned to Mexico and spent the next few years going to school, living off the graces that her trust fund allotted. Her Communist venture would not be just a teenage spasm; she still believed in the movement and envisaged real world revolution. The bloody encounter with a fractious father had only galvanized the cause, and the hot irons of Marx's utopia seared its brand on her so completely that it would leave its mark for the rest of her world-shaking days.

XXXIII

Goldman's heart was a prisoner of war, still grubbing through the lost years of captivity; the incarceration of the American argot: slang dreams, sliced schemes, an entomos lover whose *corazón* was still cut to pieces. It had been more than two years since he had last seen Mina, but her apocryphal image was still etched into his cornea as if by witchcraft. She still owned Goldman's parceled heart even if only as an absentee landlord. After arriving back in the States he thought about heading to LA. Would she still be there? Would that be the only reason to return? Then there was the prospect of the FBI awaiting him, along with other apparitions of the government, rat-bag entities intending to do his person harm should he return.

He bought a used Chrysler in New York and called it a New Yorker, even though it was the Windsor model, and decided to make the cross-country trek to California. Napa Valley was where he heard deep calling to deep, and followed the setting sun as far as it would *grow* . . . that's where the grapes were and purported miracles of arcanum transference. The secret of medieval alchemists would always hold him with the unexplained fascination of turning common grapes into purple liquid gold; where he would shut his mouth, tend its needs, and always learn its ways.

He headed south through Maryland and Virginia, where glacial notions dwarfed him before a colossus of sutured ideas: America, the land of verbal exaltations and endless repeated spans, fractal oblivion where Confederacy and Union notions are stitched in patches of a compound republic quilt, still waging civil wars yet to be declared.

He got as far as Lynchburg and was poked with a hankering for waffles. As luck would have it, he spied a large neon sign blinking the words "Dixie's Waffle Emporium". He entered the establishment that was peopled with country bumpkins and twanged-out hickory sticks, found a booth, and eyeballed the menu's plethora of waffle combinations: Belgian waffle, blueberry waffle, strawberry and whipped cream waffle, waffle and egg combo, waffle and bacon, waffle and grits . . . But his sole yearning was for a good old-fashioned American waffle dream, straight up, butter and maple syrup. His entire time in Israel he had missed only two things, Mina and waffles, and he suddenly felt crucified by the calendar with missed opportunities for the simplest of pleasures.

From three booths down, he heard a minor commotion of an unusual manner. A young black man was engaged in a slightly discordant conversation with a middle-aged, heavy-footed white waitress.

"I don't care what your policy is, ma'am. I'm a paying customer and I feel I'm entitled to my request," said the polite yet determined young man. The waitress looked as much puzzled as irritated. She cocked her hip to one side and slid her pencil behind her ear.

"I'll say it again, sir, we don't mix our chicken and waffles here."

The young man scratched his head, smiled slightly, and looked up at the overweight waitress. "All I'm asking is that you give me a regular waffle and an order of fried chicken and serve them on the same plate."

"I'm sorry sir, but mixing chicken and waffles is against the rules."

"I guess you got to know the rules before you can break 'em," he said with gallows humor.

Frustrated, the waitress turned toward the kitchen and yelled, "SARGE!"

From out of the kitchen stepped a six foot two, two hundred and fifty pound Confederate fry cook with a determined look to maintain the menu's status quo.

"What's the problem Brenda?"

She pulled the pencil from behind her ear and pointed it at the young black man.

"This boy says he wants his fried chicken and waffle served on the same plate."

The Shenandoah cook rolled up his sleeves and cracked his oversized knuckles. "We're gettin' pretty tired of you Yankees comin' down here and demandin' chicken and waffles on the same plate, and we ain't puttin' up with it no more."

"First of all, I'm not a Yankee, I'm from Atlanta. And I ain't leaving until I get chicken and waffles on the same plate!"

"Let me tell you sometin' boy, this town ain't called Lynchburg for nothin'. Now why don't you just leave before you become *one o' dem scrange fruits dat hangs fom souvern treeees.*" The cook reached over and grabbed the black buck and the two took to scuffling with mutual vehemence.

"Please, sir, I don't want no trouble!"

The cook loaded up and punched the young Negro in multiples and hurled him through the metal screen front door, crown first onto the gravel parking lot. He went back inside and flung the man's suitcase through the screen door as well.

The young man picked up his suitcase, walked out to the highway and moved dejectedly down the road. The temperate peace of the waffle house was restored and the tubby waitress approached Goldman with a relieved look on her face.

"Sorry about the commotion sir. What'll y'all be havin'?"

Goldman lifted his eyebrows and pinched his eyes tight, almost grimacing, and then looked up at the waitress with a bated grin. "Birdie yum-yum."

"Excuse me?"

Like an enlightened Buddha, he went from grinning to glowing. "I think I'll have what that negra' boy was having."

The waitress rolled her opal eyes and craned her dishwater-blond head toward the kitchen again.

"SARGE!"

*   *   *

Goldman rolled down the highway and saw the same young black man sitting on his suitcase with his thumb out. He pulled the car over and rolled down the passenger window.

"Need a lift?"

The young man leaned into the Chrysler and eyed Goldman, who was freshly garnished with a fat lip and a nasty mouse over one eye.

"You know I eat fried chicken and waffles on the same plate?"

"Birdie yum-yum. Tend to like the same myself. Where you heading?"

"Atlanta, Georgia."

"I can take you as far as the Tennessee border."

The young man got in the car and the two continued down the road with black and white battered faces and unfulfilled longings for fried chicken and waffles.

Goldman side-glanced the young man. His profile seemed to mollify hard-shelled notions of bigotry and gastrointestinal expressions of power. Two hundred miles and not a single word.

"Where you coming from?" Goldman finally asked as they approached the Tennessee state line.

"Seminary school, Pennsylvania. Semester is over, going back to Atlanta to visit my folks."

"Seminary school, huh? You plan on being a preacher?"

With a plaintive gaze, the young man spoke with converging feelings. "The world has to know that it is hell without Christ."

They rumbled down the highway in commiserating providence, where real destinies seemed enfeebled, tormenting those who suspect that they might be living the wrong life.

They rolled another thirty-nine miles when declinations of angular revelation danced across Goldman's parietal lobe. He began to speak, as if in a trance:

"You are the king . . . the one the world has been waiting for." He inexplicably blurted out.

The Negro said nothing but nodded courteously.

"Montgomery bus boycott!"

The young man nodded again and looked out the passenger window with discomfitures of feigned understanding.

"Lorraine Motel, early morning, April 4 . . . no, early evening . . . a shot rings out in the Memphis sky . . . *I have a dream.*"

The unnerved black man gaped at Goldman with rheumy eyes and dire expressions of dreaded destiny, yet slightly smiling: a mixed cauldron where sadness and gladness are gradations of the same thing.

"Please, you can let me out here?" He lugged his suitcase from the back seat as Goldman pulled the car over.

"Thanks again for the lift, and I'm happy to hear that you have a dream," said the young man.

"Every man needs a dream," said Goldman. The hitchhiker looked down then up again.

"I have a dream . . . that one day fried chicken and waffles will be served on the same plate, and ain't no one ever going to question it again." He exited the car, gave a good-natured wave, and crossed the highway.

Goldman put the car in gear and suddenly felt like he had tried to understand the depth of a puddle that was now deeper than any ocean, where exudations of American grace are released and runaway slaves become kings and high priests.

*   *   *

He crossed into Tennessee with resounds in his ears that drew him like tuning forks, where velvet hammers strike clavichord hearts and Memphis memories are cradle snatched by *Anuket* burglars. Returning to Memphis was like returning to the scene of an unsolved crime and he was determined not to touch ground in that ancient Egyptian city. He knew the associated summoning of his past would freeze dry his soul—but he couldn't help it. He needed to mourn for things he never had and laugh about things that never were, and to build elaborate bridges over a dried Nile River that connected the two sides of his upper and lower, supine and belligerent nature.

He had just about reached the city limits when something like psychic ooze congealed inside his brain. His arthropod feelers retracted and it bugged him real far to be real close, and the closer he got to Memphis the steeper his emotions begged off: gravity is falling down, energy is falling up, entropy is falling apart, and the second law was leaving rusty nail marks across his persona like thermo*dramatic* pronged forks.

He spotted a teenage kid hitchhiking with a guitar slung over his shoulder. He decided that if he had to drive through his times of yore, then he would at least shore up his ever-crumbling self assessment with some of the local Memphite gentry. He pulled the Chrysler over and the young man flooded the sedan with luminous 2K filament eyes.

"How far you going, kid?"

The teenager dismissed the question while mesmerized by the car. "Jesus Chrysler . . . wha' year is it?"

Goldman looked the kid up and down. His immediate impression was of his *sex*cellent, Greek-god good looks and consecrated Corinthian smile. He had never questioned his sexual inclinations, being a dyed-in-the-wool hetero all his straight-life days. Still, the boy's appearance abruptly challenged his psychosexual components and left him drifting in metro-sexual space.

"You want a lift?"

Without hesitation the kid bounded into the car, eyes glinting in chimerical orbits as the Chrysler rumbled down the empty Tennessee highway.

"Ah . . . ah . . . ah do appreciate y'all givin' me a rad', sir."

"My pleasure," Goldman said with a passing glance.

The lad continued looking out the passenger window as the sixty mile-an-hour wind tousled his hair and the Tennessee thicket became one bottle-green blur. He started humming a tune. Goldman had heard the song before but couldn't place the ditty. He was impressed by the kid's faultless legato pitch and his ability to hold and sustain a note with unusual vibrato and Southern piquant taste.

"What song is that?" Goldman asked.

The adolescent snarled with a lopsided grin. "Ah . . . ah . . . tha' would be *'How Great Thou Art.'* Is about da Lord."

Goldman noticed that the kid's guitar was old and worn, and the frets cradled deep gutters in the unvarnished wood. "You play that thing?"

"Thas righ't, sir, and I plan on bein' a singin' deacon one day."

He hummed a few other tunes that Goldman could not recall, and then abruptly stopped. The Chrysler was then ensconced with the contented pitch of mollified silence where obdurate laws of space and time are reduced to immaterial and the destiny of grace is understood through words not said. Goldman started humming a tune. The kid listened, his body swaying and stirring to a rhythmic backbeat that only his young ears seemed to hear.

The nameless melody then morphed into Kazuo's five notes. The C, F, A flat, G flat, and C sharp rolled over and over like the miles that languidly passed. The soporific drone seemed to weigh on the boy's shaded eyelids and he drifted in and out of phlegmatic awareness, utterly lost in its thrall. The teenager then reemerged like a young Siddhartha after napping under a bodhi tree and directed Goldman down Beale Street, past the hillbilly bars and soul kitchens, to a public tenement building—the very building that had housed Goldman's childhood years.

"Ah . . . ah . . . you can drop me off here, sir."

Goldman shook his head in deadpan disbelief. "You live in this building?"

The kid pointed to the second floor. "That's righ't, sir. Unit numba' seven."

Goldman was afraid that seeing the landmarks of his past would leave him wincing with cat-o-nine-tails scoring across his back. Instead he was comforted with ecclesiastic feelings of forgiveness for those that have lived too long to find innocence again. Maybe he had gotten over the sour memories of Memphis, or maybe the kid had something to do with his choral convergence, where unpleasant recollections withdraw under Southern charm and a polite boy's graces.

The young man smiled and thrust out his hand. "Ah . . . ah . . . ah do appreciate the lift sir, and y'all do have a fine lookin' piece o' machinery."

Through the firm hand grasp Goldman felt a mild tingling sensation that quickly transmuted into rivulets of energy shooting up his arm and grounding him, like placid lightning, to a fire now brewing in his belly. The two looked at one another like mirrored forensic photographs staring into each other's collective futures, narrow-scopic eyes privy to some great secret. Inexplicably, the teenager started humming Kazuo's five notes, but with Negro chocolate feeling and perfect Pat Boone vanilla pitch.

Goldman was suddenly awash in apparitions and cryptic parlances flowed from his mouth like pastel premonitions:

"*Hound Dog! Hound Dog!* Dexedrine, Quaalude, Oxycodone, Hydrocodone, Diazepam, Temazepam, messengers of heartbreak to your hotel. *Don't be cruel* to your much befitting pomp. You are the king, the one that the world has been waiting for."

The boy shot back with a gouging glance. "No sir', *You* are *The King,* the *One* the world has been waitin' for."

The two quietly exhaled and released their handclasp as wafting pheromone links permeated the insect-buzzing air with streaks of lavender and soft spots of May violets. The boy grabbed his guitar and gamboled past the porch monkeys and po' white trash, up the steps through the door of unit number seven.

Like a Memphis misfit Goldman continued down the highway. For the next forty-two miles the whiff of cheeseburgers and teenage poontang assailed his olfactory senses and rockabilly anthems rattled his hammer, anvil, and stirrup with twelve-bar fibrillate spasms, seraphim choirs and Vedantic thought, Cadillac angels and heavenly suspicions that we've always been everything we've always wanted to be.

XXXIV

Goldman rolled into Marin County like a penultimate refugee, where second to last is as good as first. He was short on funds and the trip had cost him just about everything. He tried to pull monies from his accounts in Israel but, after the attempted assassination, the Israeli government had frozen his *ass*ets off. The meager three thousand dollars he had stashed in a Pinot Noir bottle on the kibbutz was used to buy a plane ticket, a car, gas, and food. But he was glad to finish a chapter he knew he would never read again and was relieved to start a new one in the pages of the great California novel. Driving through Napa Valley excited his senses, and annulations of immanence circled his head with pungent ripening grapes that ovulated in the warm sun, sweetening his uterus nostrils by the mile while salivations whetted his mouth well into the cultivated night.

He was about one meal and one gallon away from his needle being on empty and needed a job, quick. At the next little grape town he pulled in front of Manzarek's Feed & Supply. He fell to talking with a fellow who had a relative that owned a vineyard not far away and the man said he would inform him that a new farmhand was headed over. By the time the sun had set, Goldman had landed a job as a tractor operator. His experience on the Simpson vineyard, and being able to speak enough "Mescan" elevated him to the senior foreman position in a short period of time.

The California loam welcomed his soles with raking enthusiasm, and it felt good to be close to the electrostatic field that farm dirt generated. The soil was a healer for Goldman and he could sense a metabolic hum return to his jittery body and balance to his renegade brain. Something about celestial mechanics, planting cycles, and ruminating in the whiff of farm dirt could flatten his sub-continent thoughts with deep valley exaltations.

Often, when living in the city, he would dream about farming. It was sexual, life giving, and superbly terrestrial; it moved not only his senses but thinned out the derma-tropic accretions that city life often laid on him. On occasion, he would grab a fistful of nutrient-loaded farm dirt and devour it with the predilection of a freakish omnivore. It was a kind of communion, a Eucharist from the mineral kingdom that left him feeling ecclesiastical with visions of god particles that waltzed in his Vienna-ballroom head.

He loved watching the massive vats churning the grapes in the distillery. The homogeneous hum of the mechanized and the macrobiotic morphing into something new always put him in an amorous mood. It was if all was well with the world when man and dirt conspired to create a spit 'n' gut elixir; an inscrutable ferment copulating in patterns of reproductive union, where consciousness becomes self-aware and neuro-peptide chemicals distill as one. Its properties and symbolic importance would always mark time between heaven and Earth, until all drank at the final feast of prodigal drunken tales.

He busied himself with the farm and was happy to be far removed from the calamitous events of Israel and his ubiquitous beefs with the US government. There could be no way that they would find him here, although that didn't exactly make him feel at ease. LA had always snatched his attention with leering winks, and in sulking silence he was homesick for a city that seemed to defame his character with minor Mina memories. No matter where he was or what he was doing, she drifted in and out of his recall with the ardor of an opaque specter.

It was her translated portrait and recollections of lotus kisses that got him through the pitched battles of Israel. She was his inspiration, even when her indifference was the only thing that he could remember. He loved her something whacky and sensed that she could love him too, but like him, was delicately guarded around the prickly rose of sharpened sentiments.

He would often regurgitate jackass, cheese-ball musings about returning to LA and sweeping her off her foot-bound feet, whisking her away to some far-off asylum where the two would tumble in blessed merriment for the rest of their daydream days. No revolutions, no wars, no bitter little men to mock their steps and piss in their garden; simple wedded bliss and the sweet routine of an Arcadian existence somewhere East of Eden.

The nights on the farm were cold and lonely; as on the Simpson farm, he had his own bunkhouse and took to reading again. He still had the probing little notebook of Kazuo, whose didactic voice ran through immutable cores like the Tiber River running through the heart of every Roman god; a torrent of inversions that upended Western pyramid paradigms. Empirical laws, taught to Goldman by his father, were embraced yet pierced by Kazuo's punctured point of view.

Kazuo was susceptible to the woo of Planck's quantum work, and had ensnared notions of a mechanical universe, mass, momentum, inertia, etcetera, etcetera . . . Kazuo's encryptions bombarded Newton's hamlet notions with insinuations of reality as a singleness of mind, and matter as only an extension of that mind. The entire universe was an electromagnetic drag-force, a colossus of ever-expanding information. All matter was mind, including man, and Kazuo believed that the mind of man was an exact replicate of the original cosmic mind and imbued with the same potential power.

Kazuo's concurred with the Magi Essenes that the true god was impersonal—science—yet all-knowing and unlimited. However, it could only find entrance into this dimension through the highest consciousness of, ironically, the limited and schismatic human brain. The Essenes had said that Goldman was the apex of that consciousness. He wondered why their declaration was so personal. And more to the point, why him? To them, the illusion of separateness was the exodus curse from the Garden: endless generations feebly trying to reenter but kept at bay by the flaming sword of ignorance.

Kazuo asserted that the building blocks of all life are nothing more than information in cryptogram form, a massive symbolic language that is understood only by the universal mind itself. However, if man could retool the brain then he too would be fluent in the same celestial tongue. It would be the default responsibility of man to realign with the original Source, and when finally liberated from the constraints of the ego—*Egging God On*—the doors of elucidation would naturally open.

Reality is the perceiver, and the seemingly abstract forms of the world cannot exist without subjective interdiction, yet you can only perceive what you allow yourself to become aware of. Nothing can be observed without being affected by the observer. In the end, reality as people experience it is the manufacturing of perception—life has no meaning other than what it is assigned and matter has no validity until it is seen. Yet, most people lived unreal existences, dwelling in the realm of unconscious self-preoccupation.

He used the example of a film projector. "We think we are conscious when caught up in perceived images, sensations, memories, and dreams of our own moving drama. Except real consciousness is the light being projected onto the screen that makes our images flicker before our eyes. The problem is that we are hypnotized within our own dark theaters, unaware of the source that makes our own movie even possible. If one can break free from the image and look only at the light, then there you will find consciousness. But we are too caught up in our entangled hierarchies that defy any tangible forms, to experience the possibility of transcendence."

All the great avatars had struggled to achieve cosmological communion, but it was as elusive as looking at yourself with your own eyeballs. For Kazuo, the answer was sound waves and how they related to the autonomic nervous system. The brain was the essential Holy Grail to the universe, the cosmic chalice that cupped liquid connections to all eternity, and man—the default caretaker—was responsible for all meaning. The problem was the sense of separation of second cause from the prime creator. Time and space had twisted the illusion of a bilateral disconnect, and the human brain was living proof of life's left and right hemispheric schisms.

Kazuo believed that a binaural beat, which oscillated at a low frequency, combined with the high-amplitude chant of the five notes, could produce a two-pronged synchronization of the right and left hemispheres of the brain. By doing so, it might be possible to achieve altered states of consciousness that could be lulled to gamma echelons, a *terra incognita* depth never probed before. At these cavernous levels, subject and object find union and deductive and inductive reason as one.

Nirvana, for Kazuo, was an inside job. The summit of the universe had been smack dead center in the human brain all along, the quantum computer, the universal touchstone, the mainframe coupler to all creation, meaning, purpose, and fulfillment. But the "I" and its chronic illusion of separation had always been the virus in the software. When consciousness devours the ego, the devil is swallowed and God is finally free.

Metaphysical leaps at this altitude were dizzying to Goldman's physics instincts, but it made perfect sense, if only intuitively. Could it be, as the Magi Essenes had said, that the Garden could be reoccupied if gene-code ignorance were dashed? Was it only matter—the emotional brain—that was out of whack and not some spiritual peccadillo?

Feeding his spirit this way made Goldman feel monkish, and spending time alone with Kazuo's theories seasoned his thoughts like an Aquinas monk—which, of course, contrasted with his *hoe-ish* tendencies and carousing through the local flesh palaces and random binges that were becoming more frequent. He couldn't find that happy medium between devotion to wisdom and the fervor for a disorderly existence. Jung's gestalt of duality thrived in Goldman's split conflagrations, wrestling between spirit-flesh, heaven-hell, and yin-yang, yet he could not find the balance in his super-positional core. For now, these disparities would have to coexist in the fallen realm of dispensation. And if he had to fall, then he was determined to fall forward, and hoped that one day he would put to rest his double-pendulum extremes and center his ever-tipping self.

XXXV

Goldman's psyche moved like a trilobite in an inverted age where intercourse with invertebrates is only a Cambrian explosion away. If only he could decode transcendent causes to ideas in perpetual disconnect, he might grow something original in his inner fallow acreage and share it with the world. He buried himself in the work of the vineyard, but his mind kept retreating to scrapheap worlds and a nagging penchant to make a run for LA. He dreamed about Mina with quotidian reliability and played over in his *heads* the night they made love. The thought of her always produced exhilarant rushes of adrenaline that gushed through his stomach like a torrent of fire, but would flame out as quickly as it had ignited.

He wondered if she was bedding down other men, maybe a new recruit like he had been, that she could cold play like a Bolshevik tin soldier, marshaled as potential field fodder and as stupid and impotent as she might have expected. Thoughts like these were constant and left him feeling desultory and aimless. He wearied of these lapses of languor that were flotsam, and vulcanized whatever softness he might have had in his spongy core.

His new boss loved him with decorous appreciation and the vineyard was having a loadatious year. Goldman's touch made even the most stubborn fields blossom with verdant succulence, a cornucopia of radical human hope that reassured nervous farmers with the arrival of its faith-filled bounty. Like the Simpson vineyard, Goldman would amble through acres and bless the vines with the laying on of his instigated hands. He intuitively understood that life was a fragile filament and handled it with a benediction that plants and even animals responded to. The bumper year was like none other and the wine was richer and more aromatic than the most discriminating palate in the valley had ever trilled.

The work was rewarding but Goldman was slipping between crags of the forlorn, dangling on his last line of optimism and tired of swallowing love's lumpy lodestones. He had to cowboy-up to the fact that Mina didn't love him, but his recollections of her exerted a mighty suction and drew his essence into fissures of sexology and the zero sum game. She was a strange cupbearer, and it wasn't about this cup or that, but what was poured in, and hers would always be an aperitif elixir that would never be had before a transmitting encounter. She possessed built-in radar that could pick up blips most people weren't even aware of, and a cunning ability to sink the disingenuous. He wondered if she even remembered him.

*   *   *

There was a bustling town just outside of Napa, a rogue settlement that once served as a waystation during the gold rush years, now a stockyard and cattle depot where the local beef was auctioned and shipped by train to slaughterhouses. The town was notorious for its rough and tumble bars and cathouses that serviced the lonely cowboys and the farmhands. The prospect of so much tendered tail easily seduced Goldman. Like a kid in a candy store, the storekeeper didn't care if the sweets rotted your teeth or if your mama didn't approve, just shut your yap and bring your allowance.

He was caught in its eddy like every other sap that needed the company of hired ass and a shot of sour mash to make the fact that you were paying for va-jay-jay less disgraceful. He felt unusually priggish about his precipitous backslide into alcoholism and piquant carnal indulgences, but its lure rapt his knee-jerk nature that slavishly obeyed the salutations of a stiff drink and a stiff prick that had no conscience and never condemned his maladjusted behavior.

The whorehouses were like holding tanks for sea-salmon women who never got the chance to spawn upstream: shit-stained panties, bloodstained sheets, poorly acted orgasms and dour cases of little girl dreams looking for daddies in twenty dollar bills. Goldman felt for them and always put down roots in the whores he plowed and shared their spirits in the abyss of their concealed grief. He had a favorite cat den and routinely bedded the same prostitute. Mary was a smart damsel who never drank and always made sure that the swords of the knights she serviced were clean and kept in rubber sheaths when thrust into her. This made Goldman feel somewhat safer, as there were, from time to time, local venereal epidemics.

One night while waiting in the lobby for Mary, he spied a chiffon-eyed ingénue standing on the staircase landing, a woman-child of frightful beauty, imperious yet generous to a fault. He was taken aback so completely that for the rest of the evening he was fixed on the seeming apparition like a child-painted portrait of the most primary colors. His interior leaped with tantric zeal and photosensitive cells discharged electrons of demonstrable bliss, filling his cup with assorted sensualities to be drunk by two from one who offers to one.

There was something deeper than his initial impulse to vector sensual-scopic beams into her tight skirt. Unspoken precedents of elucidation radiated across the room from her ethereal brilliance, moving faster than its own speed, yet maintaining a constant velocity with a non-local effect. She was that living, breathing illumination that Einstein had theorized but could never calibrate. Even while penetrating his favorite strumpet, Goldman could not take his mind off the young immortal. The thought of her made him plow hard into Mary with an explosive hormone-factory climax that they both were unprepared for. The only other time Goldman had heard a whore moan like that was when he refused to pay. The session was so gratifying that the two blushed with innocent fulfillment and, for the first time as a professional fornicator, Mary *came* with a *John*.

Goldman rolled off of Mary and stared silently at the ceiling. He was sopped in a heightened sense of guilt and scolded himself for using the pubescent image of the young girl for his *wishful sinful* fantasy. He felt a sputtering anxiety which at first was alarming, then left him feeling vaguely uneasy. He lit a left handed cigarette and exited to the right with an accusative walk and Medusa melancholy that slithered like serpents in his snake-den head. He wanted to get one more look at the lass that made him feel so inadequate, but she had disappeared like a fastidious haunt, easily disgusted by the unclean. He asked Wyoming Joe, a muscular six-foot-five lummox who was the in-house security.

"Oh, her," he said. "That's little Eurika, and it'll cost you plenty to bed that down."

Word was that she was an eighteen-year-old virgin and anyone who wanted to be the first to tap her vein would have to pay in gold, and by "in gold" they meant that three hundred dollars in gold coin was the dowry for her gilded chastity.

Goldman returned to the farm, thinking only of being the first miner to strike the mother lode in Eurika's unexplored shaft. Her image ran through the turnstile of his token mind like a *soft parade*, but he would not be paid for another month. He waited for his pay, plagued with skulking feelings that some other road apple had gotten to her before him.

*　　*　　*

He raced to town on a Friday before the sun had set and entered the house of pastiche love, eye sweeping the establishment, but no Eurika. He approached Fanny, the sizeable madam who owned the genital joint, and asked about her.

"Eurika is being saved for someone who can afford her and that will be six hundred dollars in gold." she declared.

"Six hundred dollars? I was told three hundred!" Goldman exclaimed.

Heavy blows fell when he didn't have the money, and his perving aspirations shattered on the unforgiving floor. Fanny explained that Eurika was such an exceptional sampling that she could not settle for anything less than the compensatory price of her virginity, and felt she was a commodity whose value the market could bear. Goldman wanted to at least meet her. Fanny said she would make the arrangements, but it would cost him a minimum of two drinks and a twenty for the privilege.

"I've never heard of such a thing," he protested.

"You've never seen such a thing," she wryly said, leveling her chubby palm in his volition-less face.

Why he was so rapt by the petite ingénue he couldn't begin to understand. Granted, she was ravishing and gentle on the eyes, but it was something deeper that linked her to the nexus of his inner core. A weird panic suddenly gripped him and he felt that if he didn't see her that night something inside would implode, a psychic detonation that his hand-grenade heart was unprepared for.

He laid the Andrew Jackson on Fanny's plump palm and she led him laboring upstairs to the whorehouse saloon where the uppity Johns waited their turn to ride the most prized fillies of the stable. Goldman ordered a couple of whiskeys and sat edgy on the bar stool, anxiously wringing his hands in tremulous anticipation. A few minutes later he heard a slight, delicate voice emitting from the unspoiled vocal cords of a sylphlike angel.

"Are you here to buy me a drink?"

Goldman turned. He was surprised that he was not floored by her up-close exquisiteness. Instead, he was bowled over by a wave of truth that illuminated every dark lie that lay hidden in the corners of his empty closet. Black dust bunnies that had accumulated over his venal years were immediately blown away and a spit-polish shine came across his face. Her youthful grace did not entice, seduce, or provoke, but was a soft runner that dashed through old men's visions, and he was leveled with one clean shot to the heart.

"Yes," he said. He listened intently to the silence behind her smile, and the tender slang between her puce lips. She sat at the bar and took a sip of rye from a shot glass etched with the cathouse name: "Fanny's Fanny Fantasies". They were awkward, simultaneously turtle faced, mirroring each other's movements as they made darting glances into the reflecting ponds of their almond-shaped eyes.

Goldman took a sip of whiskey; he found it difficult to steady his nerves long enough to hold her in his vector even for the briefest of moments, spellbound by untrimmed thoughts and slight vagaries veiled by her simulacrum face. It was an invigorating milieu that permeated the most enigmatic expressions, like looking through a generation of aggregations stitched together in a long-forgotten patchwork quilt. Every word bubbled like a crystal-spring fount from her childlike mouth that made him feel amenable, virtuous, and still. With a hydraulic yawn he sucked in a lung full of air and his eyes tipped heavily as he listened to vowels and consonants form from her delicate thorax.

What began as clumsy attempts at repartee grew into a meaningful exchange. She professed to be eighteen, but looked fifteen or sixteen, though elegant and composed well beyond her babyish years. By the end of an hour their affinity for one another was apparent and Goldman had to deposit another twenty into the madam machine, and was obliged to buy two more drinks for the privilege of continuing their farrago of words and jumbled feelings. All through the shining night their conversation was tempered by the isolated chance that at any moment a fire-breathing dragon might pay the six hundred dollar dowry and steal away his virgin princess.

Something in her orb was sanctifying and consecrated Goldman's torn essence and he felt magnified by her solace. Through peeling and revealing, their common ground was marked by tombstones of buried respites, where tension for who you think you should be are traded for repose and who you really are. They exchanged heartrending tales of calamity; both had lost their parents at a young age. She wouldn't, however, expound on the circumstances that shrouded her past.

The idea of this princess earmarked into the loathsome world of prostitution gnawed like a woodworm in Goldman's soulful church-spire gut: the diminution of her arabesques core, abdicated innocence, and unpunished wickedness that left him feeling marooned in his own sermonic base compromise.

Roaring waves of hoarse talk and riotous laughter from the saloon drowned the soft tones of their trickling conversation. He tried to dig deeper for the fossils to her past, but she was cagey and they would not be unearthed. She would only admit that she was fretful at the prospect of losing her virginity to a strange man; if someone paid the six hundred dollars, she would be bridled and mounted like the rest of the mares. Until then, she would remain on a tight rein, by Madam Fanny and Wyoming Joe.

After an evening of potent talk and watered drinks she was ushered off to the sex parlor where the house tarts were put on painted-lady display. The thought of her being there was a mule kick to Goldman's breadbasket, winding him with moral indignation and the vilest of rage. He yearned to conceal her from the uglies of the world, but was contradicted by his own predatory appetite. Like an insatiable satyr, he would not be satisfied until she was his.

*   *   *

Goldman saved the six hundred dollars he needed to consummate the carnal contract, and after another month of anxious waiting he laid the bag of soft yellow coin on the madam's hard mahogany desk. Fanny dumped out the treasure and ran her thick fingers through the shiny bullion, methodically counting it three times. She told him to wait in the saloon upstairs. He ordered a drink in an attempt to steady his jittery wires and nervously paced the parquet floor in geometric patterns.

Fanny soon entered with young Eurika, who appeared transformed, mineralized like Venus de Milo before the passage of time had stolen her appendages and worn down her polished veneer. Fanny led the two to a decorous room that was striking in contrast to the forthcoming event, and closed the door. They stood motionless, statuesque, like marble monuments to people who had done something enormous in a past life.

Eurika was uncontaminated, like a snowflake before it hits the steamy gutter, where an irregular world melts flawless symmetry in its grubby grime. Her six-sided perfection defied all depiction and her golden ratios added up to perfect rational numbers. Like Goldman, she was tiffany nervous, and the two looked at one another with a powerful resonance that assailed their absconded wits. Guiding instincts stirred from one, then to the other, an odd perigee circle as they orbited one another's center mass. She put her arms around his carotid neck and relinquished a kiss.

"They told me never to kiss the guests but I can't do this unless I do."

Goldman was suddenly struck by thin-air guilt that permeated the vacant quadrants of the room, like a thief sneaking into heaven by a back door that someone carelessly left unlocked. A screeching ring whirred in his ears as he tried to collate his defecting feelings.

"*Touch me*," she said.

"I feel this isn't right," he balked as he sat on the edge of the bed, rubbing his bead-sweating brow. He looked up. "I'm a selfish pig who doesn't belong in the same room with you."

She was salved by his consternation and sat next to him, resting her sculpted head on his chiseled shoulder, perched in a nonce that left them both perplexed, yet tranquil. She put her slight palms on his face and turned his heavy head in her direction. "*My eyes have seen you*, and you are a most decent man. I would rather my first time be with you than with one of the other guests."

Goldman was relieved, but lacked any piloting skills to navigate this fragile terrain. She looked long into his face and then moved senselessly to his lips, obeying some foreknown calling with its own predetermined rules.

Her mouth night-blossomed like a tuberose perennial and they embraced as their tongues danced lightly upon the other's fragrant spit. Goldman thought he would not be able to control the trouser trout that had been thrashing on his zipper line for the last two months, but he was gentle and patient. He had not remembered feelings like this since his school days, when he had first kissed Rhodesia, or the night he made love to Mina in the warehouse. His head was like helium balloons wreathing in circuitous wrappings; his extremities tingled numb and the most minuet traces of saliva evaporated in his Gobi mouth.

Her kiss was delicate and the air that bellowed from her petite young lungs winded through his mouth like baby's breath. His entire rogue essence was consumed by a single immaculate kiss and the two fell irretrievably as one, a crucial link that pulled cycles of eons into avers twinkled eyes. They collapsed onto the bed like feathers falling on new ground, an etymology in primary words of symbiotic love. They doffed their clothes and fitted their nakedness together, and, prone to surrender as they were, laid down their arms in a relinquished passion play.

Nature is a whore, Goldman thought, *it just doesn't feel good unless it's sick 'n' nasty*. But this was different, reverential, blinding and magnificent in its significance. The two withered under a blitz of impalpable ambiance that devoured any crumbs of logic, and an unseen world impinged on them where they unconsciously drew their significance.

Their fabled night was filled with sorcery, incantations, and abstruse utterances as their collective mortality locked in an extant state of chaos; wrestling with spastic tides that wreak havoc on full-moon nights, when celestial bodies move in elliptical paths and are at their most potent. Like some great polyphonic opus that plays in perfected pitch, graced by sour notes that are disordered and contradictory in a song of faultless morphic resonance. There were cries that wailed subterranean; tortured inner chambers where the unransomed and the unredeemed are beaten from the grapes of fury. For these two, the night brought salvation in the form of a runaway train that took them from station to station, blood to blood, and then to there.

Goldman left Fanny's Fanny Fantasies thinking that it was the best six hundred dollars he had ever spent, and was lifted by oratorical wings and declamatory boastings. It was a spectacle never before witnessed, intensely stupendous, yet a fog descended and left him evanescent and temperately disturbed. All through the working week he was vexed by the unrelenting fact that she was not his. The six hundred dollars was for her maidenhead, a rental for the night and now that she was no longer a phial filly, the stall's gates were open and she would be nothing more than one of many in the stable; a deflowered for hire, a soiled dove, a hired-hand working for the company, that's it.

This intolerable fact left him with a bad case of myopic loss aversion, entangled with a single-minded neurosis. He could not imagine that the cultivated ground that he had so meticulously seeded would be furrowed by other paying Johns who would slop all over his virgin soil with their territorial spray. No matter how he tried to get his head around it, the unseemly fact left him vacant and fraudulently sore. He felt like an operate afflicted with fraud; anathema hovered over him like sulfurous smoke and under-divulging tremors rattled stress fractures in what probity he had left.

XXXVI

Goldman fell into a light-shaft that denuded the cephalopod shell that he had carried for some thirty years. Eurika's illumination had laid him open like a vacuum-sealed clam and his mollusk core had no place to hide, and he didn't want to. She was the only foal in the stable that meant anything, and now she had become everything. No longer a gilded virgin but a courtesan, status: Circassian.

He could not keep away, and his misreckoned love for her was crazy. Sometimes he paid for her services and the two would do nothing but talk late into the abstinent night. Something exuded from her diminutive exoskeleton that provided support and protection to Goldman's arthropod interior, arresting his insect-like pensiveness with a cooling balm for his scorching sin-burn sores. When he was with her the very federation of his spinning world would cease and the stillness massaged the contractions of his compound heart. Their collective essence was so laudable that he felt duty bound to free his captive princess from her corset collar and tower of doom.

She wanted to leave, but fear always clamored, rattled, and hummed in her innards. She was a moneymaker and Wyoming Joe and Madam Fanny kept her in perpetual sexual escrow. Goldman protested that no one owns anybody, and could not understand why she felt obliged to them. She resisted revealing the reason for her indentured servitude, but after relentless cajolery she finally caved.

She explained that her mother had sold her into the nefarious white-slave trade and that most of the women in the establishment were victims, some willing, but still victims. Her mother had incurred large gambling debts and bartered her daughter as a tangible asset to her creditors.

This drove Eurika to tears, and not just token effect tears, but floodgate wails. Never had he seen someone bawl so hard. She went on about how her whole life was a mess from as far back as she could remember. She groaned with racking sobs about how her father left her as a baby and how her mother had become a transient alcoholic, roaming from town to town, man to man, nuthouse to nuthouse. Her mournful cries twisted into guttural moans and long strands of snot, bitter ectoplasm, dripped onto her lap.

The dog tale was familiar to Goldman: remote, but familiar. Maybe it had something to do with his own slapdash childhood, but this was something recondite. She continued to blubber and he kept handing her tissues, wiping away her eyeliner and makeup. Under the mask of a callow storefront prostitute he could see her natural tinted beauty, her apple cheeks, organic-lined eyelashes, and blushing full lips, but mostly it revealed a very troubled girl. Every paternal instinct that had lain dormant in his tar-pit gut came forth. He pulled her close in an unencumbered squeeze and fused his dewy eyes sympathetically to hers. *You're lost, little girl* ran through his head as he continued to wipe tears from her flushed face. Then something caught his eye, something that made his ventricle valve fibrillate and suddenly pump ponderous globs of recompense to his farthest fringe.

A tottering wave that had always threatened their link suddenly broadsided his ghost-ship past with a wicked squall, flooding him with recollections from another lifetime ago. He fretfully grabbed another tissue and wiped away the residual makeup that ran from her flushed face down to her graceful thin neck. His eyes squinted at a mark just below her right ear—a birthmark—a small port-wine stain in the shape of a perfect little heart. He quavered hard and a spiraling tempest blasted his soulless barge, listing him thirty degrees to port, his head swooning, mocked, and blind as he flailed in its psychic debris. Her mouth moved but he heard nothing as he sat cross-eyed and lock-jawed.

"What is your name?"

She looked at him oddly. "Eurika."

"No, your birth name."

She thought, elongated, firm, and hesitant. "Ruth."

In an instant all the sifting through his murky waters became perspicuously clear. He felt like an unsuspecting sap, lulled to sleep by a child's bedtime story and rudely awakened by the bludgeoning of a night-stalker's bat.

"How old are you?" he asked, shaking with trepidation.

"Eighteen."

"I want the truth," he shouted at close range.

"Fourteen," she fretfully answered.

"Where were you born?" She shook her head. "Think!"

This made her nervous and she cried even more. "I don't know."

He tried to apply first-aid comfort but his acridity was too tart to put her feelers at ease.

"This is very important."

She shook her head. "I don't know."

His eyes rolled as he coiled backwards in swing time, and a creeping tide of forgotten currents pulled him under again.

"What was your mother's name?"

"I don't understand, why are you asking me all these questions?"

"Please," he bellowed.

She gathered herself in pantomime gestures and for the moment posed as someone composed. "Rhodesia."

Goldman tried to swallow the cattail prick in his throat and he felt his very being morphing into some kind of entity, a persona non grata, stripped of all externalities.

"You were born in Memphis, 1936."

The declaration hung like a double-edged pendulum swinging over their heads, and he exited the room teetering like a spinning top.

*   *   *

He returned to the farm without saying so much as goodbye to Ruthie Lee. For days he moved as a dead man on foot, a bipedal zombie, limb dragging in conjugated impasse. There would be no way to reason his way out of this, because the whole thing was so unfuckingbelievable! He deserved exemplary punishment and the first thing was a healthy dose of self-mortification. There would be no high court to appeal this miscarriage of justice, no acts of absolution or penance for the exculpation of incest, only the hanging judgment of saturnine law.

He had unleashed a cankerworm that had blighted the name of his only daughter. Even though he was reconcilably rueful and had every right to be wrong, there would be no atonement for such a sprawling gaffe. He denied himself sleep, food, even wiping his ass. He wanted to throw his carcass into the Russian River with a millstone tied around his neck, but to off himself would be too easy. No, this would be a long, drawn out, pathogenic assault. Penitent flagellation came easily to him and he was going to make sure that he suffered—not enough to kill—but enough to keep the embers of *Gehenna* burning and his teeth gnashing in shoddy damnation.

For days his anguish whipped as he tore his fleshly elements to the bone, skilled at the art of self-dismantling that came with years of refining the craft. When it seemed his carcass could take no more, a shard of light pierced his shadowy nature. It gradually occurred to him that he could not be culpable for something he had not been aware of. The more he thought about it, the more his queries unloaded.

Yes, it had been a spastic act of incontinence, but it wasn't first degree murder, but the lesser charge of involuntary manslaughter, he thought.

This perspective helped to neutralize his ad-nauseam assault and, after sorting through the details, he determined he had expiated himself adequately—not enough to be absolved, but to at least appeal the self-sentence.

He had to sort through multifarious entanglements about his daughter. He now understood why he felt so powerfully toward her; the sirens of fatherhood had sung a homecoming, but cloaked in the disguise of his fleshly hankerings. The leading edge of his emotional hurricane had passed, and unexpectedly he found himself in the empirical eye of lucidity. His resolutions were now clear. He would go commando and free his daughter from the grip of Wyoming Joe and Madam Fanny. If it meant gunplay then he was ready to get his X on and take to the grave what fate had conspired.

He waited until he could collect his pay from the winery, packed his meager belongings, and threw everything into the Chrysler. He purchased a Colt .45 semi-automatic and a nickel-plated snub nose .38. His plan was axiomatic and blatantly clear. He would simply sneak into Fanny's Fanny Fantasies and steal her away in the wee morning hours.

He visited Ruthie Lee early that Saturday afternoon and told her to be ready for anything. She didn't know what he meant but suspected something dramatic and noticed how stoic and distant he seemed. When you love someone you don't want anything from them, and it seemed he wanted nothing from her. She made attempts at osculating tangents, but he stifled her open flower kisses and left as hastily as he had arrived.

*   *   *

At zero-dark-hundred hours, while the moon eased into its cobalt horizon bed, Goldman slithered into Fanny's Fanny Fantasies like a nocturnal viper through a side window he had unlocked earlier. The women were constantly changing rooms, so it would be tricky to find her. He treaded softly, methodically casing each room, looking directly into the faces of the quiescent women. The floors of the old Victorian house squeaked so badly that he was sure to wake any light sleeper, but he didn't care if he woke the whole God-condemned town, he was getting his daughter out. With a steady creak, he opened one of the bedroom doors. He looked in and saw a woman in black silhouette slowly sit upright.

He walked over and whispered millimeters from her nose, "Get your things together, I'm getting you out of here." She answered with a fully-throated buxom shriek and flicked on the nightstand light as an echoing scream caromed from a room across the hall. Goldman turned and saw Ruthie Lee sit up in the bed across from another woman, who was squealing like a bewildered banshee.

"Get your things. I'm taking you away from this place."

Her first reaction was to resist, but there was something in his voice that was assuring and all her reservations frittered away. She rifled through her belongings and stuffed them into a wastebasket that served as a temporary valise. The other woman's scream dissipated to an annoying snivel as she reached for a pack of cigarettes, lit a fag, and stared at the two like a fire-breathing serpent. They dashed down the stairs but the front door was dead-bolted from the outside—the madam wanted to insure that none of her stable mares would take a canter in the middle of the night.

They darted for the back door when a thunderous *bang* clapped through the vestibule. Madam Fanny was screaming demon-inspired obscenities and pointing a pistol with mortal intent. Goldman pumped the clip of .45 full-metal jackets into her torso. The high-velocity shells pushed her rotund silhouette to the back door, where she dropped like three hundred pounds of blood-soaked pork rind. The odious waft of post-mortem sex, gunpowder, and the shrieks from the prostitutes brewed into a sour purée of a good plan gone bad.

He grabbed baby Ruth by the hand and moved with exigency to the door. He pushed the limp body of the madam out of the way and pulled the door open. The two ran across the street, but before they could get to the car another volley of shots cracked through the wee hour, penetrating his car with echoed thuds and splitting the tranquility of the predawn bird songs. Goldman yelled for Ruthie to duck and, in one move, trained his .38 and fired three rounds directly into the carved trunk of Wyoming Joe. He drifted and swayed, like a hulking redwood, before his tree form slammed to the ground so hard that the tremor vibrated through the asphalt. The two jumped into the Chrysler and sped off, rippling the blacktop road like loose carpet. Ruthie turned with a concluding gaze for an age that had ended. The house of horrors left her feeling like a pillar of salt, frozen in the memory of the only life she could remember.

*   *   *

They trekked through the dark remote byways of the farm country and Goldman made the unilateral decision that LA would be their refuge. They could not, or would not, say a word. Driving alone with Ruthie Lee was like meeting his daughter for the first time. He made cautious glances off her placid surface, but each time turned his head before she noticed. He knew how to act around Eurika, but not Ruthie—this was different, she was his baby now and all recriminations were supplanted by the supernumerary sensation of being a dad. They then traded coded epigrammatic stares, like fused windows pulling back curtains that kept out an unwelcome world. She moved her hand to his and squeezed it tight. They exchanged crystal-lake reflections, luminous apparitions baiting one another as the rumble of the V8 lulled them into a false calm and assured providence of their *moonlight drive*. Goldman knew that she didn't know he was her father and he wanted to return her affections, only now it would be different. She couldn't have known, and he thought that, to her, he was her knight-errant who had saved her from the dragon's lair and that now the two would be forever tied in a lovers' slipknot.

The newly conjoined coalesced into a single stanza and *I am in love with us* was the only thought that ran through their throbbing heads and massaged their aching hearts. He lifted her palm, which was holding his so tight that his fingers fell to sleeping. He brought the back of her hand to his mouth and it kissed it; he felt something warm and moist with a taste twinge of copper. He glanced in the rearview mirror and eyed a smattering of blood across his lips. He then looked at the hand that was holding his daughter's and saw that it was sealed in a coagulated red sheen.

He yanked the car over and flicked on the dome light. Like a diaphanous mirage, Ruthie Lee's death-mask looked faintly upon him. Goldman tore open her coat; the middle of her abdomen was sopped in blood. For some inconceivable reason she hadn't told him that back at the shoot-'em-up she had been stung by a wild bee moving faster than the speed of sound.

With catastrophe-driven panic, he pulled her from the car and laid her down in front of the headlights on the full-moon gravel road. He unbuttoned her dress and was instantly vacuumed by the gravity of the gut wound. She never cried or winced once in pain, but took her licks and was not about to complain.

Her life was ebbing and the snake of transience coiled around his princess with a circuitous *hssss*. He found himself paralyzed and defenseless, abandoned by any *raison d'être*, like an iridescent torch where illusions hide behind the truth of a dying flame that could not light another; two candles slowly burning, flickering, hiding its fury, promises begging the two to hurry up and wait.

"I love you, Ruthie Lee."

She looked one more time at Goldman through a grand and imposing door that was about to close, the air from her vernal lungs pushing against her baby-back ribs to air her last.

"I love you too . . . Daddy."

Her soul took flight from the only habitat it had known for four years and a decade. She relaxed lightly in the arms of a father she now knew, and, like a birthday dress that was hardly worn, her folded light was placed neatly in the drawer of impossible worlds and she was suddenly no more. Goldman lay prostrate before the Chrysler's headlights, heaping dust and gravel on his head, mourning in a river of salted last rites.

He put her back in the car and drove through the endless rows of peach trees. He spotted a tractor and upon it found a shovel. Between two peach trees he dug for two hours until the hole was deep enough to serve as an eternal bed for his fallen fruit. He ceremoniously placed her into the vented tomb and covered her face with a red bandana. Like a senseless machine, he robotically placed shovel after shovel on the stunning corpse that once was a piece of him, now forever interred in the fetal position of the Earth's womb. He stood over the sacrosanct ground, an unwilling witness to another fire-by-birth die before his eyes, before it had been able to walk, or even to run. He would miss her and he would miss them, he would miss what they shared and what they showed, the love that was there for the giving and the love that they would never know.

XXXVII

Goldman thought he would leave Napa with a bound and a bang, but miscalculated badly, and like someone beaten by a sock full o' nails, he crawled out in want and whimpers. The only thing that amended his flattened world had upended, and the only meaning that absolved his black collar crimes had ended; the urn that held any hope was now hopelessly broken. Minuscule mental monsters hurled hot-air remarks, territorial tags on his bromide walls, lampooning the death of his daughter. There was a squawking yowl that percolated from the bottom of his barrel that he would never understand, but which would live on with him in some unredeemed form. He felt wholly dropkicked to his nuclear core as he drove nonstop to LA in a China syndrome burn. He couldn't sleep or even rest along the inexorable Highway 1, pulling the graveyard shift in the factory of his automated soul. The journey had become the destination, his hypnotic highway to hell.

There were vituperative accusations that swathed his daughter's reflection in white-hot heat, then plunged her image into arctic blue waters, and her dipped memory foamed and steamed through the scathing cracks of Goldman's mind. He knew he was on the tipping side of a tight-wire act, and if he were to carve out some kind of survival then he would have to blot out all recollections of her. She was gone, and there was nothing he could do about it.

He continued southbound, on the Pacific Coast Highway, which was picturesque and, under ordinary circumstances, would have been something to be pleasured by, but it left him feeling like a microbe, cultured under the worst of septic circumstances. As he rolled closer to LA, familiar revenant gnomes hitched a ride in his head and he wasn't sure if he was ready to reenter the soup cauldron of his past.

He got as far as Malibu when he was struck with the notion to pull over and take in the view, or maybe it was road fatigue. He only knew that he had to get out of the static trappings of the car's memory or he would pressure cook into a pestilential stew. He drove the Chrysler down a dirt road to a lookout that afforded a vista of the Pacific. He pulled up next to a beat-up bench, exited the car, and was instantly smacked with an onshore breeze that massaged his tracing paper sensibilities with nuances of clemency.

He sat on the bench and tried to decompress from the unremitting ache of the circadian events. What followed was a motionlessness that transcended his self-denunciation and the doldrums of his ill-boded prospects, like a mental patient whose obfuscating hallucinations are stripped of all power and are reduced to passing contrivances. He was still, still like the soymilk moon that remained suspended from the night before, interposed, tide-pulled, impersonal nothingness.

He took off his shoes and planted his feet on the ground. The warm sun caressed his face as he doffed his blood-stained shirt to share the sensation with the rest of his body. The slight onshore breeze blew kindly through his longish hair and the five hundred mile knot that was lodged in his throat slid passed his apple and dissolved in his vinegar gut. He was close to the charged Earth again, reenergized by its electromagnetic pulse; his hair slightly raised and arced with tiny popping sounds as electrons scraped from his tingling scalp. It was a highly unusual sensation and he guessed that it had something to do with the ocean's amniotic draw. Nature had the ability to administer first aid to those conscious of its significance, and could coiffure entangled habituations and coagulate emotional hematomas of a bruised soul.

The moment seemed to reconcile the notion that he ended where his skin stopped; that the universe is not particle but a wave grid system of one—but he felt anything but one, as he tried to reassemble himself like a straw-stuffed scarecrow. He knew chance was a dog not to be feared, but fate was a mean bitch that was not to be trusted. He finally resigned himself to the fact that nothing really mattered, including the death of his baby Ruth. There was a sense of collective knowingness that permeated down to the hearth of his fire, and the ancients that inhabited his psyche were busy with sympathy for all things, even him.

He felt that he could sit on that bench for eons, so long as the electrical discharge of his troubled mind was safely grounded, but the earth broke hard under his calloused soles and he opted out of any cosmic consoling, preferring to remain shamefaced and sullen. He noticed that the bench was made of an old redwood surfboard. He had not seen a surfboard since he was stationed in Hawaii. He recalled how he loved floating in the azure water, catching waves, braising in the tropical sun as the sultry trade winds of the South Pacific stroked his tawny skin.

He closed his eyes again and continued to commune with the sun and the distant sounds of the surf crashing on the white sandy beach below. He then heard the far off accent of jousting and corporate laughter. At first he feared it might be the defecting voices that from time to time tormented his barking spider mind, but he was sure these sounds were real. He walked to the overhanging crag and saw a dozen tanned dots bobbing in the glassy turquoise-green water. A healthy swell rolled in from the deep blue, quickly turning into a translucent formidable sea-green peak that peeled perfectly from right to left. The sun-bronzed dots turned into erected wave riders as they mobbed the same break, laughing, yelling, and pushing. The sight cheered Goldman, but it was a weird thing to see tragedy and joy laminate together in space and time. His daughter freshly entombed in the cold, cold ground, while these surfers enjoyed the warm, warm fun, as if inoculated from his existential crisis and the virus of death.

He decided to traverse the steep trail down to the beach to get a better look, and maybe a dunking in the water would extinguish the smoldering pyre of his daughter's memory. He changed his shirt, stuffed a couple of books into a bag, and started down the trail. It was a private cove where the local beachcombers had bivouacked. Static radios were blaring, ice chests were full of beer, and bikini-clad girls babbled with one another like wannabe society matrons waiting for their wave warriors to turn into men of respectability.

From the beach he could see how hefty the waves were. Only the most practiced could make the steep drop. The break would pitch hard and then peel perfectly off a pile of concrete rubble from the ruined foundations of a Victorian hotel that had collapsed decades before. The concrete debris went out far and deep enough to create waves that lined up for a hundred yards. He found a place to park his perineum, and for hours remained mesmerized by the surfers. The sun had set and the last surfer washed ashore. The beer drinking, ass grabbing, and joking went on past twilight, and the same phosphorescent moon that had witnessed the shootings from the night before haunted him like an inescapable orb.

He was drawn to the revelers like an ochre moth to a luminescent globe. The gang looked to be in their late teens and early twenties. He was just shy of his thirtieth birthday and suddenly felt like a geriatric orphan who was not worthy of adoption. Every now and then the guys would look at him cross-haired. He wasn't sure if they liked him or wanted him to make like a bird and get the flock out of there. They built a fire, which made Goldman feel like a recluse, an ancient canine lurking in the dark, waiting for someone to throw him scraps from the tribal table. The guys were drinking hard and started goading him with taunts.

"Hey, buddy! This is a private party."

"If you're looking for a beer handout you can forget it, you fucking bum!" said another, which was followed by castigating laughter.

The word "bum" tangled Goldman's protuberant feelers and made him feel uninhabitable again. He hated the sensation of being a stranger, especially when people were hostile, like a stray dog that instead of being thrown a bone is greeted with a rock pelting. Still, he longed to be in their company, even if it meant being degraded by their impertinent remarks. He knew the kind of person he was, but he was looking for people he wanted to be. A man cannot be anything until he is ready to see, and a spectacled outlook was still his only point of view.

He didn't know the first thing about these foreign natives, but he had a deep-seated need to bond, nothing serious, just an honorary membership into the clan. He didn't even care if they knew his name, just so long as he could sit next to the fire and lose himself in their customs, secret signals, and tribal codes. For the rest of the evening the party raged as he sat alone in the coal-pigment night, listening to the revelry of testosterone and estrogen-driven youth and the unrelenting bombardment of the surf. With a heavy dose of heartache, he kissed the owl goodnight and nested with his hooting dreams.

*   *   *

He awoke the next morning to the smell of dying embers that filtered through his nose like a smoldering specter. A white sheet had been draped over him and the dew pressed against his silhouette like a beach blanket Shroud of Turin. He sat up and looked down one stretch of the sand and then the other, but saw not a soul. The morning was chilly and he was grateful that one of the beachcombers was thoughtful enough to have covered him, even if it was only a dirty linen sheet. He was hungry and rummaged though the discarded trash from the previous night's soiree. He managed to dig up a cold dog without a bun and some damp potato chips. After washing the sand off the frankfurter, he devoured it like a scavenging seagull. He found a beer that had not been opened and used it to chase down the soggy chips.

The swell was still working off the broken concrete jetty, a beautiful right that peeled like an unbroken apple skin. The surfers had left their boards leaning against the cliff. An empty wave with a choice of redwoods seemed a waste, and Goldman was sorely tempted to commandeer one of the logs—*carpe diem* in two secs—but not on this day. Still, he wanted to be in that water, but wondered if he even remembered how to surf. His daughter's death still beset his mind with a drawn and quartered tearing sensation, and he craved any distraction to liquidate the stultifying uselessness of his tormented parts.

He left the campsite barefoot and disheveled and walked down the beach with the dirty white sheet draped over him like a high-plains drifter of comparative religions. His single urge was to put one foot in front of the other until his thorn-piercing subsided; abscesses from his emotional inflammation were still draining through weep holes of a ground-soaked heart, and he could not be still. He walked the entire day; his survival system kept him moving through unwanted opportunities to focus on his vagrant thoughts and the certainty of his uncertainties. It was nearing sunset again, and he had made the Malibu pier. He thought he would be hungry, but surprisingly was not, although he did need to quench his thirst. He found a beach house and took liberties with the water hose, then parked himself on the sand to rest, and fell fast a-nap.

He didn't know how long he was dead to the world, but his mind had traipsed in a familiar nightmare. It was always him alone in a room painted in unreserved blackness. Something was lurking, a malevolent entity that could only be sensed but never seen. The thing breathed with whizzing gasps, inches from his face, whispering obscenities to his virgin parts. As always, he tried to wake, but instead slipped deeper, like someone whose feet were tied to stones, descending into darkening principles of lateral terror. He thrashed on a hidden diabolic line and barbed himself clear from its aquiline snare. He opened his eyes, only to find them fixed on the Malibu sands.

Even in his dreams—especially in his dreams—near misses with notions of death were always inscrutable, and left him consorting with irreconcilable elements that dared understanding. From his bag, he pulled out Kazuo's notebook. He flipped through the pages until his eyes locked onto a single line: *You will make bad choices on levels where you are unaware.* With a sustained shudder, the words struck a wire in Goldman's grid system. *To be aware that you are aware, and to live by intention not by accident,* the writer had penned. Up until then, Goldman had felt he was an actor's accident in someone else's play and was tired of being a passive observer of his own experience. All his days he had looked to people and books to interpret his existence, but it just seemed like a lot of bowel-moving to generations of the same old shit.

Kazuo felt the same way, and wrote that all internal activity must cease, that being still was our only job. It was about unconscious struggles with intractable worlds; the burden of reality's illusion was that it perceives disconnection, while the substructure of the universe was a sea of quantum fields in an all-encircling colossus of one coherent charge. Subatomic particles resonate at an auditory frequency. If deep-winded binary chants could vibrate at these frequencies then, with practice, it might be possible to clear meridians and re-wire energy vortexes that could coalesce into a multidimensional whorl.

Kazuo had worked with a physics professor from UC Berkeley, a closet metaphysician who also studied audio frequencies and their supposed paranormal effects. His experiments were highly secretive and if the school's faculty had gotten wind of it he would have forfeited his tenure and be stigmatized as a kook of pseudoscience. They investigated different chanting techniques and found that the deeper tones emanating from the lower diaphragm were more effective in establishing higher amplitudes and lower frequencies.

What was most significant and effectual was to play recordings of chanting to subjects standing in the Vitruvian pentagram while bombarded by an audio crossfire piped through a quadraphonic speaker system. Administered in this manner, the five notes had the theoretical ability to marshal quantum energy into endless potential. A real sense of peace, serenity, and love seemed to be the initial effect, healings of not only the mind but also the body: IQ increased, deep sleep cycles, significant boosts in comprehension, and in general, an enhanced sense of connection with others.

The recorded tones were used as audio therapy on patients from the mildly depressed to the delusional and schizophrenic, even acute medical conditions responded in a positive way. The two thought that they might be on the cusp of something significant, but then Kazuo had to leave for Japan. When the war broke out, all experiments ended, but Kazuo was determined to carry on the work even after his conscription into the Japanese Army. The notebook was filled with pages of mathematical equations and handwritten graphs, bell curves, and physics jargon that fried Goldman's limited understanding but, intuitively, he was able to grasp potential psychic panoramas that he had never been aware of before.

* * *

He continued to spend his days on the same stretch of Malibu beach. He had not eaten for a week, and yet, oddly, felt fine. In fact, the thought of food made him queasy. He continued to wander down the coast; it seemed to facilitate focus on intangibles that he might not have deigned rational before. He shed the sour memories of his past like discarded clothing, and his usual truculence to the idea that he was deserving of any good thing was transformed mile-by-mile, into blithe assumptions of remote worthiness. Maybe Kazuo's theory had something to do with it, but whatever the cause, his emotional load seemed to lighten the farther he wandered. Another week and a half had passed and he made it as far as Long Beach. He rested there for a couple of days and then headed back north.

He continued to read Kazuo's notebook, the contents of which were starting to gel, and he found places in his metaphysical library where its postulations could finally be indexed. According to Kazuo, there is a bedrock connectedness in all things whereby electromagnetic fields, general relativity laws, and light are wholly compatible. The trick was to integrate these laws with Plank's world of subatomic chaos, which according to him was too random to be likeminded with general relativity. Yet the anarchy of inner space defined the building blocks of an orderly universe. Kazuo believed this inconsistency was reflected in the unconscious world of humanity. There was real chaos in the human spirit that was in direct conflict with the tidy fabric of the universe. He was convinced that the East-meets-West Tibetan-five-note Vitruvian stance was the answer to man's woes. Still, it was not the silver bullet that he had hoped to fire.

His last theory proposed a radiation quotient. Both alpha and beta particles have an electric charge and mass, and are quite likely to interact with other atoms in their path. He believed that if the human endocrine system could be charged with sufficient levels of radiation, and combined with the Tibetan-Vitruvian protocol, then there was the potential for a symbiotic interface: energy and matter, spirit and flesh, quantum intercourse and the spawning of a new hybrid human. Until the day Kazuo died, the missing element had eluded him, and maybe it even exceeded his proto-scientific talents.

Goldman was grateful that Kazuo's notebook did not end up in the belly of the giant snake. He even felt an obligation to run with the metaphysical baton that had been unintentionally, or maybe intentionally, handed to him. He had limited or no knowledge of the subject and felt unqualified to carry on such a grand task, yet streams of irradiated excitement leapt in his belly and seduced him like a trove of trinkets in the hands of a Manhattan Indian.

He found a secluded area and stood in the pentagram with one palm turned up and the other facing down, as Kazuo had explained. The palm facing up would gather energies, and the palm facing down would ground them in a completed circuit. He could hear the five tones in his head as clearly as he remembered playing them on the piano as a kid, and hummed them loud and proud. It seemed ridiculous, but with patience he started to feel warm, life affirming, and still. After a time he had chanted himself into a hypnotic state of relative ease. Like a tuning fork vibrating with cosmic communion, Kazuo's five notes pulsed through Goldman in bio-luminous waves of unrelenting bliss.

He felt devoured by the immensity of the universe, while at the same time swirled in a feral energy that enveloped him like a hungry lover. It was like the exterior and the interior becoming one, as if the whole cosmos were now inside him and infinity had measurable distance. Parabolic waves massaged his innards and his evasive loose ends coalesced and reorganized. Like a somatic shaman, his consciousness was super-radiant and rippled in a cascade of lucidity. His life's film role had stopped and translated into a single photograph, one frozen frame festooned with metaphysical party favors handed out for free.

He was devoid of any need for meaning. There was no sense of movement or linear spans, just the infinite now and washings of deliverance, redeemably pristine, soul scouring. The Samadhi experience breached his mental defenses and his monkey theorem mind wanted to leap from the limb he was out on. It was like death with its gentle sweet stream, carrying the unaware in posterior bliss, but erotic terror in the sense that the soul was being molested without consent. He tried to pull out, and only with considerable struggle did he reenter the three-dimensional stratosphere, like a comet dashing across the sky, a prince of the air, a supernormal oddity. Time and ego, the dueling devils, had been obliterated and what had felt like a five-minute excursion into an ageless frontier had, in actuality, gone on for two hours.

With transcendental reverence he walked all the way back to Malibu and the surfers' cove where the perfect waves broke. The quiet dominion of the dawning sky gave way to oblique shafts of sunlight, and he was exhausted. He hiked up the steep trail to where he had left his car a month earlier and it was as if time held no authority. Other than an almost flat tire, nothing about the car had changed. A hunger pang that had been a mildly annoying candle was now a roaring flame for sustenance. The embers from the surfers' previous night's fire smoldered to the top of the cliff with the scent of food, and for the first time in weeks he felt famished. He figured he might be able to scrounge up something to eat in the camp, and maybe get some sleep while it was still to be had.

XXXVIII

He got to the cove and there wasn't a goofy-footer or ho-dad to be had, nothing but the filtrate ruins from a previous Bacchus night. He rummaged through the camp's leftovers and found a half loaf of bread, a few chilled grilled dogs, and some soused cheese. But to him, it was desert stones turned to manna, after wandering the beach wilderness for forty straight days without food. He hastily slapped together a hotdog sandwich and ate with such fervor that he bit his tongue twice, as if mastication was a forgotten gastronomic art.

He crammed the food into his mouth with dog-eat-dog urgency, but it was difficult to swallow a dry meal that kept lodging in his food pipe with eye-popping alarm. He rummaged for liquid respite and found an ice chest containing beer—a lot of beer. Between three cheese and hotdog sandwiches and four fermented malts, his fasted parts reconstituted and for the first time in weeks he felt fleshly. He then peered out at the rolling break with its glass-like silky perfection. There was a nice four to six foot swell and not a salt-geek in the drink. He had been so hungry that he was caught unaware of the caterwauling surf or of the unattended boards that were lined up against the craggy rock face . . . *carpe diem*, in two secs.

He dragged one of the wooden Goliaths to where the water lapped over his blackened feet, hoping to get a session in before the surfers were aware of the verboten offense. He stripped down to the skin suit that his mother had given him and paddled out enmeshed in a foreseeable nonce. He was spooked at first by liquid macerating snarls that growled louder by the stroke, and felt he might not be equal to the task. But when the next set lumbered in, he disconnected all trailing doubts, and his muscle memory denuded any diffidence.

He was wobbly and arrhythmic at first, but his instincts returned to their appointed places, and he rode the inaugural wave all the way to the sand. He paddled back out, and lost himself in the Zen of pristine waves and the cadence of a new lunar tide; a hermetic subsistence of solitary sealed surf, impervious to ruminations of his past or gloomy premonitions of his future. If the waves continued, there would only be the perennial now and a reconciling of his ambivert nature. By the session's end he was so rubber-armed that he could hardly bear the board across the sandy parapet.

He had not noticed the gathering crowd—and not just any crowd, but a burgeoning surfer nation: wave-running archetypes and off-center lunatics of a new surf ethos. They ruled the shores from Malibu to San Diego and were at Libido Cove for their annual jamboree.

"Hi!" Goldman said with manufactured ambiguity.

One of the guys threw him a beach towel. He wrapped it around his naked waist and returned the board with pomp and reverence. The largest of the surfers, Big Jim—a six-foot-four, two hundred and forty-five pound sea creature with dancing pectoral muscles—approached him with scrawled eyes and a looming scowl.

"You got some balls, my friend. That's my tree you're riding."

"No one was here, I just thought . . ." Before he could finish the shaky apology, Big Jim swung for the bleachers, but Goldman's eye was keen, and he slipped the haymaker with uncharacteristic imperturbability. "I don't want any trouble, I'll just leave," he said, fish faced and meek.

He backed down the sand like a mole crab as another surfer dropped to all fours, blocking his unseen and inverted path. He tripped flat on his back, like an upended crustacean, wobbling back and forth in a laughable attempt to right himself. Big Jim picked him up by his collarbones and threw him against the cliff where he landed ass-to-balls first into a sandy bramble patch. With one hand Goldman pulled thorns from his gluteus, while with the other he scratched blinding sand from his carbolic eyes.

The two beach gladiators squared off and Big Jim proceeded to put the hurt on. After a merciless piston-pumping-pounding, Goldman disentangled himself from the meaty clutches of the philistine giant and his marine training kicked in. In three moves he had the big man on his back, dead bolted in a paralyzing arm lock. It was humiliating, but Goldman's salty nuts pressed up against Big Jim's face was more agonizing than the radius-cracking arm-bar and had him squealing like a schoolgirl.

"Okay, let go, let go!"

Goldman let go and sprung into a combat stance, thinking he would have to take on the entire surfer nation. The crowd hung back in vanquished silence as Big Jim stood, massaging and re-rotating his tweaked arm, still facialized with chagrin. The tension stretched, then snapped with the recoil of collective laughter.

"Where did you learn to fight like that?" Big Jim humbly asked.

"Yeah, and where did you learn to surf like that?" asked another.

As quickly as the up-in-arms clash had started, it was over. The crowd sauntered back to Libido Cove, where the national front for the liberation of postmodern layabouts continued with slipshod verve and laissez-faire vigor.

One of the guys escorted Goldman to the day camp like a deserved pledge. "My name is Andy. Ah, don't worry about Big Jim, he comes across as a real bloody stool most of the time, but you gave him a good cocking he won't soon forget. But seriously, your cutback's real tough. Where do you surf?"

"Oahu," he said with a winsome grin.

"And what do they call you?"

"Goldman."

*   *   *

For weeks Goldman buried himself in the cove, and let the sands of the beach run through him, right side up and upside down, in hourglass tides with no recollection of their granulated passing. The surfer nation wasn't sure at first, but beer by beer and wave by wave they got used to Goldman's physical casing and his divers ways, gradually taking a fiduciary shine to him. He was an unquantifiable quirk, with his bedraggled kitchen mop hair that had grown almost to shoulder-length, and a thick carpet beard not seen since the revenant days of the Civil War. He made for an archetypal mascot and earned the honorary title of "Rasputin". They admired his surfing prowess enough to get him his own board. Not that anyone spent money, but Big Jim and another surfer liberated and rehabbed the redwood board that was used as a bench at the top of the cliff, and Goldman employed it with such frequency that it was continually spongy to the touch.

Goldman liked being around the serenading sounds of a young crowd, the "oomph" and "ahhh" of guys in their pistol packin' twenties. It reminded him of the days in the Corps, when boys-to-men fought under his command for the fate of the free world, armed with a carbine and a Hershey bar. There was an enchanted insanity about this straightjacket period in a young warrior's life; the weaned suckled years from mama's teat to the waxing transition of meat-eating manhood and its uncharted wasteland. He loved their spontaneity and the endless chop sessions that were the stock-in-trade of high-capacity testosterone factories. Sharpening one another with X-Acto knife filleting wit and scorching third-degree burns, never self-conscious and full of alacritous daring where the word "doubt" had no meaning.

The balmy night flavors precipitated madcap, rough 'n' tumble frontier sprawling and Goldman loved sitting by the fire, funny-boning at the endless energy expended on zilch. For the first, time since he had the ability or desire to recall anything, he enjoyed drinking with people. It was like he lived his drunken yen through this tartan tribe and to burn brain cells on boozily-instigated nonsense was well worth the cellular expenditure. Wrestling matches and tests of strength were a constant, and competition for the women was fierce. They were an endless source of entertainment and a curious assortment of composite parts, which made up the organism of the clan, and he reveled in its hyper-extended adolescence.

Goldman became the official leader, in an unofficial and constituent way. His enigmatic and bohemian quality thrived with the band of brothers and he felt open and unframed by his normal tableau self. Every night the parties would *beer* up like piñata-whacking fiestas, summit, and then *wine* down the soporific path of suggestibility, the lithe reeds bending easily to Goldman's placatory lead.

He commandeered their side winding leaf-mold minds with tongues of serpentine reticulation, loud whispers behind the red-coal fire that cast tinted heat waves in front of his image with cult-obscurities and iridescent qualities. He tailor-made designer chic statements, and dressed to the gills non-relative, ambiguous teachings that could only be understood by more questions which could only be understood by more questions. He opened veranda views to horizon line mysteries, vanishing points to nothing, and bedeviled their young incorruptibility with affectations of masquerade.

No one had repartee on his level and Goldman pitied them; a flock of bleating sheep with congenital amentia that could not think past the end of their dicks or the bottom of their bellies. But their minds had not yet been closed by the world, and their hearts were paragons of the sublime. It was not they that were seduced, but *he* who was beguiled by hegemony and his ascending mini-cult-star status.

He had always been uncomfortable with attention, yet the crazed beach soirees facilitated something in him that needed plaudits and praise, legitimizing his bastard complex by tribal inclusion. Goldman loved to do philosophy shots and contemplate the meaning of tequila, but in time, the wild merrymaking decreased, and the mystical fireside chats expanded as the surfers' minds were overstuffed with Goldman's lumpy ideas and loquacious speeches. He felt a binding obligation to lead the beach horde, and had become the heralded bearer, the first and last mystic to Kazuo's mystery, a virulent creed for a new prophet and his neophyte beach blanket faction.

What was supposed to be a half-hour road break in the beginning of May had turned into a summer hiatus, infiltrating the ides of September. Every day he entertained the call of the road, but he had become entrenched in a vice lifestyle that was now a habit. He proved a didactic leader, admired and maybe even loved, although the majority of the time he brooded and felt numbly alone. Most of the guys suffered from cranialrectumitis, flapdoodle blokes living on rations of beer, tits, and waves, and it was impossible for Goldman to relate, but there was one guy he took a shine to. Andy was different; he possessed a resolute sensitivity and an aristocratic intellect that reasonably complemented Goldman's philosophical and metaphysical penchants.

The two bonded in an atypical way, like big brother, second cousin twice removed partisan twins, yet Andy was besotted with unease by Goldman's imperious meekness and his collective contradictions. For all of Goldman's yawning insights, he was still plagued with flawed thinking patterns that Andy felt needed to be challenged, but he didn't feel confident enough to volley philosophical ping-pong balls against Goldman's atom splitting ways-of-the-world wit.

One day, Andy stumbled upon Goldman while he was engaged in a thickening meditation session, complete with the five-pointed Virtuvian pentagram and bellowing Kazuo's five notes. He watched Goldman chant robotically with a stone-like calm, his outstretched arms unbending under the weight of gravity, his splayed legs never quavering from fatigue. When he reemerged he was only slightly startled by Andy, who looked on with tyro curiosity.

"Don't look so surprised, Andy, this is the future."

"The future?" Andy quizzed with mild leanings of confusion.

Goldman opened up the notebook and started quoting excerpts like a Kazuo-ian ideologue. He went into detail about Kazuo's work: the five note chant, the Vitruvian pentagram, and its potential revelation to the world. Andy was halfheartedly skeptical and Goldman agreed to let him disagree, but he was taken by the irreducible propositions that were pregnant with potential and mind-expanding debris, which left him still begging the question.

XXXIX

The summer solstice was in its final degree and last calls for the road were announced with a disinclined salute. Goldman's era with the compound republic of surfers had been like a tour of duty, and his well-earned remission of sins seemed assuaged. The months on the beach were a sorely needed anodyne prescription, and the frivolous inactivity of summer dissipation—where he ruled from the sandcastle of *surf*dom—would have to be relinquished before the contractions of a new autumnal equinox. He had earned the title of Alpha Dog Rasputin without having to assert any macho shit or marking territory with odious social spray. Where he would go, he wasn't sure, but to fritter his life away on the beach was too addicting and in his sun-bleached bones he felt a greater calling.

The guys looked up to him as the undisputed Kahuna par excellence, and even the women convened around his status. At first the cliquish Gidgets thought he was weird and scary, but unconsciously they were wooed by his exotic good looks and unrefined cold charm. Eventually he had run the sex-gambit so that they became immovable magnets stuck to his refrigerated door. His long dark hair and beard with blond streaks, his semi-olive complexion, and dark eyes were vaginally provoking. But when draped in his white sleeping sheet he projected a toga-draped persona, and the young ladies with Christ-Eros fixations easily succumbed. The rest of the guys wanted to emulate him, and all those clean-cut American boys grew their hair and beards in the summer of 1950.

The waning, warm summer nights were now proper tribal gatherings, not the riotous beach bashes that they once knew—no better. The clan had become secretive, and would sit around the campfire seduced by the rhythm of crashing waves and binging on the reflective brew of Goldman's distilled philosophies and metaphysical moonshine; alterations to their consciousness, where exotic knowledge is the fermented drink of choice, novel witnesses to a revelator who had decoded the encryptions of Kazuo's theories.

The surfers believed it was the genesis of a new law, and a new religion, with a new savior. Goldman spoke with such shibboleth authority that it reminded him of Jonathan's father back in the old days at the tent revivals—only *his* revival was a cry to metaphysical repentance and a gleaning inebriation from the god of impersonal logic. Control, for Goldman, had become a neurotic narcotic, and he knew that he could easily overdose without steely temperance. It was seductive and he secretly thrived on the authority buzz released from his pleasure glands. Feral sounds of demagoguery filled the beach, and he seemed enhanced, not corrupted, by his hubristic penchant for more power.

Goldman's devotion to Mina still manacled his thoughts with irons of fidelity. He found that his nightly bonfire of the vanities was turning into a beachfront Communist-rally side dish as much as the main metaphysical course: heaping helpings of existential political goulash. He still felt beset by self-opposition as he grappled between delusional narcissism and practical self-deprecation; a splitso-schizo, bisected right down the middle, and if he was to be their leader, he needed to be a sensible Commie-commissar, not a clipped-wing deity symptomatically in need of psychiatric intervention.

The time spent at the cove was not entirely frivolous, or nearly as serious as the cult of personality. He used the diminishing days for meditation and to think and act in deeper abstractions, whatever that meant. It was hard work, but it was his moil, his labor, and his itchy house where his sweat was dried with sheets of fiberglass insulation kept wadded in his attic head. He had finished reading Kazuo's notebook. The writings were like drinking water from a fire hose. He didn't understand it all, but what he did understand he used with padded-cell devotion: the chanting of the Tibetan five notes with the Vitruvian pentagram, the philosophy of stillness, and the awareness of a quantum continuum, pervasive in all things. It had taken him years to learn to just sit and think, and now he had learned to just sit.

*   *   *

September on the beach was magic, with its fleeting warm ginger days migrating into magenta sunsets of meteorological fall. The summer was about to expire, but there was still a good swell working, which produced some marathon days and had, in fact, been unimaginably epic the entire summer.

The surfers accounted it all to Goldman and the weird and wonderful effect he seemed to have on nature's rudiments. Never had they seen a summer without one day of coastal fog, but instead continuous sunshine and an endless supply of buxom-breasted waves with deep cleavage drops. And the phenomenon was not everywhere, but only at Libido Cove.

The Santa Ana winds were blowing offshore and the water was glass. There were plenty of waves that centripetally pulled on everyone, even the dolphins. They would line up a half dozen in a row like giant canned sardines, and dash down the face of a rolling wave with their snouts sticking out like bow rudders, snorting and grunting through crescent smiles, joined by seals who skipped across the surface like big black polished stones.

On the outside, Big Jim sat patiently, waiting for the occasional swell with extra size and juice. He was always bugged by a big man's complex and wanted to show the other guys that just because he was large didn't mean he was uncoordinated or slow and that he could master big waves without the advantage of a lower center of gravity. Goldman eyed him on sporadic large sets, lifted by a piece of the continental shelf, rolling like green translucent mountains all the way to shore. He decided to paddle out farther and share the wave wealth.

He was almost within a shout-out when a commotion unfolded before his disbelieving eyes. Big Jim was wearing a scuba suit to keep warm. For a big man he was sensitive to the water temperature, which always drew taunts from the rest of the guys. He had gotten off his board to undo the rubber beaver tail that was wrapped around his groin when from the water's depths he was hurled ten feet into the air with a serrated leviathan latched to his meaty drumstick. The fifteen-foot Great White made Big Jim look puny. The shark slammed back into the water with Big Jim's leg still clamped in its mechanical jaws and pulled him under in an expanding radius of blood. A few seconds later, he bobbed back up with a water-choked gasp and a vilely hoarse scream for help.

Goldman's initial impulse was to paddle for shore in a craven act of self-preservation, but something held him in place like a deeply emoted anchor, and a contrary yen propelled him hondo pronto to Big Jim's rescue. He paddled closer, through water turning different shades of puce and burgundy, in terror that the great fish was directly under him, with only three inches thick of lumber separating him from loss of life and limb and a digested prognosis; flickering frames of solidified panic, snapshots of flesh tearing, bone snapping, swallowed headfirst diaphanous scenarios. He grabbed Big Jim and hoisted him onto his board. His left leg was virtually bitten off—the only thing keeping it attached to him was a thin strip of black wetsuit.

Goldman hollered to the others with the fetid stench of death tweaking his chords, "Big Jim's been hit!"

"Yeah, we know, Big Jim surfs like shit," they wisecracked.

Goldman paddled for shore, trailed by a stream of blood and the amputated leg bobbing like an appendage cork when, the shark threw its head onto the back of his board and the other surfers scattered like frightened minnows. Oddly, the Great White just lay there, inexplicably not finishing the meal. It was as if it was curious as to why its quarry looked like a seal but didn't taste the same. It was an enormous hulk of cartilaginous meat predation, with a piece of Big Jim's wetsuit still clinched between its razors.

Goldman proceeded to punch the monster but it was like beating a sand-finished plaster wall. He then jammed his thumb into the shark's primordial eye and the animal slid back into the water in a well-mannered and polite exit. Goldman resumed paddling and the retinue of surfers escorted him to the safety of the beach.

They dragged Big Jim onto the sand as globs of oxygenated blood pumped with dizzying volume from the mangled stump. One of the surfers ran off to get help. It was bedlam as the boys screamed and spun like whirling dervishes, helpless and panic-throttled. Goldman's war experience kicked in and he immediately applied pressure to the thigh, but it continued to bleed at a saucer-eyed rate. It then occurred to him to have the guys dig a small crater in the sand, deep enough to accommodate Big Jim's lower body.

They placed him in the hole and Goldman had them realign his severed left leg to his thigh, as if to be arc welded together. They buried the lower half of his body, and Goldman had them stand on the sand to apply pressure. He had done this trick during the war and the compressed dirt helped to stem the blood flow until help could arrive. Big Jim drifted in and out of spooky consciousness with sporadic screams, violent twists, and a pallor as white as the sea salt that had dried on his anguished face.

Goldman knew it would be some time before real help would arrive and he feared that the hole they had dug for Big Jim would soon become a shallow grave. Then something came over him and the noises in his head curiously resolved themselves. Like the Colossus of Rhodes, Goldman stood and spread his legs over Big Jim, with his arms out level to his shoulders in the Vitruvian stance.

He turned one palm up to the sky and the other palm down to Big Jim's crown. He tilted his head back in an expostulated rejection of the situation and started chanting the five notes in deep resonating pitches that soon quieted everyone, even the painful wails of Big Jim. The surfers were dumbstruck, yet they respected Goldman's weirdness enough not to question the bizarre behavior. The chanting went on for a few minutes, and then abruptly stopped. With liberating sadness and dewy-eyed tears, he slid his bloody hand onto Big Jim's forehead. Infrared heat leapt from his fingers and Big Jim responded, if only slightly.

Like stardust come to life, untamed energy bolted though Goldman's fingers as he drifted in and out of a Dark Continent trance. The deeper he went, the more frightening the experience. It was like an out-of-body occurrence that somehow violated the sacred constitution of his very essence: terror driven, but cajoled with inter-cognition and persistent bliss. The same inward perimeter force he had experienced in previous interior forays had finally sucked him down its conical vortex, all colors turning white in the centrifuge of his brain, then nothing. When the unknown is squarely faced, then all is known, or at least that's the way it felt.

He opened his eyes, looking absently at a scene that had gone from strewn chaos to placid control, and all symptoms of the emotionally charged storm had passed. He looked at the guys, who were at first mutable, but now rack focused into view. He didn't know if he was imagining it, but virtue had left him, a *prana*-based discharge of sorts. He remembered the lamb on the ship in the Bikini Islands—it was the same sensation. He shook his hands, then wrung them out and applied them to Big Jim's head again until the color of redemption returned to his pasty face.

"What's going on?" Big Jim asked with granted respite. He tried to move but the guys were still standing on the sand that encased his legs. He squirmed hard with his two hundred and forty-five pound mass, and the guys jumped off.

"Jim, don't move, you've lost your leg," they shouted with infuriation. Big Jim rolled his eyes as if it was a badly delivered joke, and kicked his right leg out of the sand. The guys kept yelling with ominous forebodings, but when his left leg kicked out as well, the silence was louder than cellular tele-traffic at rush hour. Big Jim scrambled out of the hole, his limb, still bloodied and the wet suit was shredded, but there wasn't a trace of the mortal shark bite to be seen with a skeptical eye. Nobody said a word. They looked at one another in mirrored astonishment, then back to Big Jim, then to Goldman, in collapsed comprehension.

"Why am I covered in blood?" Big Jim asked, horror struck.

The guys volcanically erupted with molten lava yowls. They kept shouting that a shark had bitten his leg off and that Goldman had healed him. Big Jim couldn't remember the attack, but was convinced by the unbridled exuberance from the guys, the tattered wet suit, and the volume of blood that something scarier than death had occurred. The surfers then attached to Goldman like metal shavings to a positive pole, magnetized with iconic awe.

"What did you do?" they demanded.

Goldman stood with Big Jim's blood still smeared on his face and hands and shook his head in thunderstruck disbelief. The surfers then gamboled down the beach declaiming to all, the apparent miracle of the ages.

*   *   *

The word spread and Goldman was daily besieged by a pitiable assortment of beach people suffering a myriad of ailments. He was confused and patently denied that he had done anything, but the act was self-evident, yet it seemed like it had happened to someone else. Crowds now followed him around like rudderless souls drifting in his photon-radiated wake. He didn't know how to act around the surfers anymore and often had to leave Libido Cove to wander the beach like a directionless sand fly, just to be alone. Every time he returned, the crowds grew bigger, needier, and more desperate. Big Jim had always respected Goldman for pinning him—no man had ever been able to do that—but after the leg incident, he all but worshipped him and was his ever-accompanying shadow and protector, chasing the crowds away with the ferocity of a junkyard dog.

Every day, the sycophantic beach mob grew more frantic and scary, bombarding Goldman with healing requests and even giving him money. He felt embarrassed and with dismissive exasperation tried to give the money back, but they were having none of it. When he could take no more, he slipped out in the middle of the night, lit by the exploits of a new nitrogen star.

For a succinct season he had been a Pythagorean cult leader and a teacher to a brood he never really knew but, like a fly in the ointment, belonged. The experience had aroused something sleeping in his bed that was waiting to be awakened. Power had been bestowed upon his charge as the initiator of some great work, but was laced with a nagging sense of vice and adversarial dominion. He fired up the Chrysler and was back on the road again, with the words, *Now, where was I?* humming through his sun-bleached head, and the V8 rumbling through his firewall legs.

XL

Yesterday is history, tomorrow is a mystery, but today is a gift, that's why they call it the present. Was it possible that he really did have a present: the gift of healing? Something spine chilling, weird, and wonderful had unveiled itself, but the bewildering details of the event would remain inscrutable. There seemed to be a new sign hanging over Goldman; Aquarius was under the precession of the equinoxes and expiations of a new moon was moving in critical degrees across his celestial equator, luring him back to the land of a million broken dreams. He would follow his ancient compass and ditch himself in the LA illusion as a much-needed guest by an unwanted host.

LA was not a destination for Goldman, but a metaphor of brute reckoning and perilous splendor. Why he felt compelled to be there, he did not know. Maybe it was Mina, or maybe it was just to put more distance between the memory of Ruthie Lee and fate's illicit plot twists. He had hoped that his time spent on the beach would be the mechanism for dismantling his yakking Babel towers, but now that he was in motion, his essence moved like a herd of wild turtles and mumbled like old women knitting with reckless abandon. He knew he could not erase the memory of his baby Ruth in one summer of inane dissipation and fantasy impulses. No amount of pretension would lessen its grip.

He had hoped that her memory would fade, and with it the ache that made his entire body throb and distorted his vision with bereaved connections to what might have been. He was shot to bits, but his mind kept shifting to the electric event on the beach, and thoughts of the impossible gamboled through his head like crazed gazelles. Did he really have something to do with Big Jim's leg being mended? Was it possible that Kazuo's extraordinary theories could be applied in the ordinary world, where abstract models become core realties?

Kazuo had written briefly about the radiation recipe, that it might be the missing ingredient in his metaphysical cake. Goldman knew his body was tainted with irredeemable levels of radioactive decay, but was it enough to have made a difference? If so, then it elated him to think that intractable paradigms could be shifted—no, shattered—beyond any reasonable recognition. But if this were the case, then the anguish of this possibility having slipped his mind when his daughter needed it the most, would dog him like a bout of *canidae* distemper. Whether he had something to do with the occurrence or not, he had to erase the ineluctable event from any recollection, or he would surely go mad with emotional high-altitude deterioration and thin-air grief.

He was glad to be on the road again, but was tempted to drive his car over the palisades, or at least to turn around and be readmitted into the beach tribe and stall for more time—time that was in short supply, time that had dulled life's wonder and stripped him of his wrapped robes of desire. But he knew that could never last. To the surfers, he was a slide-show freak from someone else's vacation, a tourist attraction that in time would become a bore. His memory, like all memories, would fade from young elastic minds that eventually calcify by the hardened cares of the world. Reality's gnaw was never far behind and his fickle Superman euphoria was shadowed by his Darkman second nature, where a gaggle of mean spirits tormented him down the gangways of high entropy and low-altitude gloom.

He rolled into LA with a frozen mind, but his body was tan, svelte, and muscular, and he looked healthier than he felt. He didn't know where to go, and for the first few days dodged himself and lodged himself in a flophouse just below the Hollywood sign, where the motel's red neon sign buzzed through his window like a macrocyte blood cell, making him feel anemic and wanly. He lay in his motel bug bed trying to fortify himself in front of the fangled flicker of a black and white TV and alcohol-induced static. Eventually, that lost its inebriating soothe, and he needed the relief of something more stringent.

He invited heroin back into his life, like asking the best-looking girl to the prom; but this date would never say no, and kissed long and hard and he didn't have to change his underwear, brush his teeth, or comb his quantum entanglements to please her. He had always thought that if there was anything worth doing, then give it all of you. Heroin was his chambermaid and he would give her his all if she would just take away the pain he dragged in train. But she came with a price, and soon all the donated money from the clamoring beach hordes ran dry.

He degraded to panhandling, and the acidic affects of a curb 'n' gutter junkie sullied to petty burglaries and even purse snatchings: not-so-petty larcenies that made advances on his spirit and soul. After weeks of ruling from the sewer, the flimsy chain mail that had held him together started to pop. *Death would be a relief,* he thought. He longed for it, but his demise wish exceeded his talent to pull it off. Even in his inebriated stupor, he was unable to shake Ruthie Lee's memory, and the scoliosis of her freighted load still bent his back low. He often wondered why his bouts of melancholy would score so deep and thought that there might be something wrong with the physiology of his brain, a chemical dark star ruling his inner universe without reason or antidote.

He possessed the symptoms of a nociceptive condition, where the anterior grid is overly sensitized to pain and cannot discern the difference between a broken arm and a broken heart. Maybe that was an exaggeration, but there was something about his torn fabric that needed hemstitching if his threadbare essence were to wear any kind of meaning. The days skulked like raddled locusts and the benchmark end to his third decade came and went, and he wasn't even aware of it. What was once a healthy thirty-year-old body had been reduced to an emaciated gulag ghoul, a dead man walking, where all notions of subject-object realities contravene into temporary lapses of an indistinct present.

*   *   *

Out of the doorway protruded a set of shoeless blackened feet. Equally black and equally worn, in a fetal position, a quiescent stiff curled on the threshold of the homeless shelter. The street derelicts stepped over him without so much as a splay-legged glance. It was Goldman's asylum and there he lingered, oblivious to palpable dangers that lurk in skidrow's distorted surplus population. Reduced to the unrealities of his dreams, he remained cataleptic, a permanent fixture among the city's discarded, and the thing he feared the most had come upon him like a mutating virus. He was a phantom without a name; *no place to live or be loved, dangling by a thread over the abyss of a perilous fate.* But the doorway didn't seem to mind.

He was seemingly senseless to the incursions of the endless foot traffic that muddled over him. A hand reached down from a jumbled whirl of street-fried humanity and rang his rickety doorbell head, but no one was there to answer. It wasn't until he heard an admonitory summons, with the authority of a court ordered voice that he retrieved some trace of consciousness where his realities and unrealities conjoin. He cracked his lids just enough to make out the features of a fuzzy figure. The unprepossessing glare of a brigandage world made him feel like a thirty-year salt miner pulled from a thousand meter shaft . . . optic fried and retina ripe.

"Are you hungry?" the blurry form asked.

"No," answered the barely audible, sweaty, spermous, fishy, malty, urinous, and musky figure.

The silhouette then re-racked the aperture of his turned blind eye to a *persona non-grata,* devoid of any recognizable features, social status, or humane rights.

"Goldman?"

The nomenclature seeped into his degraded compartments with a vague recollection. He looked closer at the hazy figure then half-cocked a foul-breath smile, and with the laryngitic throat of a polypus toad, croaked,

"Jonathan?"

*   *   *

Goldman awoke the next day in a detergent-scented bed with clean white sheets. He looked at his usually filthy fingernails and grime-embedded hide, like a hostile witness to the washed color of his natural complexion, and felt foreign in his own skin. He took a disquieting gander at the scabby tracks on his arms: abscessed, perforated, inflamed, hardened flesh, receding veins in the sparse muscle he had left. Red tributaries snaked the whites of his eyes and his head pounded like steel on steel anvils. Jonathan perched like an ancient owl by his bedside.

"Okinawa, 1945."

Goldman nodded. "And the last time I saw you . . . the May Day riot. Do you work here?"

"This turned out to be the Lord's calling. It's very fulfilling," Jonathan said with artificial predilection. He smiled, patted Goldman on the head like an inert stray, and left.

The days turned like torn, dog-eared pages, and the word count was not enough to follow their collective plot lines; the brothers just didn't know each other anymore. Jonathan talked about how he had served as a chaplain in the Navy, how the war had shaken him to his brittle core, how it damaged his faith, and how his very essence seemed punctuated with epistemic question marks: abscission syndrome, furtive God road rage.

It was a first for Goldman; a hesitant witness to Jonathan's substantiation as a real human being, not some fully clad church mannequin with a chamfer-cut religious smirk, but someone afflicted with symptoms of the real world. Goldman shared similar grievances, except his were never about holding a potentate responsible for anyone's ends and means. He was a hulking loaded atheist, which for him, helped stream line life's issues.

Jonathan said he had read about Goldman in the periodicals, about his war exploits and how *Red*vine rumors designated him a Communist. He wasn't even sure what a Communist was, other than a buzzword that meant trouble for someone. Goldman tried to keep his carapace point sheathed but even in his wilted condition he felt obliged to defend his views. It wasn't because of his servile devotion to Mina. It had something to do with his osmotic association with Socialism, the kibbutz in Israel, struggles against glorified dehumanization, and draconian governments. It didn't take long before the petty rivalries of adversarial brothers turned into acrimonious parrying and jagged quarrelsome gaffs.

Goldman was still half out of his sour-pickled brain and would spiral in Tasmanian tizzies about the immoral one percent that control and manipulate the oceanic masses while raking in colossal profits for their overflowing coffers. It made a good argument but, like the rest of America, Jonathan didn't get it. He couldn't understand why someone with Goldman's garlanded war record, and potential for the authentic American dream, would throw it all away for something so contorted.

Goldman's dramaturgical theatrics were a poorly conceived artifice to avoid the memory of his craven conduct on Okinawa, in the face of Jonathan's irritating reminders. What he really wanted to say was that he had been a coward on Sugar Loaf Hill, and was a spurious fraud. But he had determined long ago to take that tinted heirloom to his grave. Soon the same briny debates foamed to the surface, Cambrian explosion versus fossil silent evolution, purloining attempts to hone blunted points of view.

"Your purpose is to live for the miracle of God," Jonathan said.

Goldman shook his head with mocking annoyance. "There is no such *Face*."

"He is a *Face*," Jonathan argued.

"Only intelligent energy and that is no miracle," Goldman declared.

"He *is* a *Face* or He is nothing," Jonathan dourly said.

"No such monstrosity."

"If there is no G . . . G . . . God, then there is no purpose," Jonathan stammered.

"If man is too weak to stand alone, he invents a god to lean on."

"Without God, it is impossible to weave meaning into a nihilistic world," Jonathan hammered.

"The wages of stupidity is death," Goldman exclaimed.

"No!" Jonathan uttered. "The wages of sin is death and the end is coming soon!"

"You're wrong! You're wrong!" they both shouted in opposing synchrony.

*   *   *

Time at the skidrow mission dragged, like a weighted rickshaw. Goldman went cold *jake* on the alcohol, and the smack. The shelter brought a sorely needed reprieve and he was given his own torture chamber where he could go through the indignities of withdrawal in private comfortable hell. He gained weight and lucidity, and felt almost reconnected to a world that would still remain a stranger. He could stay at the shelter as long as he needed but, like the rest of the in-house residents, he had to help with the chores of running the street mission.

There were mandatory church services twice a day. He found it amusing that Jonathan gave the same phlegm-polished sermons that his father had, way back when. Watching him work the unenthusiastic pews was emptily hilarious. It was sad to think that humans are second nature creatures with yearnings to do away with their true selves and submit to creeds that corral wanderlust natures.

The Saturday evening service was the hootenanny of the services, and the street chapel was most crowded on those nights, filled with cajoling music and deliverance-bound souls. The gloves would come off as Jonathan liked to take the devil on bare-fisted. From the laying on of hands, to the discordant battles with evil entities, it was a yipping showstopper full of eerie dazzle and sordid carnival panache.

Jonathan and his loin-girded assistants would move through the congregants, sniffing out malevolent spirits that had set up shop in some vacant storefront soul, and then proceeded to evict them with the deputized law of the Lord. It was a fire-on-fire conflagration, and the demons exited with *un*righteous indignation and a commotion not seen since the days of the New Testament. Goldman suspected there were no evil spirits, only ghosts of mental illness that would naturally vacate once the subject had been properly diagnosed, medicated, or lobotomized.

The healing part of the service was what banged the mission bells, with every ailment and addiction getting gold fleeced with vestal deliverance. Goldman remembered the same worn-out rituals he witnessed as a kid, and wondered how those people had fared. Were they really healed? Or was it just one of those moments where one gets carried away and when all the pixie-dust settles they're at the same place they were before: homeless, sick, and oppressed by swells of great grief. *If God is a Face, then it is a Face that is in collusion with crimes against the poor and ignorant,* Goldman thought. Hope is an affliction, and giving hope to the hopeless was the devil's work. But that had always been part of the business of saving souls, and he was not about to challenge it. It was sad to think that no savior would come to their aid, that there was no shepherd to protect and look after the lost, and that God was consigned to an unseen dramatist.

The only saviors are us, he plaintively declared.

To him, the flock gatherings were campfire daydreams. Still, there was something sweet and genuine about serving an invented god. If it somehow served the sheeple, then that on its own made it okay. He had never seen Communists set up a homeless shelter, and he was grateful for the mission and its Christian philanthropy. It had provided him a place to moor his leaky boat and mend his storm-torn sails. He was not able to move forward with his life, and the death of his daughter still left him in emotional traction. He didn't want to think about it, but swimming in the cavernous waters of his skull were the submerged threats of Muller and the FBI, and if they got wind that he was back in town, then who knew what tomfoolery awaited him.

Goldman had to lay low, and this was about a low as one could get. He felt restless, and the grind of being at the mission was abrading him thin. He thought about Mina a lot, but did not have the verve to go by *The Daily Worker.* Maybe one day he would drum up the courage, but for now he would make his bed at the bottom of the birdcage, until his troubles tired of looking for him, or at least "throwed off" his scent.

XLI

They drove the sedan delivery truck to MacArthur Park to distribute sack lunches to the homeless. Jonathan told Goldman to go to the opposite side of the grassy commons and wait for the street refugees that would soon show up, like pigeons to a crouton convention. Goldman walked with a box of lunches to a distant bench and was immediately bum-rushed by the hungry, devouring the sacks with piranha efficiency. With nothing else to do, he found a picnic table and took a siesta. By the twelfth snore, a dozen white doves had landed on the table without him being aware of their visitation, and then they inexplicably flew away.

Jonathan was eye fastened to Goldman's outline, when what appeared to be a spiraling mist descending upon the cat-napper. The luminescent beam superimposed his likeness with gold-leaf petals, a deluge of golden folios gently rocking back and forth. It was a familiar visitation, beautiful and soporific, a sight that assailed his senses and left the logical bounds of reality with heavy eyed transience. When they were kids, it had happened just before Goldman hit the baseball that shot into the sky, never to be seen again.

The effulgent mind-boggler challenged all bounds of good sense and cracked the caissons of Jonathan's watertight reality. Curiosity pulled at him with countervailing forces, where the observer is central to the creation of its world. He moved slowly and cautiously towards Goldman, as if he might scare away whatever was happening. Not since the baseball game had he been this close to something so mind burnishing and obscenely allegorical. The gold petals were thin enough that sunlight penetrated them. He picked up a handful and it was like peering through gilded gold leaves of a Homeric deity. He noticed how heavy the petals were, yet thin and tiffany delicate. It was fascinating to let them drop, as they shattered with a tinkling sound the instant they made ground.

He sputtered with fretful steam. He was sure that if he could not find a witness to the spectacle, he would contort into a mental pretzel of irrationality. The only possible eyewitness was the sleeping Goldman, but he was hexed in an insensate voodoo spell. Jonathan shook him so hard that the gold petals that had piled on him fell to the ground like vanishing parcels of light, divine golden letters from an entelechy dimension. By the time Goldman came to, they had all vaporized without a trace.

"Did you see that?" Jonathan peevishly asked

Goldman gave Jonathan a cockeyed simper and simply walked away, leaving Jonathan whirling and poking at a phenomenon that had vanished as summarily as it had materialized.

*   *   *

The weeks passed and Goldman mended, but he was bored. The grinding minutiae of serving street derelicts did not sit well with him. He knew it was philanthropic and all that good stuff, but it was never enough to fill the gullies of his attention, and his mind constantly wandered to more picayune interests. He was highly intelligent, but an idler that required constant spurring, and trying to carry palanquin ideas with society's discards was like shooting pearl marble notions before snotty pig snouts, and his attempts to fit in were degraded by elements of charade. His time at the mission was macerated incarceration, and the inevitability of backstroke progress waterlogged him with soggy contempt. He fancied himself better than the garden-variety low-life, feeling that even his addictions and vagabond ruin were above the common and vapid.

Goldman was a puzzle of ribald scorn, but succussed with distilled wonder, a peculiar tincture of bliss and rage that burned and soothed as it congealed in his gorge and digested in the world's gastric tracts. He abased himself most of the time with urinous satire, yet he believed he was unique, leaning into the wind, knowing something big was always about to happen. He indulged in fantasy: of worlds where he was amazing, a feted shooting star, knocking elbows with the intelligentsia, living beautiful falsehoods, saving the afflicted new age with just the hem of his garment.

Maybe that's why he had gotten caught up in the Communist movement—to be enraptured by a life and death struggle always appealed to his hortatory side. He remembered the rush he got in the battles of the South Pacific and Israel, how he never felt more alive than when he was on the razor's edge of resplendent annihilation. He longed for the simplicities of meaning, and war reduced all contrivances to their lowest common denominator, a one-on-one leveler and a repatriation of conglomerate natures.

With the death of his parents, a thorny childhood, and no one to mentor his talents, all that untapped potential was consigned to a survivalist in the tornado of years that blew through him like shit through a goose. He wanted to be formally schooled, but denied the curriculum. His obsession for compiling sequestered ideas drove him on refractory quests for answers, which he tried to glean from the books he devoured and the unsavory explorations of kneading through his doughy reflexologies. It was always about illumination and where meaning's light was hidden.

As a boy he was spellbound by metaphysical abstractions, the teachings and philosophies of the Far East, the sages of India and their purported powers. It was fascinating to read about the exotic erudite who knew things about others; to envisage future events and seemingly by magic to levitate in oboe-mood rhapsodies of anti-gravitation. Sometimes the fantasies were so dazzling that for hours he would lose himself in the indulgence of reverie, while wild images ran through his mind like a hit parade of palatable rhymes.

If you don't go in, you go without, and in that world, he was a great avatar: legendary with a dedicated following; admired and embraced with cushioned sycophantic blubbers; adored by throngs that jostled and competed to be near him, palliating his wilderness wandering years of worms, shadows, and gargoyles. And the women, oh, the women, with contortionist twining legs and licentious *bocas* . . . the pick of the pussycat litter. Never having to sell himself, he would just show up and his worshipers would do his bidding.

In nostalgic reverie he pined for tongue-wagging occultism that mesmerizes crowds. He remembered how Jonathan's father worked an audience, how intriguing it was to watch him administer the snake oil, hexing spellbound spectators with serpentine declamations, and to herd cattle minds with the whip of snapping prose. He had gotten a taste of it at Libido Cove and even from his followers at the kibbutz. He remembered how the crowds roared when he entered Jerusalem a conquering hero, filling him with a self-magnificence that could not be shaken. He loved feeling iconic, but he loved feeling iconoclastic even more.

His daydreams crammed him with delight, but it always retrograded to ignominy. He was embarrassed by these nonsensical fantasies that left him convicted of a bad session of auto-fellatio. Ultimately, he was just a sleuth for truth—objective truth, not adulterated unguents. He covertly kept his options open to any belief system, and was determined to get to the prized core of life's riddles and enter the free zone of absolutes. But for now, his daze would be filled with haze and indistinct sounds of the *shaman blues*.

His biggest question was the simplicity of *Quo Vadis*. Where was he going? Why was he here, and what did any of this mean? In his water-well gut he felt a connection to the spinal cord of the divine, where deep calls to deep and distant ports are called home. It was about struggling with unseen forces, where all energy is indexed to its vibratory equivalent, balancing on the narrow arête of thesis and antithesis, where false selves do not want truth and true selves want it at all costs.

Maybe these distractions were the perfect imperfections of the arrogant. Life never came with instructions, only inaccessible directions spoken in medieval tropes, bewitching intelligence with idolatrous language. It left him wilting under the weight of his still unanswered questions, and what were once mildly intrusive images that lurked in the backwaters of his psyche, had now grown claws and fangs, and he often felt their hot breath raise the hair on the back of his neck.

He wanted to be free of his absurdness and to relegate his sense of self to cliché American vacuity: the chastity belt house with the propriety picket-lined fence, the adjudicating wife, kneecap gnawing rug rats, an alleged real job, hardened arteries, stiff joints, and necrophilic romances with mistresses of a mediocre death. No more troubling discourses about luck and fate, where fear and failure masquerade as valiant and victorious. Self-respect? Integrity? Love? *Ptui!* Trumped-up carrot mirages dangled in front of the plow horse just to get the lower seventy years tilled.

His contradictions were smart enough to keep out of hooting range, or sneering jeers at his closeted aristocratic self. He felt he was above the menial duties at the mission, and swaggered with fascist superiority. To Goldman, the hollow-eyed refugees wanted to be exactly where they were, and there wasn't one boulevard victim in the bunch. It was pointless to try to rebuild something that did not want to be reconstituted, like robbing the grave, best to leave them to their serial murdered lives. The monotony of living in the mission subverted Goldman's minimized stature, making him feel small enough to crawl into a bottle. What at first was a nip 'n' tuck had become a chug 'n' guzzle, and most of his waking hours were spent floating his battleship around.

*   *   *

He limped through the days sitting in the mission's TV room. Television had become his VHF lover and he was directly smitten by it. He was riveted by the Congressional hearings, a fact-finding Un-American Activities Committee, whose mission was to seek and weed out Communist moles.

There was something that the novel viewers in television land had not acclimated to, the collective senses of their nascent TV brains being overwhelmed by this new contraption. The scant imagery and deliberate stimuli had the power to assail their mental ramparts, and to invoke wraithlike beings that invaded their TV-land spirits and taunted their deepest cravings with synthetic joy.

Goldman viewed the front room carpet bombardments of ubiquitous advertisement as an insult to his intelligence, which pissed him off with the ferocious notions of a lovelorn fool. It was Capital prostitution at its ravenous worst, where essential dearth is seduced with sensual aspects of gluttony. Entire corporations were built in a day with a single commercial; from beer to cigarettes to hand soap, a colossus percentage game cajoling for American dollars.

There was a kind of electric-lady chic to TV, an art deco encased marvel that unlocks the unconscious, but Capitalism desecrates it and turns it into one more object of mass consumerism. America would become an abnormally-formed fiend of conspicuous consumption on a behemoth scale, where a young nation celebrates its new god: a one-eyed entity that seduces sentient beings, reducing them to insect-like creatures, *praying*-mantises before image of the beast.

Goldman found himself a pugnacious parrot, squawking obscenities at the salt and pepper screen, not only at the commercials but also at the bulbous-nose inquiries of the anti-Communist hearings. It was an idle crossed idea that the government could feel so threatened by the tagged-Communist scare. Kangaroo courts across the country were exposing patently clear criminals, connoisseurs of Commie caviar cowering in every conceivable cupboard.

This cut him deep with severed memories of *The Daily Worker* and Mina, and the hearings made him want to rally by her side. It would be a homecoming, he thought, and he fantasized that she would bear him up with open arms and offerings of prurient desire. His fear of the FBI was waning, loaded only with half suspicions now, and his courage seemed to bubble and rise, as did his deep-fried anger at the televised hearings. A churning flame was kindling in his belly, and if he didn't take action, he would have to throw the TV through the window out of partisan duty.

Goldman continued to belch obscenities at the flickering screen, which grabbed Jonathan's attention. He entered the TV room, which reeked of cheap alcohol, Lucky Strikes, and a mulish penchant for anarchy, and saw Goldman pointing his erected middle finger at the TV. He was put off by his brother's cutting tongue, and felt obliged to confront him.

"Admit it, you're a Communist," Jonathan accusingly said with coarseness in his voice.

Goldman didn't answer but continued his rant. "It's a pig circus! Fucking slubs, all of them! They have no right to do this to people!"

To Jonathan, America was God's chosen land, and that included its Capitalist system. He had always voiced his opposition to a Communist philosophy that denied the deity of Jesus Christ and God's ontological monopoly. Goldman argued with an aggrieved eye and an alcohol inspired tongue for the Communist cause, and as an aficionado of opposition to the neo-fascist machinery of the US government. The debate digressed into invective attacks against one another's character and doubled-fisted punctuation marks.

"Communism breeds antichrists!" Jonathan mendaciously shouted.

"Then kill a Commie for Christ . . . sake," Goldman shouted back with rising zeal.

Goldman's minatory insinuations mixed with strong drink were grounds for banishment.

"I can't have you here anymore," said Jonathan.

"What are you talking about?" Goldman slurred with congealment of speech.

"You're a bad influence on the others, and you're a bad influence on me. I want you to leave."

Goldman's initial impulse was to start firing at his brother's downrange face, but the words passed through his ears with a liberating sound, the only sound that could force him out of the mouse hole and push him over the crag of indecision. He would not let on, but he was grateful that he was able to beat the heat in his brother's prayer-conditioned mission. But he was even more grateful for his recrudescent return to the land of the alive, and to let the formaldehyde departed of skidrow bury their own.

XLII

Goldman scrounged up a domicile where he could set up shop, leaving the first symptoms of a contradicting second nature and a third-rate destiny behind. His kumfumbled life would be put on waivers, which meant scratching out a new start, a haircut and shave, getting a job and getting real. No more self-indulging aberrations, no more down-and-outer alcohol sprees or inner-upper black water dunking in heroin's contaminated spoon ponds. No more lurking criminal conduct that could pounce whenever inclined, or whatever rogue apostasy that might tempt him. He decided he was going to be optimistic, no matter how alien it felt, and in his strata hub, sensed that there was still something first-rate evolving in his fossil-gap tale. Life's hand still seemed outstretched with exhalations and, on occasion, it would breathe through him, but lately drafts of dispensation left him lightheaded with flakes of sanguinity that he hoped would last.

He was monumentally alone, but resolved not to procure the reptilian services of side winding strumpets. If he could not find a legitimate woman, then he would celibate his life as a mendicant monk. He had determined that he would not be the butt of his own joke anymore, and whatever parody he levied on himself would wind its last in the rustle of a panting wheeze.

These were productive days. Not so much for the legal tender that was exchanged for his gulag labor, but fructifying in the sense that he was spending healthy quality time getting close to his itchy skeleton, and understanding better his unsaddled equine frame. Self-analysis requires boots on the ground and a willingness to shoot anything that moves downrange, and he constantly scanned for targets with an existential thousand-yard stare.

He took odd jobs that were soul-sucking and only fit for molasses-witted misfits. It was a derogated way to eke out a living, but it paid the bills and he had been sober longer than he could remember. At first, it was terrifying to be clean but on occasion he would face terror just to see what it would reveal. He had a good run before his reconstituted body and glassy mind began to feel starless and subdued. In some perverse way, too much wholeness seemed unnatural to him. It didn't take long before the nuisance of boredom closed in on the quotient of his sobriety and what at one time felt open and sane, had become claustrophobic and bane.

His obsolescence returned like an ordure guest that you invite to stay the night, and which calcifies into a two-ton effigy that won't leave your sunken bed. He complained incessantly to thin-air omniscience about loss of detail, misshapen melancholy, and sibylline oracles that courted him with chivalrous necromancy. He had learned to turn a blind eye to cortisol inspired gloom, but in some way sadness to him was natural. Bouts of melancholy measured distance between reckless happiness and the consequences of jerk'n 'n' gherk'n mind chatter.

The years had taught him how to cope with the black dog of depression, but the bi-polar bear of loneliness he had no natural defense for. He couldn't find a woman, which chafed at his failed art self-esteem and chided his inability to be loved. It was overshadowing exaggeration, yet he could not escape the feeling. It seemed a delicate balancing act between the character he was, and the character he wanted to be, and all those muddy faces in between; a cross between Dracula and the Greek mythological character Narcissus; Narcissus who gazed at a reflection that he loved but did not understand, and Dracula, who never had a reflection and had to live on in immortal invisibility.

His curse was that of a remarkable mind manacled to a disobedient imagination, both fighting for his attention. Like a parable from the *Tao of War*, where restless warriors long for a fight but are utterly incapable of mounting an attack on an enemy that harasses them throughout the night and by morning is always gone. For some inexplicable reason, if he didn't have someone or something to fight, then all that acidic blistering would turn on itself. He had to be with people that were bigger than his own pitiable self, but he was tired of being with people that were only worth seeing once and he missed-da-Mina with felony conviction. How often she would blow through his interior and lately his nostalgia for her had become gale-force winds.

*   *   *

It was an overcast day, drizzling slightly, the kind of day that left one feeling like an infant marsupial curled in a furry pouch and sucking on mama's lactating teat. He crawled out of bed at the crack of noon with an irritating hint of a cold, and turned on the TV. He hated this new technical phenomenon and it was the one addiction he could not kick. It was his only friend, a window to the world that brought the intimacy of human conductivity without the uneasiness of having to relate to another being.

A local news channel was running a report on the Soviets, who had recently detonated their first thermonuclear bomb and were now building an arsenal of hydrogen monsters to dwarf the Hiroshima atrocity; a preamble nuclear death grip by the US and the USSR. Folks started digging bomb shelters with sarcophagi beds and tombstone pillows; certified MAD sorcery, and the clock ticked with the upwelling of apocalyptic fervor—a nuclear midnight that would bring in the New Year with sticks and stones and the matricidal murder of mother Earth never known. The broadcast shifted to live coverage of a downtown demonstration. The street reporter ranted with frothy denunciations of American Communists, "This demonstration is just another symptom of Soviet saber-rattling in America's front yard!"

On the TV screen, Goldman saw an ample woman leading the pack with raffish style, aristocratic and levelheaded with a degree of stately detachment. The reception on the TV was bad and he crazily wiggled the rabbit ears until they contorted into a metal pretzel, but the reception didn't get any better. Still, he was sure it was Mina. Who else would head a demonstration with that kind of flouting glower and swaggering eloquence? He grabbed a tissue, blowing his nose and his mind, and made a hot diggety dog dash out the door. He didn't care if she didn't want him there, and he didn't care if the FBI would be there. He only knew that if he weren't there, then he would be nowhere. In an instant he recognized that the cause would measure his meaning, and he would reclaim himself under the red banner of *The Daily Worker*.

He drove through the soggy streets like a man inseminated with unimaginable timidity but unblinking certitude. He trailed the crowd along the side of the wet street and followed the scent of battle, pulling him into an escalating fracas that was sure to come. He caught glimpses of Mina but was rampantly hesitant, wrestling with contradictory feelings of exhilaration and rejection: *Will she remember me?*

In the most crucial moments his shambling emotional snags had the ability to ensnare him when he needed it least. This was not a drill but the real deal, time to dance the Aztec two-step and let it rip. He watched her lead the demonstrators like a cleavage-busted Zapatista radiating with an iconoclastic lure that pulled him into her beaten path. He infiltrated the protest stew and elbowed his way to her, as her shadow cast no doubt on the path he had now chosen. If it meant serving as a soldier of misfortune in Mina's forgotten war, then he would throw his cuirassier self into the frying pan*demon*ium of her delusion.

Before he had time to reconsider his upshot, he grabbed the first protest sign he saw and thrust it high above the heaving mass. Mina swiveled her head as she scanned one side of the street to the other, shouting in sinewy Spanglish about revolution and other *Red*bone Party-line rhetoric. Her eyes fell on Goldman and delivered a thinly veiled glance with apparent indifference.

The shouting crowd rolled around the corner for a finito rally at City Hall, where they were greeted by a hefty contingent of construction hardhat workers who formed a phalanx of muscle and pissed off chiseled faces. They snarled and shouted stenchy obscenities, while the Commies responded with phonetically incorrect roars of premature triumph. Goldman worked up enough lion-hood to sidle up to Mina with feigned eunuch-like blasé.

He hailed her with a hesitant "hi", but before he could start his manicured speech, she parried his salutation by raising the bullhorn and sounded off with more menacing threats. He and others noticed a couple of men in black suits and sunglasses taking photos. This infuriated the Reds, who knew that it was a government thing; building anti-American profiles and fusty dossiers for the regime.

Goldman's initial impulse was to skedaddle, but a rolling roar interrupted his momentary dithering. The construction workers charged the demonstrators like the British rearguard smashing headlong into Napoleon's attacking cavalry. The sound of slapping flesh and snapping bone could be heard as far as Chinatown. Fists, bats, and sticks joined in the fracas, until the police had enough entertainment and arrested the Communists and only the Communists . . . again. Goldman was cuffed and loaded into a paddy wagon. As he was being driven away, he caught the features of an unwanted face that he had not laid a glower eye on in some time. Muller stood on the sidewalk with two of his associates, Cyclopsing him through the diamond-mesh cage.

*   *   *

After spending the usual incubating time in jail, the Commie birds were hatched and released. Goldman found himself mucking about with Mina and the other sprung revolutionaries on the still bloodied and wet street, debriefing. He tried to start a *tête-à-tête* but, like a seized camshaft, he couldn't get his motor to turn. She knew that he was thick tongued around her, but watching libidinal dominance squirm under inundations of the devil's choir always made perfect sense to her, and was even required. She was a pitiless queen of a matriarchal cult, gratuitously cruel, and endowed with the natural ability to knock a man's dick into the dirt and to make one feel invisible and utterly inconsequential.

The cold reception was in striking contrast to his ticker tape and confetti, corndog, cheese-ball, castle in the sky, Johnny Comes Marching Home fantasy. Like a devoted dog, he faithfully waited and, to his horror, was suddenly overcome by rabid disgust. Her underlings fanned out and he was about to do the same when she turned to him, appraising his value with the single-eye gaze of a shorthaired pointer. She said nothing as Goldman's manic feelers leapt every synapse, and her assessing scrutiny lulled into a supercilious smile.

"The Marine, right?" She asked with an imperious accent.

Goldman tried to form a shred of comprehensible verbiage, but could only shrug his shoulders and bob his spring-loaded head. She finished her hewing appraisal and, like a fleeting blip on a radar screen, was gone. His good sense batted its wings and flew hither 'n' yon, an unconfirmed orb flashing in the zero-sum game. She never said hello or goodbye, and, once again, he felt utterly negligible in her marmoreal shadow, his essence dripping onto the drizzling street like a drooping, drooling drone. Her features were as striking as ever and her beauty had been predictably obstructive to his receding horseshoe pattern self.

She walked up to a brand new Mercury convertible and dug through her Louis Vuitton for the car keys. Goldman followed: slouched, gawped, and drawing deep in the well for a leaky bucket of words. She looked at him, washed up and motionless, a piece of driftwood on her high-tide shore and, for a moment, testily deliberated her converging feelings. But the sun broke through the scudding sky, casting unusual beams of sun-flecked warmth across his semi-olive rubicund face. She was caught off guard by his rugged good looks and a boyish vulnerability she'd not detected before. They hadn't seen each other in nigh on three years, and he looked different. He seemed libretto versed in the vagaries of attractiveness and seasoned contraventions of new broken ground. His strewn countenance was as susceptible as ever. Words formed in dribbles.

"Do you always park your car next to the jail?"

She nodded and fished out the car keys from her purse. "I know where it always ends."

She sat in the Mercury and closed the door with a placid *click*, and started the engine. She dripped of sex, even doing the most ordinary things. Even her pressing the dash button to ease down the convertible top massaged Goldman's pleasure glands, speaking commercially in pituitary tongues and oral fixations. The sun streamed into her glittering, squinted eyes and her heavy lids went half-mast, like windows with the Venetians half drawn. She whipped a duster around her head and slipped on a pair of black Ray-Bans that sharply contrasted yet complemented her moue, red lips. She was leaving, and he couldn't find a gimmick in his grab bag to stop her. She put the car in drive but left her foot on the brake, sizing him up again, this time with remnants of ephemeral fondness.

"I want to show you something. Get in."

*   *   *

The two drove down Sunset and up the Pacific Coast Highway past Malibu. Mina pulled the convertible to the side of the road, to a cantilevered crag over a hidden cove just north of Leo Carrillo; the same Libido Cove where Goldman had spent the summer with the crazy surfers, the endless waves, and the forgotten miracle. He wondered if they were still there but, for the moment, he didn't care. She was all that mattered. The timing of their arrival was immaculate, with the sun resting on the rim of the ocean's semi-clouded silver horizon. The two sat speechless, like glass-eyed mannequins perfectly posed for passing window shoppers that he hoped would not browse.

The retreating sun turned and spun its dappling colors in a fading kaleidoscope of orange, gold, and amber-pink. Shards of billowing purple sky danced between the green and white tuck 'n' roll leather seats and their California-glazed skin; an epidermal lightshow of static electric bolts popping and snapping between fingertips, lips, and genitals, fusing flesh under spangles of swirling light. They made love in the Mercury under flaxen moonbeams until the moon too, sank along the path that the sun had blazed the day before. Like spent reactor rods, the two drove back to her somniferous apartment in a radioactive buzz, where she prepared homecoming Tapatio eggs and toast for a forgotten hero. They shared their over-divulged bodies for one more assembly, then entered their respective comas and slept for the better part of the day.

XLIII

It was close again—that predator who knew his quarry by name—like a sinister accountant of his sins, who kept an ongoing spreadsheet accurate to the last cent. He could feel the entity moving from side to side, hovering millimeters from his face, its nearness sucking away all oxygen, a fiery back draft waiting for someone to open his door. He felt as though his throat was being throttled and a large hand was covering his mouth and pinching his nostrils tight. One day he would call the strangler by name.

The cracks in his eyelids allowed the mid-afternoon sun to leak through, like a rude alarm clock ringing his bell until he fully opened his eyes. He then remembered Mina. She had the ability to leave the senses jumbled, which took considerable disentangling after an encounter with her. The fact that she wasn't there was not unusual. She thrived on being mercurial, and her fickle temperament could be a threat to one's sensibilities if you were not of her persuasion.

He rolled out of her brocade-covered brass bed with the squeaking springs, lurched to the *salle de bains*, and took a bulging bladder leak that was an eye-popping orangish-silver color. He felt as if his body was inundated with bumps and knots, yet his skin was smooth to the touch. The streams in his system were babbling with photons of radiated threats, speaking a peculiar destiny through a catastasis not yet understood. In the bathroom mirror his eyes caught the reflection of the baby grand piano in the front room. He was pulled forward, as if by a reacquainting string, and sat before the ivories like an old friend.

He played a Liszt sonata with oblate adagio piety. The keys felt holy under his proffered hands, as the vibration from the soundboard grasped his body with kneading resonation. He finished the piece and went directly into Kazuo's five notes. Over and over he played the C, F, A flat, G flat, and C sharp, enlightened, his body static and transcendent, clearing out psychic cobwebs and uninspired civility. The power of sound was like a needed legal penalty for Goldman, confiscatory and, in a way, more important than sight.

Life's algorithms had sequenced through him all his life and it wasn't until recently that he had even become aware of it. Kazuo had written, "The mathematical sound representation of reality is beyond human projection, but sounds from the god particle are to be found in those who practice the repetition of the Tibetan five notes." Goldman sighed, and for a moment laughed with humiliated farce, always a metaphysical desperado, grabbing at mystical saplings that snapped and left him floundering in the quicksand of his ever-sinking reality traps.

He was bored, and started nosing through the underpinnings of Mina's digs. It was lavishly appointed and obvious that money was of no concern. It all made sense: her cultural snobbery and aristocratic tongue, the fact that she did not have or need a job—the cadres of *The Daily Worker* in her employ. It was all her. He had rightly deduced that she possessed globular doses of wealth and had been fartin' through silk her entire life. Palpable irony was everywhere, and the bittersweet scent of hypocrisy hung heavy in her Shangri-La palace. *It was so typical of the idle rich to bankroll pet projects, like revolution*, he thought. He supposed it was a way to lessen the money guilt and keep overactive shame mongers from self-denunciation for their filched positions, as if needing to give moral kickbacks to the honest inferior.

People with money never do the heavy lifting of waging revolution, but Mina was a proven exception. Still, he was intrigued. Why would someone with access to copious amounts of wealth feel compelled towards world revolution? Why not be a philanthropist and just give heaps of cash to causes that commensurate? The idea collapsed a vital lapse in the last lap of his clap clasp thinking. Once again, maybe he had this Communist thing all wrong? The idea of being wealthy titillated deeper yearnings that he had not fondled since his experience with the moneymaking kibbutz in Israel. Just being in proximity to the glut of money suddenly filled him with status anxiety, and less critical about the spoils of free enterprise.

This kind of contradiction he understood. He realized that they were both raging hypocrites, imposters even, hiding from unwanted schlockism and impoverished desires. He knew, and he was pretty sure that she knew, that this whole Communism thing was a floating dream, suspended by her Miss Adventure capital. Rallying around causes for underdogs would always be an exercise in vainglory. Ultimately, self-interest would triumph over altruism—America was living proof of that.

The privileged class would always feign charity on altars of ritual sacrifice, *du jour artifice*, mystical commercial rites to insure that crops are good, livestock is healthy, and babies are not stillborn. To them, it is a hallowed sacrament. It looks exalting to consecrate industrial-strength blood, just so long as it is not their own. The rich stand portrait tall, but they are elevated on the bent backs of others who are always just out of frame.

None of it mattered to Goldman. He had come to a place in his life where he knew who he never was, but wasn't sure what he had become; a conscience, and remnants of pride, were no longer within his budget. From now on he was sticking to the basics. His boorishness would rule until he had accrued enough credit to buy some distance from his knuckle-dragging past and reptilian tendencies.

Why he assumed Mina was the great love of his life he could not say, but he loved her like a dumbstruck brute, but he'd had enough of his Eucharistic sacraments for her. He knew only too well what kind of woman, womb-man, worm-man, she was: a Dinkenesh-Lucy, an evolutionist. And not just any evolutionist, but a porncore Social Darwinist who, in her own way, exploited the weak—ironically, the requisite to a Capitalist call, not her limousine liberal egalitarian-festooned fraud. If the world was about survival of the fittest—the opportunistic species living off the weaker—and if her genus were like the rest of the animal kingdom, then there she would always test, poke, and prod, and if you could not ford her chromosome river, you ended up on the scrap heap of the genetically challenged.

Mina's panoply could withstand the most flagrant of emotions. She prided herself on self-reliance, that she did not need a man to complete her. But things were changing. The devil that had stuck close to her over the years was now being threatened by a devil she did not know; no longer the budding perennial, that red-banner-waving teenage revolutionary, but a fully-flowered rose with a prickly stem, jonesing hard to cross pollinate. What was once a passing incursion into the hunting grounds of men was now turning into penile dementia, splendiferous concoctions of testosterone and muscle, where covetous estrus arrest us. Her nightmare was someone who possessed something that she needed, and Goldman, who was once only a mild distraction, was turning into a threat . . . even worse, a proprietary need.

From the very beginning she had been testing his essential stock and his bathetic contrivances for her had always left him in a compound conundrum. He didn't know from one day to the next whether she would kick him out of her life, or let him amuse her until she tired of him. If like a black widow she took his head and devoured the rest, then it was his choice to crawl into her web. He never questioned if nature was a whore—it was obvious, and he had always been her best customer. For now, he would stick to fiat points of view, and all authority would flout to the leadership of his *Johnson* and his convex head would be solely responsible for his concave heart. The fact that he wasn't able to decode her didn't matter, either, the only thing that mattered was that they could hump like Schnauzers, and at the very least he knew that mattered to her . . . and him. They were two minds orbiting in the same body now, their atom smashing had fused them into one charged particle, and both would be last to admit that their former selves were fading.

*   *   *

It was one of those contusing sex conferences that sacked her honeysuckle and sapped his man chowder. There was no running away from the fact that Goldman was yoked to her, no matter how hard he tried to reduce its sublimated quirks. He would hold her long after their cuckoo coital coupling, not out of some pathetic neediness but as a dimpled nestling and as a courtesy to fables of female farrago. With Mina, his usual slant to avoid post-sex closeness was not even detectable. She had a way that was markedly different, that left him with redoubtable calculations and fearsome desires of inquiry. The shards of his innards felt whole and healthy when she nuzzled into his nook, that taboo sweet spot where schoolgirls become obsequious lovers to daydream daddies that never were.

In this situate, her voice would change as she baby-talked and cooed with gibberish sounds that only the father of a cosmic orphan could understand. Her lilac body bouquet aerated subtlety, and he would get lost in the maze of its fragrance, touching her face with his eyes, drinking her breath with his lips, losing himself in the garden of earth and water called worm-man, womb-man, woman. He could not remember when he had felt like this before. It was one of life's rare occasions, which linked prolonged bouts of amoral vacuity with gooey, fuzzy, otherworldly love that visits the Earth-shackled from time to time. The heart is a lonely hunter. How effortlessly he failed to resist the delicacy of love's barbed-wire entanglements.

Their shared pleasures were elegant, yet vaguely uneasy for him, as he found himself drifting into the gaping arena of guilt. The undertow of Ruthie Lee's opposite flowing plot twist tore through the pages of his mind, and he was in love with a woman whose brother he had killed off—like some badly scribed fiction. There was something about the reciprocity of joy that shot down to his sore heels with sciatic postmodern distrust. Happiness was so unfamiliar that he didn't know how to behave in it. It was enlivening, yet spooky, devoid of any relativity or points of reference, leaving him out of sorts, spellbound—witchcraft.

All he wanted to do was marry the woman, but like every other desire, it was booby-trapped with contingencies that forbade being defused. For the first time, he wanted to share an islet piece of his life. He wanted to take care of someone, not as a comrade-in-arms, but as a husband in-her-arms, and hew out their own cause. The problem, of course, was that she was already married to a jealous aficionado that would fend off any potential suitors who might threaten her matrimony with world revolution.

He forgot that he was not going to encumber his life with the countenance of compunctions; the only thing that was going to matter was the ordinary, the common, and the vapid companionship of the shameless now. He was determined to erase the past—as far as he was concerned, everything that is called the past is literally nothing but present memories anyway. He was with Mina, and that was it, and if the unrequited sound blips of love did not echo back, then he would liquidate his overstocked emotions for her until demand for its inventory might one day be needed. But for the present, he was not going to let his eternal now be contaminated with the eternal then.

If we have not enjoyed the last hour we have wasted it!

*　　*　　*

Mina dragged red-lipped on a white Pall Mall, raking her red nails across Goldman's neck. She then eyed the quarter inch hole in his ear and slid her little finger through it. She moved her mouth to the opening and tickled it with lingua lashes. She was an odd one, this woman, who savored physical wounds like a benchmark wale, yet never once had asked about the hole in his ear. She then started poking at something that was protruding from the middle of his shoulder blade: a distended nodule that stuck out about a half inch, with the color of a ripe field turnip and the texture of cauliflower.

"What is this?" Mina asked.

"I don't know. I was hoping it would go away."

She fixated on the little anomaly and kept fondling it. "Kind of sexy, in a horrid way."

"Look serious?" Goldman asked with a dissipating smile.

"I think you need a doctor to look at this."

He didn't want to think about it, but lately had sensed something amiss in his endocrine system, and this seemed to be another precipitator to a skirmish in the undeclared borders of his body. He rolled Mina onto her back, with instigations of a sultry evening plowing through his core.

Love me two times, three times, four, five to one, waiting for the sun until I can't see your face anymore.

*   *   *

The weeks moved laggardly, and could not keep up with the escalating pressure of the days. Mina was becoming more paranoid that government agencies were taking a keener interest in dismantling *The Daily Worker*. A deluge of threats bombarded the organization's mailbox. Headquarters was under constant surveillance, which wasn't so unusual, but the government's shadowy activity had increased since Goldman's bald-faced return. She knew they had a valid beef with him, and that her operation was almost inconsequential by comparison. The military tailor-made its war heroes and fine-tuned its propaganda machines; but to them, the creation of Goldman had become Frankenstein's monster, unleashed on the peaceful village of America.

He was a marked man, a flea of defamed character and a bloodsucker on the hide of its American host. For the first time, Mina felt threatened by her association with him, but in a dramaturgical bend, she was elevated by his earned role as an enemy of the state, which kept her in the limelight and shed new credence to her cause.

He had become the American Che Guevara, and she respected him now with laudable tribute and proliferating potential towards the struggle. To her, he was more than just a Red wine comrade, but an amethyst brew that had distilled the posy of her heart; her magnanimous smooch, and for the first time . . . she realized she loved him. Not because they hated the same things, but because she loved their differences, where their common insecurities thrived and were wholly compatible.

She wasn't naïve. She knew what he really wanted. She had been ogled by men all her life. From the get-go, she knew he was a gecko, like all men a lizard of lust, never a committed Bolshevik. Still, his fidelity to her was tacit devotion to world revolution. It was costing him everything he could have been, and his dedication put a unique slant on her Euclidian vector. There was an aura of humble devotion she now felt for the man, and the imperial tiara that she had placed on his brow was different than that of any other lover she had ever crowned.

*   *   *

It was another Communist demonstration, marching with the full pageantry of Marxist banners, protest signs, and political fire branding by Red devils that had the godforsaken gall to reinvent themselves in their own image. In the lead were Goldman and Mina, moving at an arm over arm blustering clip. She reached over and slid her little finger though the 6.5 mm hole in his ear, and turned his head to bend his other ear. Amid the hoof beats of herded demonstrators, her winsome smile conspired with the obliging curl of her lips.

A bucket of consonants and sorted vowels poured from her mouth, but Goldman could not understand so much as a cup's worth. She shouted the words again, but they jumbled in a dyslexic alphabet soup of orderly disorder. With stochastic guesswork he descrambled the syntax, and the words rearranged clearly in his ears.

"Marry me!"

Goldman instantly ear*gasmed* as halos wreathed over their heads, and the dirty, shitty avenue had suddenly become a *love street*. The two stopped in the light of solitary plurality, and the biggest syllable of his life clipped between his tongue and palate, hissing through his clenched teeth, like sibilant steam from the boiler room of his heart.

"Yessssssssss."

Without even so much as a kiss or any indication that something titanic had occurred, she jackknifed head first back into the demonstration pool and continued with the ordinary business of lighting the world on fire.

XLIV

King of the road and Queen of the highway, it all felt right, everything: the sultry desert air blowing through the youthful color of their seventy mile an hour mane; the purr of the V8 engine rumbling through the floorboard, gently vibrating their hardened bones and massaging their soft organs. They would never look this good or be this naïve again, and the nonce would never be more critical.

Mina stuffed her hand deep between Goldman's thigh and the green and white leather seat, while watching the fading details of the desert-scape turn in conical bands through shades of gold, purple, and pink. Long stretches of stratocumulus clouds lay just above the horizon, giving the illusion of great landmasses in an endless ocean of intricately woven blue, like a frozen snapshot, one of millions of snapshots in the vast tracks of time yet to be played out in their incunabula launch. It was frosted cream dreams, angel cake schemes, and devil's food icing—life's dessert finally served.

The sun dripped and tipped late into the afternoon, as the affianced bookends sat cheek-to-jowl rolling north on Interstate 15; Las Vegas, neon-light fairy tale dreams—five hours to the inaugural ball. They had made good time and, if they got there by dark, they could make the midnight chapel. It had been nigh a week since Mina leaped out of character with the wackadoodle proposal, and Goldman was still jigging and capering.

He would have done the entire blasted thing, the ring, the flowers, on his knees, the whole cliché, but he never knew what combustibles might be in her tank. A proposal that blew up in his face would have been tough to handle with casual detachment, and would have tapped out what little self-esteem was left in his emotional cistern. It felt weird, freaky even, to have her ask for his hand, but he was boundlessly thankful that she had taken the initiative.

Goldman's philosophy was simple anymore: It ain't where you're from that matters but where you've been, and what matters is not what you do, but whom you do it with. And he would do it with Mina for the rest of their days. The two had surrendered their contumacious crowns for interwoven regard, where awareness is neither transparent nor opaque, where incantations and sorceries are transformed by seductive charm and hysterical spells of connubial bliss, voluptuous and yielding, where falling feels like flying, hurtling to the ground at the speed of meteoric love.

Goldman was nearly hypnotized, lost in the desert's barren vanishing point, when the appearance of a black sedan in his rearview mirror snapped him out of his trance. He remembered seeing the same car when they made a pit stop for burgers in Baker. He would not have given it much mind, except that he also remembered seeing two men dressed in Hawaiian print shirts and mirrored shades who promptly turned away when he looked squarely into the reflection of their sunglasses. He then remembered seeing the men jawing with a parked California Highway Patrolman, the three powwowing in an unholy trinity.

They crossed the Nevada line, and the black sedan still trailed about a thousand yard clip. He slowed down to let the other cars pass, figuring it would force the sedan to do the same, but after crawling for miles, the sedan still trailed behind. He then punched the Mercury's dual-quad carburetors and exploded the four hundred horsepower convertible to sub-mach speed, transforming the highway's broken white line into a single pallid blur. The black sedan accelerated, but had no reasonable shot at the Mercury. Mina had known something was amiss ever since they left Baker, but hadn't said a word. She possessed spider sense about potential trouble and could handle it with an unruffled cool, but she hushed in silent fear that she might be a widow before she was a wife.

"We've got someone spoiling for a fight." said Goldman

Mina turned to see that they were putting distance between the cars.

"You're beatin' 'em Marine!" she triumphed.

He had put about a badland mile between the cars, but now they were creeping up on another car, and not just any car, but the same California Highway Patrol cruiser that Goldman had seen in Baker—a set up as sure as a novella's antagonist. He figured the big V8 had a shot against the patrol car and made his move, whipping the Mercury into the opposing lane. The two cars kicked it in and were running neck and neck to a final photo finish, when oncoming traffic barreled in like two ton chrome and steel angels of death. Goldman pulled back into his lane without passing.

The black sedan caught up to them, and the convertible was now pinched between sinister opposites.

In an instant, all of Goldman's prized dreams were in jeopardy of utter annihilation; his sylvan paradise dissolving before his deliquescent eyes. He jerked the car back and forth in a mongoose and cobra game of feints and dodges. He sniffed out an opening and jerked the Mercury past the centerline, then whipped back onto the sandy shoulder and gunned the convertible with a one hundred and eighty psi lead foot. The maneuver worked, and he was in front of the patrol car, spraying gravel and desert debris at the rolling mischief-makers and putting a generous distance between them. The apprehension that had clenched their jaws tight faded, and their facial muscles eased into sanguine grins. Mina's scarf blew off her head and snagged on the black sedan's windshield wiper, and the two laughed at their Spic 'n' Span-clean getaway.

Fate's penal codes were blotted out, and providence pulled them closer to Vegas. But their moment was as short-lived as it was spectacular. The ear-busting sound of a blown front tire echoed across the tranquil desert. The Mercury pulled diabolically to the right, Goldman hotly countered to the left, but over-cooked it, accelerating their collective fates into a sand embankment, catapulting the car with twenty-one rolls of crushing steel, rubber, and flesh. The amorphous mass finally halted upside down in a dustbowl heap with the V8 still roaring like a wounded tiger.

The black sedan and the patrol car pulled over and they exited their vehicles, filing out like fetid fowl perched on a power line; birds of prey, whose quarry's stench filled the air. The spectacle inexplicably invoked spontaneous remorse from the miscreant three, who had their hearts of stone pulverized by ignominy. They returned to their cars and pulled away, like vultures abandoning flesh too putrid, even for their carrion taste.

The betrothed lay motionless, like supernovas reduced to starry-eyed dwarfs, objects of dread on the searing desert sand, as the wasteland's curtain lowered on tales of unforeseeable impermanence and lovers' black-velvet night dreams.

XLV

Goldman's insensate remains jerked with primal reflex and he attempted to move, but bolts of salient pain seized a body that now demanded an explanation as to why it was at the thin edge of life. He tried to assemble some recollection of the insensible, but his survival check valve was flowing in only one direction. His ears were barely in range of droning tidbits, nonsensical voices devoid of any meaning. He tried to open his encrusted lids, but the normally dilated and fixed spheres were frozen. The only thing that seemed to be working was his nose; smell data, and a mélange of rubbing alcohol, bedpans, and triage fear.

His eyes came open a slit and he focused enough to see that he was in a sallow room trimmed in stainless steel, filled with official-looking strangers clad in pale attire. A hospital? Snapshot proofs developed in the emulsion of his mind. The accident was as dreamlike as his waking moment.

"Mina?" he faintly groaned, arousing the attention of two nurses and an intern.

"Please, don't move," the nurse admonishingly said.

"Where is she?"

"You've sustained some injuries. Please try not to move."

He was oblivious to his own flesh-knots and hematoma leakage: swelling, abrasions, hemmed lacerations, brain inflammation; the only pain that registered was the noxious throb of Mina's unknown fate.

"She's here in the hospital." said the intern. "I think you'll be fine. You got a lot of scrapes and contusions, but no broken bones and no internal injuries. You're a very lucky man."

"I didn't ask about me," Goldman said with a plaintive voice.

The floating anxiety in the room was statically charged and silently arcing. The doctor made clumsy attempts to form an attenuated evaluation and said a lot of long and narrow things, but not the right thing. He did explain that she had survived the accident, however there were complications. A scopulate creep shuffled across Goldman's back as he anticipated a gloomy forecast that loomed as a threat. The doctor driveled into medical rhetoric and remedial yak.

"Spit it out," Goldman said with a fluttered spew.

He sucked in a lung full of valor and whispered in semi-cipher code, "Paralysis."

Goldman craned his ear hole toward the doctor's mouth. At first, the word evaded any meaning, but like a dry sponge soaking up sour milk, he slowly absorbed it.

"What does that mean exactly?"

The intern made feeble attempts at putting on a face that would fit the occasion, but was a poor disguise for clinical detachment.

"Her neck is broken. From the sixth cervical down she feels nothing."

The meaning of the word crystallized, leaving Goldman hangdog faced and dangerously suspended. He remembered seeing spinal injuries from the war, gunshot wounds that tore through the spines of fellow marines: in an instant, vibrant young bodies exchanged for decrepitude. His wits caved under the infernal thought of Mina's stunning physique shrunken to creaky bones and dewlap flesh: bed sores, bed pans, breathing apparatus and daily feedings, wiping shitty cheeks, changing menstrual rags, brushing graying teeth; a litany of the unthinkable.

The whole thing was gossamer, dream-able, as seen through a viscous film, Greco-tragi-hysterica, back thrashing and belly kicking contractions, womb dilating, nine pounds of terror crowning into his new world. The doctor asked if he wanted to see her, but he lay flash-frozen in minute cubicles of space and time, brain frozen, and senseless. Tentacles poison tipped with bewilderment squeezed between the threads that kept the cap of his sanity screwed on. Hope is oxygen to the suffocating, but any thoughts of hoping were now reduced to coping as he gulped for commiseration.

His ample imagination and its pernicious spread started to rationalize the impracticalities of being a concierge to an invalid. To his astounded horror, he wanted to abrogate his commitment contract with the woman he had forsworn would complete the abandoned project of self. He spiraled down the staircase of onus abstractions, and dreary obligations, to a dungeon where ragged madness speaks its own language, accented entreaties of the condemned.

Goldman hadn't bargained for a wheelchair-imprisoned future, and he certainly had not signed up for custodial nursing of a woman who still had many difficult years ahead. He could not react to semaphoring reflexes and involuntary shock signals of bare-naked truth: his Amazonian queen was a warrior no more. Fear and sap pumped through the veins of his mawkish airs, and unbidden obscenities whispered like dragon's breath into his hardening heart. His rat button alarm was sounded and sent him running out of the hospital like an abraded naked goblin. He climbed the nearest tree and perched in it like an opossum, feigning dead for the remainder of the evening.

*   *   *

He awoke to a stone pelting and the mulish berating of the hospital security.

"What the hell is wrong with you, boy?"

"Why are you throwing rocks at me?" Goldman demanded with just-awakened surliness.

"Hospital rules, no one is allowed to climb the trees naked."

"Well, what if I was clothed?"

"That might be different. Now get your ass down from there and bring your wiener with you too."

He climbed down and was escorted back to the discomforts of the hospital room. He spent the entire day weighing in on issues hidden in the remote recesses of his translating interior, where wheedling banshees scream, *Run! Why? For your life.* But, of course, that was too perfunctory for a thinking man. He still loved Mina with the incendiary flames of a vile-eyed arson. *The finest steel goes through the hottest fire. Tough problems build strong virtuous character, while easy problems make people soft, lazy and mediocre, but this is ridiculous,* he thought. This new reality was too absolute and too desolately defined. Goldman always functioned best in areas of gray, whereas dialectic truths of black and white challenged his nature born ambivalence, where precise vagaries are open vistas of moral interpretation.

Something caught his eye, a phantasmal blur of what looked to be a man in a black suit and trilby hat striding past his room. He leaped from his bed and looked down the hall, but could only make out the back of the nonentity that was rounding the corner. He made a barefoot dash in a perspired attempt to intercept him. The sound of an elevator door *pinged* as he reached the corner. He lunged for the elevator just as the door closed on the indistinct features of someone who he feared looked like Muller. If it was him, was he here to finish the devil's work? All of Goldman's pig-jowl tendencies for self-preservation deserted him and he could think only of Mina's safety.

He bounded down two flights of stairs and crossed the threshold of room number 212, where his eyes were buffeted by Mina's motionless form connected to a respirator. He sizzled like a drop of water hitting the frying pan floor and his feet nervously danced as if flames of the un-expiated were licking between his toes. He forgot about the specter of Muller and saw only her entirety, as all disparate feelings evaporated into altered states of hallucination. Her portrait bust was locked down by a stainless steel halo-brace, bolted to her sweet skull with a dour heavy-metal grip. Her inert body, strapped to a board, gave the illusion that she might levitate had she not been belted down.

She looked as capacious as ever, as if she could easily house a pantheon of oral-poetic gods; her body still bursting with prurient potential and skin-deep translations of libidinous tow; her complexion an even cream coffee, her raven hair combed straight, crow-tailed. He lightly lifted her hand and held it close to his thumping sternum. His heartbeat in recognizable rhythm, crossing boundary lines of her sleep, the windows to her soul opening, all dreams penetrating reality, reality-defiling dreams and the smoldering eyes that were once full of fire were now slow burning embers, black coals of filtrate catastrophe.

"Take me out of this place," she begged from her molten core.

Goldman wilted like a saggy-jowl maw and he could not resuscitate a single word but only solicitously gaze at her as if from afar. He kept a bedside vigil with hesitant sincerity as she sobbed in free verse; unguent weeping that, for the moment, soothed the two with the salve of correctness.

Recollections of Big Jim squeezed his diaphragm and rattled his dismissed mind with the possibility of another miracle. Could he do what he had done at Libido Cove? Did he have the power to untangle another horrible plot twist? As Mina dozed in and out of consciousness, Goldman assumed the Vitruvian position, with one palm facing up and the other directly over Mina's trammeled head.

He began chanting Kazuo's five notes over and over with the urgency of a triage metaphysician. But something felt different. He tried marshaling his powers by descending to his cavernous interior where he had previously encountered the terror and the might of a quantum world that seemed to move at his behest, but something was blocked. After an hour of chanting her condition remained the same. Whatever spec-ops ability he thought he might have possessed now seemed utterly cold, stripped and impotent. He collapsed from fatigue and failure with no place for his colluding thoughts to conspire. His head tipped to the high-polished hospital floor as he methodically counted the black dots in every twelve-inch square tile in the room, 2157, without once looking up.

*   *   *

Goldman garrisoned the hospital until the doctors said he could leave. Mina was another story. The cartographers of her journey still had to map out her arrangements with new acquaintances and the ravages of her novel destiny. The immediate danger of infection and the possibility of pneumonia had passed. She would be transferred to a special facility where she would remain hemmed in and suspended indefinitely. Her family's vast treasury would procure the best medical care, but "what she really needs and will continue to need is Goldman's sustained commitment and categorical support," said the doctor in uneasy tones.

The weight of the responsibility was brutishly unwieldy, ill mannered, and gauchely sneering with unwarranted wrongness. Goldman wanted the *très bon* life of status courtesans and squires, the *fantastica fornicatio* wet dream, to enjoy everything and not be responsible for anything. His distaste of moral imperatives lay bare for all to see and the room's atmosphere grew charged with direly cast eyes.

In the first days of his bedside night watch he had convinced himself that he could fill the gaps in the line, and that he would be with her until the annulations of the world ended at the beginning of their wedded rings. But the realities of caring for a de-deified quadriplegic were daunting, and the insoluble obligation became clearer as the dog land days dragged into weeks. They were preparing Mina to be moved, when a resident doctor pulled Goldman aside.

"I want you to know that after the accident I did a full examination of you."

"Yeah, I know, you said I was fine, right?"

The doctor nodded. "However, I found a mass of tissue on your back. I had a sample of the growth sent out for biopsy. I got the results back today and I am relieved to tell you that it tested benign." Goldman tipped his head with relief, and the doctor continued. "I also did your blood work, which, curiously, tested positive for high amounts of radiation. Do you know where you might have been exposed?" Goldman shook his head as a punctuation to end the subject.

"Your RAD readings are high enough that you should be dead . . . ten times over," the doctor flatly said.

Goldman stood motionless as he vacuumed in the rug debris disclosure. It was bad enough to suck up Mina's fate, but this was a new assault on his constitution that left him psychologically fragile, but physically robust as a cockroach.

*   *   *

Mina was put into a special hospice and adorned in a Stryker frame that would be superimposed on her body for the rest of her horizontal days. She would have a private room, a private nurse, private adverbs of Mephistopheles, and private admonitions of perpetual private torment. Her obstinate defiance was showing signs of wear in her broke-back shell, and a psychic discharge congealed in globs into her brave new world. *How fickle is devotion*, Goldman thought, *and how conditional it is when your own needs will not be met.* What was he going to do with her, sexually? He supposed she could still give head. Would that be enough, could he mount her lifeless body for dead fish intercourse? He suddenly felt like an interloper, with petty thoughts of money slithering through his snake den head. Goldman had always felt starved in the face of Mina's opulence and now, to his horror, her affluence had become a purloining issue. He hadn't gotten the chance to marry into her fortune. Would he still marry her, and would it now be for that reason? The untidiness of his new calamity made him feel boorish, incandescent with rage, and boiling in sincere lout-ness.

Mina's cadres were at the hospice to greet her. They were quietly quarrelling about the future of *The Daily Worker* and who would take charge. It was a partisan matter, but Mina would not permit dissent. They tried unsuccessfully to change the thick weltering climate in the room by making thin-air comments on the accommodations, pointing out that there was even a fine view of the ocean. Goldman and Mina made dim, shielded eye contact, glancing blows of barely controllable feelings. He thought if she looked too deep she might read his unraveling intentions and know that rabbit was in his blood. One of the Communists approached him.

"I want you to know how terribly sorry I am. Your devotion to comrade Mina is to be commended." Goldman nodded and leveled his eyes at the polished floor. The man went on to say that despite Mina's inopportune mishap, the cause would go forward, and that maybe Goldman should lead. He then whispered in his ear, "You need to keep an eye out. The FBI is turning up the flames. Two of our best ended up dead."

The unsavory piece of info pushed Goldman's systems failure to the overhang of a bottomless abyss. All the endorphins that had fired when he had joined the Party were now relegated to bitter chemicals associated with fear and dread, producing maculae marks on the skin of a scoundrel and acidic compounds in his noncompliant thoughts.

The Communists vacated the room; Goldman and Mina were left alone with only their curdled expectations to tie them together. What was once a grand panorama swathed in colors of gorgeous possibilities had shriveled to blights on an optic disk. Mina had always reveled in the unkind laws of natural selection and the cold steel skewer of Darwinist law. But the cruelty of syllogistic rules left her deep-shadowed beneath rolling dark clouds of impending doom. *Quadriplegics don't make good lovers, therefore Goldman will not love me.* She could hear the hapless notes of a funeral dirge and the requiem of their love was breathing its apparent last.

"I know this is not what you had bargained for, Marine. Your duty to my stillborn revolution is no longer required."

Her full lips coiled into a muddled smile and she turned her wanly eyes into the sun's refracted colors. A prison's prism rainbow filled the hospice room and their storefront lives were laid vacant. No expiatory gestures of reassurance were produced, no volumes of Emerson to be recited, no praiseworthy laurels entitled to a spouse. They both knew that when he walked out that door, the path that the two had beaten would diverge into tales of singularity. Like an icy avalanche, a chilly sensation ran down Goldman's back and caved-in his hollow hearted interior. A sterile thought then pierced his conscience. *What we have we deserve, what others do not have, they deserve. It is justice and it reigns.* Goldman fixed on her with his rootless wandering eyes that spoke decrees of an American gothic tale, and a long sigh wheezed through his sunken chest as he realized that, in the end . . . we are all alone.

XLVI

Quadrants of reason and visual deflections were interstellar benchmarks in Goldman's murky Milky Way. After the ignominious abandonment of his barefoot *Contessa*, he drifted into uncharted waters of submerged obscurity. He had to navigate to falling stars in his new sky and longed for the days when Mina shared his boat and the two sailed into the warm trade winds of love. What little bit of himself he had left was siphoned off with intact dilation and evacuated with procedural precision. He had aborted her like he had aborted himself, and any gastrula possibilities had been shit-canned in a bloody heap. It was 1951, and all hopes of bringing in the New Year with great expectations were dashed with the snapping of Mina's fair Grecian neck. This was the year of the rabbit: delicate and unsettled, self-centered and deceptive, where consequences of running compulsions stir passionless inspired mishap, *"touché du monde!"*

It seemed a fitting description, and Goldman's wasteland wandering baffled his antithetical reckoning, fragged again by enemies yet to be identified. He threw himself into the abyss of dissipation with such ferocity that something new and pathological mixed into the meat cauldron of his life. His usual descent into mindless days of reckless drink, and self-obliteration was to be expected. But this bout was different. It wasn't some side effect from foggy alcoholic epochs, but something in the very fiber of his flesh was conspiring against him.

The face and body that God had given him had retrograded into the nonagenarian face and body that he deserved, and at thirty-one, he had wizened beyond his era. It had taken three decades to learn the art of absurd ballroom brawling, grand facades, and wanton deeds that walk a vertiginous tight-rope around the narrow rim of suicide. He had slithered out of Mina's life and into the void. Now he would slink on his belly and eat the dust of the world for having whispered schlock deceptions into her ears. So many mistakes, but of all his mistakes, she was his best.

Goldman had vowed never to find his twisting path on skidrow again, yet there he was, a cesspool lifeguard responsible for a lugubrious zombie population, the king of congenital idiots. His once handsome physical form was reduced to a lank haired, beard matted, bipedal anthropoid, and the small growth that had colonized on his back had metastasized to every quadrant of his hat-rack physique. There were a variety of tumors that peppered his epidermal-scape with pink and purple cauliflower growths, like uranium flak on the skin of an alien craft. He was a deleterious sight to behold and smelt like how he felt, an atomic biohazard in radioactive decay.

He always knew, somewhere in the pit of his plum, that the fruit of radiation poisoning would come into season. He was terrified at the prospect of his fragile mortality, and his natural desire to die old and leave an ugly corpse, was inverting—now he would die young and leave an even uglier corpse. Loneliness and hunger were his constant companions, and the ceaseless gnaw of survival prodded him on until it was the only thing that made him feel like he was alive.

Street cadging, and digging in trash cans for discarded sustenance, made life pitiably uncomplicated. If only his inner-workings were that effortless, he lamented. Curb 'n' gutter existence is a ghostly experience and spook people like him were only acknowledged with purloining glances. But when one is encrusted with scaly purple and pink nodules that look like the most absurd monster costume a B film could contrive, it's hard to expect anything other than an execrable reception. He couldn't remember the last time he had eaten, and the only thing he had to fill his gravel-churned gut was a fermenting pint of Ten High. His steady intake of rock-hard alcohol put him in peril of organ failure, but it was the only medicament that could fend off a fated psychic virus that had infected him and feelings of self-minatory perpetuation that he had contracted. The alphanumeric cells that together made up the grid of his gross eccentricities finally resigned to total senselessness as his meiotic mind split and slipped gently into mental illness.

He knew that if he didn't get help soon his human membership card would expire, and he would join the myopic zombies exhumed from his past, but as hard as he tried, he could not figure out how to excavate his molted soul. To retreat to the skidrow mission and to have to face his brother would be a trebuchet-hurled boulder to the groin. Even though he was famished, homeless, and marooned, it would be a piece of humble pie that he could not gag down.

He roamed aimlessly, knuckle shuffling in eclipses of black and white, grainy images, unblinking mementos of spent *Dachau* days, a misanthropic lunkhead deprived of name and humanity; goulash groused into the discarded human inventory of warehoused bodies, indexed souls and stock number tattoos. *Surely the world must know?* The water of his life reduced to a trickle that was barely-detectable between the dry cobble of his irreducible mysteries, where inner-action and authentic heroes are forever lost.

He spied a fellow street ghoul who was devouring a sandwich. The sight of food made his eyes water and his dusty mouth salivate.

"My good friend, where did you acquire such a handsome-looking sandwich?" The bum stared at Goldman with truncated breaths and an unobstructed length before words could form. Even by a homeless sewer rat's standard, Goldman was an unholy sight to the eyes and an offense to the soul.

"Th . . . th . . . they're handing out sack lunches at MacArthur Park," he said with false enthusiasm. The thought of food put just enough vim and vigor in Goldman's step to move him at the speed of a tree sloth. He thought it nauseously ironic to go back to the same park where he had handed out sack lunches. No matter, he could not take the pangs of his ravenous jabs another minute. He hoped he would not run into someone he knew, or even worse, Jonathan.

On the way to the park he happened by a storefront window with a mannequin mirror, when out of the crook of his eye, a sight stunned his most basic sensibilities. He stepped back into his reflection and was plowed under by the macabre exhibit, offensive by any standard. It had been a long time since he had taken in his likeness. The scene was surreal, like something from Dante's *Divine Comedy*, and he laughed with a panic-driven guffaw, tremolos of rapid cackling horror. The facial features he recognized as him were barely visible. Instead, he looked like the exterior hull of a fishing schooner, encrusted by sea barnacles, muscles, and other soft-shelled creatures.

A woman exiting the storefront was so startled that she belted out a rattled scream and dove back into the store where she collapsed. Goldman thought it was hysterical—hysterical in the sense that he felt the same way, but sobering to know that he was probably dying. The sight of his condition faded as he forged ahead, pushed by the growls of his stomach and visions of sandwiches that were already masticating in his salivated maw.

He turned a corner and a white dove fluttered in his face. It caught him so off guard that he instinctively backhanded the bird, which ricocheted off the windshield of a passing bus and fell dead to the street. He stood motionless in a moment that was neither prosaic nor incredible, but seemed rolled up with lumps of potential meaning. Something about the creature having to lie in the gutter felt indecent and he decided the only considerate thing to do was to bury it. He picked up the dead fowl and had walked only a few steps when his solar plexus were sucker punched and dropped him to his rickety knees. Maybe it was the pain of not eating for days, or a delayed reaction to the revelation of his face, all he knew was that the sensation had robbed him of all voluntary movement.

He fixed on the dove again, which seemed to be a touchstone that detonated ordinances stored in his emotional ammo dump and a welling up in his throat had turned to retched blubbering. He held the small animal, soiling the top of its feathered crown with tears from ducts that had not been used in years. Mourning for the fowl made him exceedingly self-conscious of his lilting psychodrama. It then occurred to him that his cry was oddly in the pitch of Kazuo's five notes. It was a significant gesture and the notes exited his throat with powerful ease, but enough was enough.

He found a vacant dirt lot and with his bare claws proceeded to dig a small shallow grave. As he did, he kept looking at how perfectly beautiful the dove was, whiter than snow and without one worldly blemish. When the hole was ready to intern the animal, he turned to see that the dove had righted itself and was on its haunches. He was certain that the bird had been dead: *Maybe it was just knocked out*, he thought, but it wasn't breathing and was limp as a white satin handkerchief. The dove got its bearings, looked up at the monster, and took flight. Before departing, it circled Goldman seven times, *cooing* with seeming gratitude and fluttering its wings in genteel homage.

Goldman found the incident perplexing, albeit not entirely mystifying. What befuddled him was the inexplicable plunge into the baby pin of a squalling child; the sudden grip of stacked emotions that he was unable to control or conceal, but trying to break that down had low priority, as his hunger was heckling him louder than a pack of hyenas. He made his way through MacArthur Park to where a small crowd of mad ragged bums were being handed lunch sacks. As luck would have it, Jonathan was among the sack handlers.

He hesitated at first, then moved into the crowd with an attempted anonymous, not among us, hidden fungus, head turned down, nameless if not faceless maneuvering. He was so disfigured that Jonathan probably wouldn't recognize him anyway. Nonetheless the reactions from the street varmints did anything but make him feel invisible. Startled screams and frightened squeals were enough to draw unwanted attention. He kept his bulging face and bulbous nose bowed to the ground, thrust out his knobby hand, and hoped. A brown paper bag was pushed into his paw and he gamboled out of the homeless pack like a kangaroo on Quaalude.

Sitting on a park bench, he unsheathed the first wax paper-wrapped cheese sandwich when, from across the commons, his watery eye caught a solitary white lamb gazing directly at him. It let out a faint chain of bleats, turned and slowly walked out of the range of scrutiny. *Weird*, he thought, and turned back to his meal, his paroxysm for food, the only thing that could hold his attention. He devoured the sandwiches as fast as his rotgut could take them and it was a while before he acknowledged an inquiring voice that hovered just above his shoulder.

"These are strange days, my brother, days when sullen knives are buried breast deep in the ones we love the most."

Goldman turned his gnarled face to the brother of a prodigal son.

"And you are a man after Caesar's own heart," Goldman countered.

Jonathan sat down next to him. "Let's get you cleaned up."

*   *   *

Other than an occasional golden shower, compliments of street indigents, it was the first hot shower Goldman had taken since he could remember. The street's filth and grime penetrated deep into every square inch of his tattered body. Like a mange-afflicted dog deloused for the first time, an endless stream of liquid brown and black flowed into the shower drain with mounds of fungi, funk, and fleas. It was hard to wash his skin as the tumors had to be individually scrubbed, seemingly resistant to being cleaned. Maybe it was their porous wart-like surface that made it so tough, and a shower that should have taken ten minutes took forty-five, even then he didn't feel or look muck free.

He stepped out of the shower and stood before a full-length mirror. Seeing his reflection at the storefront was only a preview to the coming attractions of this horror matinee. The growths had almost completely covered his carcass: ghastly skin eruptions, pustules, and various sized tumors, some as small as pencil erasers, others as large as golf balls. For whatever reason, his genitals were entirely unaffected. He panicked and just wanted to pull off his radioactive costume and return to Normalsville, but it was not about to be cold-pealed from his frame.

Goldman turned to see Jonathan approaching him, slowly and cautiously, and handed him a towel, visually inspecting the moon-like surface of his body.

Goldman lowered his head in embarrassment then looked back up at his brother.

"*Ecce homo*, behold the man."

"Have you seen a doctor?" Jonathan plaintively asked.

Goldman wrapped the towel around his waist and shook his Sasquatch hair and beard.

"I have."

"Well?"

"Well, other than the fact that I have enough plutonium circulating through my veins to kill a dozen men, I'm fine."

It was impossible for Jonathan to look at him, but just as impossible to avert his eyes. Goldman's skin was like his aura, double buckshot blasted with irregular protuberances and cavities, and where smooth and defined lines should have been, there were instead tributary bumps and gullies in the lopsided silhouette of a spurned imposter. Goldman opened his arms wide, in a crucified golden ratio, a slowly turning carousel of the obscene. Jonathan took it in like a stomach-churning sideshow.

"What are these wounds?" Jonathan asked, his voice deliquescent.

"Those with which I was wounded in the house of my friends."

"I don't understand."

Goldman drew a deep breath as if it would take a lot of hot air to explain.

"It's funny. I fought and dodged bullets for this country and was even awarded the Congressional Medal of Honor, a real hero that the government has now labeled an enemy of the state. So they went pig sticking, turning me and countless others into wretched oink pinks, radioactive swine, shanghaied into the atomic tests on the Bikini Islands. I survived, but my shipmates weren't so lucky. I guess they thought I was Superman, so they decided to pump kryptonite directly into my veins, just to see what would happen. And now you see what has happened. What you are looking at, is the cremains of an Atomic Cocktail . . . shaken not stirred, with lots of olives and a twist of sour lemon."

Jonathan could scarcely believe the story. "I want to say a prayer over your body . . . and soul." Goldman quailed in flimsy terror and could hardly keep his see-through composure as his trigger finger nerves hovered over his panic button. He read Jonathan's face like the cover of a paperback horror novel, and would have convulsed in laughable hysterics at his unrestrained reaction, had it not translated into something so positively unnerving. He readied himself for prayer only because he didn't know what else to do. This was not the day of unilateral revelation. He had been bagging and tagging body evidence for months, umberglazed with changes of biblical proportion, but he could not muster up enough grit to literally face the revelation of his new reality.

He had even made eclectic entreaties to the pantheon of godhead possibilities: Buddha, Jesus, Jehovah, Allah, Zeus, Zoroaster, cosmic electricity, positive thinking, and even Kazuo's five notes. But no one or no thing had come to his aid. He thought that maybe Jonathan might have the inside track to God's Grecian oracle, where presages are altered and pleas for deferred mortality are granted. Jonathan tentatively moved his hands close to Goldman's head, avoiding any contact.

He proceeded with a long, heartfelt petition, the sounds of a puzzling language filling the air. To Goldman it sounded like saintly abstruse utterances devoid of any real meaning. He wanted to believe—really believe—that there was something out there other than cosmological mythology. Some people are constituted for great faith but he could never drum up enough, and he sensed in Jonathan that enough was never enough. Sadly, the prayer seemed compulsory, derision worthy, impoverished.

"I want you to come to the mission services tonight."

Goldman was reluctant, but he knew the drill: church and chores were required in hell's kitchen.

"I'm going to have the congregation pray for you."

Goldman shrugged his bulbous shoulders, crinkled his deformed face, and nodded his clunky head.

* * *

There were only a few regulars in attendance, which didn't dampen Jonathan's manufactured zeal. He gave a searing sermon on the evils of sin, salvation and the alchemy of souls. Goldman sat in the back pew and tried not to be noticed. But no one could help feeling imposed upon by the alarming image of a Neolithic monster. At the end of the sermon Jonathan explained who the strange-looking man was and said that his condition was a direct assault of the devil, and that they were to pray for the immediate expunging of the satanic malady. No one was about to lay hands on his crocodile hide, as was customary to do, so Jonathan had them direct their hands in remote-controlled prayer. Goldman felt disconsolately self-conscious and knew there would be no healing; the spectacle was embarrassing and farcically pitiful to him.

Jonathan continued with bottomless supplications to the Almighty, praying in circular motions that spiraled to a blaring peak. As the congregation soaked their dipped heads in marinated prayer, Jonathan saw a strange yet familiar materialization of light fogging over his brother: the gold petals manifesting again right before his unquiet eyes. He glanced at the congregation, whose heads were still bowed and unaware of the apparition or anything that might be out of place. Even though the phenomenon had the effect of vacuuming terror, he didn't question it anymore. Either he was hallucinating or this was something for his select eyes only. Still, the sight was intensely fascinating, and for a long period he said nothing and did nothing, but watch the eerie manifestation do its thing.

The moment passed and not one gold petal was to be retrieved. Goldman's distended head still hung glumly, and then tilted up. Whatever the prayer was supposed to achieve left him looking and feeling no different. He lowered his head again in a posture of obeisance, when he felt a slight touch on his distorted face. Looking up, he was greeted by the guiltless visage of a little blond girl, incarcerated in a wheelchair.

"I'm praying that you will get well, mister."

Goldman was politely relieved that there was someone who was not entirely repulsed by his Methuselahated hide. The little girl's bonhomie splendor clipped the memory of his own daughter and he was intensely moved by her stricken condition. His mind darted to Mina and how he had frigidly abandoned her, and he felt the same sharp pain in his gut that he had experienced when he held the white dove. Like the spear of Longinus piercing his thorax, blood and water gushed from the side of meekness and filled him with sickly sweet sorrow. He reached out to the girl in selfless ministration; the two hugged each other with palsied limbs and bumpy tomb-like grasps, embracing broken body dreams, and fusing as a single lighthouse for lost ships drifting too close to any morally jagged shore. The feeling was like heroin, only authentic, pure and innocent, and for the moment he was happy not to be thinking of himself.

The congregation remained quiet and respectful as the two possessed each other, rocking lullaby babies, coeval souls dreaming in born again dreams. It was a certifiable moment of the highest form of human interaction, the kind of moment that turns systemic norms into expressions of faithful piety. Something peculiar, yet familiar, leaped inside of Goldman, and once again he felt like something had been jettisoned. He could only equate it to a kind of magnetic discharge, like an electrical sneeze, and for the briefest of moments he was out of control. The feeling was startling at first, but like any heartfelt sneeze, it was good to get it out. The foundlings released their embrace and the girl wheeled herself back to her mother's side. The congregation ignominiously exhaled in collective guilt, ashamed for not having the naïve yen to do what the little girl had.

Even Jonathan shamed morosely. From the moment he had seen his brother he would not touch him: possible contagion, possible revulsion, but definitely the expectorated spewing of a man he still envied. He led the congregate in a hymn that climaxed with a collective "Amen". An eerie quiet vacuumed the chapel, except for the single fragile voice of a ten-year-old angel. The girl in the wheelchair was humming: C, F, A flat, G flat, and C sharp. A palpable presence, defying all mortal instincts, hung in the five tones' lilting melody, and then silence.

The tepid air was suddenly interrupted by an expulsion of untreated emotion, and whirling gasps filled the chapel as the crippled girl stood. She quivered out of her rolling steel chair, putting one fragile foot in front of the other, trembling and wobbling down the aisle. Her steps became firmer and all equilibrium returned with instantaneous muscle regeneration. The congregation buzzed with skepticism, when the hush was split by the ignited wail of the child's mother. The little girl threw her arms around Goldman as if he was the most handsome man at the church dance.

"Thank you for healing me, mister."

Pandemonium erupted as everyone enveloped the wheelchair-liberated child and one by one hugged and shook Goldman's gifted hand. He sat stunned and amazed that people thought he had anything to do with the bizarre event. He even laughed at the idea, but an accumulation of phenomena had followed him around, which was now creating cracks in his insouciant dismissal of the implausible. His entire essence soft-boiled in the warmth of attention, and for the first time since he could remember, he felt connected to others.

XLVII

Three days had passed since the miracle of the little girl and Jonathan could not scrape the stupefying event from the cracked walls of his mind. He knew the girl and her mother well. The two had always been homeless, and refuge at the mission was an ignominious routine. Jonathan had laid healing hands on the child many times, but her condition always remained unchanged. She reminded him of the other little girl that he had tried to heal years before, with the cancerous tumor that had gnawed through her femur bone. He had failed so abjectly then, that he had hoped to make restitution with this little girl, but that ended in goaded frustration as well. Polio was the devil's weapon of choice and had left her rolling-chair-bound all her young life. The fact that she had never walked was evident by her withered legs, and for her to amble on appendages where muscles had never developed was beyond explanation. It was a God thing all right, but of all the God things that Jonathan ever witnessed, never had there been a manifestation on this echelon. The real question was: how did his brother fit into the equation?

*   *   *

The room reeked of swill and pigs as Jonathan sat like an exigent witness to Goldman's cross-examined body, soul sleeping, cocoon-psychoma. A white sheet that draped loosely over his undulating form made him look as if he were morgue interned. Jonathan pulled the sheet back like a spectator at a carnival freak show's main attraction. Goldman's chest heaved with his breathing, spastic and disordered, percolating air through fluid lungs with a sickening congested necro-wheezing. Flies buzzed around his malformed exterior and spasmodically danced across his lumpy face, but it didn't bother Goldman in the slightest.

Jonathan noticed that in addition to the numerous excrescences, Goldman's skin was developing a shiny leathery glaze like that of a snake or a lizard. Different parts of his body randomly quivered as if electricity were arcing just below his potholed skin. He emitted a detestable scent, a bittersweet toxic odor that initiated auto gag-reflexes with undignified shudders. He was a sight to consider, and it was vexing to Jonathan to see this once handsome specimen reduced to such a disfigured heap of dewlap flesh, yet he furtively derived *schadenfreude* pleasure from his brother's misfortune.

Goldman's mouth began to quaver and he mumbled something. Jonathan drew close and heard what sounded like some kind of prayer, spoken in dead tongues, shaken loosely together with bad breath English; garbling straggling shoots of the nonsensical.

"The thirty-eight parallel is crossed by the northern hordes of Korea. Sixty thousand American dead. Tet Offensive! The serpent of the South China Sea swallows fifty-eight thousand American boys. The *Beast* of Belshazzar devours the *Dog* of Kuwait and the *Eagle* sends its talons deep into the throat of Babylon. September eleven, the two towering *ones* are subtracted and the pentagon is now *four*. Afghan dogs run to the hills and piss on the *Bush*, Obama buries Osama, extinguishing flames in the sea of retribution. The great *Bear* invades Asia *Minor* with its *major* Muslim hordes and fornicates on the scales of Israel's mountains."

Goldman opened his blood-blasted eyes to see Jonathan's fixed features, two inches from his face, and bolted straight up. "What are you doing?" he yipped.

Jonathan flailed backwards and fell into a saddle-worn chair and crashed to the floor, splayed in a horizontal X. The spectacle of Goldman's inanimate form suddenly animating violated the bounds of anything normal, the tumors quivering and shuddering as if possessing a life of their own.

"You've been sleeping for three days. Are you okay?"

"I guess I haven't been feeling well."

The two looked at one another with scoured thoughts and gnarled notions of a previous event.

"I've been thinking and praying. I believe that the Lord has given you the gift of healing."

"Listen, I don't want to get into a whole religious thing, but making me out to be a healer is plain poppycock," Goldman said with dangling ambiguity.

"Something happened," Jonathan said with a somber chill.

"I don't believe there was anything wrong with that girl in the first place." Jonathan rolled his eyes with staggered bafflement. "You would be very wrong. The church members have been bringing the sick and crippled and you must see them."

"I have a very full schedule," Goldman groused.

"If you want to stay at the mission, you'll pull your weight, and right now your weight is to lay your hands on the sick"

"Why? So I can make a fool of myself like your father?" Goldman caught himself but the peevish comment cut quickly to misdemeanor memories and felony fraudulent pasts.

"I'm sorry, I didn't mean that."

Jonathan glowered down. "Then you'll do it?"

Goldman threw up his arms in exasperation. "Just this one time, so I can prove you wrong."

He rose from the bed and left the room with an oblique lurch, leaving in his crop-dusted wake an indescribable smell of over-heated flatulence that buffeted the air like mustard gas . . . instabarf. Jonathan cupped his hand over his mouth and nose and gagged slightly. He then noticed the bed sheet was traced with an opaque grease grime, sweat-soaked shroud negative of Goldman's ghastly form.

*   *   *

Rumors were abounding of a supernatural *voila* that had taken place at the mission. Most folks thought it was just a reactionary yarn that refused to die, but when people saw the once wheelchair-bound girl walking and running like any other hale 'n' hearty ten-year-old, there was no denying that a San Andres-scale spiritual reckoning had shook. The mission chapel was chock full with a myriad of the ailing, waiting patiently for the ugly man with the beautiful gift. Some were in wheelchairs, others leaned on crutches, some were coughing, but most were there as signatories of curiosity. The service started with decorous hymns, the praising of a manicured god, and pastel shadings of heaven yet to come. The event was charged with bated expectancy, and carn*evil* deliverance was painted like a sad clown on every circus-church inspired face.

After the obligatory word, Jonathan motioned to a reluctant Goldman, who approached the pulpit, piqued by a sense of dread and embarrassed concealment. Goldman thought it gauche to try to repeat something that had been so sweet, special, and spontaneous, reduced to a discounted dog 'n' pony show. It was sheer idiocy to him, and he figured the sooner it didn't work the sooner he could lay the myth to rest. But in the backroom of his mind, he suspected that he might be storming against a presumed destiny, and that he indeed had everything to do with it.

"A tremendous work of the Lord occurred here three nights ago and it was the holy work of the Spirit. God can and will use anyone to carry out His will, and if it is God's will that no one should suffer, then only *He* can heal." Jonathan began the compulsory praising and lifting of his hands with embroidered benedictions, enjoining the congregation to follow suit. He then motioned for the infirm to queue up in front of Goldman, who vaguely recalled the practice of laying-on of hands from the days of the tent crusades. He felt self-conscious and absurdly clumsy.

"Just touch them," Jonathan whispered.

Halfheartedly, Goldman placed his hand on each individual, but with an intervening sense of fraudulence. He figured that to keep it authentic he needed to make some kind of hand gestures. He began with nonsensical waving motions that grew into wild, bizarre hand gyrations, but nothing that resembled the Cross. One by one the sickly fragrance of the enfeebled drifted back to the pews until all had been touched. There was a period of silence except for Goldman's peculiar humming. Kazuo's five notes resonated from his pulsing throat over and over. Weirdly, he stood in the Vitruvian pentagram, one hand turned up, the other turned down, Cheshire smirking to Jonathan.

After a period of hushed weeping and praising one of the faithful stood, a blind man with a white cane, hurled it across the chapel, almost hitting an old woman who had to duck for cover.

"Good Lord Almighty! I can see!!"

Another man, who was wheelchair-bound, started jumping and screaming, "I can feel my legs!"

From across the room a deaf woman shouted, "I can hear!"

The congregation began to spontaneously shout out their healings. People that had been in wheelchairs and others who had slouched on crutches belted out shouts of praise and danced on their newly bequest legs. Others with just about every other conceivable disease, bellowed out declarations that they, too, were cured. The entire flock shook and lurched on the chapel floor, jiggering and quivering well into the wee hours of the miracle-requisitioned night.

*   *   *

Word of the incredible happenings at the downtown mission had spread like wild burning trash, and the once scarcely populated skidrow chapel had turned into a holy shrine of standing room capacity. After days of querulous denials, Goldman reluctantly surrendered his chink-penetrated opposition to the fact that people were actually being restored to health with just a touch of his miracle requisitioned hand. Jonathan tried to bolster Goldman and told him that he should be happy that the Lord had found him worthy of such a gift. Goldman, of course, never felt worthy of anything, nor did he believe in anything, especially the coquettish divine. Something quantifiable had transpired though, a real sundering phenomenon that peeled onion dome layers to its tearful core. He could only credit the miracles to Kazuo's five notes and the Vitruvian stance. Deeper still, he had begun to realize that *he* was the missing radioactive ingredient to Kazuo's theorem, the outré recipe to his metaphysical cake.

He had learned long ago that there was no such thing as miracles, but he didn't know what else to call it. If it had nothing to do with Kazuo's theory then the source eventually would have to make itself known. For now, he had to earn his keep, and a healing gig beat changing bed sheets and washing dishes.

The twists and turns of an emerging providence stirred boyhood memories of working the crusades. He remembered how unseemly it was to entice the vulnerable into counterfeit deliverance from their corporeal curses. Now he was plying the same trade, but actually doing the very thing that Jonathan's father could not. It felt a trifle bizarre but was, in a vicarious way, vindicating.

*   *   *

What at first seemed inept and artificial began to take on a hauteur life of its own, and what looked like a derisive stage act was turning into an unctuously crafted form full of murk and refined contrivance. Goldman, who was at first dubious of the attention, let his freak flag fly and was now enjoying the adulation with high-altitude delirium. He had become so emboldened that before each healing service he would vociferously chant Kazuo's five notes with operatic theater, and stand for long periods in the Vitruvian pentagram before the spellbound crowd, creating an atmosphere pregnant with pretensions of a Euripidean drama.

He developed different techniques for the laying on of his hands. Sometimes he would touch the afflicted on the forehead and they would instantly drop. Some would shake and shudder and assistants would have to drag them off the deck like flopping tuna. Sometimes he would just blow on them and in a Bethesda whirl whole groups would collapse, healed. He quickly became addicted to performing in front of the ever-growing crowds and loved spellbinding the congregate with kinky spiritual demonstrations that kept them suppliant and begging for more. His priory was expanding from auteur expressions of deviant creativity, and he imitated the techniques of Jonathan's father and even Mina's fillip wordplay.

*   *   *

Goldman was a media darling. Soon the entire city was aware of his otherworldly exploits. Every night was sardine-crammed standing room only, and there was not one of the infirmed that did not walk out with a complete and instantaneous physical overhaul. Unprepared eyes that lay upon his image would sometimes scream in sprawling alarm, collective gasps and entreaties of sympathy when Goldman walked to the pulpit.

"How could something so hideous be an instrument of God?" people murmured. His squalid exterior belied the power that lay within, but eventually they accepted that this was how God had packaged the miracle worker: a spectacle to behold, the man with a glut of distorted knots, bumps, and tumors was doing the unimaginable, delivering real curative healing to an unsuspecting world.

Jonathan knew it was God's power, but what left him feeling so anxiously bile was that Goldman, an avowed atheist, was contemptuous of anything religious. The peculiar way he hummed the strange notes before and after the service and the occult pentagram stance made Jonathan feel intensely ill at ease. Goldman never brought glory to the Lord and never commanded illnesses to leave in the name of Jesus. *There is something divergent about a displayer of the divine who does not recognize the diviner*, he thought. These facts threw Jonathan into an anal-tight spiritual spin, dizzying to all his theological assumptions and a genuine threat to his assumed religious prerogatives.

At the beginning of the services, Jonathan made sure the congregation got a good dose of the gospel. It wasn't so much that he was committed to his sermons, as it was a way of competing with his brother's gift of the elect. With mock determination he explained to the growing crowds that the yuletide healings that were about to take place were the gifts of Christ's Mass, not Goldman's. Goldman never uttered a word that might be in agreement. To compound the insult, in one of the services Jonathan heard him voice the unutterable: "I heal you." Not in the name of the Lord or any other deity, just "I heal you." The crowd was not aware of the heretical faux pas, but Jonathan was, and he was incensed with the egregious oversight.

One night, after the mission's healing service, he sat Goldman down, determined to set him on the fundamental good foot.

"You need to understand something, my dear brother. It is not you who are doing these miracles, but it is *my* God using you. From now on, you are to heal in the name of the Lord and the spilt blood of Jesus."

Goldman laughed like a Transylvanian that had robbed a blood bank.

"Your God has nothing to do with it. For some time I've been trying to figure out a way to explain the unexplainable, and now it's so clear. You see . . . the chemistry in my body has mutated and my brain is now non-hemispheric. There is no left side or right side. There is only the singularity of one. If I do anything in anyone's name, it will be in the name of Kazuo."

The explanation ruptured Jonathan's vacuum sealed standards, leaving him devotedly defensive.

"What is a Kazuo?"

"The voice of one crying in the world's wilderness," Goldman said reassuringly.

"You see, I am the missing element in Kazuo's formula. My irradiated cells work as a chemical conductor, and when combined with the five notes and the Vitruvian pentagram, I become the portal to the universe's nexus and the prime directive of quantum power is conveyed directly through me."

"What are you talking about?" Jonathan asked with gallivanting confusion.

"I am the genetic model, the first gene machine altered with the highest doses of a nuclear brew. It is *I* who loosen the grip of the electron. It's through *me* that the subatomic universe opens and is receptive to *my* sound therapy, bringing wholeness to the body and spirit. It is *I* who alter the very magnetic fields in my internal space and emit a field of bio-photons that change ailing energies. It is *my* power that realigns the aberrant waves of a malevolent world's condition to their proper frequency."

"Why can't you heal yourself?" Jonathan asked.

Goldman stood noiselessly and tipped his head at an unbalanced slant.

"My own condition is an unfortunate side effect to the Atomic Cocktail that I have no control over. I guess the price of healing comes at the price of the healer, but what savior hasn't paid that price?"

"You're mad," Jonathan said with percolating incontinence.

Goldman scudded across the room like a Shakespearean artiste.

"I am the epicenter where the universe becomes aware of itself and all secrets are revealed. Life is a grand drama to be played out on a homogeneous level, and the wounds that the world inflicts cannot be repaired by some anthropomorphic god performing spiritual surgery from the corner of the cosmos. We have to be our own doctors and treat our own wounds, right here, right now, on good old fallen Earth. It has nothing to do with primitive god entities that act a certain way based on offerings and sacrifices. We have to be our own god, our own healer, our own power and wisdom. This is my annunciation: I am living proof of Kazuo's theory, and I will proclaim *his* good news to the world."

Goldman tried to explain that every epoch had its own revelator: Moses, Mohammed, Buddha, Zarathustra, Ashtavakra Gita, Jesus, Gandhi, Kazuo, and now Goldman. These people, including him, were each living holographs illuminated by different aspects of the same superluminal truth. The problem was, and had always been, that a dark and corrupt world wants no part of the light, especially the church that hides under its own consecrated rites and self-diluting beliefs.

"The years of heartache and pain have purified, cleansed, and distilled me like a fine wine completed at the rebirth of a new vintage." Goldman flounced out of the room with a *touché* swagger and a semi-godlike spook that left Jonathan's thoughts inverted and narrow, like looking backwards through the telescope of his soul. The blasphemy hammered his wooden framed edifice and loosened every nail that fastened his meager beliefs together. For him, Goldman's mind had unraveled like a *Zeitgeist* mummy, and now there was only the freeze-dried casing of someone who had gone completely insane.

There was no chance that he would let him get away with spiritual larceny. *Yet how could he do such things if God were not, in fact, with him?* Didn't even Jesus have to defend Himself from the Pharisees when they accused Him of healing people in the name of Beelzebub? Jesus had deftly answered, "A kingdom divided against itself cannot stand." And did He not also say "Do ye not know that ye are gods?"

Jonathan hated entangled paradoxes that could spin his mind in sticky webs of circuitous logic. Goldman was a self-confessed atheist, and if God was in fact behind this, and He must be, then how could He employ an antichrist to carry out the sacerdotal work of Christ? The whole thing put him into a holy scamboly meltdown, where credibility gaps nag stories of empty sepulchers, and heavenly ascensions are potentially reduced to dematerialized myths. It was an anomalous quandary, but he was determined to roll away the stone of his compartmentalized ideas, where belief and doubt stink the same tomb. Pungent truth was the only smell that mattered to him, no matter how odious and he was determined to bring the glory of God's fragrance back to its source, to the very Ark of the Lord's Holy Temple.

XLVIII

FREAK HEALS THE MASSES splattered the front page of the *Los Angeles Times*. Every local news channel covered the ongoing saga of the bizarre wonder man who packed the mission chapel and turned out the healed like a curative stamp-press factory. Most thought it was cocktail party sensationalism but when the mayor caught wind of Goldman's purported powers, he brought his ailing wife who was in stage four of ovarian cancer and counting her final sunsets on the fingers of her bony hands. After Goldman's Midas touch, the mayor took her to an oncologist who declared that there was no trace of the malignancy and she fully recovered.

Goldman went from being *Homo sapiens* nonentity to a *Homo luminous* super entity, and his ever-expanding hubris craved more. He sensed something percolating in his interior like a steaming geyser, and putting his hand into its gushing rapids transferred to him the command of an esoteric supremacy, drawing him deeper into uncharted levels of metanoia. *Yes, the river knows.* This would be the beginning of his destiny, his priest-craft calling, a *humanimous-maximous-anomalous*, the likes of which the world had never seen.

His confidence grew to gargantuan proportions and his ambition would stop at nothing to fulfill his calling as a supernatural being. The power he wielded was mindlessly intoxicating, and he thought that maybe the trade-off for his perverse appearance was worth it. When word got out that even the mayor's wife had been eased of her dis-ease, the downtown mission became a Mecca. The chapel could not contain the crowds, and street riots broke out among those who could not get in.

Security was becoming a concern. What Goldman had not counted on was that religion, or anything that resembled it, can bring out an acute weirdness in some folks that is insalubrious and glycerin volatile. People questioned how he was doing what he was doing, and some even called him the devil. One maniac attacked him with a meat cleaver, screaming,

"Antichrist! Antichrist!" and hacked off one of his bulbous tumors. The man was dropkicked and almost beaten to death by a contingent of fanatics with the zeal of jackbooted storm troopers.

Word spread of the attempted assassination, and a few days later eleven young men with shoulder-length hair and matching beards arrived at the mission and asked to see Goldman. He appeared before them like a sojourning king and there ensued a portrait reunion the likes of Jacques-Louis David's, *Oath of the Horatii*. The Malibu surfers and their Rasputin had not seen one another since the days of Libido Cove, and their meeting was ebulliently jovial and full of febrile tribute. Big Jim and Andy approached Goldman and dropped to their shaky knees, their eyes fixed on his affliction with shock and awe.

"We've been reading about the miracles in the papers and we knew it had to be you," said Andy.

Goldman smiled through his misshapen mouth. "Well, you know the papers, they always exaggerate."

"We have come to offer our help," said Big Jim.

Goldman motioned for the two to stand.

"You need protection, and as a token of our esteem we are here to render our services and to declare our loyalty to you," said Andy.

Big Jim embraced Goldman. "From the day you first walked into our lives we knew you were someone special, and after you healed my leg I knew that I would devote myself to you. Whatever your cause, we will follow."

The eleven genuflected before Goldman like his Knights Templar. All vowed undying allegiance and to forgo their former lives as beach deadbeats to be disciples of Goldman's annihilating and transcendental authority. From that day there was never a time when at least one of the surfers was not by his side.

* * *

Jonathan, like the rest of the city, was caught up in the mystical events unfolding before their unbelieving eyes. He was so preoccupied with the immense undertaking that he lost sight of his responsibilities at the mission, upstaged by Goldman's meteoric rise. His brother had already tipped to iconoclastic profanity, and without Jonathan's sermons, the services would more aptly resemble a pagan fest, devoid of anything that resembled a Christian crusade.

Goldman resented Jonathan's reprimands and he tired of his continual niggling. He wanted to get rid of him, but he needed his help to implement the enormous undertaking and his religious legitimization of the crusade. Staggering amounts of money were being donated and it wasn't long before the two were seduced by the non-taxable cash that dropped into their coffers like leaves falling in a New England autumn wind gust.

Goldman wasn't so dimwitted as to usurp entrenched beliefs. He understood that the people who came to the services were god junkies, and if the healings were not presented in a way that appealed to their sentimental sacraments, the donations would cease and the influence that cash afforded would soon dry up. He recognized that the herd needed to be fed from the same old trough, but, like any cattle thief, he also knew that all he had to do was modify the brand ever so slightly, and in time . . . they would bear his mark.

*   *   *

The press got hold of information about the enigmatic icon and articles circulated details of Goldman's war record: the first Jew to receive the Congressional Medal of Honor, orphaned as a child, a common man committing rare acts of the stupendous. It all made for enticing reading. The articles went so far as to say that he was a natural leader, and even entertained the idea of him running for president. To the papers, he was a gilded lily and a publicity bonanza, but Goldman feared the uncovering of his not-so-glorious past, and the more exposed, the less mystical he felt. Like a recluse spider, he lived as an outsider on the inside, hiding from the world's hard-shelled queries.

He only felt comfortable with his retinue of surfers. Paranoia became an on going conundrum, and any perceived enemies were to be squeezed under his knobby thumb. To him, the world was now becoming psychiatrically disordered; and like all mad men, he thought everyone was insane but him. He feared that wangling nut jobs might want to off him, and knew that it was only a matter of time before Muller and the FBI came snooping.

Muller was all too aware of Goldman's latest rise to glory and of his devoted following, Red-cell meiotic and growing into legions. A card-carrying member of the Communist Party with a marshaled colossus was potentially political napalm and if Goldman were to use his platform to promulgate a radical Socialist agenda then he might incite a national insurrection. Muller was frustrated and desperate to take some kind of action. He decided to leak stories to the news affiliates, of Goldman's Communist associations, his arrests, even the killing of Miguel Contreras. When the FBI provided photos of him marching with Communists, a thin Red line was drawn and people started shoring up sides. Some said it was a government conspiracy to discredit him, while others believed the stories, but no one knew for sure, as the photos looked nothing like the disfigured man that they slavishly followed.

Regardless, Goldman was still an article that garnered reckoning. From Los Angeles to New York he was a sensation, and soon became worldwide front-page news. The FBI was so frantic to besmirch his reputation that they spread tabloid yarns that the man was not even from this world; replete with credible sources and firsthand accounts, of a flying saucer landing in Central Park and Goldman exiting the spacecraft. They feigned another story that he was half-man, half-armadillo, and that he fiendishly ate barbequed babies. The public didn't know what to think, they only knew that he was a spectacle and a living testimonial to inexplicable good.

To the FBI, he was still a clear and present danger, but there wasn't a lot they could do in the absence of any interdicting laws. If they arrested him they might ignite riots, and if they did nothing he would be free to do and say as he pleased. Muller had hoped that the deadly amount of plutonium they ran up his arm would be enough to render him *corpus non grata*. Instead, it had turned him into a radioactive demigod that could not be controlled and would not die. Even after the seemingly fatal car crash in the Nevada desert, he lives on in unredeemed form. The agency resigned itself to the fact that they were powerless to do anything radical. They would keep a "big brother" eye on him, and if he started to peddle revolution then they would resort to draconian measures with mortal consequences. To the government, the death of one was still worth the saving of a nation.

Goldman's Ministry, as it was known, was humming like a fine-tuned ecumenical machine. Even the largest arenas were filled to standing room only. One night he healed twenty thousand people. FBI agents infiltrated the crowds, and reported to Muller that Goldman wasn't inciting Communism but was preaching a message of some kind of brain reconstitution, which was somehow being implemented with the weird five notes. Goldman would work the crowds until all were chanting Kazuo's five notes in an incessant monophonic whirr, which theoretically squared its power to exponential levels, supercharged by Goldman's Vitruvian stance. He was the grand conductor and holy coil to the universe, electrifying and transforming the herded lemmings into super-radiant beings.

To Muller it was preposterous, but he feared that if it were somehow true then Goldman's followers' brains might become non-hemispheric, as Goldman had said, potentially endowing them with their own powers. It was like something from a poorly scripted sci-fi movie, horribly conceived but magnificently executed. If all these brains were Communist inspired and all-powerful, then the government would be in danger of being trampled underfoot by a new movement of Communist mega-brains.

"Unfuckingbelievable, the whole flippin' thing!" Muller yelped in frustration.

*   *   *

Jonathan had been in charge of all the finances and the money was gushing in such volumes that it started to lose its meaning, and they had to hire fulltime bean-counters. Thanks to Jonathan's, fiery religious sermons, the donations were tax free and legitimized by the IRS, but he resented being a Jiffy-Pop subordinate, playing court minstrel dirges to Goldman's grand symphony. For him, the lunacy of the ministry had hit an all-time absurdity, with zealous legions mindlessly worshiping Goldman as if he was the one to be glorified.

The impious ruse was intolerable, and he demanded that Goldman set the people straight, and relinquish his illegitimate throne to the Lord. What really grated on him was the fact that *he* was a true believer and had devoted his entire life to a healing ministry that had failed so abjectly. Now a renegade Jew, who did not believe in the Old Testament, let alone the New, was doing the inexplicable, and all in his own name. It left him so infuriated that he wanted to wash his hands of the whole mind-warping thing.

The truth was that underneath the veneer of his outrage he was secretly electrified by his brother's abilities. For the first time in his life he felt he was a part of something that was real and was more authentic than any religious experience he had ever had. He was elated to be associated with something so euphoric, especially when it allotted him the opportunity to preach to huge captive audiences. It was all so seductive, the cash that was coming in gave him a salary that was excessive, and to walk away from it would be testing.

Some nights there would be mountains of greenbacks, and Goldman would roll in it in a disgusting display of surfeiting excess. His shameless cash seeking was like a horde of greedy pigs that required constant feedings, but still squealed that it was not enough. The purgative display of evacuating lust reminded him of how his father had barefacedly coveted money and Jonathan's own perverse hankering for riches made him feel power drunk and money mad even as he faked temperance. He was torn between conviction and temptation, but should he stay or should he go? To return to the grind of the downtown mission would be to return to chronic discontent and molting of the soul.

He wrestled with the angel of the Lord through many a sleepless night, but never got the blessing, and in the morning always felt like his soul was out of socket. Yet the Lord blessed his brother's chicanery, just like the flim-flam sham of his father's ministry. He hated the fact that by the end of his best sermons the crowds just didn't care. Often he was interrupted by the mob's humiliating jeers or drowned out by their chanting of Goldman's name.

Jonathan loathed the fact that Goldman was so mawkishly adored and dignitaries from all walks of life clamored to meet him. They loved to take photos with the gifted metaphysician and groveled shamelessly at his feet. As if holy vestiges, people would fondle his sacred tumors; they were entrancing to the eye, fleshy ornaments dangling heavily from some twisted Christmas tree. He was a living breathing holiday and an international celebrity—more than a celebrity, a mortal incarnation of the divine.

Goldman's status was pile-driving his brother's fading-flock heart. For Jonathan, Goldman had become a despicable and sinister article, but now there was something about him that raised the possibility of the unthinkable. Could it be that he might be the Angel of Light, Lucifer himself. He even counted the letters in his name, David Oliver Goldman, which was a total of eighteen letters; if he counted the three sets of sixes in the antichrist's name that would be eighteen and the alphanumeric equivalent of 666.

The acronym of his name backwards was *GOD*, but more fitting forward was *DOG*. And to Jonathan, Goldman was a dog, a pathological carnivore devouring the lost. More correctly he was an antichrist, but was he *the* Antichrist of Revelation? Could it be that his brother was the Antichrist that his father had preached about all those years? If so, were these the final days of cosmic cataclysm and the end of the world? Would the Seven Plagues of Revelation be released and the Seven-Year Tribulation begin?

He remembered reading in scripture that in the last days false Christs would appear and perform great signs and miracles to deceive even the very elect. The possibility sent waves of galloping panic that bolted from the balls of his feet to the top of his tingling scalp. For a fleeting flash he understood the quintessence of evil and the possible reality of who his brother might really be, and that he, might be Goldman's unwitting Mephistopheles and false prophet. Jonathan laughed nervously and dismissed the thoughts as coincidence—a hell of a coincidence, but still a coincidence . . . Or was it?

Nevertheless, he believed there was a grand deception at work. The miracles were big and getting bigger, like the tumors on Goldman's ever-expanding body. None of it could be explained away rationally, and Jonathan came to resent him even more. All the spiritual struggles that he had sacrificed a lifetime for had been reduced to pointless platitudes that implied that he would have to live on in the indignity of his brother's long shadow. Even the gold-leafed petals that manifested over him seemed a declaration of the elect. God had chosen Goldman's altar over his, and the spirit of Cain raised its fists to smite a fatally flawed brother whose sacrifice was somehow more acceptable.

These superseding facts were such an intrusion that Jonathan felt like a caricature in his own pathetic gag. To carry on as an inconsequential esquire for the knighted messianic prerogatives of Goldman was intolerable, but to carry on believing in a mega-nebulous being that he furtively resented would be a greater pretense. The seeming indifference of his potentate tore at Jonathan's cobbled guts and choked what little flow was left in his spiritual pipes. Billows of religious monoxide were suffocating his cankered heart and the beatific light that once poured from the windows of his soul had dimmed to stillborn visions of opaque anger and illegitimate piety.

XLIX

Goldman's ministry was in Palm Springs giving an outdoor sunrise service and he had healed some five thousand people. When the crowd started to murmur that they were hungry as there was no place to buy food in the middle of the desert. Someone produced a loaf of Wonder bread, a carton of milk and a bag of beef jerky that immediately multiplied into thousands of cheeseburgers, fries and milkshakes and every believer ate until they had their fill. It was a spectacle beyond belief, yet Jonathan despised the incident, but it was the best damn cheeseburger he had ever had.

Shortly thereafter, the ministry had booked a healing revival at the Pomona fairgrounds. It was a typical Goldman service, with Kazuo's five notes pumping through a grand PA system. Jonathan had finished another monotonous sermon that the locals had tolerated and only when Goldman walked onto the stage did the crowd come to life, heaving with roaring cheers and plaudits of tribute.

For twenty minutes Goldman stood in the outré five point pentagram, lost in waves of transcendence, while Jonathan stood behind him, lost in waves of absurdity. A sobbing woman pushed a beautiful blond teenage girl in a wheelchair toward the stage. Jonathan instantly recognized the two from his failed attempt to heal the girl's cancerous leg years before. He was so aghast that he hid his face and ducked behind the PA amplifiers.

Goldman opened his eyes. The mother pulled back the blanket that covered the girl from the waist down, exposing the teenager's missing limb.

"Where is the girl's leg?"

The mother cocked her lamenting head. "A false prophet allowed God to take it."

"God did not take it. It has only been misplaced."

Goldman motioned to Big Jim and Andy to bring the girl up on the stage. They laid her at Goldman's feet and covered her waist again with the blanket. He bent down to his knees, placed his hand on her stump and drifted into a diaphanous daze. *With liquid fire eyes, he arose with his arms outstretched and* Rex Judaeorum *beams of assurance radiating from any crucified doubts.*

"It is not God's will for this girl to lose her leg," he confidently proclaimed.

He gave a large smile to the mesmerized crowd and started humming Kazuo's five notes. Before he could even get to the fifth note, the girl screamed and threw the blanket off, jumping to her feet, leaping like a young gazelle on her *two* legs.

The girl's mother shrieked and swooned. The audience collectively gasped and a tsunami of humanity hurled themselves at Goldman's feet, prostrate in genuflecting worship. Behind the amplifiers, Jonathan stood alone, contorting under sneering forces of incredulity as he watched the teenager frolic up and down the stage. He was so hard-bitten by the event that for a week he could not get out of bed.

*   *   *

Goldman thrived on the waves of oceanic adulation and the building of the perfect beast. A nuanced profile with an enchanted sense of buoyancy lifted even higher his stratospheric stature, in striking contrast to his accustomed sense of self-dissolution. There was something about the tang of power—real power—that was otherworldly and godlike, gnashing jaws of power that masticate life while it's still moving. Hegemony fed his barbarous appetite for marinated regurgitations of self, but somehow never satisfied. Any qualms about commanding the paranormal were allayed, and not just any power—Goldman power—obliquely confirmed with torque-induced precession and the right-angled touch of his hand. He wanted to believe it was all him, yet sensed a parasite inside that was passing itself off as a host, and clandestinely functioned under retrogressions of a malefactor.

He was a heliocentric force and the world was caught in his pull and had not seen anything like it since the days of the New Testament or fabled tales of mythical paganism. Often people wrangled over scripture, whether Christ actually did heal, and if so, then only God could do that. This was a ponderously gifted man who handed out heavy doses of deliverance, but nonetheless just a man. Or, some questioned, was he? People began calling him the Messiah. This created a querulous chasm; some believed the Messiah was still to come, and others, especially the Jews, believed that it might be Goldman.

The ultra-Orthodox Jews took a keen interest in the matter. They were aware of Goldman's Hebrew lineage, but did he come from the line of King David and was he born in Palestine? After a good deal of Septuagint speculation, many a Jew was convinced that Goldman indeed was the fulfillment of scripture as the deliverer of the chosen people: according to enciphered text, now that the holy land was in the hands of the Zionists, the Anointed One would come. For others, there just wasn't enough evidence to proclaim Goldman "King of the Jews". For the crypto-apocalyptic desperate, just the fact that his name was David was enough: "He had no beauty or majesty to attract us to him, nothing in his appearance that we should desire him." And: "By his wounds we are healed," they quoted.

Others thought he was a grand deceiver and that through the power of mind control, he was only making people think that they were healed. Either way, the fact that he was even controversial made Goldman drunk on accretions of legitimacy, self-importance, and immune to thought-snagged ideas that might eclipse his emerging now from his faded then. He felt that he was destined to hold the high ground of perpetuity, a fixed summit of godlike infinity that had the potential of constellating broken fragments of a fallen world into a true, scheming political machine.

The press was constantly interviewing him, and when the cameras were rolling he held forth semi-Socialist agendas. Communism was still a dangerous snake to handle, but Goldman liked to flirt with it; a contentious scarlet minuet, dancing center court in rings of star-spangled controversy. He knew his garrulous claims would incite the fury of the FBI, but his burgeoning sense of authority made him feel armor plated, and he grew reckless with his provocative *lingua-franca* tongue.

*   *   *

The crowd was stacked into a rodeo arena in Dallas, Texas. A large wooden stage had been built in the middle of the dirt-manure stadium with a special pulpit just for Goldman. Jonathan was giving a full-throated sermon to the unenthusiastic Lone Star audience. The crammed arena tired of his bloviating drone and started a deafening chant: "Goldman! Goldman!" Jonathan raised his placating hands, but could not mollify the herd, and once again he was driven from the pulpit under a wave of humiliation. Goldman's surfers took to the stage under the relentless Tibetan five note piping through a PA system. The throbbing whirr of Kazuo's echoing tones mixed with the relentless roar of agitated anticipation from a crowd tipping on the arête of hysteria.

Goldman rode into the benighted arena on a white stallion, clad in a sequined cowboy suit and hat. Hundreds of tiny battery-powered light bulbs imbedded in the outfit shone like a miniature galaxy of twinkling stars. He dismounted and took to the stage in a raffish incandescent glimmer, obliterating the senses with irrational numbers, seducing multi-layered aspects suffused in the subconscious of the untutored yokels.

He had adorned himself with expensive Italian sunglasses, custom made for his enormous irregularly shaped head, and his hands were fitted with large diamond rings specially fabricated to adjust over his bulky fingers. His hair and beard had grown long and were coifed to Nazarene specifications, eliciting splendor and cultic wiles to a vulnerable audience arranged like layered targets to his oratory hail.

The crowd hushed as he sashayed like a sequined Liberace to the podium. He stood motionless, a ghastly Quasimodo wax figure flanked by the eleven surfers. The sequins on his outfit refracted the tiny lights from his electric suit onto his dark sunglasses that looked like mini fireworks as he robotically scanned the obsequious audience. Holding Kazuo's black notebook, he raised his lumpy hands and began speaking in iambic pentameter, where his hushed low notes echoed from the crackling PA system.

"Fortieth page, third chapter. 'What you are looking for is what you are looking with,' sayeth Kazuo.'" He angled the black notebook toward the crowd, then placed it back on the podium and fanned through the tattered pages.

"Seventy-second page, first chapter. 'Your brain at one time was non-hemispheric and later became bipolar, lateralized, and almost separate. The hemispheric brain as we know it is a deformity, a sin, the result of human unconsciousness, and its chronic sense of spatial separation has hoodwinked the human race in its short history.'" He waved the notebook in the air.

"Because of this, the matrix of the world has made you its slave. But I have come to free you from your bondage and at this very moment your brains are being rewired into rational sentient beings by the sounds of the five notes. Do you hear it? Do you feel it?"

The crowd let out a voluminous roar.

"I know that you have come to find healing for your bodies, but you must also find healing for your mind sores. We must emancipate society at large from exploitation, oppression, class distinctions, and class struggles.

Wall Street is sick and the Capitalist system in America is sick and your bodies are symptomatic of that sickness. Until we rid ourselves of the cause, the symptoms will remain."

The ushers then passed out buckets for donations that were soon filled to overflowing. Goldman continued his semi-black mass in fluctuating tones.

"It is I who herald a new kingdom. It is I who give life. So now you must give and it shall be given unto you. Communities share, isn't it beautiful? That's what Communism is. Follow me and let us bring revolution to the world. Revolution! Revolution!" he shouted with unfettered glee.

The crowd echoed back with full-throated enthusiasm, "Revolution!"

Goldman proceeded with the routine healing of every *Tejano* when, out of the crowd, a wisplike boy with barn-door ears and burnt-orange freckles approached him, toting a heavy cache of lostness-in-a-bag, and swinging like a pendulum between bare terror and sacrum-cracked bliss. He stared at Goldman with *tabula pasa* eyes, blank slates waiting for anything to fill them. Something about the boy made lapidary etchings in Goldman's touchstone heart, a familiar longing to fit somewhere and be prized.

"What is it that you want me to heal, son?"

The boy looked down in embarrassment and then shyly tilted up his pale face. "I want my life to mean something."

Goldman was floored. Never had he heard a request that seemed so significant. He knew how to cure suffocating maladies, but this request was finely tuned, bewildering with evocative detail.

"I'm sorry, I don't know what to tell you," Goldman said with a shuddery breath.

The boy's faraway eyes looked up at him with languid anxiety, vectoring in where Goldman seemed to have no resistance, an oscillated frequency that was his quintessence of synchronicity. He moved to the lad and cupped his innocent freckles and big ears in his hands and smiled. For a moment, time ran backwards and he was twelve again, only safe now, as the two exoskeletons seemingly embodied the same shell in one protected soul.

"Can I be a Communist like you?" he asked.

Again Goldman was flattened by the appeal. He had his first convert to the cause and laughed out loud with glee.

"Yes, my son, yes." He then placed his hand on the boy's head and gave an impromptu prophecy.

"This boy will single-handedly spread world revolution and fight for the freedom of the oppressed. This very city will bear your name, for with a single blow you will bring down a corrupt Camelot and the entire world will remember your deed."

The boy seemed satisfied and a conjoined quiet came over him. His timorous nature vacated and he felt confidence fill him. He handed Goldman a large spook-grin on a stick.

"Thank you, sir." He turned and started to walk back into the endless recesses of the churning throng.

"Hey, boy," Goldman shouted. "What's your name?"

He turned with a *Babushka* smile. "Lee Harvey Oswald!" he hollered proudly.

Goldman gave the boy an approbating nod, watched him dematerialize into the anonymity of the Dallas crowd, and was potently moved to tears.

He continued with the handheld curing until all the sheeple were restoratively sheered and healed. Inspired by the boy's prehensile eloquence, he returned to the stage and digressed into a sprawling twenty-minute indictment of the US government and its shadowy agencies, working up the crowd until they were ready to raze Dallas and storm the capital of Austin. A single gunshot split the Texas night sky and a spray of brilliant red peppered Goldman's face. The surfers tackled and covered him as the manic crowd went salty-cashew-nuts. Goldman was whisked to Parkland Hospital, where a doctor bandaged a perfect quarter inch hole in his other ear as Goldman rambled in maundering circles about government conspiracies and blood-dappled abrogation of morality and murder.

L

The brazen assassination attempt drove Goldman underground like a perforated mole with matching 6.5 mm pierced ears. *Only Ronan could have made that shot, and if he's here in the good old USA, did he do it at the behest of the Israeli government, or the FBI?* Either way, Goldman knew his bullet was homing in, modulating in its inevitable delivery. He had been branded for eradication, but seemingly extended another professional courtesy from his *coup de grâce* appointment and the end to his unconscious suffering.

His Communist agenda was coming at a heavy price, and his life now teetered on the precipice of an absconding government that was not *for the people* or *by the people*. It so angered him that his pretense as a crypto-Communist was abandoned. Goldman held a press conference with a two-hour denunciation of the evils of the US government and their botched attempts on his life. In no uncertain terms he proclaimed to the world that he was indeed a Communist of rigor and purity, and that those that followed him were hoof-footed with sharpened teeth and horns, bloodthirsty Socialist who eat strangled animals and feast on lambs boiled in their mama's milk; hyperbole and rhetorical excess, probably and finally, the revolution was on. But revolution is like venereal youth, fast and contagious, and now that it was here, he feared the forth-coming third-Red scare with second-rate enthusiasm for the first-time.

He remembered his father's admonition: *"Real revolution is a steep slope that has the potential to turn into a runaway train. True revolution has to be done with exacting measures if there is to be a real utopian society. Speed would be its demise, and like any train that cannot slow down at a sharp turn, its own momentum would end up a pile of philosophical wreckage, if not engineered with temperance."* After the press conference he went back into hiding, a hermit maestro, day-lighting only on brief occasions.

*　　*　　*

The sniping incident frayed Jonathan's nerves like over-heated copper conductors. He entered Goldman's headquarters and marched directly to his office door, which was dead bolted from the inside and now steel reinforced, but it wasn't enough to keep Jonathan from confronting a madman emblematic of moral crimes. He pounded on the door with deputations of an avenging angel. The surfers heard the commotion and threw him to the floor, warning that if he attempted to do it again he would be repelled with doubled fists.

The door finally cracked just enough to expose one lens from a pair of Italian sunglasses.

"You are the mother of harlots!" Jonathan hissed.

"Is there something on your mind, dear brother?"

"You are a liar and have stolen from the flock." Jonathan pounced.

"I'm not like your father. My followers give out of the goodness of their heart and I have healed all their maladies. What is it that you think I have stolen, and to whom did I lie?"

Goldman opened the door and Jonathan entered, but now felt stripped of anything legitimate to say. He knew Goldman was right. He was painfully aware of his unrequited devotion to God and that if he could not get satisfaction from the object of his desire then he would lash out at the object of God's own elect. The only pretense he could muster was that Goldman was pushing the new-fangled practice of Kazuo's teachings whipped with a Communist agenda, a confection of sweetened lies and sour truths, pilfered dreams and idle crossed seduction. Goldman produced a Gila monster smile and laid his heavy, skin-rumpled arm on Jonathan's shoulder.

"Let's be real, brother. Most of those that I touch go home to a hopeless future, and there's nothing I can do about that, but Socialism can."

"You're a highwayman who separates the needy from their money. That's why someone took a shot at you!"

"It's the destiny of distribution. You want to see the collections as avaricious seizures, but we have a lot of expenses to cover, including, I might add, your very healthy salary."

Goldman pulled off the sunglasses that he had worn continuously for a month. Cat-like pupils now cut through the center of his iris; his chocolate almond eyes had turned puke green, and the whites of his eyeballs, a sickly piss yellow. A chill raced down Jonathan's spine and finished with an arc in his tailbone that made him jump like someone poked with a pitchfork.

"This is just the beginning. I've decided to turn our operation into a traveling tent revival. You know, like when we were kids. When this shooting thing blows over, then we'll get started. First it's Los Angeles, then every city in the country, then the entire globe. I've realized I'm not here just to heal the broken, but to save a malignant and decaying world," Goldman animating with his arms in wide circular motions.

He blathered on about how he needed Jonathan's help to streamline the healing process. It just took too long to have individuals go into explanations of their ailments, but he'd brainstormed a solution. Before each service, Jonathan and the surfers were to hand out forms for people to write down what ailed them. The healings would be itemized and priced by particular disorders. Deafness would require a minimum five-dollar donation, blindness, a ten-dollar donation, heart disease, twenty-five dollars, all types of cancer, fifty dollars, spinal cord injuries, seventy-five dollars.

"It'll be a healing menu. Isn't that fantastic?" he balefully grinned. "Once they make their donation, we mark their hand or their forehead to show that they've paid and, *voila* they get their healing. Isn't that bountiful?"

It took a while for Goldman's statement to slow the frenetically moving parts of Jonathan's runaway reason until a combustion of disgust detonated from his dissonant hub. He laughed so hard that he dropped to his knees and the deprecatory spectacle lodged in Goldman's craw.

"You're a hypocrite and a flim-flam profiteer," Jonathan chortled.

"Quid pro quo . . . whole societies are built on hypocrisy and profit!" Goldman said with bile admonishment.

Catching his breath, Jonathan stared at his brother, a man whose very pheromones had the ability to affect his better judgment, and he remembered what he had once almost forgotten, that people have entrenched beliefs stacked up neatly in the closet of their lives and don't want them scattered by logic. Goldman's truth was laser sharp, blistering perfection that tore though Jonathan's dead matter like a diamond bullet, scattering his stacked logic into jagged shards of moral relativity.

He had no rejoinder to his brother's exactness, and realized that all his life he had tried to understand the world according to what someone told him it ought to be, and not what it actually is. Suddenly the reason of a predator's lobe made perfect sense to him, and he saw that Machiavellian ambitions were not only necessary but honored. He knew Goldman was nuts, but Jonathan suspected that his beliefs were irretrievably ensnared by the claptrap of his own psychosis, and that he himself was quite possibly as mad as a rabid dog.

Goldman impudently declared: "You and I have much in common. Its souls we're after. You hate me because I'm doing something you can't, and that is preaching the good news of *my* salvation. The blind see, the deaf hear, and the lame walk, not because of the crumbs of manna that fall from *your* God's table, but because of the full loaves of bread that *I* feed them!"

Jonathan rose to his feet and took a long hard look at the thing before his eyes. He knew he could have nothing more to do with a man in flagellant torment who was sliding into the precipitous waters of total insanity. There would be no absolution for having desecrated the holy institution of soul saving, and there would be no waking for someone who willingly descended into a sleep-induced psychosis.

Goldman was right, though, Jonathan was envious, and a major-rager before his God for allowing the seed of Satan to do the work of angels when it should have been *him*. He was tired of dying by a thousand paper cuts from the pages of the Bible, and felt like a single contaminated wound left open for too long. He knew he would have to amputate his infected self from the body of Goldman's work and his own suborned attachment.

Jonathan feared it was only a matter of time before someone took out the Mad Hatter and he would be no party to that. Like a carnival puppet, he cut his strings and walked out of the center ring of his brother's circus, resigning himself a mere footnote to the spectacle of Goldman's show—bamboozled, he was sure, by the greatest showman he had ever seen or would ever see again.

LI

Jonathan returned to the anti-universe that he used to know and still reviled, and the dour prospect of running the mission again emptied him of his remaining self-worth. To be relegated to an innkeeper for derelicts left him feeling contrary and agitated. Like his father, he didn't know how else to make a living as he grudgingly took on the mission's dreaded mission. He already missed the excitement of Goldman's Ministry, and the healthy salary, too. But he could not go on as an impresario to Goldman's operatic play. He had heard enough that it again shook the shoddy fabrications of his spiritual outhouse theology.

The idea of collectivism, the call for communal contribution from all spheres, chipping in to make the social order work, seemed evenhanded and reasonable. No more hoarding, everyone sharing in utopian harmony, actually seemed sane. If Socialism were implemented then skidrow missions like his would become obsolete. The days of taking care of street dullards and idle deadbeats would be over, and each individual would have to pull his own bedraggled lazy ass weight.

Goldman's candor had spilt truth's light onto Jonathan's lap. He recognized that he had no love for the indigent and the morally lost and even despised their mislaid souls. Goldman's ability to render simple ugly facts with blinding truth brought his own hypocrisy to the forefront. His brother was a master of douchebaggery, but he had the ability to live in the mystery, while Jonathan felt like a pig without questions, and spent most of his life pretending that he had life's complications squarely pushed through round holes. He resented Goldman's ability to expose cracks in the edifice of his self-deception that laid him open to the cold winds of moral relativism. He unlocked the church doors and reluctantly prepared for the morning's service.

"Tell me, Pastor, are you part of the Communist conspiracy?"

The voice startled him. He turned to see Muller and another agent sitting in the pews, flashing their FBI badges.

"Does your mission support Communist insurrections?" Jonathan froze, staring in soundless reticence.

"You know, just being associated with that Commie radballs is enough to get you some hard time," Muller threatened.

"For what?" Jonathan enquired with blood vessels constricting.

"You are a promoter of a foreign subversive. Under the Communist Control Act, that is a Federal offense."

"I'm not a C . . . Com . . . Communist!" he stammered.

"That may be, but your working relationship with one will bring an indictment."

Jonathan's blood iced and bubbled like someone who surfaced from the cold deep too fast, his nerves scattered. "I'm not a Communist!"

"We don't want you . . . we want that man."

Muller sauntered up to Jonathan's ear hole, whispering, "We need to take Goldman into custody. Nothing serious, just want to ask some questions."

"And you want me to set him up?"

"You pick a public place where he'll feel safe. You're his friend and he trusts you. We'll slip in real quiet, take him into custody, and you can slip out just as quiet. No big deal."

"Was the FBI behind the Dallas shooting?"

"I dare say that the medical insurance companies and the pharmaceutical conglomerates, that he is single-handedly putting out of business, would like to see him dead. A lot of kooks out there, but it wasn't us. We're trying to keep him alive but we need your help to do it."

"So . . . I'm your Judas?"

"Listen, there's a gamut of anti-Communist feelings out there. An indictment will stick. This ain't rocket-surgery, you've got a family to think about." Muller reached into his pocket, and pulled out a small paper bag, and pushed it into Jonathan's perspiring hands.

"That's fifteen thousand now and another fifteen thousand after his arrest. That's a lot of non-taxable charity, Pastor. Weigh your options. You'll see it's the smart move." The agents left the mission with Jonathan holding the bag.

His mind tumbled as he tried to justify the betrayal. Maybe it was God's will that Jonathan end the skullduggery that Goldman had pulled on the world. Maybe Goldman really was the Antichrist, and he was the only good man left that could stop him?

His imagination got the best of him with his pathetic fantasy about being the instrument of God. Still, if he had to turn on him, it would be Goldman's comeuppance. He wrestled with the prospect of conniving treachery, and as bad as that was, it was the thirty thousand dollars that felt so persuasive. The web of his confusion spun even deeper: *What if Goldman really was an agent of God?* Then he would not only be betraying a brother, but heaven itself, and then there would be hell to pay. He wrestled with the dilemma for days and with reluctance, arranged a meeting.

*　　*　　*

Krieger's coffee shop was a downtown joint that didn't have a lot of clientele. There was a bit of a stargazed commotion when the two slipped into a booth but they ordered food just like everyone else. Jonathan wasn't interested in saying a whole lot, but looking through Goldman's lumpy exterior from across the table, he caught glimpses of the boyhood friend that he still envied but respected. The two took in one another with a palpable sense of stewardship. They were a double-sided portrait in the same frame, and both understood that, somehow one could not be without the other, but to what end, neither knew.

"I never understood why your parents had to die. It just didn't seem right. Why do you think that happened?" Jonathan asked.

"A bowel movement of the universe, poop just happens," replied Goldman with insouciant dismissal.

Jonathan was caving under the weight of his dark matter mass and an escalating sense of doom. He was sitting with his brother for no other reason than to orchestrate a rat bastard betrayal. He remembered the night Goldman was sodomized by Pastor Jack, and that he'd done nothing to stop it, and remorse suddenly filled him with fetid waves of destructive interference.

"So what's so important that you wanted to meet with me?" Goldman asked.

Jonathan waxed. "I just want to say I'm sorry. I'm sorry for a lot of things. Can you forgive me?"

"Forgive you for what?"

Jonathan hung his head. "For whatever I have done to you . . . or will do to you."

Goldman reacted with a cat eye quirk. "Look, we all got to let shit go, or the past will continue to mirror our present."

"I want to apologize for my father's behavior, and I'm sure it doesn't mean much now, but he was an ambassador of Christ, and I think the Lord deserved better and so did you."

"You are absolved," Goldman tittered.

"I'm serious."

"I have a great memory for forgetting. You were always a good friend. We've had our differences, but I always loved you like a real bruddah."

Goldman's authenticity heaped brazier coals on Jonathan's arctic heart, and there wasn't enough of him leftover to deal with that.

"I hate these intimations of my inabilities," he lamented. "I'm tired of trying to add up the pieces of my life that never make me whole."

Goldman looked at him with the profundity of a Pythagorean mathe*magician*. "I've learned not to add my life in fractions. I find the lowest common denominator and round off all other irrational numbers."

"I don't understand." Jonathan said.

"When I finally understood that one is an indivisible number, a sigh ran through me like a running ghost, and I realized that the central story of our lives is barely noticeable. If you can crunch that number, then the rest of the world is gravy. Learn to eat what life puts on your plate and let that fill you up."

The two sat in itchy silence as their eyes glanced off one another, around the coffee shop, and back to the table again. Jonathan watched Goldman fidget with the official Communist Party pendant that Mina had given him—a talisman of sorts that kept the memory of her alive.

"I think I understand why you became a Communist. It was a way of belonging somewhere, right?" Goldman half nodded and stroked the pendant with his ballooned hands.

"You know, the Book of Acts describes the early church practicing true Communism. Everyone gave all they had and shared everything equally."

Goldman smirked at Jonathan's naiveté. "I'm afraid my motives are not as elegant. I became a pinko, not to banish aristocrats, but to bed down a beautiful Argentine commissar. I only wish that my intentions had been genuine, but that's the real story."

"What was her name?" Jonathan asked.

"Mina, *Mina* than a motherfucker." Goldman laughed sumptuously.

"Were you in love?" Goldman nodded. "I was to marry the woman. For a very brief fraction of time we were one, happy and indivisible. But there was an accident and she was paralyzed. That was one irrational number I could not round off, and I was gone."

"But what happened to her?"

Goldman laid his misshapen melon in his hands, leveled and silent.

"To not heal is a sin, and that includes her." Jonathan said.

"I can't," he mumbled.

"Of course you can. My God has given you a great gift from heaven," Jonathan enviously claimed.

Goldman squirmed. "It has nothing to do with your God or any god. I just happened to stumble onto something that has existed since the dawn of eternity. Like Edison discovering electricity, it seemed like magic, until he exposed the trick."

"I see only magic," Jonathan edgily said.

"It's not magic to the magician," Goldman dismissively sneered.

"Then what is it?"

"Just your everyday Vitruvian, chemical-electrical sound phenomenon, mixed with mortal levels of radioactivity and getting one electron to dance around another . . . trick, that's all."

"Why can't your magic heal you?" Jonathan asked in frustration.

"Because God is a malevolent prankster, and too cheap to answer the sixty-four thousand dollar question."

They both broke out in paroxysms of laughter, as if the universe had just delivered the punch line to the joke of their collective fates.

The weather then changed in Jonathan's eyes. "I don't want to drop the G-bomb on you but, give your life to the Lord before it's too late. The world is ending. Can't you feel it?"

"I know . . . We're all waiting for the world to end right on time, but we have to wait until the last soul is saved, right?" Goldman sardonically asked.

Jonathan reached over and gave Goldman an *au fait* pat on the shoulder.

"These are strange days my brother, days when sullen knives are buried breast deep in the ones we love the most."

Crash! The plate glass window exploded and Goldman ungainly slumped forward. Jonathan instinctively ducked with one eye peering over the tabletop.

Goldman gawped at his brother with a gimlet grin. "And you are a man after Caesar's own heart."

Another *crack* split the coffee shop void and a single bullet smashed through Goldman's crown, and he rolled onto the blood spattered floor.

Big Jim and Andy ran into the coffee shop and tried to resuscitate the dying gasps of an emperor cult.

Blood from the head wound and the threadbare chest hole pooled together in a sticky dark red pond, *terminus mortalium*. Jonathan shouted for an ambulance at the circle of spectators standing around Goldman's teetering form. Goldman gasped for oxygen as tiny blood bubbles percolated from his mouth, floating in the air like small red balloons, popping into a fine scarlet mist. He exhaled a gurgled breath and quietly gave up his moniker spirit with little or no fight as the room fell into an eerie silence, peppered with groans of astounded disbelief.

On a Thursday evening, April 2, 1953, at 8:55 p.m., David Oliver Goldman was pronounced dead. Jonathan told the hospital staff that he was the next of kin and took his personal belongings. For the rest of the evening he sat in the dark grotto of his mind, and compressed his deadened chest into a chasm and stamped it with the steel anvil of the damned. He was now an ordained Judas priest of a new pagan guild where the hanging of his self seemed worn and clichéd. What practical decency he might have possessed lost all standing, and for the rest of his dung-beetle days, he would push the Sisyphus stone up the hill of his brother's memory.

*   *   *

Goldman was stretched out in the LA City Morgue. The pathologist dissected the brain to establish the path of the slug while Muller also examined it with an unsteady yaw. He thought for sure that the brain would be different, or non-hemispheric, as Goldman had so often proclaimed. But other than the intractable path of the 6.5 mm bullet, it was like any other bilateral lame brain: perfectly normal, perfectly inert, and perfectly dead.

LII

Goldman's body lay in state at the skidrow mission. It was an arabesque funeral, full of solemnity and spectacle. The death of Goldman was surreal; no one could fathom the turn of events, especially Jonathan. For three days, thousands queued up in the pouring rain to view the postmortem remains, and dignitaries from around the globe attended in awe and reverence. The devoted were psychologically mauled by the murder, and promulgating conspiracies were running rampant. Goldman knew that the government wanted him dead, and the time spent with his surf disciples had been filled with diabolic talk of his inevitable demise.

The possibility of their own martyrdom spooked the surfers with predacious panic. They strapped on brave masks, but eventually flung them off and scattered like wolf-stalked sheep. Only Big Jim remained. Goldman's devotees pointed accusing fingers at the American regime and took to the streets with a newborn Communist fervor. Thousands marched, protested, and demanded justice from a government that they were convinced had assassinated their theocratic leader. To the shadow powers that be, Goldman had become potentially more dangerous below ground than above.

*   *   *

For the better part of the day Muller sat behind his desk listening to live news feeds from the mission. Across from him sat Ronan. Muller's voice was stripped of its resonation after ranting about the infuriating turn of events. He had counted on Goldman's death breaking the master link of his Socialist chain, but it had instead set a backfire along the inner-edge of an American Communist Party fire-line whipped in new directions by developing popular winds. Ronan slumped in a reticent lapse. The killing of Goldman sifted through the vagaries of his moral landscape, and the shame of illicit power induction was fraying his formerly impenetrable conscience.

Muller glowered. "If you had finished the job in Israel, or in Dallas for that matter, I wouldn't be dealing with this now."

Ronan dragged his fingers through his prematurely graying hair and snapped his head back and forth to ease a pinched neck nerve. "A bullet through the ear is a good warning. A bullet through the other ear is an even better warning. He was earmarked, that's all he deserved. I grieve his loss like the rest of his followers."

Muller snuffed out his last cigarette, rose and straightened his exhausted suit. "Your assignment is complete. Another ten million in arms is being shipped to Tel Aviv as we speak."

Ronan rubbed his bloodshot eyes and tweaked his neck again. "If you don't mind, I think I'll stay for the funeral." He walked out of Muller's office like an adjunct to an inquisition, quibbling to flush out his indignations with pernicious censure.

Goldman's funeral snowballed into something that the government could not possibly deal with. Tens of thousands had come to the mission chapel, waving Marxist banners and hand-painted signs demanding justice. Muller's best hope was that the dust would settle and the Red-eyed virus of Goldman's legend would finally be laid to an ignominious rest.

Jonathan was petrified that word might leak out that he had a hand in the assassination. He wanted to tell the whole world that he was duped by the FBI but how could he prove it? His despondency left him limp-brained and in rude health, but he still had to make the arrangements for the funeral. The FBI paid him the balance of the thirty thousand dollars and the money hung around his neck like a millstone tie. The funeral and burial were set for that Sunday. Goldman's body would be interred at the *Hollywood Forever Cemetery* on Santa Monica Boulevard.

*   *   *

It was a beautiful Sunday afternoon, and after days of unrelenting rain, the weather finally broke. Warm Santa Ana winds whipped through the San Bernardino Mountains and into the lower valleys. It was standing room only for the open coffin ceremony and the entire city came to a standstill. For the legion that could not get into the chapel, thousands lined the street outside. The mourners stood in inimical grief as they waited for the ceremony to commence, listening through a vast PA system to Kazuo's five notes in Goldman's honor.

International news crews covered the solemn event, and reporters from around the world translated the service into dozens of languages. A crosscut of the world's citizenry spoke at the podium, sharing anecdotes about Goldman and the immeasurable effects he had on their bromide lives. The Communists used the occasion to further the cause he had championed. They vowed that the movement for world Socialism would continue in his name with revitalized gonzo gusto, and, if it meant confronting world governments, so be it.

After hours of showering accolades it was time for the final tribute. Jonathan approached the podium with an abashed feeling of unease and a cavernous tow. He briefly went into the particulars of their lives—how the two had grown up together. He expounded on Goldman's war record and the meritorious deeds of a humble and reluctant hero. *It's funny*, Jonathan thought, *that when someone dies you only remember the good stuff.*

He chronicled Goldman's implausible gift but, for some reason, did not defer his supernatural ability to God, nor did he feel inclined to turn a worldwide audience into a proselytizing event. Maybe it was out of respect for the dead, or maybe it was barren perfidy for having been a patsy in the killing of God's elect, or maybe he actually believed that Goldman was a divine being; he didn't know anymore. The source of his paranormal command would linger as an unsolved puzzle, and the ingredients would remain a sunken treasure buried in his brother's pirate cove grave.

Jonathan could not keep his eyes off the corpse, and its image fastened to his center. Goldman was draped in fine white linen. His hair was as long as his beard and his tumors had flattened like deflated colloid tires. Folds of scaly skin were all that was left of his once ponderous and bulbous physique. Even through the funerary shell of the man, Jonathan could see the friend and brother that he had always betrayed, and he felt so lachrymose that his voice trembled throughout the eulogy. When he could take no more, he collapsed under a gush of super-positional grief, and threw himself on the casket, weeping like an old woman. The audience was stirred by the spectacle and racking sobs and abreacted wails broke out among the mourners. Big Jim pulled Jonathan away from the coffin and tried to sit him in a chair, but he was determined to finish the service. While he attempted to regain his poise, the large front doors of the mission suddenly blew open and a torrent of hot Santa Ana wind ripped through the little chapel.

The congregation turned toward the battered doors, but just as quickly as the wind blew through, it departed, leaving loose paper swirling and floating like large pieces of confetti. The congregants turned their attention back to the coffin and were thunderstruck to see Goldman sitting upright. Screams and howls bellowed through the little church and some folks collapsed out cold. The street crowd heard the commotion and stormed the chapel. Among them was Ronan, who stood stupefied before an impossibility that had become unbelievably possible. Goldman's huge Frankenstein-stitched head moved from side to side like a turret on a tank.

He lifted himself out of the coffin, smirking like a corpse prepared by the skill of a gifted mortician, and assumed the Vitruvian stance as a thunderous roar from the hot Santa Ana's blew through the doors again. With thin air defiance, he then levitated over the spectators, drifting between the rafters, smiling at the bedeviled onlookers like monstrous pagan statuary.

Utter bedlam erupted and the crowd spontaneously broke out in worship and hymns before the scaly gryphon-like visage. It was petrifying and eerily otherworldly and as beautiful as it was terror soaked: his satanic majesty, rictus grinning, arms stretched out wide, draped in flowing white, his long hair and beard whipping in the wind; a transmogrified angel hovering over his followers, an icon of humus to luminous, transfiguring between life and death, man and god, inner-sized and exercised all quotients of reality.

Jonathan could not take another second of the bedazzled specter. He and Big Jim ran out of the chapel in unrestrained terror, along with others who could not begin to comprehend the wraithlike spectacle. Ronan looked on as the thing that he thought he had destroyed made psychic advances in his shrinking head. Ectoplasm poured from the holes of his sallow skull as his form darkened in the shadow of Goldman's *maximus dramatis personae*.

LIII

Goldman's status as a holy healer was one thing, but when word spread that he had raised himself from the dead, the world's reasonable physics instincts were reduced to being wistfully obsolete. His anomalous being merged mortal and legend into a divine closed system that seemed to violate its own laws. The man's ability to heal terminal conditions was now eclipsed by his ostensible ability to raise the dead, or at least himself, and the mob that once besieged him for the salvaging of their corrupted bodies now beseeched him to resurrect their dear departed ones. Rumors spread that he was clearing out entire graveyards.

He was back, bigger and badder than his previous incarnation, but the ordination of the unofficial title of a god had affected him worse then that of a divine healer, and his *deus ex machina* plotline made him feel expressively contrived and corporeally racked. It was tough for him to render his own mystical facts; like reading a sentence backward, he got the words but it had no meaning, and something changed when he returned from the land of the departed.

Like Osiris, the underworld god that granted life to all, Goldman was informally deified, but felt out of place in the mortal land of the living. He was not nearly as enthusiastic about performing in front of crowds and was fearful of another assassination attempt. He knew the government still wanted him dead, but it wasn't just the government, and sides were being drawn. Many of his former followers now believed he was a heretic, or the very split-hoofed, brimstone breathing, Satan himself. His life seemed to be threatened by every malcontent who would not be satisfied until his protuberant carcass was finally in the ground.

He had an ocean of devotees, who still would fight and die for him, but he was almost more troubled by them; excessive idolatry was too much even for Goldman's psychopathology. He knew that he was something extra, extra ordinary, but what he really needed to know, was whether he was just earthenware man or in fact the Potter Himself. For years he had encased himself with amorphous divinity syndromes and through the years was compulsively driven to increase the illusion.

He didn't know how he had resurrected himself, and if he was God, then it seemed reasonable that he would know. *It is a pathetic riddle, being this "I am."* he thought. He had become his own greatest mystery, an aggregation of forces in different degrees of condensation, a dynamic center in which he was the rightful master. Yet he could not redeem his own body or even begin to calibrate his divine inner gears.

The apocryphal resurrection had somehow affected his physical condition, retrograding his fleshy form into the impossible. A bony mass emerged from his forehead like a keratin horn and his body grew larger tumors. Like a giant horned toad goblin, his skin turned green, dorsal barbs grew from his spine and his tailbone had elongated with six more vertebrae. A swarm of flies constantly buzzed around his face and his breath smelt like a rotting corpse. When he burped, coughed, or sneezed, long blue flames now shot out from his nostrils and mouth. It left him flummoxed and fretful to see that the more gruesome his looks, the more potent his powers. Levitation was a common occurrence, and even manifestations of telekinesis were becoming frequent—hurling objects across the room with just a single glance.

It seemed he held the keys to life and death in his transmigrated shell, and that every wayward daydream he had ever indulged in had come true far and beyond his pilfered fantasies. But now that he had it, it meant nothing, and given his appearance, it meant even less. He could not escape himself, or his iconoclastic symptoms, and all that had pained him. Enmity with his self was his inability to change, and to change what you get you must change who you are. He could not outrun his shallow shadow, and now he could not outrun his even shallower followers.

The fanatics were begging him to give the order to commence with world revolution, and if it was Communism at the end of a gun barrel, then they were locked and loaded and ready to be goaded. He had tired of being their alchemic touchstone and just wanted them to find their own destiny. He came to despise his loutish fascist followers, but still could not kick his addiction to the drug of mass flattery and public adoration. But like heroin, it was an insatiable itch where he could never get enough scratch. He needed to raze his in-house structure of self-worship and the only way was to go cold turkey dinner from public feasted tables.

*   *   *

Without Jonathan to buttress Goldman's compromised foundation, alcohol, dope, and cultic prostitutes became his sanctuary. Drugs and booze was an easy out, but for a woman to bed down with his likeness was a tall order, even for the most calloused whore. Not just because of his hellish appearance, but because most people viewed him as a god-animal, and engaging in carnal adventures seemed zoophiles, frightening, and possibly sacrilegious. But with enough money he could buy just about anyone. He employed a gaggle of sex nymphs for his private harem-scare-em in the basement of a whorehouse that became his personal house of horrors; the confining pit where he secreted himself from the world and employed his basest harlotry and spellbinding pharmakia.

Despite his pernicious condition he had a prodigious craving for sex. He spent days on end licking, sucking, fucking, and mortifying prostitutes' bodies, desecrating their vacant souls in the habituations of the devil's workshop, where minatory sexual shrieks wailed into the harrowing nights. With his sexual compulsions replete, he would indulge in straightjacket benders that lasted for days, lost weekends where *blue Sundays* were a reprieve from alcohol rigor mortis.

His appetite grew to gluttony, and his gluttony to Heliogabalian proportions. In a single sitting he would eat more chicken and waffles than any man had ever seen: a half a dozen baguettes, twenty raw eggs, ten bottles of Coca-Cola and a gallon of rocky road ice cream. Finally sated, he would bathe his dirty soul in boiling spoons and stainless steel syringe dreams, where his subverted contumelious nature rode brown sugar tracks still laid out on his perforated arms. When he could not get a mainline to cooperate, he would shoot into a tumor that served as a blood reservoir, dispensing heroin directly into his circulation like a fleshy-floppy hospital IV.

With this discordant self-abuse, his conditioned worsened. His eyes became snakelike, his hide, wattle and iguana-textured with large imbricate folds that molted in piles like ghastly transparent body pods. Some of the tumors grew to grapefruit size and had a gelatinous texture. Insects would burrow in and lay eggs that would hatch and he would regularly be covered with hundreds of spiders, fly larvae, and black ants. Every now and then, a tumor would spontaneously combust, spraying anyone within range with liquid fire that continued to burn like a black-oiled wick.

Once, while in a drunken fume, a tumor on his neck exploded and ignited his hair and beard. He couldn't put out the fire and in desperation dunked his head in a toilet. When there was not enough water to extinguish the flames he flushed the commode, but got his long hair stuck, and the water filled the bowl to overflowing, almost drowning him in a holy shit baptism.

The intransigence of his iniquities filled his sty of a room like carrion flesh, there was a hot thick blanket of humidity that hung in the unventilated air, and the atmosphere always reeked of the unimaginable. Even when he used the crapper his turds moved of their own accord like electric eels and his urine was a cross between blood red and piss yellow, a sickening burnt orange that reeked of burning trash.

Goldman's perving diversions were fleeting interludes and he was running out of things to occupy his time. He procured an upright piano, and went berserk with Beethoven; over and over he played, sobbing like an ancient Aryan baby. *He had heard babies bawl before, but while most were trying to satiate some selfish need, this weeping was old; a vintage cry squeezed from the grapes of fermented souls, souls who knew they had missed something gigantic in the puny lives they had led and were powerless to do anything about it.*

There were a lot of people who would pay top dollar to find him. Not that Goldman was a fugitive, but he brought something to the world that it needed, and it was more than just miracles. He was a yardstick by which people could measure their desires, fears, and fantasies. Like a rogue wave, he had crept up from the fathomless deep and capsized the world's floating paradigms; a grand oeuvre that could be interpreted as anything one might be inclined to think him to be, and he brought a catharsis to the average blowhard who felt short listed in the stunted lives they led.

With no news of the incredible man, the world was hopelessly bored, and so was Goldman. Even the most spectacular news would pale in light of the headlines that he once commanded, but he hated it as much as he loved it. Sometimes he would daydream about being back on the vineyard and working for old man Simpson with meager pay and a normal face and body. How sweet it would be to be a nobody again, without powers to heal or futures to predict. It was moronically mocking, he thought, that when you get what you want, all you want is what you had.

He longed to have Mina ministering to his stricken condition, but he knew she would have nothing to do with him, certainly because of his contaminated tadpole gene pond, but even more so because of his gene-deficient lack of reasonable character. He dreamed that one day their besetting paths would converge again, but mordant reality was the only imposter he ever knew, and he could not find a way to wake up and honestly say, "I have become myself." He would sometimes wander the streets late at night, and he felt safe walking in the *Homo solitarius* haunts of the dark. It was the only time his prowling thoughts would cease; *I do not think, therefore I am not,* and there he remained invisible. He even wished he was back at the mission doing chores and sitting in Jonathan's tired chapel, listening to one of his tired sermons about his tired God and wishing he was any place but there.

LIV

The early morning precipitated with dwarf stars that buzzed like luminous sodium lamps, and the LA blue moon reclined crescent and half asleep under an indigo Aurora sky. After weeks of pathological debauchery, Goldman's decanted libations on the altar of Bacchus fell afoul, and panic hit him like a snapped cable from a San Francisco trolley. Demon-vexed, hair tearing, teeth-gnashing anxiety attacks were common, but this one launched his blood pressure like a sulfur-fueled rocket, imploding sweat glands and blood, soaking his shirt like a dirty dishrag and made his atomic tumors leach like calcified nodules. His moratorium from the world had induced a nerve assault on his already shorting circuitry, and his psychological listing could be tipped by a single aberrant thought.

Whenever possible he avoided mirrors. Seeing his insalubrious condition stark close was a harrowing ordeal, worthy of fear and loathing, and when on occasion it did happen he would slip a cog and go on an iniquitous bender to forget the egregious sin of his reflection. It took considerable effort for anyone to acclimate to his looks. If he moved deliberately and slowly and talked normally he could almost be tolerated. But if he acted anomalous in any way or made nippy physical gestures, it was amplified a thousand-fold by an appearance that was alarming even to the most fortified eyes.

There was a full-length mirror in one of the bathrooms, so he always made sure that the light was off when he used the guano bowl. He was taking a plutonium leak when one of the shag-hags accidentally flipped on the light, leaving him with a compound dose of his hunchback burlesque face. He smashed the mirror in a fit of primordial rage, and like a stampeding rhino, proceeded to tear the whorehouse apart.

He charged out of the bordello and ran into the darkened streets, howling and trunk trumpeting like a wild wounded elephant, screaming at the top of his tormented lungs, "Somebody love me!" He wasn't sure, but it looked like men in black were following—the FBI, he thought. Like a giant hurdy-gurdy monkey, pursued by shark-suited hounds, he found the nearest tree and swung his hulking figure up the branches. He perched there for hours until his hysterical mechanisms retracted and he fell asleep. By morning he was awakened by a rock pelting and the sudden sense that, like an overexposed Dracula, if he didn't get to his basement coffin soon he would surely melt by the light of day. He looked down to see two Chassidic Jews with full beards and black matching suits.

"Why are you throwing rocks at me?" he cholericly asked.

"Because you are a grown man hanging in a tree," answered one of the Jews.

"So?"

The other Jew pointed at him. "Cursed is the man who hangs upon a tree."

He tried to lumber down, but a branch snapped and he dropped to the sidewalk with a remarkable thud. His head hit the concrete deck, but a large fluid-filled tumor broke the fall, rupturing like a nasty water balloon.

"Are you all right?" the Jews asked.

He tried to stand, but his head spun like a broken gyroscope and he passed out.

*　　*　　*

"Are you the One we have been waiting for?"

Goldman awoke and shook his head in an attempt to understand. "What?"

"We are the Messianic Jews of the *Final Millennium*. We believe we have been waiting for you."

Standing about him were more of the same Chassidic Jews with black suits and mystic beards. He looked around and saw still more facing him in a semicircle. His hands and feet were tied to a large wooden chair.

"What are you talking about?" he asked.

"That's right, Mr. Goldman, we have watched your exploits for quite some time.

We have taken a keen interest in you and your activities. You are a Jew?"

"Why am I tied up?"

The head rabbi, Shlomo Riezen, ascetically pierced him with steel blue eyes and an expression of perfervid conjecture. "Are you the promised Messiah the Zionists have been waiting for, the Lion of Judah?"

"What are you talking about?" He squirmed in the chair.

"Do you come from the line of David?" asked another.

Still another shouted out. "His name is David and I think that is close enough!" Garrulous excitement filled the room as the rabbis fixated on his appearance.

"'He has sent him to proclaim freedom to the prisoners and recover sight to the blind,' Isaiah 61. He has fulfilled this. He healed the blind and did time in jail. I have his arrest records right here."

Other Jews wildly gesticulated with their hands. "'He had no beauty or majesty to attract us to him. Like one from whom men hide their faces,' Isaiah 53. Look at him!"

"Were you born in Israel?" Someone hollered.

"No!" shouted another. "But he did fight for the birth of Israel, and I think that means the same thing!"

Rabbi Riezen motioned for calm and addressed Goldman directly. "We believe you are the Chosen One and we will follow if you are the One that we believe you are . . . *Immanuel* . . . are you God, with us?"

Their stony questions were relentless and Goldman was taking a brain beating. He didn't know what or how to think. His bio-systems were so shwasted from weeks of binging that he zonked out cold in the chair.

*   *   *

When he awoke again he was lying in a king-sized bed with clean sheets and pillows. He felt as drained as a leech-treated cadaver and just wanted to be safe somewhere and the only place that felt safe was lying in that bed. Over the next weeks he scoured and detoxed his tainted system with distilled water and distilled thoughts. Rabbi Shlomo befriended him and yakked his perforated ears off with versified mystical revelations, exegesis of the Torah, and the imminence of the last days, and for the first time, Goldman felt at ease with his mother's religion.

The more Rabbi Shlomo expounded on the significance of the Torah, and other pseudepigraphic scriptures, the more he persuaded Goldman that *he* was in fact the Anointed One. The rabbi's endgame revelations altered the atmosphere with shifting metaphysical dimensions and quantifiable religious quirks, and were so persuasive that Goldman was almost swayed.

He convinced him to return to his calling, but secretly as the Magistratus Messiah. Goldman was reluctant, but if he had to return to the limelight of the un-illuminated, then he would take it out in trade for his Marxist

agenda, if not for himself then at least in homage to foggy recollections
of Mina. It seemed a fair exchange: the rabbis could have their savior and
Goldman could spread his Socialist schema. When the time was right, the
Final Millennium Jews would seize the world by force in a *coup de raison*
and commence the thousand-year reign of Communist bliss and messianic
demo*crazy* by force; *Novus ordo seculorum*—the new order of the ages.

With their media influence the rabbis would arrange interviews on
television, radio, and in the newspapers, and gradually ease the world into
the light of Goldman's celestial truth. For now, they would assert that he
was merely a great Jewish prophet, who could heal the masses, and help to
bring peace to a lost and reprobate world. Goldman was still not entirely
convinced that he was the Chosen One, but reluctantly agreed to employ
his gift as a cosmic metaphysician, and if he really had to, the redeemer of
the world.

*   *   *

Goldman returned to public scrutiny with the pomp of a culture
warrior and a conquering Roman god, illumined by the radiance of his
purloined image. Rabbi Shlomo was his liaison to the world. For security,
he was protected by a contingent of fanatic ultra-Orthodox Jews armed
with celestial weaponry and automatic guns. The Jews dressed him in a
Chassidic black suit, a *Tzitit* sash and a fur-lined *Shtreimel* custom fashioned
to fit his munificent head. His newfound Jewish fervor was confusing at
first to his followers but they were still recital pledged and devoted. It was
the beginning of a new human era but veiled in illuminati cover.

The Jews began construction of a temple for Goldman on the corner of
Fairfax and Santa Monica Boulevard. Jerusalem was not in the hands of the
Zionist, so this would become the new nexus of the universe, or at least,
LA. When the day came for the world to end, Goldman would be ushered
in as *Praetor Maximus* with an inner-court to dispense law and legislate
from the new throne of David. America had always been an apocalyptic
country, and, fittingly the City of Angels would be the New Jerusalem; the
portal to heaven where veneration for earthbound stars are worshipped
and homilies are conferred to Hollywood carbon chauvinism, benevolent
despotism and the clinically insane.

*   *   *

Muller had Goldman in his sights again, but what could he do that he hadn't tried before. He called on Ronan one more time to finish the dirty little chore, but his agents found the sniper in the downtown Morrison Hotel with the Manlicher-Carcano stuffed in his mouth and a 6.5 mm hole through his head. Pinned to his shirt was a blood-soaked pizza box upon which Ronan had scrawled: *THE END* OF THE GOD ASSASSIN. Muller didn't know what to do. Unless they blew Goldman up into thousands of itty-bitty Bolshevik pieces that could not be reconstituted, he would just resurrect himself like an exhumed god-creature. But to let him carry on as a national security threat would be intolerable.

The government had always been a master of systemic studies and religion was its prime tool for controlling society. Prospectus threats of hell or earned treats from heaven would always be leveraged to egg-on decent citizenry and cattle-called obedience. The security apparatus was spooked at the prospect of antichrist-anarchists rolling over America, but more alarmed at the implications of the thing turning into an outré religious crusade; martyrs were always the greatest threat to the established order. Even if Muller succeeded in completing the act of deicide, he could count on every major city going up in flames, which, ironically, would be tantamount to a Soviet nuclear strike. The FBI had to retool its game, and for now, it was better to leave Goldman's head on his shoulders than mounted on a wall.

The hubbub of Goldman's seemingly fictional tale acted on Muller like a virulent pathogen that had, over the years, systematically stripped the walls and the balls of his virile sanity. It could never be business as usual, never really knowing who or what Goldman was or how to stop him. Muller was not aware of counter transference, emotional entanglements and paranosic sympathy for the god-man. He was Muller's antipode, yet also his authenticity, where the badlands of rapid-eye dreams are finally realized. Muller began to shirk his duties as a special agent and willingly drifted into estuaries of salted psychosis and Black Forrest lycanthropy. Living in a mental world of possum moons and wild beasts, eating grass, grubbing for shoots with his long nails, and mumbling incessantly, "To drive the stake in the heart of the dragon you must first get past the flames. Goldman, Goldman, the night's fire-breathing serpent and destroyer of the American day."

LV

Rabbi Shlomo arranged for Edward R. Murrow, the most noteworthy television reporter in the country, to do a live interview with Goldman. It was all part of their plan, a systematic approach to acclimate the world to who he really was and the heralding of a new human epoch.

Goldman had thought a lot about what the Final Millennium Jews were saying about him. He probed the Torah and Kazuo's notebook for passages that might help to shed light on his situation and festschrift the two into a syncretistic metaphysical heap. After little time in reclusive carrel and even less time, soul searching, he believed he finally had explanations for the mysteries concealed in his cashew-nut case.

Murrow sat across from Rabbi Shlomo and Goldman, dragging on a cigarette.

"How is it that you came to wield such power?"

Goldman drew a long breath and glowered at the studio camera, but before he could speak Rabbi Shlomo cut in. "Goldman doesn't wield power, he just directs it."

Murrow looked quizzically at the pseudo-interlocutor then directed another question to Goldman. "Who are you, and do you have an agenda?"

He opened his mouth, but again the Rabbi interrupted. "Goldman is a prophet and his only agenda is to bring goodwill to the world."

Murrow took a long drag on his Chesterfield and blew the smoke in the Rabbi's direction. "If you don't mind, I am here to interview Mr. Goldman."

Murrow again turned his attention to Goldman. "Why do you look the way you do?"

Goldman spoke in a cool monotone. "The US government is engaged in a great conspiracy. There are evil puppeteers who pull strings in high places to control the Federal Reserve, the military, the FBI, the Justice Department, and even the White House."

Murrow's eyebrows rose. "What is it that the government is doing that justifies your accusations?"

"This government has conducted illegal atomic experiments on me, that's why I look the way I do. But they didn't anticipate that the weapon they formed to destroy me did not prosper. Instead, it has given me mystical supremacy to heal, but also the ability to prophesy."

Murrow guffawed. "Well then, give us a preview."

Goldman closed his eyes then opened them again.

"There will be a great rocking and rolling and a shaking the world has never seen. A boy king will rise from the south and from his scepter he will rule from the house of Memphis. But tidings from the east bring fear and trembling to his throne and then the invasion will begin. *Beatles* will '*Yea . . . Yea . . . Yea*' while *Stones* find '*Satisfaction*' and roll over all who stand in their way. The plague will continue, and the *Animals* will take dominion. The young will exclaim, '*We got to get out of this place!*' and, like a '*Backdoor Man*' they will exit through the *Doors,* then *Nirvana* will come, but it '*Smells Like Teen Spirit.*' Men will walk on the moon and women will walk on men, and men will be women and women will be men. Gasoline will get to as high as one dollar per gallon. Muslims will blow up New York City and a Communist Negro will hold the highest office in the land; *Obama* is a comma and a question mark, but *Barack* will attack the America that you once knew but never loved."

Murrow tilted his head as if that might him help comprehend the convolution. "Sounds like a bunch of gobbledygook. How about predicting something that people can understand?"

"Okay . . . how about I predict that in five minutes you won't have any eyebrows."

Murrow produced a wistful grin. "Look, the world has only one question. Who are you, or what are you?"

Goldman weighed the question and then returned a derogatory smile. "I am many things and yet nothing. I am you and you are me and we are all together, sayeth the egg man."

"So you are the egg man. What does that mean?"

Goldman sneered through his lumpy flesh mask. "Which came first, the chicken or the egg? Did God make man or did man make God? The truth is . . . *I am* the creator of this world, for I made me."

Murrow bowled over, speechless, as Goldman smiled into the camera with a frozen android gaze.

Rabbi Shlomo Riezen jumped to his feet. "He is not God, just the savior of the world!" Goldman slapped his hand over the rabbi's mouth.

"You are a god?" Murrow asked.

"I am more than a god; I am the full embodiment of all divinity."

"You mean you were made in the image of God?"

Goldman slowly turned his head back to Murrow with his hand still clamped over the rabbi's mouth. *"I am that I am."*

"How do you know that?"

"If you don't believe me, then at least believe the miracles. No man could do what I do unless, in fact, he was God in the flesh."

"Then why can't you heal your . . . flesh?"

Goldman weighed the question with infernal scrutiny. "I rejoice at the outer crumbling of the house, for it is necessary if the inner-temple is to be revealed. I willingly wear this ramshackle dwelling to remind the world of its sin."

"What is the sin that the world needs to be reminded of?" Murrow asked.

"They are victims of primeval stupidity, rank idiocy, and false consciousness, causing war, hunger, ignorance, and death. They create these realities, but what they do not understand is that they are illusions and they can change these illusions by climbing to a higher vibratory level of consciousness that is within their fundamental nature. And I am here to guide the sheep to their awakening."

"My understanding is that God is omnipresent, omnipotent, and omniscient and I doubt that you are any of these," Murrow said dismissively.

"The man with experience is never at the mercy of a man with only an argument."

Goldman countered.

He pulled his hand away from the rabbi's mouth and thumbed through Kazuo's black notebook. "From the book of Kazuo, forty-fifth page, second paragraph. 'We are here as boson particles igniting between heaven and Earth.' But I am here as *the* boson particle to extend the quantum viewpoint to ordinary life, and to expose cracks in the structure of scientific materialism and religious mysticism."

"And that means what, exactly?" Murrow asked.

"The world is a picture of alienation, frustration, and a hopeless search for completion. All along it has been an illusion that has pulled on us even before we arrived. But it's a game, a colossal cosmic game, a fantastic Holly*weird* production designed to suspend our disbelief about who we really are."

"Who are we?" Murrow inquired.

"God particles disguised as stardust."

"I don't understand."

"The world experiences duality and is therefore ineffective. To live with God and not as God implies separation. It has taken a lifetime, but I have made the hero's journey with countless sorties into the staggering vastness of the great within and found consciousness with the only true God."

"If you are God consciousness, then what does that make you?"

"I am beyond consciousness and so in consciousness I cannot say what I am, yet, I am that I am . . . the great I am."

"If you are *the* I am, then what does all this mean?"

"Meaning finding itself negates itself and meaning, and proof of meaning is matter and antimatter. When they meet they cancel each other out."

"Well I don't think that's what the Bible says," Murrow admonished.

Goldman sarcastically smiled. "The Bible is like anyone. If you torture it long enough, it's liable to confess to anything."

Murrow pointed to a slide projector and clicked on the screen. "I have something I want to show you." The first slide showed an arrest mug shot of Goldman, one of many mug shots. "And you would have us believe that this is God? I have other interesting photos courtesy of the FBI."

He continued with a hodgepodge of candid shots: Goldman with prostitutes, drunken in public, shooting heroin, leading demonstrations with the Communist Party. One photo depicted him and Mina marching side by side, and that was enough to shred his nerves like a steel fork dragged across broken teeth.

"So this is what God looks like?" Murrow snidely asked.

Goldman fumed with vitriolic ire, his tumors turning different shades of red, purple, and pink. He yanked the microphone from around his neck and sneezed on Murrow with a blue flame that singed his eyebrows clean off. Murrow scrambled off the set like a flaming Roman candle. Goldman then levitated off the floor, smashing all the studio lights with just a tilt of his telekinetic head, and punched the producer in the eye.

*   *   *

The fallout from the Murrow interview was total. Goldman was ridiculed around the country and the world for his blasphemous declaration of Godhood, and his once adoring faithful turned on him with hyena treachery for not being a bigger god. He did not dare show his face in public, and death threats were constant. His fall from grace was a fire-fall plunge that had come to an obliterating crash, and all his infertile aspirations were shattered by the impact of a temporal dream that was no more.

*   *   *

Trees oxygenated Goldman and had always been a dependable refuge. He roosted in those that were high enough and strong enough to support his podgy weight and hide him from prying eyes. He had an uncanny ability to keep his balance while sleeping in the saddles of branches, and could stay motionlessly perched long enough that birds often nested in his hair. Like a night stalking, urban-grimed atomic animal, he competed with raccoons, coyotes, and opossums for scrounged trashcan bits of food, and spent his days in the upper limbs where other marsupials, squirrels, and birds fought for the best spots.

He had not slept for days and finally drifted into a cavernous slumber in the nook of a eucalyptus tree. He was visited again by the same reoccurring dream, that black haunter of his night years. It was always the same; stygian darkness in a cold room where the entity lurked, always skulking but never exposing its identity. The thing had the ability to inject terror the likes Goldman could not articulate, let alone understand, and to open his eyes would surely mean death, the second death, and then judgment. It was a fearsome experience to face judgment, and he was sure that every sin he had ever committed would be in full view for all eternity, and that it would be for him alone to pass the only verdict . . . *guilty*.

He knew that one day he would have to confront the creature and this time he was determined to face his tormentor with damnable revelation. He pried his ominous eyes open and was face to face with the beast of his ever-hidden anguish. Before him stood a being that defied any earthly adjectives, illustrations, or symbolic meanings. The years peeled back in layers, like skipping bloodstones across the surface of existential proclamations. The center, finally exposed and the tormentor at last revealed . . . a twelve-year-old Goldman, eternal, ephemeral . . . *lost.*

*   *   *

It was an overcast day and there was a slight drizzle. Jonathan was returning home from another day at the skidrow mission. It had been months since anyone had seen or heard from Goldman. After the fallout from the Murrow interview there wasn't a rock big enough for him to crawl under or a tree high enough to climb. As he pulled into his driveway he noticed something large in his California oak; Goldman, roosting like a flying elephant, completely naked.

Jonathan exited the car and looked up into the tree.

Goldman looked down. "I know Jesus loves me, but the rest of the world thinks I'm an asshole."

"I would appreciate it if you would get out of my tree," Jonathan retorted.

Like an extinct giant sloth, Goldman lumbered down the trunk, and with a wobbling gait approached Jonathan, grotesque, burlesque, and absurd.

"The papers say you're running for your life."

Goldman shook his enormous head and shrugged his hunched shoulders. "You know the papers, they always exaggerate."

"Playing God is a serious game." Jonathan said.

"Well, I'm still pretty sure I'm God."

Jonathan glanced at him like a shipwrecked space invader and shook his head.

"And the serpent said, 'Eat from the tree of knowledge and your eyes will be opened and you will be like God.' But now you are naked and the whole world sees it."

Goldman squared up to Jonathan's circular logic.

"You're jealous. You've always been jealous of me. You only wish you could do what I do. And the reason I can, is because I have the guts to believe in *me,* and you don't. That's why you got me killed . . . I know it was you."

With the hostile stare of a foreigner the two stood with their visages melting one into the other, unfriendly aliens in a ground zero setting.

"These are strange days, my brother, days when sullen knives are buried breast deep in the ones we love the most." Goldman declared.

"And you are a man after Caesar's own heart," Jonathan rejoined.

They looked at one another like falling trees in a forest of doubt. Goldman turned and ambled down the driveway, a walking epic. Like granite, his image would eventually erode by the relentless drops of time, and he too would disappear as had the pantheon of gods that had come before him: a vacated celestial monarch, an anthropic *prince*-iple, incompatible with the ordinary and forgotten among deified stars that never were, nor would ever be . . .

LVI

With maladroit steps Goldman trudged into the hospice where he had deserted Mina eons before. He wondered if she would be able to recognize him through the hedgerows of growths that had become fleshy chaparral ranges on the bodyscape that she once loved. But, what was more vital, would she receive him? He knew his exigencies would be morbidly objectionable, and hoped that his appearance, inside and out, would not alienate him in an unwanted welcome.

He walked into her cosseted room and was struck by a heady aroma of lilac and bifurcate possibilities. In shades of another world's imagination, she was fast asleep. How often he had dreamed a woman's dream of being a good man and he didn't know if he should stay or go. If he stayed, it would require a super-sentient being to collapse her wave-like vision into reality. The room hadn't changed in the years that had passed, and neither had his former bride-to-be. It was if the sands of years refused to slip through her hourglass figure, and the metronome of time decay had altogether stopped ticking.

Her beauty was exquisite, and even unconscious she exuded an efflorescent increase. He suddenly felt like a brackish dog for allowing her to remain in that condition. He had tried to heal her once, but something had blocked his curative path. Now he realized that the something had been him all along. His unconscious and supine gripes had materialized as that of a malefactor for whom amoral self-gratification and narcissistic reprisals are selfishly justified.

Something inside had coldly detached him from the mainframe of normal sympathy. It was the power of *No* that had etched an emotional vendetta deep below his fossilized veneer. Mina had used it on him for so long that, for once, his petty contrivance would use it on her. It was payback for her indifference to his insufferable devotion, and to look upon her beauty made it patently clear. Even though she loved him enough to marry him, his arti*choked* heart made sure that she suffered and waited, just as he had suffered and waited. It was her turn to be *feeble and malformed who by natural selection would be unfit for mating rites.* There was a sad sickness that ruled Goldman's inner-poverty, and like a sadistic harlequin clown, he secretly savored perverse humor in the ones he loved the most.

He stood by her bed, a misanthropic beast, watching his beauty's breasts gently rise and fall. Her eyeballs stirred under heavy lids and then opened and turned to him. Her vacant stare cast his image with seemingly dour and dismissive inflections, tangoing in her optic nerves, and he waited for the indignation that would surely assail him. But, she had kept his memory in a locket close to her leaking breasts and without so much as a blink from a butterfly; her eyes spoke celestial decrees of inviolate love and divine particles fluttered in the air.

"I've been waiting for you, Marine."

*   *   *

The cameras swung into position and zeroed in on Edward R. Murrow, sitting in a padded leather chair in a studio mockup of his front room, dragging on a Camel and noticeably devoid of any eyebrows. He looked directly into the one-eyed god that spoke scruples into the cottage industry ears of America.

"It's been years since the disappearance of David Oliver Goldman, the enigmatic faith healer, the man and the myth, who on this very set claimed to be God."

Inside their synagogue Rabbi Shlomo Riezen and the eyes of the Final Millennium Jews were vacuum-tube sealed to the television as Murrow continued.

"He was loved by many, and yet vilified by most. In my opinion he was feared by those who loved him as well as those who hated him."

Rabbi Shlomo rolled his eyes and chimed. "Oy veh!"

Murrow's monologue carried on. Watching the TV screen in an ineffable hush, a healthy and vital Mina stood tall and strong, mixing cake batter while her almond eyed little girl held onto her shapely gam.

"A healer," said Murrow, "a Communist apparatchik, a decorated war hero, an atomic monster . . . What do we call him? I think we call him a man much like any other man."

On a couch sat old man Simpson with his four ugly daughters, sipping red wine with a half-baked smirk in front of a glowing black and white set.

"A complex man of ineradicable contradictions, a man who got caught up in his own monomania, and who rattled all of our comfort zones. Maybe that's why he was put here, to remind us all of our untapped potential and even our own mystical connectedness. Where he is now? God only knows. But I know how he affected me, an objective reporter, in the most subjective way and I unquestionably know I will never be the same, nor will the world, I suspect. This is Edward R. Murrow bidding you good night, and good luck."

From the flicker of the salt and pepper television screen Jonathan melts, slack jawed, alone, in the dark . . .

*   *   *

On the corner of Broadway and First, a grime-covered man with long lank hair and a matted beard burrowed through trashcans. His eyes made a ricocheting glance across the street and off the distinct features of a well-dressed ghost he had not seen in years. Goldman crossed the busy avenue and the two greeted one another with a hardy handshake that turned into revivifying hugs, and they walked to a nearby coffee shop.

Seeing Goldman from across the booth left Jonathan scrawling in thought-ascending verse, like a poet diplomat ornamenting the incomprehensible with riddles and interlocking puzzles. His faulty long-term memory had forgotten about the growth-inundated monstrosity that was once Goldman's face. Every cursed tumor and tubercular skin affliction had vanished without the slightest hint of the epidermal war that once waged on the frontline of his body. There was not so much as a pimple to tarnish the man's perfect complexion and even the matching 6.5 mm holes in his ears had completely smoothed over. Jonathan, for his part, had not fared as well over the hard and intractable years, and the book of his life was dog-eared and torn, every page faded, homeless, and yellowed from an abased life on the streets.

"What happened?" Jonathan asked with resolute curiosity.

Goldman drew a double helping of air and let the chronicle seep through the tale.

"I just woke up one morning and knew I couldn't do it one more day. I wandered aimlessly until I washed up at Mina's door."

"Tell me you healed her."

Goldman looked to the floor and back up again. He drew another breath. "At first I couldn't muster up a shred of decency to do it. I was

Frankenstein's monster, and so long as she was imprisoned in that bed she would be the monster's bride. Then it occurred to me that if my life was to amount to anything, I would do this one good deed, and then throw my devil flesh to the dogs of hell."

"And she recovered?"

"Miraculously. But the greatest miracle is that she didn't leave me. Even after I confessed that it was me who killed her brother. All that time, broken and abandoned . . . she cried out for pity, and the Lamb came to her with salves of comfort and otherworldly love. The only love she had ever known was the love of power, but it was the power of love that put her on her back, and there she found the most extraordinary view of God."

Jonathan squirmed in agitation, like a single cell dividing and then interacting with itself. Being around his brother was the perfect split portrait of his honest imperfection, stripped of worn illusions where his naked truth still hid.

"What happened to you?" Jonathan asked.

Goldman smiled. "I just got tired of carrying counterfeit coins."

"What?"

"The mystery of iniquity is found in the temple of denial, and I was its chief priest. All my life I tried to squeeze out my spirit, but no matter how hard the contraction, the holy of holies was undisturbed, and in the end, it was your witness that showed me that God hungers for mortality."

Jonathan rolled his eyes with static annoyance, but sensed movement skulking beneath the floorboards of his purgatory life.

"How did you get healed?" Jonathan predictably asked.

"My condition worsened, if you can imagine that, and if not for Mina I am sure I would have died. It seemed the more unconditional her love, the less room there was for my radioactive hate, until the tumors, like rumors . . . just . . . disappeared."

"That's the answer?" Jonathan derisively asked.

"When love is involved, there are no burdens, and only when you are fully known will you be fully loved . . . I never knew who I was until heaven's healing gate opened through Mina, who had enough faith to see me whole."

"No more Vitruvian pentagram, the five notes, the non-hemispheric brain . . . no radiation power?"

"It was a boat to get to the other side. Now that the river is crossed, I guess I no longer need it," Goldman said.

"I don't understand. You climbed to heights only dreamed of."

"Yeah, but I leaned my ladder on a wall-of-voodoo."

"But the ladder was still right . . . right?" Jonathan anxiously asked.

"As long as we have a person, place, or thing to hold onto, however convincing, we will only see *electricity's* dazzle and not the *Face.*" Goldman waxed.

"I don't understand."

"Grace is the *Face* and until *He* finds a face to plug into, God will never be anything more than cosmic voltage."

Jonathan wheezed out a lungful of sardonic steam. "Goldman, the icy atheist saved by the fire of God?"

Goldman shrugged in an extraordinary way as Jonathan re-interned his depleted self, from whom all meaning had been stripped and forever banished.

Jonathan spoke plaintively. "There was a time in my life when being close to the fire was all that mattered. But to keep the flames alive you have to spend more time and go greater distances gathering wood until, one day, you return to ashes and burned-out consecrations. You taught me well. It has taken me an empty lifetime to admit that God has no *Face,* nor do we."

"Your purpose is to live for the miracle of God," Goldman said.

Jonathan shook his head with mocking annoyance. "There is no such Face."

"He is a Face," Goldman argued.

"Only intelligent energy and that is no miracle," Jonathan declared.

"He is a Face or He is nothing," Goldman dourly said.

"No such monstrosity."

"If there is no G . . . G . . . God, then there is no purpose," Goldman stammered.

"If man is too weak to stand alone, he invents a god to lean on."

"Without God, it is impossible to weave meaning into a nihilistic world," Goldman hammered.

"The wages of stupidity is death," Jonathan exclaimed.

"No!" Goldman uttered. "The wages of sin is death and the end is coming soon!"

"You were right! You were right!" they both shouted in opposing synchrony.

The coffee shop patrons turned to the clamor of swapped paradigms. The two lapsed into a peculiar hush suspended in a quantum cocoon where their true selves caromed between the spaces of their thoughts. Goldman looked into Jonathan's hard-shelled facade, etched with deep lines that connected the dots of alluded illusions, and pitied a brother who had spent a lifetime asking for bread and fish but was instead given rocks and serpents.

"It's two minutes to midnight. The Communists are in Cuba pointing missiles at our backyard. Kennedy says that a nuclear attack may be imminent. Is this the end of the world that you had always talked about?" Goldman respectfully asked.

"You're the one blessed with prophecy. You tell me."

"They weren't blessings but afflictions, and like my growths, are no more." Jonathan looked long and lean at a man he had always stood under but now, for the first time, understood.

His emotions started to log jam and he rubbed his salty eyes. "So what's your take on your Commie friends aiming missiles at us?"

Goldman laughed, jarringly. "They're not my friends. I had a radical conversion to the dreaded bourgeoisie and turned in my hammer and sickle a long time ago. I own a vineyard in the San Fernando Valley that I bought from an old man."

"An old man?"

"A piece of unfinished business. We grow a pretty good Cabernet in our garden."

Jonathan paused, piercing his brother's visage with discarded street eyes. "You have inherited great gifts," Jonathan enviously said.

"Sometimes a great inheritance is spent on ignorance. All this time I thought *the world was a mean mistress and sensitive souls did not fare well in the face of her bigotry and contempt of new world shakers*, but if you have the infatuation to court her, you'll see that she has been a lover all along."

"And that means what?" Jonathan asked.

"It's a lover's riddle . . . and so are we," Goldman said with fraternal ease.

They left the coffee shop and walked down the busy street, but did not or could not say a word. Jonathan kept sneaking dry glances at his brother, who had exposed dusty skeletons that he thought he had buried long ago. It seemed to him that even at Goldman's worst he still came out on top, when everything *he* did ended up on the threshing floor.

They stopped at a red light and were waiting for the green when, out of nowhere, a white dove flitted onto Jonathan's shoulder. They looked at it with dismissive bewilderment, and then it flew away. The light changed and the two continued in a bubble of silence.

Seeing Goldman again was a fine thing, but it was a freighted occasion almost more than Jonathan could bear. *He's too heavy to carry*, he thought, *so he must not be my brother*. It was always Goldman who had infused substance into his dirt encrusted self, and he had given up his own concealed notions about who or what grew from its ground. He had spent his years plumbing the abyss of his nothingness, scavenging for bones of faith and always looking for his halo, and in the end had been left with pieces of dried theodicy and feeble attempts at reconciling a good God to an evil world. But his greatest disaster was that he was unable to reconcile a good world to an evil god.

Questioning faith had ultimately brought him to a profound dread of lostness, exile, and of being totally alone. Yet "there is a kind of strength in knowing you are alone," as Goldman used to say, and Jonathan's strength was measured by the greatness of his enemy, which had been him, all along.

Beneath the scudding autumn sky, they walked toward the bus stop. On the corner of Broadway and First a Lamb lies down as the balmy Santa Ana winds whipped through the streets. Trees swayed and women's skirts were blown up and men's hats were blown down, dancing fedora jigs on the warm windy sidewalk. From down the block a city bus approached. The brothers clasped hands and hugged.

Jonathan then looked at Goldman with a brooding question-marked face. "Explain something to me? Why are we who we are?"

Goldman thought for a moment and then linked with his brother's averting eyes.

"Yourself can't be explained, only experienced."

Jonathan gazed into the firmament then back to Goldman. "You know I hate God."

"Why?" Goldman asked.

"Because He is not love."

Goldman stared at Jonathan like someone doing time for someone else's crime but kept silent before his accusers. "He is love," Goldman said. "But for God to see His wonder He needs our eyes and without our mortal heartache and essential despair, it is a love He cannot possibly know. And in that corner of the universe we are heroes, and He washes our feet, eternally grateful to us, for walking where no god could possibly go."

Jonathan tipped his head in abstract submission, and then looked up. "You taught us all a lot. An Atomic Cocktail that made the world drunk on possibilities."

Goldman grimaced. "Nothing is more tragic than to live another's life. Your blessing was my curse. I was the wrong man for the job. It was your destiny all along." Jonathan hooted at his fate and had given up with hollowed resignation long ago.

"Do you still climb trees?" he asked.

Goldman smiled. "I don't go out on a limb anymore."

The bus pulled up and the double-glass doors swung open with a mechanical clanging *swish*.

Goldman slipped Jonathan his phone number. "If the world doesn't turn into a nuclear winter, you call me sometime. Otherwise, I'll see you on the other side."

Jonathan squinted through the dark clouds of his beset self, and shafts of light faintly streamed through the teeth of his clenched smile. The mawkish moment was broken by a loud *bang!* From out of the marmalade sky a baseball crashed off the top of the bus and landed directly between the two.

Goldman stooped over and picked up the ball, the two, bedazzled, stargazing at the apparent apparition. He turned the ball over and etched across the leather were the words, *Let the miracle happen.* They looked at one another with a perplexity that siphoned off all language. The event, penetrating their collective pasts like the years that the ball had defied gravity, space, and time; where prophecies hibernate and reenter worlds with sounds of lightning and sights of thunder.

They stood face-to-face, bookends to the same antinomy tale.

Goldman handed Jonathan the baseball and said: *'You are a man of miracles and no weapon formed against you will prosper. Whatever you have in mind, go and do it, for the Lord is with you. You are The King . . . the One the world has been waiting for.'"*

He entered the bus and jutted his head out the window. *"Now don't think about the ball or nothing, just feel it. Feel it in the middle of your gut and let it happen."*

"Let what happen?" Jonathan yelled.

Goldman shouted back with entreaties of mythic fortune. "The miracle!"

"What miracle?" Jonathan hollered.

"It's your turn to save the world!" Goldman exclaimed.

An avalanche of eerie love, and a peculiar sense of stewardship to the divine, flooded Jonathan's vacant heart. The bus pulled away and Goldman fixed on the receding figure of Jonathan holding the baseball, standing alone on the sidewalk like a Greek bronze, timeless, poised, and significant. He then saw what could only be described as a misty fog envelope his brother, and then a single gold petal appeared. First one, then two, then a deluge of gold quietly fell onto his frosted silhouette without anyone, or even Jonathan, apparently aware. Goldman shook his head and rubbed his incredulous eyes but the apparition remained. He turned back around and settled in his seat to begin the long ride home, his head swimming with trilling memories bound in shards of alien bliss, otherworldly mumblings in parables of phonic joy, and . . . sighed.

"He then looked at his own soul with a telescope. What seemed irregular, he saw to be beautiful constellations and he added to his consciousness hidden worlds within worlds, within worlds, within worlds."